PRAISE FOR *THE D...*

WINNER
Costa Children's Book Award 2011
BC Book Prize for Children's Literature 2012
Le Prix des Incorruptibles 2012/2013
Cybils Award for Fantasy and Science Fiction
Prix Utopiales de Nantes 2012
ALA-YALSA Best Fiction for Young Adults
Coventry Inspiration Book Award 2012
Rib Valley Book Award 2012
Spellbinding Book Award 2012
FAB Award 2013
BC Stellar Award 2012/2013

"A shot of pure adrenalin. . . Exuberant, exciting and charged with emotion, its powerful, pared-down prose draws us into a world of adventure. . . Novel of the year"
Amanda Craig, THE TIMES

"This vision of the future is hellish and frightening but if you wanted anyone in your corner in that place, then Saba's your girl"
TELEGRAPH

"Saba can be a tough heroine to root for, sullen and ungrateful to those who try to help her, but fans of the Hunger Games' *Katniss will find in her similar reserves of hidden good nature and ferocious fighting abilities. . . Young has leveraged an intriguing action-romance story into a* Mad Max-*style world that'll leave readers both satisfied and eager for more"*
BOOKLIST

"This book raises the bar when it comes to the genre. . . Not only will it satisfy the cravings of Hunger Games *fans, but it is – dare I say – better than* The Hunger Games. . . *This book will blow you away . . . a truly remarkable reading experience"*
MTV

"This is a must-read, where girls rescue boys, and where the future looms up full of hope and loss, struggles and archetypes that give the story a timeless, classic edge"
GLOBE AND MAIL

*"*Blood Red Road *has a cinematic quality that makes it white-hot for film production. . . The fervour is more than warranted"*
LA TIMES

"A post-apocalyptic story with the flavour of a western. . . Powerfully narrated in a spare vernacular. . . A sure-fire transporting holiday read"
SUNDAY TIMES

MOIRA YOUNG is from Vancouver, Canada and now lives in the UK. She was an actress and an opera singer before becoming a writer. Her prize-winning debut novel, *Blood Red Road*, first in the *Dustlands* trilogy, was published in 2011 to international acclaim. The *Dustlands* are published in 30 countries.

www.twitter.com/Moira_Young

RAGING STAR

MOIRA YOUNG

MARION LLOYD BOOKS

To Sophie McKenzie, Melanie Edge, Gaby Halberstam and Julie Mackenzie – friends and companions of the road – my ever-grateful thanks.

Thank you to my excellent Dustlands editors: Helen Thomas at Scholastic Children's Books, Karen Wojtyla at Margaret K McElderry Books and Marion Lloyd. Thanks to Doubleday Canada for their wonderful support and encouragement; also Gallimard Jeunesse, S Fischer Verlag, Otava, Gyldendal Norsk and Raben & Sjögren and all at Aitken Alexander.

Special thanks to Gillie Russell and Andrew Beacham. I'm indebted to John McLay, Gill McLay and Julia Green for giving me a push when I needed it most.

Above all, thanks to Paul Stansall. For everything. Always.

in loving memory of
John Elgin Stark
dreamer, artist, teacher

I bin dreamin of my long-dead mother.
I used to every night
when I was nine,
ten.
Her life bled out birthin Emmi,
Pa's grief more than awful to see.

He set her on the pyre,
her funeral pyre,
that he built with his heartbroke hands.
Over an over, he wept her, he kissed her,
her face, her lips, her hair.
Don't die, don't leave me, sweet Allis don't go.
My golden beauty.
My life.

Then he lit the fire to send her,
his heartsoul,
back to the stars.
What was best in us burned to ash.

She walked in my dreams,
my sunlight mother,
every night fer them first two years.
An the same fer Lugh.
Lugh an me, the same.
It was some kinda comfort,
I guess.

As her light faded our darkness grew an she walked in my
dreams no more.

But now, she walks agin.
In the dark of my dreams,
she lives
agin.

First published in the UK in 2014
by Scholastic Children's Books
Euston House, 24 Eversholt Street
London, NW1 1DB, UK
A division of Scholastic Ltd.
Registered office: Westfield Road, Southam, Warwickshire, CV47 0RA
SCHOLASTIC and associated logos are trademarks and/or registered
trademarks of Scholastic Inc.

ISBN 978 1407 13677 6

A CIP catalogue record for this book is available
from the British Library

Printed in the UK by CPI Group (UK) Ltd, Croydon, CR0 4YY

1 3 5 7 9 10 8 6 4 2

www.scholastic.co.uk/zone

the
Eastern Defile

We run. Through the night. The five of us. Through the white night-time woods of New Eden. Lugh an Tommo an Ash an Creed an me. The five of us. We run.

Dry tree litter cushions the ground. Hushes the pound of our boots. Our breath puffs steam in the chill. We're all sharp, tight with intent.

Lugh's got the rope, slung around his chest. I carry the blastpack. Swaddled in cloth, tucked in my sack, along with my meagre gear.

Long-looker. Sleepkit. Medicine bag. Flint. Waterskin. Salt twist. Cooktin. Shirt. Knife in my boot sheath. Bolt shooter. Ammo belt. My whiteoak bow an a full quiver. An the heartstone hangs at my neck. Cool in the hollow of my throat. That's pretty well it. It ain't much.

Guerillas travel light. An fast. An that's what we are. We're the Free Hawks, reborn. Set to fight fer the right to live in New Eden. Good land an clean water's scarce in this world. But it's here in New Eden. An it's the birthright of all. Weak an strong. Old an young. People an beasts an all that share the earth. Not jest him an his Chosen ones.

Him. DeMalo. The Pathfinder. His Chosen ones, the Stewards of the Earth. Pure young people. Strong an healthy. Breeders, workers fer his shiny new world. Forced to his service at gunpoint. To be flattered an wooed by him. Convinced an overcome an bent to his will. Kept in line by his Tonton militia.

Tonight we thread through the trees. We each map our own course. We leap over streams. Over rocks. Then a sudden slowdown to pick-pick safe passage through a gangle of overground roots. We cain't afford no injury. No slips or twists or breaks.

We're at the dreg edge of New Eden. In the far southeast corner, where it bleeds to the bleak of the Raze. This is deadbone country. No settlement or farms. It's ridges an hollows an hills. Here the land holds itself close. The earth spreads thin over rock. The trees root wily an tough.

As much as we can, we keep to the high ground. Our forest world's clear-lit. Washed cold white by the moon. We move outta the shadows. Into the light. Then back to the shadows agin. In an out, over an over. We're silvered. Whitewashed. Ghosts on the run.

An Tracker's my ghostly wolfdog. Rough-haired lord of the woods, his great body skims at my side. High above, Nero crow-surfs the night. Ridin the wind on a sea of stars. A sea of restless stars.

It's star time. Star season. In these short days of the year when the light fails early an things perish, the stars streak through the night. They're the unquiet souls of the dead. Returnin to earth on unfinished business.

I run at the front fer the most part. But I slip back now an then to save my breath. East, that's our course, due east by the Plough. It warn't my plan we should run all the way. It's jest what we did, what happened. As we left the cave where we'd stopped to rest, I started off a quick walk pace. A few strides later, we was runnin. We're too wired, too buzzed to go slower.

I keep sharp-eyed from the off. I'm lookin fer Jack's first waymark. The start of his white spruce trail. White spruce, a

3

tree like no other. Stunted an twisted. Easy to spot, night or day. When I clock the first tree, his first mark, I smile. He's done jest like we said. On the tree's north side, on a shoulder-height branch, he's hung a twist of root. He's tagged me this shortcut every half-league. It's our secret. His an mine.

An Jack's my secret. Everybody else believes him to be dead. They think he got killed a month ago. When we blasted the Tonton stronghold, Resurrection. An that's how it must be. He's gotta stay dead. Jack has few friends among us. Them I run with tonight in these woods ain't his friends.

Ash an Creed hate him fer his time in the Tonton. Jack joined the enemy, sure. To work aginst them, though, not with 'em. But he got tainted by blood. He was there that night, at the Darktrees slaughter when the Tonton killed our friends. The Free Hawks an the Raiders. He took no part in that bloody deed. In fact, he saved their lives. Creed an Ash, that is. Maev too. An he helped us at Resurrection. He was the one who blew the place up. His quick thinkin spared Emmi's life.

None of that stands to his credit. Not with Ash an Creed. They lost their tribes at Darktrees that night. Their souls was cut deep an fer always. Jack rode with the killers, that's enough to damn him. If they know he's alive, they'll betray him fer sure.

Lugh's got the biggest hate fer Jack. Tommo comes a close second. Both of 'em fer reasons to do with me. Slim don't know Jack. Molly an Emmi love him. As always with Jack, it ain't simple. So we decided, him an me. We cain't trust all of 'em, so it's safest we tell none. To them, he has to be dead.

If only they knew. Jack's on our side. He's my scout, my spy. Busy workin his tiny network of New Eden rebels. He's

4

got a few insiders, clear-eyed Stewards who share our aims. An some outcasts. So-called Treedogs, becuz they went to ground in the woods. When DeMalo seized their land, they chose to stay. To stay hidden an cause him trouble.

Jack's helped me plan this first action. He scratched maps in the dirt. We talked tactics an ammo. He tagged our trail all the way, jest over two leagues from the cave to the bridge. The bridge that spans the Eastern Defile, to join New Eden to the Raze. The bridge that we're set to blow.

It's bin newly built by slave labour. DeMalo's a builder of roads an bridges. Faster travel fer the Tonton. Easier passage fer his Stewards of the Earth as they work their stolen farmland. We aim to smash all of 'em, bit by bit. Way out here's a good place to start. We'll test our drill, our discipline, our method. Without no fear of disturbance.

Good thing Jack marked the way fer us. We know New Eden pretty good by now. But till they built this bridge, there warn't nuthin in this lonely corner. We know it in general, not particular.

I slipped to the rear a while back. Keepin my eyes peeled fer Jack's final waymark. There's a white spruce ahead. This one hunches alone an apart. As I come up on it, I slow a bit. Yes, there it is. The twist of root on a branch. The Defile an the bridge lie jest ahead. Hot excitement kicks in me. Now I'll lead the way agin. As I surge forwards, Tracker keeps pace.

Creed's a little off to my left. He's shirtless, like always, tattooed neck to waist. An he's bootless, also like always. He says his feet map the land as they touch it. The chill's nudged him into a dandyboy frock coat. Its shabby swallowtails stream in his wake. As I pass him, he flashes a wide, white grin. Silver rings gleam in his ears.

Ash stretches out in a casual lope. Long legs easy. Shoulders low. Her hair flies behind, a waist-length banner of plaits. I nod as I shift past her. Almost there. Her square-jawed face cracks a rare smile. Ash ain't no misery, not by a long shot. But she ain't cheerful by a long shot neether. Unless there's trouble or danger or a fight ahead. Which is what she'll be hopin. But not in a bad way.

I press on to Tommo. Come right up, close up to him. He shuns me. Ducks his head so's his hair hides his eyes. But I know what I'd see if I could see 'em. Hurt. An anger. I touch his arm to let him know we're near the bridge. He shrugs me off. Quick. A bit rough.

Tommo hates me fierce right now. An he's justified. Steppin on his heart like I did. Heedless, careless of the fallout. At fifteen summers, he tips between boyhood an manhood. An I played them both false, man an boy, with a kiss. A lover's kiss that was a lie. Now he nurses the bruise of my deceit.

Me an Tracker forge ahead, closin in on Lugh. He's bin holdin fast as leader fer some time. I noticed he wouldn't yield to Tommo a little while back. I s'pose he's makin some kinda point. What that might be, I ain't got time to consider.

Lugh! I keep my voice low as I pull alongside him. We're nearly there, I says. I'll take it from here.

He throws me a glance. His beauty's whitewashed by the moon. His birthmoon tattoo stands out darkly sharp. High on his right cheekbone, jest like mine. Put there by Pa to mark us as special. We two, rare Midwinter twins. The boy made of daylight, gold as the sun, child of our mother's heart. The girl, me, dark as the night-time, born in her brother's shadow. You'd hardly take us fer kin, Lugh an me, let alone think we shared our mother's womb.

Fall back, I tell him. I'm leadin us in, you know that.

He don't acknowledge me. Jest stares straight ahead, with his chin set to mulish. He starts to speed up. So I do too. Before I know it, we're racin each other. Neck an neck. I glare disbelief at him. Cut it out, I says. C'mon Lugh.

He makes no answer. He's pushin hisself. Breathin hard. Nostrils flared. Jaw clenched. But he's bin flat out runnin too long.

With a shake of my head, I kick up my speed. Fine! I says. Be like that!

I pull away easy. We leave him behind, me an Tracker. I glance back. He's stopped. Bent double with his hands on his knees. His chest heaves as he pulls in air. Ash, Creed an Tommo hafta swerve around him.

What a time he picks to lock antlers. I'll hafta have speech with him later. Fer now, that problem's parked. Now, we got a bridge to blow.

We crouch behind a cluster of rocks, well up the hill above the bridge. We git our breath back as we take in the lie of the land. Tracker flops between me an Ash, his tongue hung out to cool.

Nero sails down onto my head. His claws needle my scalp. As I pick him off, I see the tiny scroll of cherrybark tied to his right leg. It's a message from Jack. Outta sight of th'others, I untie it. It might be somethin I need to know right away. He's scratched a pyramid on the bark. No, not urgent. He's changed our meet place fer tonight. He'll see me at Irontree. I tuck the scroll in the small leather bag at my waist.

I train my long-looker on the bridge an terrain all around. It's jest like Jack drew fer me, with a stick in the dirt. An how I drew it fer my crew as we stepped through this op. To a tee it's how he said it 'ud be. He's a good detail man, Jack, that's fer sure.

They've built on the iron remains of a old Wrecker bridge. Added some wood support struts an a new bridge deck an beams. Plain an sturdy, forty foot from start to finish, it spans the steep gash of a rocky ravine. The Eastern Defile. A savage axe-slash in the body of the earth. In its belly, far below, runs the wrath of fast water. A thread of river, silver in the night, fumes an foams as it bucks downhill.

Ash gives a low whistle. Hope you got a head fer heights, she says to Lugh. If you wanna trade jobs, my offer's still open.

What? You don't think I'm up to it? he says.

She blinks at his chippy tone. Don't git the hump, she says. You know I jest like blastin things.

Specially if it's built by the Tonton, says Creed.

Slaves, you mean, she says. They're the ones buildin New Eden.

Okay, I says, let's run through this one more time. I tap Tommo's arm. Jest barely touch him. He looks at me. Tommo, I says, advantages.

His dark eyes glitter, unreadable in the night. There's a mocky little smile on his lips. No cloud, he says. Sharp moon. Small bridge. Quick job. Okay? His rough voice lays down each word over-slow, over-clear.

Heat scorches my cheeks. Of late, he's bin makin like I talk down to him. Which I most absolutely do not. Maybe a deaf boy shouldn't fight from the front. Ike used to worry about that. But Tommo don't ask fer no quarter fer his deafness. He don't need none. We fought our way outta some real tight spots an Tommo ain't never let us down. Not once have I treated him special. So it stings that he makes like I do. He knows it irks me. That's why he does it.

Good, I tell him. Okay, disadvantages. Creed?

He scans the road. That's our main problem right there, he says.

While he talks, I start takin what I need from my sack. A shrill tin whistle on a cord that I hang around my neck. Our emergency signal. Two blows means split up, run, meet at the rendezvous. Next, the blastpack. Like a brick in size an weight. Wrapped in oiled cloth, the long nettle fusecord in a tidy bundle.

Our sightlines ain't good, says Creed. Tommo an me's only gonna have a clear view a hunnerd foot this side, not more'n seventy on the far side. Eh, Tommo? Tommo nods agreement. If anybody was to come around these hills, says Creed, they'd be right on top of us an that means quick decision time. Shoot or don't shoot.

The narrow dirt road runs from west to east. It hugs the curve of the hills an sweeps into our view at the last minute. Jest like Creed called it.

Yer informant, says Lugh. They're absolutely sure the Tonton don't patrol this far out?

Positive, I says. But we stay alert an keep cool heads. An that means all of us, Creed.

What? he says. I'm some kinda hothead? I'm like ice.

Ash, I says, you an Tracker's our early warnin system. Where you gonna stand lookout?

She's usin her own long-looker to con the hills all around.

9

She points to the scrubby hogback ridge that runs along, high behind us. There, she says, no question. It's the highest point around.

Okay, Tracker's with you, I says. Good luck. Go on, boy, go with Ash.

He hesitates. Obedient, but torn. He's a one-woman wolfdog. Mercy's dog when I met him. Then somehow – many days distant from his home – I found him. Rather, he found me. An he claimed me fer his.

Tracker, go, I says.

As he sprints off with Ash, Creed an Tommo take their position behind the rocks. Advantages, disadvantages, the best spot fer lookout, we knew it all before. We talked an walked this entire op agin an agin, but this is the real thing. To repeat everythin now that we're here sets it in our eyes an minds. I shove three small birch torches in the back of my belt an tuck the blastpack unner my arm.

You sure that thing packs enough power? says Lugh.

I'm sure, I says. Slim knows what he's doin. Okay, this is it. We'll work fast as we can.

We gotcha covered, says Creed. He's all business now, hard-faced an sharp-eyed as him an Tommo load their bows.

Lugh an me hurry down the slope. Nero flies ahead of us. We hit the road, run the few foot to the bridge an scramble down the rocks. It's dark unnerneath the bridge. A strong smell of fresh-cut wood. As Lugh shrugs off the rope he's bin carryin, I lay down the blastpack an light a torch with a spark from my flint an steel. I hold it high so's we can see the structure.

It's simple. Like a flat roof held up by a peaked roof. The two main girders left from Wrecker days – iron, dead straight, a foot wide – they ram deep into the sides of the

Defile. From there, they rise at a angle to meet at the middle of the bridge deck. There's one vee of new wood struts on each girder. No surprises. It's all jest as we espected.

I dare a glance at the canyon below. An wish I hadn't of. I look away quick. The Defile plunges dizzily, steeply down to the deathly rage of the river. I light Lugh with the torch as he loops his rope around the girder, jest at the point where it spears into the side of the ravine. He ties it off with a slipknot. I light th'other two torches from the first. Then I stick all three into the rocks so's the unnerside of the bridge is lit.

Meantime, Lugh's passed th'other end of the rope around his chest. Another slipknot to secure him an he's ready to go. He straddles the girder. I hand him the blastpack. He tucks it snugly in his coat an starts to hitch along. Up up up towards the middle of the bridge. I pay out the rope as he goes.

Easy now, no hurry, I tell him.

I ain't got it in mind to run, he says.

He reaches the vee of the new wooden struts. Now he's gotta pick his way past 'em. Gimme some play on the rope, he says.

Usin the first strut to help him, he gits into a crouch. Then he stands up on the girder. My breath stalls as he makes his way around, over an between the two struts, huggin 'em as he goes. It's awkward. He places his feet with care. I make sure the rope don't hamper him.

Then he's done it. He smiles. Slippy fer the feet, he says. His teeth gleam white in the gloom.

Once agin, he straddles the girder. Once agin, he inches hisself along. Along an up towards the centre of the bridge as I pay out the rope. Unease pricks my skin. Don't listen to the roar of the river below. Don't think about the sharpness of the rocks. He slides the blastpack from his coat.

Make sure you wedge it tight, I says. Go slow, Lugh, be careful.

Would you hush, he says.

A wolfdog howl shivers the air. It's Tracker. It's the signal.

Someone's comin, I says.

Git the lights, he says.

But the rope—

Douse the lights!

Don't move, stay there, I order you! I drop the rope an rush to snatch the torches. I shove 'em flame first in the rocks to douse 'em. As I grab the last one, as I turn to make sure Lugh's okay, I see him reach out. Reach to jam the blastpack into place.

Reach.

Lose his balance.

An fall.

I scramble down the rocks. Leap to grab the rope. With a rush, it snaps taut. Reefed to full length by the weight of Lugh's body, it catches on the vee of the struts.

Lugh hangs in thin air, high above the river. Held by nuthin but the rope around his chest. In one hand, he clutches the fuse cord by its end. The blastpack dangles far below him.

I fling myself onto the girder. Scrabble along it as fast as I can. Nero swoops an screeches in a panic. Shut up, I hiss.

I clamber into the vee. Wedge myself in. Reach down. Grab hold of the rope. To do what, I dunno. The blood's poundin in my ears. My gut's like water.

Lugh stares up at me. His face tight with terror. He twists an swings. The rope creaks.

Then we hear it. Faint at first. The beat of hoofs on the road. Comin at us from the west. A horse snorts. Bridle jingles. Metal. That means primo gear. Two riders. Not in a hurry but not laggin neether. Then they're upon us. I don't dare breathe as, not five foot above me, iron-shod hoofs clatter over the bridge. As Lugh hangs from it below. As he twists. An creaks. One rider says somethin. The second one laughs. Two men.

They pass onto the road. I breathe agin. The sounds of 'em start to fade. As the road curves around the hill to the east, I git a clear sight of their backs.

They ride well-groomed mounts with polished kit. Their leather knee boots gleam. They're turned out neat, with short cropped hair. Dressed head to toe in black. Long black robes. It's the Tonton. DeMalo's militia men. In the middle of the night. At the edge of nowhere. What the hell're they doin out here? They disappear around the bend.

Tonton, I tell Lugh.

Swing me, he says.

What?

Swing me to the side!

I git what he means right away. There's bushes an tough little trees rooted in the steep sides of the Defile. If I can swing him – some ten foot or so – he can try to grab hold of one an climb to safety. I start workin at the rope. Towards the rocks, then back agin. I'm strong, but I'm crammed an cramped an Lugh's a dead weight. He hardly moves.

Keep goin, he says. Harder.

I pull. Let go. Pull. Let go. My muscles burn. My shoulders scream. Inch by inch, I labour. I rage the red hot. Make it forge my strength.

Work with me, I gasp. Breathe with me. Out on the out. In on the in. An lean yer weight.

Our eyes fix on each other. We start to work together.

13

Breathe together. Out as I pull. In as I let go. An he leans his weight … on the out … an the in. Bit by bit, it goes more easy. We swing him out. We swing him back. He goes a little further with every breath.

There's a rush of feet an Tommo hustles down the side of the bridge. Sent by Creed to see what's wrong. He takes in our plight at a glance, with a curse. He scrambles down the rocks, further into the gash of the Defile. He finds a handhold on a sturdy scrub tree. He gits in position to grab Lugh the moment he swings close enough.

We swing once, twice, an—

Now! says Lugh.

His arm reaches out as he sails towards Tommo. Tommo stretches to meet him. They grab hands. The force of Lugh's backswing sweeps Tommo off his feet. They let go. Rocks shower as Tommo scrabbles back from his death. He braces hisself more firmly.

Ready, he says.

This time, as their hands grasp, Lugh's that much closer. Tommo gives a mighty tug. Lugh grabs the tree an they tumble on top of each other. But he's safe. Lugh's safe. They both are. I let go a gasp of relief.

While Lugh clings to the tree an recovers his wits, Tommo hauls up the blastpack with care. I motion him to bring it to me quick. He clambers to the bridge an hitches along the girder to where I'm wedged between the struts.

We should abort, he says.

Hand me the pack, I says. Go help Lugh.

I don't like the feel of this, he says.

Tommo, do as I say! I tuck the pack safe inside my shirt. I git myself around the struts an then, not lettin myself think, not lookin down, I start to move. Along the girder, inch by inch, in the pitch dark unner the bridge, till I feel my head touch the deck. Then, movin slow, oh so careful, I slide the pack out an, with one hand, I feel it into place. I make sure it's jammed in tight, then I hitch myself backwards, payin out the fusecord as I go.

Then I'm back on solid ground. It's done. Lugh an Tommo help me down. As we hurry up the hill, a bank of low cloud tumbles in. Damp an white an thick as woodsmoke. I cain't hardly see my own feet. We run the fuse as straight as we can. Over boulders, between bushes an trees. By the time we reach Creed, there's a foot or so to spare.

He's got a lit spill ready. What the hell happened? he says.

Later, I says. Light it, we bin here too long.

The fuse don't catch right off. Damp, says Creed. It's this damn cloud. You know what this means? Ash won't be able to see nuthin. She won't hear so good neether.

Lugh's shiverin with shock. I hug his shoulders. Okay? I says.

Thanks to you, he says. An you, Tommo. He grabs Tommo's hand. Thanks, man. You saved my life.

I dare to take Tommo's other hand. To my surprise, he don't pull away. I couldn't of done it without you, I says. He gives me the tiniest of smiles.

C'mon, c'mon, Creed mutters. The fuse catches. There's a hiss. It starts to sizzle. But it's sluggish. C'mon, burn, he says, burn you beauty, gawdammit.

Jest then, Tracker's wail shudders the cloud. Our heads shoot up.

Tommo mouths, What? at me.

It's Tracker, I says.

But if Tracker's wailin agin, that means—

My thought dies. The wall of cloud splits an rolls open, like a door. Down below, three Tonton ride into view. Comin from the west, jest like the other two. Behind 'em, two horse-drawn carts rattle along. Creed curses. I snatch my looker.

In the first cart, straight-backed on the driver's bench, a boy an a girl sit side by side. In the white cloudlight, the quarter circle brand stands out starkly on their foreheads. Stewards of the Earth. DeMalo's Chosen ones.

There's a spotted kercheef tied round her neck. Her hair ripples loose down her back. She ain't seen more'n fourteen summers. Him, the boy, about the same. Strong an shinin with health, like all Stewards. So young, they're probly newly paired outta Edenhome. Chosen fer each other by DeMalo, like the top breedin stock they are. The cart's piled high with table, chairs, tools an other necessaries fer a life on the land. A life where, though? Surely not the Raze. It's a wasted, desolate place.

But it's the second cart that stops my heart.

One Tonton drives. Another sits facin backwards, firestick at the ready, keepin watch over their load. It's slave workers. Maybe ten, maybe twelve of 'em. Men an women, crammed tight together. Sittin on the floor of the open cart. Shaved heads. Iron collars around their necks. Chained together, like slaves always is here. By the ankles when they're workin, by the ankles an hands an necks fer transport.

Eight more mounted Tonton bring up the rear. Two great hounds pace beside them. Smooth white skin. Raw pink eyes. Massive heads with powerful jaws.

Ghosthounds, says Creed. Dogs of war.

My eyes flick to the fuse. It's burnin, still sluggish but steady. Headed fer the bridge an the blastpack. Slaves. Innocent blood. I'm on the move. Throwin down the looker, snatchin my knife from its boot sheath.

Tommo grabs my sleeve. Too late, he says.

I fling him off an I run.

Saba, come back! says Lugh.

I pelt downhill, keepin low, chasin the lit fuse. Gotta beat it. Gotta stop it. Lucky it's damp. I'm gainin on it. I pass it. Do a quick swing about. Snatch at the unlit fusecord, sweepin my knife in, ready to cut, to kill it.

My feet hit some scree. I slip. I'm fallin. I slam to the ground an I'm gone. I slide on my back, boots first, down the hill. Now the fuse burns brisk, hissin past me, racin home. I wing offa trees, crash into bushes. I flail with a wild hand, reachin fer somethin, anythin at all to stop me. I grab a thick root. Sharp jolt, wrist to socket. I jerk to a sudden halt.

I am. Too late.

The first three Tonton ride onto the bridge. Their horses sound soft thunder. An right behind 'em, the Stewards' cart, loaded high, rolls onto the boards. The sizzlin fuse nips outta sight. Now the slave cart's about to hit the bridge. I throw myself face down. Arms around my head, clamped tight to my ears.

It blows. A thick boom shakes the earth. I'm thrown in the air. I land with a thump. Stones an dirt shower down. On top of me. Around me. The sound of the world's gone dull. Like listenin from deep down in water.

I raise my head. My throat's choked by a warnin scream. A scream I never gave voice to. I squint through the shift of the cloud. An as the boom starts to fade to heavy, shocked air, I see. In flashes. Like dream shards. Through the rain of debris, I catch glimpses of our work. An my skin shrinks to my bones.

Gone. The three Tonton. All gone. The Stewards in their cart. The blameless beasts. Animals an people, now bloody

17

lumps of flesh. Flung like so much bad meat. On the rocks of the Eastern Defile. Bits of cart. Sticks that was chairs, a table. They smash, slide, tumble an crash. Head fer the river below.

No dream, this. A nightmare. The sight seared cold to my soul. I git to my feet. A cart wheel hurtles from the clouds straight at me. Vengeance slammin down from the sky. I scramble an duck. It hits the ground. Bounces wild. Strikes my shoulder an knocks me flyin.

Fire gobbles at the bridge. Orange flames score the night. Smoke billows an rages.

Then. Sounds fade in. Horses. People. Screams. Cries. Through the smoke an cloud an chaos. A Tonton's bin crushed by his horse. It strains an thrashes as it struggles to its feet. The slave cart's shattered. Bodies spilled, sprawled still on the road. Still chained at the wrists.

Somethin flutters down to land on my arm. I pick it off an stare. It's a tatter of spotted cloth. The Steward's kercheef, the long-haired girl. It's wet. Dark wet with her blood.

With a clatter of scree, Lugh skids in. C'mon! He hauls me to my feet. Starts draggin me uphill. What the hell, Saba, what was you thinkin?

The words stick to my lips. I tried to stop it, I says.

There's a shout from below. We glance back to the road. Tonton. Gittin to their feet. Dazed. They've seen us. One points at us. Shouts. Gives orders. Six start to run in our direction. The ghosthounds come with 'em, howlin pursuit. A high-pitched wail, like a winter north wind.

Hurry! Creed an Tommo speed us on with anxious hands.

I grab the whistle. Blow two long blasts. Run! I yell. Go! Run!

Creed grabs Tommo an they're gone. Scattered to the

18

woods above. Ash'll hear it too, wherever she is. She'll head right away fer the meet point.

Go! I tell Lugh.

No, I ain't leavin you!

We meet at the rendezvous. Dammit, Lugh, go. Go!

I shove him in the chest. With a curse, he scrambles off over the hill. I head the opposite way.

The red hot's wild in me. Floods me. Speeds me. It flies my feet as I flee through the woods. As I leap felled trees. Vault over rocks. Nero flees with me. He's silent. Smart bird. Don't caw, not a peep, or they'll find us.

Sounds of pursuit. Shouts. The Tonton. Headed away from me. Good, oh good. No, they could be chasin one of th'others. Maybe Lugh. No, not Lugh, please oh please. They'll hurt him if they find him. Revenge, they'll want revenge. Fer what we done. What we done, ohmigawd. The blood an the screamin an the blood an the flesh an bits of body blasted an flung—

My stummick heaves sour to my throat. I stumble to a halt an I'm sick. Thinly, wretchedly sick. Bent over, one hand on a tree. With a gasp, a sob, I run on, swipin at my mouth with my sleeve.

Wait. What's that? Banshee yowls knife the air. Wails that slice to my bones. It's the ghosthounds. I falter. Listenin. Fearin. Oh gawd, they're comin this way. Panic sweeps me on. Faster. Faster. I cain't outrun dogs. No way. I need water. A stream. Gotta lose my scent now.

I crash through the forest. Think, quick quick, think. Water. The bridge. The ravine. The river. Yes. Where did it fall from? Think. Nor-nor-east? Yes. Where am I now? Wind's lifted the cloud. I see Jupiter. Low, behind me. I peel off to the left. Nero sticks with me close.

I scramble over rocks. Stumble. Race on. My lungs burn. I start to hear somethin. Faintly. A rush. Wind in the trees? No, more like water, I think. I follow the sound. The unearthly yawl of the ghosthounds ever louder. Closer, closer, ever closer. My skin reeks of fear. My trail must hang sharp. Faster, faster, run faster.

Then I bust from the woods, I'm free of the trees an – yes. A river. Narrow an fast. Clear an – oh merciful – shallow. A foot or so deep, no more. I hurry downstream. Dodgin low-hangin boughs, takin care to flag my direction. A snapped twig here, a cracked branch there. Nuthin too much, jest enough. I go a little ways along, then double back an head upstream. Roughly north. That's good. North. The right direction.

Nero scouts ahead, flappin low to the water. I keep my head movin. Check this way, that way, all around. But it's quiet. The shallow rush of the river. A redthroat warbler tunin up. The soft sounds of a wood as it gladdens to the day. Not long till dawn, not long now. The hounds ain't wailin no more. Could it be? Did I manage to throw 'em off my trail? What if they found other quarry? Tommo or Creed or Lugh? I cain't hear nuthin though, not a thing. Surely I would. Shots or shouts or somethin.

I scoop handfuls of water as I go. Swill my mouth clean an spit.

Jest ahead, a dead pine's toppled. It bridges the river. Blocks my way. Nero lands on it an goes fer a bug. Stabbin the bark with his beak. I straddle the tree an grab him.

Find 'em, Nero, I whisper. Go find the dogs.

I launch him high to the air. He soars above the woods fer a bird's-eye view an disappears from my sight. The grey sky's smudged to palest pink. Dawn's on the break. A new day.

I slide off my bow an nock a arrow. I slip back into the water. Armed an wary, I track upstream. Above the water's chatter, the air hangs heavy. Intent. It's a stalker's silence. My heart ticks in my throat.

The river curves. I edge round the bend. A few strides on, it widens to a pool, calm an peaceful. The woods huddle close. Tangled roots sprawl into the water. As I wade through the pool, it deepens. To my knees. Then my thighs.

Nero dives at me. From nowhere. The world explodes. A racket of howls an wails. The ghosthounds! There! White terror streakin through the woods straight at me. Here, they'll be here any second. A wild glance around as I shoulder my bow. A sturdy big cedar sweeps low to the pool. I leap from the water. Grab a branch. Pull myself up an start to climb.

The ghosthounds blast from the woods. They land with a splash in the pool jest below an throw theirselfs up in the air at me. Their bodies twist. Fangs slash. Jaws snap. I snatch my foot away jest in time. I scramble higher, higher. Their hot rage blasts me. They snarl an slaver. Claw at the air. Crash back in the water an leap agin. They're frantic to tear me apart.

I go high as I can. I crouch tight to the trunk. I cling to it, huddle among its thick boughs. I'm tremblin. Hand on my heart. My rackety heart, set to bust from my chest. The heartstone. It's hot on my skin.

The heartstone? I grab it. Hot. That means Jack. But – Jack? My lips move, soundless, as I think his name. Jack's leagues away. I don't unnerstand.

Skoll! Hati! Down! A man's voice commands the dogs. Come, he says. To me.

The ghosthounds hush. I can hear 'em splash from the pool. Hear 'em pantin fer breath. That voice. That voice.

Down, the man tells 'em agin.

There's silence fer a moment. Then he laughs. A short, this-ain't-funny kinda laugh.

Treed like a cat, he says. I was wondering when you'd show your hand. Come down, Saba. I know you're there.

That voice. Deep an dark. Cold panic grips me.

It ain't Jack. Oh no. It's DeMalo.

DeMalo. It cain't be. But it is. That means he was at the bridge. He must of bin with them Tonton at the rear. Ridin among his men, like he's wont to. DeMalo. Here. I don't believe it.

So, not dead after all, he says. Not that I ever thought you were. He's outta breath from the chase. His anger's leashed tight. You see, they brought me her body right away, he says. The girl in red. Your friend, the Free Hawk.

Maev. At Resurrection. Shot by the Tonton. Her hand pressed hard to her side. Her lifeblood drippin to the floor.

Gimme yer dress, she says. That's all they seen, a girl in a red dress. Help me, Saba. Quick.

We'd rescued Emmi. Nearly got away clean. Jest me an Maev left in the fortress. Then I made a mistake. An we got found out. The Tonton gave chase an shot Maev. A mortal wound. She was done an she knew it. Her final act was to save our lives. All of our lives. By puttin on my dress.

Not a bad idea, says DeMalo, her wearing the dress I gave you. I'd think it was you who fought to the death. You who held off my men so your friends could escape.

Now git outta here, she tells me. As far as you can, as fast as you can. Go!

That was my last-ever sight of her this side of the stars. As I jumped to the lake far below, I glanced back. Her head held high, hair loose to her waist, a shooter gripped in each hand. Maev. The Free Hawk warrior queen. Frozen in that moment in my memory.

They said she was fearless, says DeMalo. That she fought with blazing courage. I laid her on the pyre myself. Honoured her with full warrior ceremony, in case you care. What a tribute to her sacrifice, Saba. You, cowering in a tree. She was worth a hundred of you. Whoever she was.

Blood slams to my head. I scramble the tree an drop to the water. I face him. Bow drawn. Arrow nocked.

Her name was Maev, gawdamn you, Maev, I says.

We're ten foot apart. Me in the pool, thigh-deep. Him standin at the edge, the two ghosthounds eether side. They're laid down all obedient, tongues drippin, their raw pink eyes fixed on DeMalo. He ain't armed. Jest a shooter in his belt. He wears knee boots, britches an shirt. A black cloak drapes his shoulders. Slung across his chest is a worn leather bag. He holds my barksack in his hand.

Oh I see, he says, So I'm the one at fault here, am I? He dumps my sack, throws off his cloak an steps into the pool.

Come any closer, I kill you, dogs or no, I says.

He don't pay no heed. He moves slowly towards me. Who left their wounded friend to die? he says. Who blew up that bridge? Who killed those people? Twelve at my count. What do you make it, Saba?

I pull my bowstring tighter. I mean it, stay there, I says.

But on he comes. Dark eyes fixed on me. Let me remind you what you said, he says. That night you came to my room. You said, there's no point to this life if we don't at least try to make things better. You do remember that?

Shut up, I says. I cain't think fer the noise in my head. It's screamin, Shoot! Finish this! What's the matter with you? Shoot, fergawdsake! Shoot him!

He wades silent, intent, towards me. Do you remember what else you said? You said, I want to work with you, Seth. I want to make the world a better place.

His voice is rich brown earth.

We can't go on as we are. We need to find a new way. That's what you said, Saba. Is this your new way? Destroying? Killing? I'm creating something. I'm bringing order to chaos. I'm making a new world, one blade of grass at a time. Healing the earth and its people. I thought we wanted the same thing.

Shut up, would you? Jest shut up! I grip my bow tight. Tighter. C'mon, c'mon, I tell myself. One shot an this'll all be over. Chop off the head of the snake. Do it an be done. Do it now.

He stops two foot away. He opens his arms wide. He's givin me a clear shot to kill him.

His silver bracelet gleams on his wrist. His thin white shirt hangs damp. Through it, I can see his Tonton blood tattoo. The red risin sun over his heart. My skin tightens at the smell of him. Darkly green. Warmly juniper. The sun trickles shy through the trees. It trembles on his hair, thick an black as Nero's feathers. His broad cheekbones. His smooth, unreadable face. His watchful, beautiful face.

I cain't. I cain't do it. Slowly, I lower my bow. I says, gawdamn you sonofabitch.

He brings his arms down. Another perfect chance wasted, he says. Just like that night in my room. Whatever you put in my wine to knock me out, another drop or two would have killed me. Isn't that right? It would have been so easy. But you didn't. Why is that, I wonder? He steps in close. Touches the heartstone. It burns in the hollow of my throat. Sweat trickles between my breasts.

He touches my bare skin. It shivers at his touch. His hand brushes against the heartstone. It's hot, he says.

It's a heartstone, I says. The closer you git to yer heart's desire, the hotter it burns.

He says, Am I your heart's desire?

No no no. Step away, step away from him now. He cain't be trusted, he's dangerous, my enemy. But I don't. I don't move.

Why can't you kill me, Saba? he says.

I could ask you the same, I says.

The first time I saw you at Hopetown, he says, I knew you. Who you really are. Who you can be.

You don't know me, I says.

Oh, but I do, he says. You have a rare fire within you. The power to change things. The courage to act in the service of something greater than yourself. And you lower yourself to this shabby misadventure. What are you doing?

I'm silent.

I'm doing good, he says. I'm guiding people, freeing them from want and hardship and suffering, showing them the way to a better future. You were there at that dawn, in that bunker. You witnessed my visions of the world as it was. The lushness of the land, the richness of the seas. Those magnificent creatures. Unimaginable wonders. You do remember?

I couldn't ever fergit what I seen at that dawn.

At this moment, he says, in this place, we have a real chance, maybe our only chance, to start again. To do right by the earth this time. We can make a better world. We can know some of that wonder. Don't tell me you don't want that. I was watching you. I saw your face. Your tears. You care just as deeply as I do.

His words slide softly around me. They grip. Tighten. Pull me towards him.

You kill people to git what you want, I says.

So do you. You've just done it again, he says. But this isn't about what I want. I'm doing what's right. I'm making difficult, real decisions every day. Allocating what scarce resources there are to those who can make best use of them. I'm behaving morally. Responsibly.

Morally, I says.

Most people just survive day to day, he says. I have a higher calling. To serve the greater good. Any violence is regrettable, but it's a means to an end. You might even say, a virtuous necessity. You remember what I told you. We're cleaning the infected wounds of Mother Earth. Did you weep when you destroyed that cesspit Hopetown? Did you lose sleep over any scum that might have burned in its flames?

I cain't make no answer to that.

No, he says. We are so alike, Saba.

A virtuous necessity, I says. Is that what yer Stewards call it when you murder their newborns?

There's no killing of infants, as you well know, he says. The weak are left in the open overnight. If they're still alive in the morning, they get another chance. It's the way of the world and everyone here understands that. Does a bird feed all its young equally? Of course not. The healthiest and largest grow and thrive. The weak fall back and perish. If we have any chance of healing Mother Earth, we need the strongest and the best. The greater good must always be served.

His eyes persuade. His voice woos. His words caress. We have a destiny, he says. Together, Saba. We're born to command, not obey.

At last, at last I look in his eyes. Eyes so dark they're almost black. Heavy lids that hide who he is. In the night-time mountain lake deep of his eyes, I see a tiny reflection. It's me.

I ain't yer creature, I says.

I don't want you to be. I have plenty of those.

He bends his head. His mouth so close. His warm breath kisses my lips. Oh, my traitor soul. What is it in me that cleaves to him? To blur me melt me lose me.

I lose myself in the touch of him. The taste of him. The smell of him. Till I feel the moment when the edges of me start to blur. I lead him to his bed. We lie down together. An I melt to the dark, blank heat.

My skin trembles. Jest barely do I whisper. But I do. I whisper,

You will not … have me.

He goes still. Perfectly still. In the silence between us, the day holds its breath. Then,

I step back. From him. Away. From him. Air floods my lungs with such a rush that I'm dizzy. To heal the earth. That's right. But how he's doin it is wrong. Wrong wrong wrong. The greater good. Moral. Virtuous. He can twist lies into truth an truth into lies till I don't know one from the other. An he can twist me. Till I don't know who I am. Till I don't know what I believe.

We did wrong today at the bridge. An he's wrong. He is wrong. What's right must lie somewhere else. Between us maybe. Or beyond us.

If you keep on with this course, he says, more people will die. Maybe even people you care about. Your sister. Your brother. How many are you? Ten? Twelve? You're out of your depth. If I were you, I'd weigh my chances carefully.

I says, This earth belongs to everythin that lives here. Not jest yer Chosen ones, them that you deem worthy. Clean water an decent land is everybody's birthright. You cain't take it. You cain't own it. The Free Hawks ain't goin nowhere.

Well rehearsed, Saba, he says. Who put those words in your mouth? He's silent fer a moment. As always, I cain't read nuthin in his face. Not a hint of what's goin on inside of him. Then he says, I'm going to make you an offer. It's a generous one, in the circumstances. You'll formally surrender to me, all your weapons and your fighters. I'll guarantee everyone safe passage over the Waste, your family and friends. I'll provide them an escort as far as the Low China Pass. From there, it's a decent trail west through the mountains. This is all, of course, with the strict understanding that if they ever return to New Eden, they're dead.

An in return? I says.

You, he says.

A prisoner.

No. My wife.

Same thing, I says. I'll see you in hell first.

You and I are on the side of the angels, he says.

He wades to the edge, grabs a branch an pulls hisself outta the pool. Water showers offa his britches an boots. As he picks up his cloak, the ghosthounds rise. I'll rebuild the bridge in a week, he says. If you hit me again, I'll hit you back tenfold. When you've had enough, if you're still standing, come and find me. My offer's good until the blood moon. Like I said, I'm feeling generous. After that, I'll have your whole misstarred mob hunted down and killed. Wherever you run to. And that includes you, Saba. Believe me, I'm not sentimental.

So you say, I says. You had yer chances, jest like I have. I'm still here.

This is the endgame, he says. We play by new rules from now on. He starts to go. Oh! He turns back, like he's jest remembered somethin. I don't suppose you're pregnant, he says.

A swift move, my bow's up an I fire. My arrow close-shaves him. Spears the tree next to his head. The dogs move. Ready to go fer me. A lift of his hand halts 'em. DeMalo didn't dodge. Didn't flinch. His ear drips red on his white white shirt.

New rules, I says.

The blood moon, says he.

With a bow of his head, he disappears among the trees, the great white dogs at his heels.

I don't move. Not a twitch. My tight twisted heart tracks DeMalo. Not by sound. He moves silent, him an his dogs. No, I track him by the heat of the heartstone. It fades. It cools. Then it's cold. He's gone.

I let down my bow. A long breath shudders out. My

bravado whimpers an dies. His will drags at me, strong as a fast river current. It takes all that I got to resist.

I wade my shaky legs to the bank an slump among the mossy roots. Gawdamn heartstone. Not DeMalo, my heart's desire. Never, never DeMalo. I rip the thing off. Pull my arm back to fling it, drown it, rid myself of its hot lies. But I hesitate. I cain't. It was my mother's. The only thing I ever had that belonged to her. I shove it deep in my pocket.

I ease my achin shoulder. Only now do I feel it. That cart wheel at the bridge slammed into me hard. I'll have a bruise an then some to show fer it.

DeMalo's rattled me to the marrow. His last words grip my head like a vice. I ain't with child, I sure as hell ain't. Oh, help. First that nightmare at the bridge, then him trackin me, huntin me down with them unearthly hounds. Can he really mean what he says?

The blood moon. The first full moon after the harvest moon. Think now, think. Last night, as we ran through the woods. The moon was on the wax. A quarter moon. That means … when? Seven nights from now? Seven. Generous, he said. That ain't nuthin. He could be lyin. Bluffin. No. We're in the endgame, he said. New rules.

If you keep on, more people will die. Maybe people you care about.

I lost so many that I care about already. An we ain't no further ahead. Seven days. We'll never defeat him. We'll hafta run.

I'll have you hunted down and killed. Wherever you run to.

He will too. An I'm instantly hot with shame I'd ever think of runnin. Like I'm some common, everyday coward. That jest proves how he gits to me. We're all set on this fight. But Emmi. I need Emmi away from danger. I should of done it long ago. I'll send her to Auriel Tai. Back to the Snake River camp. She'll be safe there. If we was to die, she'd have Auriel to raise her to a woman. Lugh can take her there. No, he'd never leave me an he won't have a star reader raise Em. Tommo, then. He can go with her.

So. Stand an fight. An win. But we ain't gonna win by blowin bridges.

If you hit me again, I'll hit you back tenfold.

There must be another way.

A cautious quork comes from the tree above me. Nero sidles out from wherever he's bin hidin all this time. This is the crow who's fought wolfdogs with beak an claw. Who'll rush to defend me from all dangers. Unless, of course, that danger's called DeMalo.

Fat lotta good you are, I tell him. Thanks fer nuthin. You led him straight here.

He drops onto my lap then climbs my front to nibble on my ear. He always does that when he feels guilty. The thing is, he likes DeMalo an he knows he shouldn't. He'd of gone fer the dogs in my defence, no problem. But he'd never harm DeMalo an the dogs was with him, so he must of got confused.

Whose side are you on? I says. I hug him close an stroke his breast feathers. They're growin back good. Where DeMalo's hawk wounded him, where DeMalo stitched him – a month ago now – it's healed well. Who am I to talk? I says. Whose side am I on? I had him an I couldn't kill him. I couldn't. What the hell's wrong with me? I kiss Nero's head. We cain't tell nobody about this, you hear?

He chitters agreement. Nero. Th'only livin creature I can speak to freely these days. I gotta guard myself close with everybody else. A leader tells her people as little as possible,

31

only what they need to know. That's somethin I learned from Slim.

More people will die. People you care about. Your sister. Your brother.

Lugh, I says. Ohmigawd, Lugh, of course. C'mon, we gotta git to the rendezvous. Make sure they all made it okay. I jump to my feet. Nero spills to the ground with a squawk of protest. As I gather my gear, I says, They'll be wonderin where we are. Emmi'll be inside out with worry. Nero, we gotta go. C'mon.

He plays deaf. Beak deep in his birdy armpit, mutterin somethin about a mite. He'll catch me up later. When it suits him.

I shoulder my barksack an bow. As I pass, I wrench my arrow from the tree.

It's the first time in my life I ever shot to miss.

I'm cautious as I leave the pool. I set a course due north fer the rendezvous at Painted Rock. I keep my eyes sharp, my ears keen, my bolt shooter ready in my hand. All clear. Nuthin untoward. No sound in the woods but the sounds of a wood. The bubble chat of warblers. The sigh of the wind. The creak of trees as they ease their bones.

After a couple hunnerd foot, I start to relax. Then. Behind me. A shift in the air. Not a sound, but somebody's there. As I start to move, a gun shoves me in the neck. Hard to the base of my skull. I stop dead. I know the feel of that snubby nose. A shortbolt shooter. A fast blast. A messy end.

The voice comes from close behind me. I'll be takin your weapons an pack. An it's all the same to me if I have to kill you for 'em. You're gonna drop your gun first, then your bow. One at a time, nice an easy.

It's a woman. She's steady-handed with the shortbolt. I can tell by the angle she's taller'n me. A whisker below six foot.

I let my shooter fall to the ground. She smells of earth an sweat. She sounds of hard years an hard choices. Somethin starts to jig at the edge of my mind. I hesitate a moment.

I said, the bow! She presses the shortbolt fiercer, deeper into the tender spot between my spine an skull. I slide it offa my shoulder. My rare whiteoak bow, the gift of a shaman. I toss it carefully to one side. My quiver follows. I don't think she's clocked my knife yet. It's tucked away in my boot sheath.

She snatches it. Quick as a rattler, she moves. The knife's gone an the gun didn't budge. She's good. Must have long arms.

Let's have your pack, she says.

I drop that too.

Hands up, she says. On your head.

I do it.

Now, she says. On the ground. Kneel.

The red hot flashes an I'm back at Pine Top Hill. With Emmi, prisoner of Vicar Pinch. The rest of us beat by him an his Tonton. Outfoxed. Outnumbered. I knelt at his feet an begged fer their lives.

I don't kneel fer nobody, I says.

She grabs my collar. Kicks me. Back of my legs. I'm down. On my knees. Gun hard to my skull.

Didn't your pa ever teach you manners? she says.

Them words. The very same. An I'm thinkin, me an Emmi in a sweetgrass valley. A cabin by a stream, bowls of stew an tough kindness. No. No. It cain't be her.

Nero drops from the sky. He's a screamin fury. Full attack, with beak, wings an claws. He slashes, beats an screeches. The woman staggers back an I'm free. I scramble around. Jump to my feet. An it is, it's her. It's Mercy. Ma's friend Mercy. We thought she was dead. What's she doin here?

She's on the ground, scrabblin to git away from Nero. Arms huggin her head, pertectin herself. Her hair's bin shaved to snow-white stubble. Around her neck there's a iron collar. A slave collar.

Nero's at her. In a flurry of feathers. I can see he's drawn blood. He means to do worse. Nero, no! I yell. Stop! Go on! I shoo him away an he takes to a tree to glare at me an grumble. Mercy's lyin on her side, folded in on herself. I crouch at her side.

Mercy, I says. It's okay, Mercy. It's me. It's Saba. Allis's girl. Willem an Allis. I touch her hand. Lightly. Jest barely. In case she's a shade, a shadow. But she's warm. She's real.

We came to you at Crosscreek, I says. Half a year back an more now. Me an Emmi, remember? When Pa got killed. When the Tonton took Lugh. I found him, Mercy. I got him back.

Slowly, slowly, her arms come down.

Here, I says. Look! I pull the heartstone from my pocket.

She stares. Dazed. Disbelievin. Ma gave the heartstone to her, long years back. Well before I was born. Then Mercy gave it to me. From friend to friend, from friend to daughter.

Saba, she says. Can it really be you? I help her to sit. She stares at me. She lays a work-rough hand on my face. It ain't possible, she says.

34

I feel tears prick my eyes. I smile 'em away as I hang the heartstone around my neck. I say what Jack always says. Nuthin's impossible, I says. Unlikely, but not impossible. That's one thing I learned since last we met.

An much more besides, I'd say. Her shrewd brown eyes is readin me. Seein further, deeper than I'd like. A raw girl came to me at Crosscreek, she says. I don't see that girl no more.

Lemme help you, I says. I hand her to her feet an we stand there. We take a long look at each other.

Tall an lean an weathered an tough. An so strongly alive an wise. Mercy was like some magnificent tree. Livin free an alone in her little green paradise, hidden away deep in the woods. A handsome woman with high cheekbones, cropped white hair an dark brows. Now her flesh clings to her bones. Her mean hemp slave shift hangs ragged to her knees.

In body, she might be less. But in spirit, she's somehow more. She wears her slave collar like the finest Wrecker gold.

We thought you was dead, I says.

I nearly was, she says. Some bugger blew up a bridge just as we was about to cross it. But I thank 'em just the same. Gave me the chance to slip my chains. It's easier to steal the key from a dead guard. Not to mention his gun. Speakin of which—

As she goes to collect the shortbolt from the ground where it fell, I says, Yer welcome. My pleasure.

She turns, startled. It was you? she says.

Me an some others, I says. I gotta rendezvous with 'em at a place called Painted Rock. Four leagues north. Yer comin with me. I gather my stuff as I'm talkin. The scattered weapons an sack.

I'll do my best to keep up, she says. If I slow you down, you leave me.

I wince at the sight of her arms, bloody where Nero attacked her. Sorry about Nero, I says. Are you okay?

I'll survive, she says. I've had worse. Thin white lines, the scars of a whip, criss-cross her sun-tough skin.

How'd they git hold of you? I says.

Later, she says. Let's move. They might still be about.

She readies her shortbolt fer action an I do the same with my shooter. She grabs my barksack an shoulders it. Kills my protest with one fierce look. I ain't dead yet. Lead on, she says.

I whistle at Nero. We set off at speed, alert to any sound, any movement. An me an Mercy head fer the rendezvous.

He was caught soon after they'd all split up. Hijacked by the mist, tricked by the terrain, he ambushed himself at a dizzy steep ravine. As he reeled back from the edge, there they were. Three Tonton, their firesticks aimed at his heart.

He braced himself for the shots. The flare of the muzzles. The impact. The oblivion, swift and sure. He was calm. Blue calm. He felt a beat of wonder at that.

But no shot came. Death, his choice. To turn and leap and cry out for life as he pedalled the air to the rocks below. No blue calm there. He surrendered. Hands bound behind him, hooded and gagged, they led him stumbling through the woods. Half a league or so, he reckoned. They stopped in what he took to be a clearing. He was made to sit on the ground.

They waited. The four of them waited. He could feel when the mist began to lift. The day warmed itself on his skin. Time passed. They waited.

Suddenly, they were scrambling, hauling him to his feet. His hood was taken off, his gag untied.

The two ghosthounds came first. They slipped through the trees into the clearing and sat right away, panting. A few moments later, he appeared. The man they were all waiting for. He'd been more than half expecting it – who else would the Tonton wait on with such disciplined patience? Still, his heart lurched and quickened.

Up close. Full power. The night dark gaze tethered him. Circled him. Considered him. Then. In the black water deep of the Pathfinder's eyes, there was a ripple.

He smiled. The smile of a man who'd found what he'd been seeking.

We have much to talk about, he said.

I'd fergot about Mercy's crippled ankle. The one she broke an had to set herself. Did a bugger of a job – her own words – an got left with a limp. Her spirit's bin forged by hardship. Her body's tough from a lifetime of toil. She don't ask fer no favours. She don't let herself fall behind. But she's taxed by the pace, I can tell.

By mid-mornin, she's slowed down considerable. We've only gone two leagues, jest halfways there. Weak to begin with, her flight up the hill an through the woods must of tapped her out. It's only sheer grit keeps her goin. I hate to, but we'll hafta stop an rest soon. I bite down my frustration. If I was on my own, I'd be runnin flat out.

Deadbone country's given way to a scrubby grassland. The day's bloomed to a muggy fug. Hot an sticky an close.

We skirt a leery path around a lonesome farm, keepin to a narrow ribbon of jack pine. Some cack-handed fool's bin hackin it hard fer firewood.

Can you believe it? Mercy shakes her head in disgust.

A few steps on, we see the fools. In a field in front of a tyreshack, a Steward couple quarrel furiously over a broken plough. A pair of kids, fifteen or so, bein kicked in the pants by nature. They're managin to keep around the shack clear an the track to the road too, but that's it. Billows of bramble an chokeweed romp the fields. Tethered to a spindlebush next to the shack stands a neat red pony.

Wait here, I tell Mercy.

Keepin low, I dash through the chokeweed, slip the pony's tether an lead him quietly back to her.

He'll make yer goin easier, I says. Lemme help you on. She steps in my cupped hands, I boost her onto his back an we hurry away without notice.

Once we're well gone I says, They'll find life a bit harder without no pony.

From the look of 'em, says Mercy, I'd say it might well be the last straw. Them two got no skills, no knowledge. You can see there ain't no trust between 'em. They probly hardly know each other. It won't take much to make their house crumble. It don't stand on strong foundations.

Let's hope, I says.

That was a half-decent place, not so long ago, she says. Resettlement, the Tonton call it. I call it what it is. Stealin. Whoever had that bit of land stole from 'em, they was earth-wise. Not like them hopeless kids. No, they would have watched an listened an worked through the seasons. They would have learned from their patch of earth. What it needs. What it don't need. How they could live together. That takes years.

38

I know she's thinkin about her green valley at Crosscreek. The cradle of her toil an care an hope. Wonderin if it's in good hands or gone to ruin. Her small wooden shack shaded by pines. The red bench by the door. The murmur of shallow water over stones.

If Lugh saw that mess, he'd spit fire, I says. It's his dearest wish to have some good land. To work the earth. Fer us to be settled.

An you? she says. Is that what you want? A life workin the land?

I ain't thought about it much, I says. That's fer later. Right now, I got bigger things on my mind.

The blood moon. That's what's on my mind. Seven nights away.

I told Mercy a lie. I have thought about it. A life workin the land.

Lugh's always wanted the same thing. To be planted in one place. To live by the heartbeat of the earth. Its rise an fall an rise an fall. Where nuthin changes, but everythin changes. When we was little, he'd kneel in wonder to the first grass of spring. I'd trample it as I tried to do the same.

I wanted what he wanted, though. Of course I did. We belonged together. We was made together. Two halfs of one whole. Boy an girl. Fair an dark. We took it as a given that we'd be together all our lives. It would never of occurred to us that we wouldn't. But that was before. Before the Tonton came to Silverlake an killed Pa an took Lugh an everythin got changed ferever.

This time we're in now, this is after.

After is like this man Pa told us about. He got gangrene in his arm an had to have it chopped off, jest below the shoulder. He'd bin without it fer years when Pa met him, but he swore blue he could feel that arm still. The weight of it. The urge to reach out with his long-gone hand. I could never imagine that. Not at all. Then Lugh got took from me. The first cut was made. An before we knew it, before eether of us could stop it, he got cut from me an me from him. By fate an chance an destiny. By death an betrayal. By wounds to the soul too big to be spoke of. By secrets an half-truths an lies.

When I lived in before, I never thought there'd be after. Now I know how that man must of felt.

I still got stones in my boots from the bridge an Mercy's badly in need of food an water. A half league on from the farm, I call a rest stop at the ruins of a small Wrecker temple. The few pine trees growin within its crumbly stone walls grant us some welcome shade.

As the stolen pony gits to work on a patch of late nettles, I tip a stream of tiny pebbles from my boots. As Mercy loosens the cords on hers, a shadow of pain tightens her lips.

You okay? I says.

She nods. I hand her the waterskin an she takes a long, parched pull. That's good, she says.

I drink an pour some in the cap fer Nero. Once he's

dibbled his fill, I trickle the rest over his head to cool him. He shutters his eyes in pleasure. I rummage in my sack fer eatables. A cake of dried bitter-root wrapped in a leaf. That's it. Sorry, I says. It's slim pickins.

Not to me, she says.

I give her it all. I ain't hungry. I gather a lapful of fallen pine cones an crack 'em open fer the nuts. I give most to Mercy. A few to Nero fer a treat.

She chews slowly. Makin each bite last. Pine nuts an bitter-root, the taste of freedom, she says. Who'd have thought? An who'd have thought it 'ud be you come to my rescue? The ways of chance are strange indeed.

Some chance, I says. Meant to be, I'd say.

She smiles. There speaks the daughter of a star reader, she says. Who knows? You may be right.

We're silent as she eats. The weight of our unasked questions grows ever heavier. Hers to me. Mine to her. An I feel somethin else growin too. Inside of me. The need to say somethin. To tell. To confess.

A lot happened after I left you, I says. When we got to Hopetown – you did warn me it was a bad place. It was worse than bad. I done some … things. So many things along the way. I killed some people. Not becuz I wanted to, I had to. It was kill or be killed. Is that wrong?

I didn't mean to say all that. I really didn't. Hell.

That's a big question, says Mercy. Is it ever right to kill another person?

I'm jest openin my mouth, jest about to ask how she got slaved when she says,

The Tonton came to Crosscreek one day. To run me off or … burn me out or kill me an take my land. That's the first time I felt the lash of a whip. But when they found out I heal,

41

they decided I'd be useful. I was set to work in one of their babyhouses. I'll help any woman give birth. I will not be party to leavin a newborn outside overnight, to be took by a beast or killed by the cold. That's what they do with the weak ones.

So I'm told, I says.

Exposure, they call it, she says. The baby's left out, naked. If they make it through the night, they're judged tough enough. They git another chance. But I ain't never seen one brought back. I used to sneak out to try an save 'em. Oh, I had all kinds of schemes, but I never managed it. Always got caught. They whipped me plenty, but I kept on tryin. They got fed up with me in the end. Decided to wring the last little bit of life outta me labourin on their roads. We was headed to start work on a new one when you blew the bridge.

What's all that about? I says. A new road in the Raze an settlers. The Raze is a deadland.

No idea, says Mercy. I'll tell you this, though. Them big hounds that was runnin the woods –

Yeah, I lost 'em in some water, I says.

– they came with this Tonton, she says. He showed up with the dogs when we was well on our way. He just started ridin at the back. None of 'em said a word, but they knew who he was all right. They rode a lot taller from then on. If they send somebody important like him, I figger it means the job's important.

I figger you might be right, I says.

I'll tell you this too, she says. That road in the Raze would have bin my last. There ain't much left of me.

We'll git you strong agin, I says.

She pops another nut in her mouth. With a frown, she eases the iron slave collar.

Is it heavy? I says.

The worst thing is how fast you get used to it, she says. She tips her head back an closes her eyes. Where Nero pecked an scratched her, the blood's dried. On her arms an shoulders an a couple places on her neck. I dig my medicine bag from my pack. I wet the end of my sheema from the waterskin, kneel at her side an commence to dab her clean. At the first touch, a little smile curves her lips.

Don't git yer hopes up, I says. I ain't no good at doctorin, not like you. Remember you fixed my hand that got shot? I show her my right hand. You did a neat job, I says. I tell you, I collected a good few scars since then. I got goatweed unction. You want some?

Thanks, she says. As I smear it on her wounds with a careful pinky, she looks at the heartstone. Our eyes meet. My face starts to warm. I drop my gaze to my task.

Feels like a lifetime ago I gave you that, she says.

What is it? It's pretty, says Emmi.

The pale rosy stone feels smooth an cool. Shaped like a bird's egg. A thumb's length in size. The light gleams through it, milky an dull.

A heartstone, says Mercy. It leads you to your heart's desire. The closer you get, the hotter it burns.

It burns fer Jack. It burns fer DeMalo. Desire, yes. An danger. An betrayal. That's what the heartstone's led me to.

I remember that mornin well, says Mercy. Crosscreek looked like paradise. After a moment, she says, We slept in these wooden sheds. Us slaves, I mean. Crammed together, chained together, men an women. My first night, I was lyin there an it was silent but ... there was such a clamour from all them souls. So, after a while I said, My name is Mercy. My home is Crosscreek. A sweet green valley that sleeps in the sun. They was all quiet. Then one of the men said, The name's Cade. I ain't got no home but the road. Don't need no roof but the sky. One by one, we all spoke. Our name an where we come from. After that, we did the same every night. Just before we went to sleep. Every night without fail. To remind ourselfs. So's we didn't forget.

Jest like me at Hopetown, I think. That's what I did. Night after night, in that cellblock. In the dark, on my own, with little left to anchor me to this earth. Knowin that the day would see me brought to the Cage, to fight fer my life, agin an agin. I came so close to losin myself. So very very close.

Right, I says. I'm done here. We better make tracks. I pack my barksack an she cords her boots. I reach down a hand an help her up. Slim's got a junkjimmy friend'll git that collar offa you, I says. He can be trusted not to talk.

She grips my hand tight. So can I, she says. An I'm a good listener too.

Thanks, I says. I'm okay.

She touches my cheek. You look so like Willem, she says softly. He was the finest man I ever laid eyes on.

It's the way she says his name. As if, long ago, it flamed in her like a sunburst. An suddenly I know. She loved Pa. Mercy loved my father.

Amazed questions rise in me. How? When? Did he love her? Did she keep on lovin him, even though she couldn't have him? He was so crazy about Ma, it must of hurt her to see them together. An yet, she was Ma's true friend. She birthed me an Lugh. She kept Emmi alive.

I don't git the chance to ask. She's read my face. Realized her slip. Slammed the door on her secret. Her face is a careful blank as she goes over to the pony. I think I'll call him Tam, she says. She climbs aboard without my help. How much further? she says.

I squint at the sky. We should be there by middle day, I says.

As I set a fast pace an Mercy follows behind on the pony, I ponder. On the dark seam that runs through my life. From before I was born to this moment an beyond. Chance. Fate. Destiny.

That I should meet with Mercy agin. At this time, in this place. It's fer some reason I've yet to know. But time will tell. These days, if somethin seems like chance, my muzzle lifts to the wind an my ears prick.

Oft-times I hear Pa. His voice still echoes in my head, in my blood. Our lives was fixed in the stars the moment the world began. You cain't change what's written. Fate. That's what he believed. So I did too. Till I started to think fer myself. Pa's very last words to me was a warnin from the stars. Maybe the only truth they ever gave him.

They're gonna need you, Saba. Lugh an Emmi. An there'll be others too. Many others. Don't give in to fear. Be strong, an never give up. No matter what happens.

Them words, his last words, they've kept me goin time after time. Given me strength when I was weak. How strange that Mercy should love my father. Her, rooted in the wisdom of the earth. Pa, who looked in vain to the stars fer answers.

I wonder what Mercy would make of Auriel. How they'd git on if they was ever to meet. I'd sure like to talk with them both together.

Auriel. Auriel Tai. The star reader girl with the wolfdog eyes. Granddaughter of a warrior shaman. Namid the Star Dancer, maker of my whiteoak bow. Auriel's rare. She's the real thing, not like Pa was. She walks the thin place between the earth an the stars. The place of dreams an light an spirit. What she knows an how she knows it cain't easily be explained.

If it warn't fer her, I wouldn't still be in this life. I was nearly lost to the madness of grief, seein the dead day an night, when Tracker led me to her at the Snake River. Auriel helped me, she healed me, she spurred me on. She gave me hope an purpose. Fer the first time, she made sense of everythin I'd bin through. She was the first one to say the word to me. Destiny.

There are some people, Saba — not many — who have within them the power to change things. Through their actions, they turn the tide of human affairs.

To turn the tide aginst DeMalo is my destiny. That's what she said. She said all of my roads lead to him. An she's bin proved right over an over.

Turn the tide. I thought I knew how to do that. That the way ahead looked clear. Hit him hard where it hurts. Hit him often. Weaken his grip. But after today — I need to think agin. If only Auriel was here. She wouldn't even hafta think what I oughta be doin. She'd know becuz she'd read it in the stars.

Well she ain't here. I need Jack. Right away. But I gotta hold myself in patience till tonight. When I meet him at the Irontree. Together we'll figger out what to do.

He jest cain't know. About DeMalo. The blood moon. The endgame.

Painted Rock rises high among the trees. It ain't one rock but three of 'em, crowded close together. Great old buffaloes of sandstone, their backs hunched aginst the sky.

In the middle day brightness their worn flanks blaze pink an gold. All is silent. Nero swoops ahead to herald our comin. The rush of his wings flicks the hush.

Mercy sniffs the air. There's a hint of cooked meat, rich an deep. Somethin sure smells good, she says.

That means Molly ain't cookin, I says. Lucky us. It's the devil's work when she's at the cookpot.

I cup my hands to my mouth an give our daylight signal. The three-cheep call of a pinewax. I wait a count of two, then I call once more. There's a cheep in reply from the top of the rock. A small figger appears.

There's Emmi, I says.

Light glints offa the glass of her looker as she trains it our way. I raise a hand. So does Mercy. A shriek of excitement cracks the silence. She disappears.

She's seen you, I says. Brace yerself.

Camp's in the middle of the three great rocks. We ride through a wide gap between two of 'em into a big circle space, open to the sky. This is one of the old places. A site of long memory an much use. The ground's bin worn smooth by many feet. Many hands down the ages have scarred the rock walls. Words an pictures scratched into the stone. By dreamers, idlers, artists an fools.

The Cosmic's parked up. Slim's medicine cart, the Cosmic Compendalorium. Fourth of its Ilk, says Slim. Whatever the hell that means. Painted bright yellow, with suns an moons an stars all over, stuffed to the gunnels with potions an cures. The horses bunch together, jostlin noses over heaps of dry grass. There's Molly's Prue, a placid mule called Bean, Slim's carthorse, my own Hermes, eight beasts in all.

Every head turns as we come through the gap. Horses an people alike. Slim's at the cookfire, ladlin stew into Ash's tin.

47

Molly's sat on a rock, eatin. Nero's already on the mooch, hoppin around her, beggin fer a share. But no Lugh. No Creed. No Tommo. My gut tightens.

Where are they? I says to Ash.

No sign of 'em yet, she says. When you blew the whistle, I jest legged it. What happened? I heard the blast go off. Loads of smoke. Damn, I wish I'd seen that.

We got chased, I says. They should of bin here by now.

You only jest got here yerself, says Slim. What was the Tonton doin there? I thought yer contact swore they didn't patrol that far out.

It warn't no patrol, I says. They was headed fer the Raze. Resettlement. A work party. It all went to hell, I – gawdammit, what's keepin 'em? Not even one back yet.

Simmer down, he says. They probly jest had to take a roundabout route. We'll debrief once everybody's back an settled in. Here, where's yer manners, you savage?

He makes a waddly beeline fer Mercy. We're used to Slim's quirks, but to her he must look a odd fish – jobble-bellied in a patchwork frock the size of a tent, grubby eyepatch askew, muttonchops an hair in a mad dandelion frizz. A mangy old rabbit's foot dangles from a chain on his belt. Young folk today, they got no couth, he says. Wouldn't know polite if it walked up an slapped their face. We'll jest hafta make our own innerductions an shame on them. Doctor Salmo Slim, TPS. That's Travellatin Physician an Surgeon. Inchantee, ma'am.

I'm Mercy, she says.

She was with the work party, I says. Managed to free herself in the confusion. An, as chance would have it, she's a friend of the family. That there's Ash. An that's Molly.

Mercy's drawn an exhausted but she manages a smile. Glad to know yuz, she says.

Me an Slim help her down from the pony. Mercy's a healer, I tell him.

A fellow perfessional, eh? In that case, I am double-delighted to make yer acquaintanceship, Miz Mercy. As he bows, all gallant, over her hand, they take each other's measure with keen eyes. I'll have a gander at that ankle if you like, he says.

Thanks, she says. What I'd really like is to get rid of this collar.

Slim peers at it closely. You need a junkjimmy with a cuttin tool fer that, he says. I know one'll git it off, no trouble. We'll git you over there aysap.

Ash says, In case yer wonderin, ma'am, yes, that is a dress he's wearin. It belonged to his late mother.

Don't let that faze you, though, says Molly. He's a blue-chip quack, is our Slim.

Mama Big Doe bequeried me three frocks, her wood leg an two left shoes, says Slim. A salt johnny from Pooce bought the leg an a shoe, but her frocks fit me – an as you can see, I'm a awkward size – so, waste ye not, says I. I'm a fashion free-wheeler an damn the torpedoes.

Mercy! Emmi yells. She comes runnin through the gap with Tracker right behind her. It's you, it really is! We thought you was dead!

As she rushes at Mercy, Mercy sees Tracker an he sees her an, as her mouth falls open an she's sayin, Tracker? Can it be? he's flyin at her, barkin with excitement. Then she's bein hugged by Emmi an Tracker's turnin hisself inside out, lickin everywhere with his long sloppy tongue an the whole thing's a giddy jamboree. Mercy says to me, How on earth did you find him? Why didn't you say?

Sorry, I fergot. I'll tell you later, I says.

49

She's lookin dazed. Em's already bolted into a breathless gallop about how Tracker found us, so I go over, sayin, All right, that's enough, you can tell her later. I peel Emmi away from her.

Slim helps Mercy to a seat by the fire with Ash an Molly. He bustles about, fillin her a tin of food while he clackets on in his usual cheerful way.

What took you so long? Emmi clings to me. Her legs clamp my waist. Her skinny arms bindweed my neck. Where's Lugh? Where's the boys? I bin watchin ferever.

Hey hey, yer stranglin me, I says. Git down, yer too big.

She twines me even tighter. Grabs my face in her grubby hands. Worry clouds her blue-sky eyes. I was worried an worried somethin bad would happen to you. An it did, she says. The Tonton came. Ash said. What happened? Where's Lugh an Tommo?

They're on their way, I says. Now lemme go. On yer feet.

She slides down reluctantly. Her hands might be dirty but fer once she's washed her face. In fact, she's clean an neat. Positively respectable. Her wayward brown hair's in a plait. Her shirt's tucked in. Her britches buttoned. She's even laced her boots. This is Molly's doin. Left to herself, Em's a scarecrow of a girl.

She stands with arms crossed, all sulky chin an scrimped up mouth. What did I do now? she says.

Don't gimme that mardy face, I says. Listen, Em, yer a Free Hawk now. You cain't go screamin around like you done jest now, like some little kid. I told you before.

But I—

Who's on lookout?

Me, she says.

So what're you doin here? I says.

50

She heaves a sigh. Well, pardon me fer bein glad you ain't dead, she says.

Git back there this second, go on, I says.

Saba? says Slim. There's fruit bat gumbo in the pot.

I thought somethin smelled good. Lugh's voice comes from the entranceway. I whirl around. He's all in one piece. His smile stretches ear to ear as he opens his arms wide. Anybody miss me? he says.

I did, I did! Emmi dashes at him, leaps at him. He twirls her in a circle. You bum! she cries. I bin worried sick. Did you see Tommo? Creed?

What? They ain't here yet? Sorry I bin so long, he says to me. I had to cut out wide to lose them Tonton. They took some shakin.

What did I tell you? says Slim.

Look who Saba found. It's Mercy, Emmi says.

What? Then Lugh's shakin Mercy's hand, sayin, I sure wanna know how this came about. It's bin a long time, ma'am.

You must be starvin, son, says Slim. Everybody come an eat.

That's it fer Em goin back on watch. I'd hafta drag her there by her pigtail. An, after all, it's daylight. We crowd around Slim's cookpot an he loads our tins. Tracker an Nero make fast work of a stringy squirrel he tosses their way. They keep a wary eye on him, anxious not to splat him with guts. Last time they did, he banished 'em from the fire fer two chilly nights. We're jest gittin stuck into our meal an all wantin to ask Mercy this or tell her that, when Tommo pitches up at last. He tells the same tale as Lugh. He had to go off his set course to lose his pursuers. He falls on the food like a jackal.

Then a short while later, Creed arrives. He's bare chested.

His frock coat's folded, tucked unner one arm. The other arm's streaked with dried blood. There's a arrow stuck in his shoulder.

Creed lounges aginst a boulder while Molly stitches his wound with a fine bone needle an gut thread. He looks like some spirit of nature. Wild curly hair, silver rings in his ears, tattooed waist to neck with twined vines an serpents.

Molly bends her head to her work. As always, there's a scarf tied over her long blonde curls. Pulled low on her forehead to hide her brand. That loathsome letter. The lie that the Tonton seared in her skin. W. W fer whore. But it don't mar her beauty. Nuthin could. A face to make angels weep fer joy. That's what Ike used to say of Molly. An lips that detoured many a man to her Storm Belt junkshack tavern. In the hope that she'd serve them a smile with their drink.

She ain't smilin now. She's got her Creed look on. It says, if he does it agin, if he declares his love fer me in front of everybody I'll slap his head from his neck. But Creed's so punch drunk in love with her, he cain't seem to stop hisself. He's only got the one tactic. Open desperation. He must think she'll be flattered or take pity on him an eventually give in. As if a delicious woman like her would ever go fer a hobbledy boy like him. Molly's used to swattin off lust-lorn loobies from her tavern days, but Creed's a whole new world of aggravation.

I go over to crouch beside them. Give her some relief. I says, With all them tattoos, I'm surprised you can see what yer doin. How deep did the arrow go?

Not very, she says. Surprise surprise, he's makin out it's worse than it is.

Creed says, Anythin to keep you close to me, darlin.

I ain't yer darlin, she says.

Cut it out, Creed, I says.

He leans his head in close to hers. I'm crazy fer you, Molly. Marry me, he says.

She slaps him hard. Almost slaps his head off. Everybody turns at the sound. The angry crack of skin on skin. Her brown eyes spit. In a voice of low fury she says, I've told you an I've told you but you don't pay no heed. I'm sick to death of this buck-at-the-rut pursuit. If you was a man, I'd of shot you by now. Fer once an fer all, Creed, leave me the hell alone!

She ends on a shout of frustration. There's a fat silence as she goes to the fire an sits. Nobody dares move fer a long moment. Then they start eatin agin, with nervous caution. Not so much as a tink of a spoon. In case the sound sets her off agin.

I should never of let it come to this. Me an Slim had a talk some days ago. We agreed I oughta call Creed to order, but I bin puttin it off as ticklish work.

He looks at me with a plea in his eyes. The mark of her hand blooms ugly on his face. She's left him half-stitched. The needle's stuck in the wound, the thread danglin. I'm a nervous doctor but I sit down. I pull out the needle an, with clammy hands, I start to sew. I start in on him too, my voice hushed.

You gotta stop this right now, I says. It don't jest vex Molly, it unsettles all of us. You know she's still mournin Ike. It's only bin six months, fergawdsake. Show her some respect.

He's silent, frownin.

Are you listenin to me? I says.

53

I gotta make her see, he says. What can I do?

Be a man, Creed, I says. Accept that she don't want you an leave her alone. There's too much at stake fer us to fall out. We gotta be able to depend on each other, stick tight together. Okay, I'm done here. I'll git Emmi to bandage you, she's got neat fingers.

I jest don't unnerstand, he says.

I grab his knee an shake it hard. Molly ain't fer you, I says. Accept it. Capeesh?

He looks at me. No, I mean, I was so sure, he says. That first time I seen her, my heart knew. It went … oh, it's you, yer the one. How can that be wrong?

Yer heart, I says. More like yer britches.

I stand up an he does too. A storm brews in his grey-blue eyes. Yer really somethin, y'know that? he says. Depend on each other. Stick tight together. That's rich, comin from you.

I start to hear the pound of war drums. What's the problem? I says. Say what you mean an be done.

He raises his voice so everyone can hear. Yer the problem. That's what I mean. We're all thinkin it, he says. I'm th'only one's got the guts to say it. What the hell was that, Saba? Back at the bridge? You, chasin that fuse? We should of bin long gone, safely away. Instead you nearly got us all killed.

You know why, I says. There was innocent people there. Slaves, like Mercy.

That's their bad luck, he says. Whose side are you on? We're yer people, not them.

I jest bin told what went down today, says Slim. He fixes me with his watery one-eyed pebble stare. Creed's right, he says, we agreed the plan. Set the charge, blow the bridge an skedaddle. In an out, quick an clean.

Around the fire, every head's turned to look at me now. Emmi's wide-eyed worried, seated at Mercy's feet.

Killin warn't part of the plan, I says.

It's called collateral damage, says Slim. Would you rather yer comrades got killt? You keep yer eye on the goal an you keep discipline an that includes you.

Sometimes you gotta change tactics, I says.

Agreed, he says. But that ain't what you did. You change tactics fer two reasons. To win the goal or save yer crew. You'd already won the goal. What you did was risk yer crew. That's a bad leader.

Ash says, I don't git you, Saba. What about Darktrees? The Tonton slaughtered our friends while they slept. Forty lives. Free Hawks an Raiders. Have you fergot that? An Epona an Maev. Ike an Bram. They all died fer this fight. I'm sorry, but Creed's right. Where's yer loyalty?

I am loyal, I says. I ain't fergot. Not Darktrees an not one of them you name. Far from it. But this ain't about loyalty, I—

It is fer me, says Tommo. Loyalty.

But it's different now, I says. Doncha see? Here in New Eden, I mean. There's too many people caught between us an the Tonton. Innocent people.

We cain't afford a weak leader, says Ash. Me an Creed bin down that road before, with Maev. An it leads to defeat an death. Yer strong. Certain. Single minded. You ain't that bleedin heart we seen today. Gawdammit, yer the Angel of Death. Yer epic, Saba. That's why we all lined up behind you.

Maybe you ain't got the stummick fer this no more, says Creed.

I go cold still inside. Is that a challenge? I says.

He says, Be who we need or stand aside.

That's enough, says Lugh. He rises to his feet from

55

his place by the fire. He's bin listenin all this time. What happened at the bridge was my fault, he says.

Everybody looks at him. Surprise on their faces.Puzzlement in their eyes.

How d'you figger that? says Creed.

I got spooked by them first two Tonton, Lugh says. I was unner the bridge with the blastpack. Saba ordered me not to move but I did. I slipped an fell an she came to save me. If it warn't fer her an Tommo, I'd be dead. I defied a direct order from my commander. I'm the one who broke discipline. I put her an the rest of yuz at risk. If Saba did anythin wrong, it's becuz I rattled her. She couldn't depend on me. The blame fer today is mine entirely. I'm sorry. I let everybody down.

He's said all of this lookin straight at me an no other. My throat's tight.

After a moment, Slim says, Well, we got lucky this time. Nobody got killt. So, I say we accept Lugh's apology an leave it at that. We learn, we move on. But we cain't afford no more mistakes. Not from any of us. An that includes yer contact, Angel. Whoever they are, they gave us bad info. Not on purpose, I ain't sayin that, but if things're changin quick here, they gotta keep pace. Our lives depend on their intel. Now, I want you two – he waves at me an Creed – to shake hands, make yer peace.

As they all turn back to their meals an quiet chat, I hold my hand out to Creed. His eyes still hold a knife to my throat. Then he's smilin an pullin me to him fer a quick one-armed hug, sayin, Sorry, you know I git assy sometimes. Thanks fer the stitches. I hear what you say about Molly.

An I wonder if I imagined that look in his eyes.

56

Night Seven

It's the time of year when the dark crowds the light earlier an earlier each day.

I nab Slim on his own the moment I can. When d'you think's the blood moon? I says.

I don't think, he says, I know. He looks at the moon, fatter than last night. Includin this one, he says, seven nights.

Could be eight though, I says. Or nine. You cain't say fer certain.

I bin livin my life by that lady's wax an wane goin on fifty year, he says. I know her faces an if I say it's seven, it's seven. Fer certain. He peers at me closely. What's the fret about?

Nuthin, I says.

Tommo heads off to sit first watch, high atop Painted Rock. The rest of us gather around the fire. Me, to wait belly-tight with nerves. Fer the time to turn till I can leave to meet Jack at Irontree. No point goin early. He never appears before the time. I bin early to meet points more'n once an had to kick my heels while I waited fer him to show.

We settle in fer the evenin. With knees creakin, Slim grunts hisself into his slingchair to smoke a thoughtful pipe. Ash an Molly roll hemp twine fer bowstrings. Nero tucks in my coat fer a snooze while I dry my damp boots by the fire.

The waters might look calm, but I can feel it. Runnin jest below the surface. The sour current of dissent. Another mistake by me an it'll rise agin. I don't hold 'em to blame. I'd feel jest the same in their place.

We gotta hold together. Hold fast. I look at them, my family, my friends. The dance of flames chases shadows on their faces. Their familiar, unknown faces. This is old, what we do, in this old place here. It runs in the blood of time. People by a fire. With dark closin in all around them. DeMalo's words circle an tighten my thoughts.

If you keep on, more people will die. Maybe even people you care about. Weigh your chances.

Weigh our chances. I cain't git my thoughts straight. But I must. Right away. Seven nights. I need to talk to Jack. I try not to check the sky too often. Try not to show how antsy I am.

Lugh an me sit close together on a log, thigh to thigh. He nudges me. Got a meet tonight, huh? he whispers. I look at him. You keep checkin the sky, he says.

They all know I git regular intel about DeMalo an the Tonton an what's goin on in New Eden. They know I cain't say who or where they are. They think I meet with Bram's old network. The little gang of contacts, informants an insiders that he managed to set up before he died that day on the road to Resurrection. Jack runs them now. He's information. I'm action. Together we plan. I don't ever meet nobody but him.

Creed's bin mendin this little hand squeezebox that Slim got from Bobby French, a trader pal of his. Now, he tries it out fer the first time. Sweet melancholy wheezes from its cracked leather lungs.

Good gawd, it works, says Ash. Where'd you learn to play?

Travellin show, he says. Squeezebox, tightrope, fire jugglin … the usual.

59

Ash looks at him askance. Tall tale or truth, with Creed it's sometimes hard to know. You was never a showman, she says.

You think I tell you everythin? he says.

Huh. Well, she says, it would explain a lot.

He noodles quietly on the squeezebox while a skin of Molly's latest brew gits passed around. Stink currant rum this time, but it's always the same. Brain-killer hooch with a kick like white pain. I give it a miss. I need a clear head.

Emmi comes to sprawl across our laps. She buries her nose in Lugh's shirt. I know jest how he smells to her. Safe. Home.

An it strikes me. We ain't ever bin like we are at this moment. Never. I mean, the three of us takin comfort from each other's nearness an company. It was always me an Lugh, with Em on the outside. Fer the very first time, this feels like brother an sisters together. Lugh smiles at me over Em's head. I smile back. Tonight he seems lighter somehow. He seems … lifted.

I cain't bear to think of sendin Emmi to Auriel. Of bein without her. But I must. It's the only way to keep her safe. I'll speak to Lugh in the mornin.

As the stars shoot the sky, Creed idles their way on the squeezebox. Its ancient sighs fade the echo of harsh words. Smooth balm over anger. Drift our troubled day to the night.

I ain't ever known a star season like this one. Molly watches 'em, shakin her head in amazement. So many shooters, she says. If they keep on at this rate, there won't be none left.

Mercy's bin lookin at Lugh. Really starin, like she cain't help herself. It's makin him flushed an shifty. At last she says,

It's uncanny how like her you are. Your eyes, they're just the same. The face, the smile, even how you turn your head.

She's right. Lugh's the spit of Ma. He shrugs, but you can tell he's pleased. Time creeps. My stummick's in knots. Hurry on, hurry on, I need to see Jack.

Ash stands an stretches mightily. My watch, she says. Better go relieve Tommo. None too gently, she nudges Slim with her boot. Hey, sleepin beauty, don't you be late fer me.

He cracks open his good eye. Fret ye not, he says.

On silent feet, bow in hand, Ash heads into the shadows.

Emmi says, What's that tune, Creed?

No idea, he says. Probly the last song this old thing played. It's like it's bin waitin. It ain't quite ready to come, but it will. In its own time, it'll come. He keeps playin softly an, sure enough, before long, the song shows itself. It's slow. Spare. Worn an warm from its passage down the ages. Ah, says Creed.

My throat thickens as I reckanize it. As it sounds in my heart. The tune settles. It waits. Fer the right voice to claim it. It waits. Fer Molly. An she sings.

Dreams to sell, fine dreams to sell
Angus is here with dreams to sell.

Memory slashes me. Ma, singin me an Lugh to sleep. The sun scent of her skin. Her fingers smoothin my hair. It's bin ten year. But this music cuts deep. To the place where the wounds never heal. Lugh's arm circles my shoulders. He hugs me close.

Hush now, my baby, an sleep without fear
Dream Angus will bring you a dream, my dear.

The song halts from Molly, raggedly tender. An I know, without knowin it, that she sang this to Gracie. Her child with Jack, fever-dead after five months of life. Em leaves us, goes around the fire an lays down with her head in Molly's lap. Music at Silverlake died with Ma. Not once was there a lullaby fer Emmi.

Molly sings while Creed plays. There's a truce, even a smile in their eyes fer each other.

One more note, I'll be undone. An at last it's time fer me to go. I give Lugh's hand a squeeze. Then I slip away, Nero still huddled inside my coat. Tracker rises from his spot at Mercy's feet. Slim raises his pipe to my goin. Creed nods. Molly smiles. They're all used to my night-time junkets by now.

I scoop up my quiver an bow. I leave the warm an the light an my folk an Ma's song. With Tracker at my side, I head fer the night-deep woods.

I set Nero to fly an we head north. Irontree, where Jack changed our meet to, is a good two leagues from here.

I pause, jest a moment. I give our night-time signal. A two-note widowbird shiver. So our lookout knows who's on the move in the woods below. Answer floats down from the top of Painted Rock. It's Ash. She's took over the watch from Tommo. He'll be on his way down to the comforts of camp.

Saba, wait up! It's Lugh, hurryin after me, dodgin a path through the trees.

With a snap of impatience, I stop. What? I says.

I jest wanted to – that song, he says. I couldn't stay. It's too much.

I know, I says. I bin dreamin about her lately. About Ma.

It's strange, he says, we bin without her fer so long an you think yer okay an you are, but then Molly starts singin an – all these feelins an memories came rushin outta nowhere an I was right back there. That last time she sang to us. Lugh lets out a shaky breath. It hurts, he says, but … I felt like she was with us fer a moment.

She was, I says. Listen … Lugh, I gotta go, I—

I know, but I thought maybe I could … walk with you a ways? He looks at me, uncertain. Like I might not welcome the offer.

Oh, my poor heart. Like Molly's song warn't enough fer one night. Here's Lugh takin a step towards me. I bin waitin fer this since the day the Tonton took him from me. Long months ago.

I'd like that, I says. More than anythin I would love that, but … Lugh, I got some hard thinkin to do. I really appreciate you speakin fer me like you did, but you an me both know I done bad work today at the bridge. They're right. It ain't good enough. I gotta do better, a lot better, startin right now. I got some … concerns that I—

We could talk, he says. Maybe I could help. You an me, we always bin able to figger things out together.

I could walk with you a ways. We could talk.

That he should even hafta say it. My very blood quickens to Lugh. To tell him everythin, anythin … or not hafta tell him becuz he'd already know.

I wish we could, I says. But this is somethin I gotta work out on my own. I do wanna go fer that walk though. Soon.

You bet, he says. I'm here any time. Always here.

I turn to go, then remember. I gotta talk to you about Em, I says. I wanna send her back to Auriel at the Snake. It's wrong to have her here. A fight like this ain't no place fer a kid. If somethin was to happen to her, I – I cain't even think of it. Or if somethin was to happen to us. We'd wanna know she'd be okay.

I won't have it, he says. Even if I would, I sure as hell wouldn't send her to Auriel Tai. We're family, Saba. We've fought hard to stay together an we will, no matter what. She does need to step up, though. One minute she's smart an tough an you think you can rely on her an the next, she's actin like some dizzy little kid. I'll speak to her.

But I—

We ain't gonna argue this, he says.

I gotta go, I says.

As I move away, he takes hold of my arm, sayin, Hang on a sec, I— He almost but don't meet my eyes as he says, I need to … I want to apologize to you. Fer the way I bin actin since you saved me from Freedom Fields. Turnin away from you. Blamin you fer everythin. Bein so angry. The thing is, after Ma died, I only had one thing to do an that was pertect my sisters. Make sure you survive. I had to be the front line. Stand in front of you an take the shot, like with Pa.

You know we don't talk about that, I says.

Night-time in the hut. In the months jest after. Pa blind drunk an ragin his grief. At us. At hisself. Why should we live when she was dead? *Where's my gun? My knife? Where'd you hide 'em this time? Don't lie to me, son, don't make me beat it from you.*

When I do stupid things, like try an race you to the

bridge? It's becuz I need to git there first, says Lugh. Front line, you see? It's all I know. But when I got took, you managed fine without me. You an Emmi both. You grew stronger. Smarter. An I'm proud of you. But I bin feelin, I dunno … useless. But no more. No more, I swear. Today changed everythin.

An I know the moment it happened, I says. There at the bridge, when I was holdin on so tight to you. I bin there myself, Lugh, I know that moment. When death leans in to kiss you, to take you, when it's so close you can smell its breath. An you say no. No, you sonofabitch, you will not have me this time. An you want life so bad an you pull yerself back into it an suddenly everythin's so clear.

He's starin at me an I realize I got my fingers diggin into his arms as I speak, like some crazy person. You got it, he says. That's it ezzackly. Yer th'only one who'd know how to say it.

Saba? It's Tommo. He's standin not ten foot away, among the trees. Can I talk to you?

Not now Tommo, I says.

But I only—

Later, okay? Lugh turns on him, impatient.

There's a moment's pause. You cain't read his face in the shadow of the trees. Sorry, he says. Then he's gone.

He's stuck on you, says Lugh. You took his hand today. He'll take that as encouragement.

We ain't talkin about him, I says. We're talkin about you.

Yeah, well … today made me realize… He shakes his head. I wish I was good with words, he says. I realized I want so much, Saba. The sky above my head an the sun an the stars an … I wanna feel the earth beneath my feet, in my hands. It's so little but it's so much, y'know, it's …

it's everythin. An yer everythin to me. You an Emmi. You gotta know that.

He pulls me into his arms an we hold fast to each other.

Tears heat my eyes. I bin missin you so much, I says, you got no idea. I'm sorry I hurt you, Lugh. I never meant to. I bin selfish an stubborn. Not jest about Jack, but—

He's gone, that's all finished, he says. It's gonna be okay, Saba. You an me, we're as we should be. We're us agin.

Some good came outta this day after all, I says.

We got the power to git what we want, he says. One day soon, we'll have a piece of this good land fer ourselfs. Fer the first time, we'll live a life that's worth somethin. Jest like we always dreamed. An we won't be shackled by the past no more. Don't worry about Em. We'll keep her safe.

I give him a last hard squeeze. I really do gotta go, I says. I start to walk backwards, away from him. See you, I says.

If I don't see you first, he says.

Such a tired old clunker. But it makes us smile every time. I leave him there in the trees, bathed in moonlight. When I take a last look over my shoulder, he's headed back towards camp.

My feet skim me through the woods. I'm all speed an starlight. Wolfdog an crow, my companions. An hope don't jest whisper within me. Now it shouts loud to the night.

My brother has come back to me.

There ain't no better outrider than a wolfdog. Tracker runs on ahead, then fans out an loops around behind me, over an over. We had a month of this, so he's well-trained. Me, on secret night journeys to meet Jack. Tracker makin sure we don't run into nobody we oughtn't. Nero cruises above the treetops, keepin pace with me here on the ground.

That surge of joy speeds me on the first half league. I'm pure happiness. Lugh took the first step. He opened his arms to me. But as my thoughts creep back in, my feet start to slow.

It's gonna be okay, Saba. You an me, we're as we should be. We're us agin.

I'm foolin myself. To be us would mean that the truth would flow between us like clear water. Jest as it used to. But now I measure it out in fearful drops. Even if I could tell him, even if I told Lugh every single one of my many secrets, until he knows that Jack's alive an finds a way to accept him, we ain't got no chance of bein us. Not even a new kinda us.

Lugh took aginst Jack from the off. I thought he'd be grateful to him. If it warn't fer Jack, we'd of never reached Freedom Fields in time to save his life. Maev was the one who told me why. Said I was hopeless not to figger it out myself. The way Lugh sees it, Jack stole me from him while he was weak an helpless, prisoner of the Tonton. I'm sure that's right. After all, twins ain't like any other. Till the day the Tonton took him from Silverlake, Lugh an me together was bindweed.

Fer now Jack's dead an must remain so. But if we win this fight, he'll step back into life an it won't jest be Lugh not overjoyed to see him, there's Tommo an Ash an — this ain't the time to think about all that.

If we win this fight. To win. In seven nights. Seven to the blood moon, if Slim's right. An he is he is I know he is.

A new plan. Fast. I gotta think of one, make one. Another blown bridge or road or checkpoint an DeMalo will do like he threatened.

You hit me again, I'll hit you back tenfold.

If he unleashes his full power aginst us, we won't survive. We'll be jest like the Hawks at Darktrees, butchered in the night as they slept. There, he was only gittin rid of a possible problem. They warn't nowhere near New Eden an barely even a thorn in his side. His reach is long an bloody.

I'll have your whole misstarred mob hunted down and killed. Wherever you run to. Your brother. Your sister. Weigh your chances.

I bin foolin myself. We're all fools. Deluded to think we can beat him. We're the few. The weak.

The few an the weak. Suddenly it hits me. It's bin starin me in the face from the start. It's only thanks to DeMalo that we're still alive. This whole time – today at the bridge, an way back to Hopetown an Freedom Fields, the fight at Pine Top Hill, then Resurrection – we bin bold an reckless an oftentimes lucky. It ain't that we didn't fight hard. We did. We do. Sometimes we even fought smart. But we ain't bin smart or lucky enough to keep us alive. Not if I'm honest. When it came to the point, DeMalo pulled back from destroyin us. An it's bin about me every time. Whatever it is that he wants from me … that's what's kept us alive.

I'll guarantee everyone safe passage over the Waste, your friends and family.

An in return?

You.

Me. Marry him. Death ain't so bad. You only do it once. Married to him, I'd die each day.

Nero's bin dippin in an outta the trees round about.

Almost like he's keepin a eye on somethin. Now, a little ways ahead, Tracker's caught a scent on the wind. He's stopped dead. Stiff-legged. Head high. As I come up to him, I'm shruggin off my bow an nockin a arrow. The scrub pine crowds thick here. I cain't see nuthin. I motion him to me an we slip behind a tree together. I tighten myself fer action.

There's a sudden commotion. In a flurry of branches, three little mosstails crash from the woods. Huge eyes red in the night. They spring across our path, not twenny foot in front of us, with Nero chasin behind. So that's what he was on about.

I relax. Tracker stares after 'em. He'd never chase. Never beg. He's too noble a beast. But, nose to tail, he quivers with desire. Not jest one mossy, but three. He looks at me. Nero shouts at him, anxious, urgent. I remember their lean squirrel supper. The chance of such a feast is rare.

Go on then, I says.

He's gone in a streak. I can hear the mossies crashin about, changin direction in their desperate race. Almost right away, I curse myself fer lettin 'em go. They're my sentries, Nero an Tracker. They can see things, hear things, sense things that I cain't. Damn. That was stupid. Dammit.

I go on, but it ain't long till fears rise. What if DeMalo's had me followed since this mornin? What if he never meant to let the bridge go unpunished? Why should I trust him? He said it's the endgame. New rules apply.

I double back a short ways. Start to beat a trail east. At a scatter of rocks, I haul off my boots an cross them barefoot. After a weave through some rootsprawl, I lose any trace of my passage on a carpet of hard blackmoss that ribbons among the trees.

Then I race north in the starfall night. I keep my bow nocked an ready. North to Irontree to meet Jack.

He followed her. Keeping well back, slipping cat-footed among the trees. Easy for a canny tracker like him.

Tracker had sniffed him out right away. But no need to raise the alarm over a friend. He kept looping back to check on him. Guarding the hunter and the hunted at the same time.

Not that he was hunting her. It was Jack he wanted in his sights. It was Jack he'd promised to deliver.

He hadn't seen him since that night at Blackwater Tarn. When he'd watched them from the rocks. Seen them together on the shore. Ever since then, she'd been meeting him. He was sure of it. She had a certain look about her when she'd been with Jack. Nobody else would notice. Only him.

Like Tracker, Nero kept an eye on him. Making sure he came to no harm in the night. Dipping in and out of the trees. But he always flew a forest that way. There was nothing to draw her attention.

Then he surprised a tack of grazing mosstails. And they surprised him. As they panicked away, he took cover. She'd want to know the cause. She'd bring Tracker. Flush him out. His heart pounded the excuses he could give her. She didn't come.

When all was still again, he found she'd moved on. Tracker and Nero had gone after the mosstails. He picked up her trail again. But not for long. She'd done a quick double back and headed east. He managed to track her as far as some blackmoss.

There, her trail went dead. He'd spooked her. He'd lost her.

He could hardly believe it. He cursed himself. He had no time for wasted chances. Hand Jack to the Pathfinder by the blood moon. That was the deal.

It had never occurred to him this might not be easy. Now the thought crashed on him. Crushed him. What if he couldn't deliver on time? All kinds of things might happen to prevent it. So much was out of his control. And he'd made a mistake, a basic one, already.

The Pathfinder wasn't the kind to accept excuses. You couldn't welsh on a deal with such a man.

Panic gripped him in a sudden, hot wave. He should never have done this. He was out of his depth. This could end in all sorts of trouble. He started to move through the trees. With his thoughts tipping, he was careless, unseeing. He stumbled on a root. He fell to his knees.

And he saw the crow lying dead on the ground.

Relief floods me as I spot the Irontree. It rises high above the canopy ahead. I've worked myself into a fine old rattle. Thinkin that every movement in the shadows is a Tonton. This ain't like me. First time in my life I bin spooked by a night-time wood. That'll teach me to keep Tracker an Nero nearby.

The Irontree stands in the Ironwood. Some big Wrecker place must of bin here once, way back when. There ain't nuthin left now but some of its bones. Huge iron girders that rise from the ground like they're rooted. They ain't in plain view. You don't notice 'em at first. That's becuz they bin swamped by the forest. As the trees grew, they took the iron into their bodies. They swallowed it. Embraced it. An the king of these trees looks down upon the rest. Irontree.

71

A great oak of mighty girth an splendid branches. Jack's built hisself a little eyrie, a platform, in its topmost reaches. It cain't be seen from the ground.

I give our signal, Jack's an mine. The quiet krik of a nightpip. I wait. No answer. I track forwards, cautiously, my bow ready to fire. I don't see no sign of his forest pony, Kell. I call agin. No answer. Where is he?

I'm at the foot of Irontree now. It's all quiet. Bloody Jack. He's late agin. With a sigh, I let my bow down.

There's a whoosh sound above. I look up. A man plunges at me from the sky. Boots first. Straight down. His hands grip a rope. His black robes fly, his head wrapped in a sheema. Fear kicks me. The heartstone's warm. It's him it's DeMalo he's here!

I duck, go to run. But he's hit the ground, snatched me round the waist an we're bouncin in the air. Up, light as birds, soarin high. The rope's rubber. I gasp. Clutch him tight fer dear life. My bow an quiver tumble to the ground. The red hot's wild in me. The heartstone's hot. Before I can think we land on the platform, high up.

As he unhands the rope an lets go my waist, I haul off an deck him. A swing at his chin sends him flyin. He lands on his back. I snatch the knife from my boot an I'm on him, I'm on top of him, my knife high, ready to slash. I'll kill him, I will. This time I'll kill him if it kills me. He grabs my wrist, we grapple an twist an then he's sittin on top of me. I struggle an thrash. I rear up to bite him. Hand, arm, anywhere I can reach. He holds me off, his eyes flashin outrage. His silver moonlight eyes.

Silver eyes. Not black. Not DeMalo.

I freeze where I am. Jack? I says.

He clamps a hand to my mouth. Yer bein followed, he hisses.

In the woods below, somethin's crashin through the trees. Headed this way. Movin fast. We scramble to our feet. He pulls two shooters from his belt an throws me one. From the edge of the platform, we part the hangin moss so's we can see what's goin on below. My bow, my quiver an arrows, spill all over the ground.

A gang of flathead pigs come stampedin through the unnergrowth below. Not one of 'em's higher than my knees. There's maybe eight of the little beasts. As the sounds of 'em start to fade, jest as I'm openin my mouth to blast him, Jack shins to the top of Irontree. He scans the forest with his looker. It's gone quiet. He shakes his head an climbs back down.

Flatheads! I grab his sleeve. I don't believe it, I says. Are you crazy or what?

He eyes me warily as he feels his chin an jaw. An jest when I thought you was startin to mellow, he says.

What the hell was that? I says. Swoopin down on me? I could of killed you.

How? Bit me to death? he says. You was bein followed, Saba. I was watchin out fer you from up there.

Yeah, pigs, I says. Save me.

Use yer head, he says. Somethin startled 'em. I mean, the woods're dark an I couldn't see who an I guess I couldn't swear to it, but it sure seemed—

Seemed? Couldn't swear? Oh, yer quite the lookout, I says.

Aw, fergit it, he says. We'll be arguin the toss all night long. Anyways, I guess if there was somebody, Tracker would of sniffed 'em out. Where is he, by the way?

Here, I says, somewheres around. I don't dare tell him that I sent Nero an Tracker off huntin. He'd tear a strip from me an no mistake.

Jack pulls off his sheema. Ruffs his short hair to confusion. Anyways an by the way, Saba, what's got you so edgy? he says. You must of known it was me. He flips the hot heartstone with a finger.

Some Tonton comes flyin at me outta the sky, I don't stop to think, I fight, I says. An speakin of by the way, what's with the gear, Jack? An the words *infiltrate the Tonton* better not cross yer lips.

I give him my hardest stare. His gaze slides away.

We agreed, I says. We agreed you wouldn't, you know damn well we did.

I agree that we agreed it was too dangerous, he says. We never agreed that I never would. So I can also agree that we never agreed.

None of yer eel talk, speak plain, I says.

I only done it once or twice, he says. Today an ... okay, maybe a few times. But only when I know it's safe. Information is power, Saba. An we need as much inside information as we can git. How d'you think I found out about the bridge? Keep yer friends close an yer enemies closer, right? He gestures to his robes. Who better than me? I know their ways, how to blend in. We ain't gonna git no closer'n this.

If only he knew how very close I bin to the enemy. He cain't ever know. Nobody can.

What if the Tonton know you helped us at Resurrection? I says. That you warn't one of them but a fake an a plotter? They could all have orders to find you, to watch you, follow you.

Nobody follows me. He heaves a sigh. Look, he says, we demolished the place. There was fifty men killed. It was complete confusion. If anybody spared me a thought after the fact, they'd figger I got blown to the sky. Jest like yer Free Hawk gang do. If the Tonton knew about me, we'd all of us be heads on spikes by now.

Don't ever say that. You take too many chances, I says. Don't do this no more, Jack. Promise me. Promise.

No, he says. If we don't risk, we don't win. This ain't no cakewalk, darlin.

Don't you dare talk down to me, don't you dare, I says. If you git yerself killed, I swear I'll … I'll kill you.

My fury boils. With him. With DeMalo. With the whole gawdamn world. Fury I'm beset by doubt an weakness. Reduced to a frightened girl. Me. The Angel of Death.

Take off that gear, I says. I hate you in it, I hate it, d'you hear?

I attack his Tonton robe. Start yankin at it. But it tangles in his weapons belt, so I pull that off him an dump it. Jack stands there, not helpin, not hinderin. I drag off the robe, grab a fistful of shirt an walk him backwards, fast, till he hits the tree trunk. I hate it, gawdammit, I says.

Then I kiss him. An I kiss him. An I kiss him.

I'll burn DeMalo from me in the fire between us. I'll stoke the flames high with my lies an secrets. Feed 'em with my weakness an my fears. I'll lay waste to myself in the heat of Jack's body. Melt the flesh from my bones. Blaze my bones to ash.

A breath of night breeze stirs the haze of my mind. He ain't kissin me back. He ain't touchin me. He jest stands, not movin. His shirt hangs open. Did I do that? I don't recall. I press closer, ever closer. My fevered hands roam him. Reckless. Hell-bent.

Uh-uh. He grabs 'em. Firmly. Stop right there, he says.

I'm dazed. Halfways to scorched, but nowhere near burnt.

Why? I says. What's wrong? You want me, you know you do.

He makes a strange noise. A strangled-at-birth kinda laugh. He's all rumpled an ruffled an hot silver eyes. He takes a deep breath. Boy, he mutters, this is a first fer me.

We both know that ain't true, I says. I go fer his lips agin, but he steps back. Puts space an air an coolness between us. What's the matter? I says. Why ain't you kissin me?

Becuz you ain't kissin me, he says. Right now, all you want is a warm body. Mine jest happens to be the closest one. I'd say the state yer in, pretty much anybody'd do.

I bristle, shake free of his hold. How dare you? I glare. What the hell're you talkin about?

He smiles his quirk of a smile. An cue righteous indignation, he says. Never bullshit a bullshitter. I know this one, Saba. I bin there, I done it. He shakes his head, rueful. You dish it out, eventually, somewhere down the road, somebody dishes out the same to you. I jest discovered I don't much care fer the taste. Ain't that how it goes. Measure fer measure.

Spare me the sermon, I says. When did you git so gawdamn virtuous?

He swipes a gentle finger down my cheek. I dunno, he says. The moment I seen yer face?

That takes the wind from my sails. I stare at his chest. The marks an the scars. From shoulder to hip, three thick puckered lines. The rake of a hellwurm's claws. The red risin sun inked over his heart, the blood tattoo of the Tonton. The same as DeMalo's. DeMalo agin. Always, always DeMalo. So. There won't be no oblivion fer me.

Tell me what happened today. Jack's voice is quiet. Determined.

Fer the first time, I notice what he's done. He's made a bower at one end of the platform, with branches of fir to soften the floor. Rainbow shimmer discs hang all around. As they turn an swing, they play in the moonbeams. There's a cold roast fowl, bread an a bottle.

He went to a lotta trouble. It's beautiful. Special. It makes my heart hurt. I hug myself tight to stop it from weepin. I see you bin thievin agin, I says. Whatever happened to virtue?

Overrated, he says.

I'm sorry, I says. My timin always did stink. Especially when it comes to you.

I cain't argue with that, he says. Let's eat. We'll talk.

Fate had nodded his way. Shown him the dead crow. He'd instantly known what to do. It hadn't been dead long. He tucked it inside his shirt and went in search of Nero.

The mosstails had left a trail of broken branches in their flight. He followed it to the killsite. Nero was there. Gorging himself on the carcass of a tiny mossjack. Tracker was nowhere in sight. It looked like he'd made a quick kill for his friend and gone after a bigger beast for himself. He'd done such things before.

He couldn't let Nero know who was taking him. His scent shouldn't give him away. Crows had a weak sense of smell and Nero's beak was deep in a heaven of blood and flesh. Still, he'd better make sure of it. He'd already slipped out of his coat. Now he silently scooped handfuls of rotting forest floor into it. Crows always know a face though. He wrapped his sheema around his head.

He'd only get one chance. He waited among the trees for the perfect moment. As Nero burrowed deeper into the guts, his greed was greater than his caution.

He edged closer. Closer. Close enough. He threw the coat over Nero. Then he grabbed him and hurried away.

In fact, I talk. Jack eats. An he drinks. An he listens. We sit cradled in the bed of fir boughs an I tell him how it all went aginst us. About Lugh's brush with death. The fog that meant Ash couldn't warn us in time. How the convoy was on top of us before we knew it. That I tried to stop the blast an failed. I talk of the slaves an the beasts. The Stewards an the Tonton. I cain't speak of the unspeakable. The noise an the smells an the nightmare realness of the death we dealt them. I tell him it was dreadful an leave it at that. Then it's Creed wounded, the curious joy of findin Mercy, an Creed's challenge. I don't tell the untellable. DeMalo. The blood moon.

Jack don't say much. The odd question an once or twice, he nods. I can tell he's thinkin hard.

We did wonder why they built that bridge, he says. But a settlement party – slaves too – headed to the Raze. What do they want with a wasteland like that? What's DeMalo up to? You can bet he's got a plan. We need to find out what it is.

I want Jack to know that DeMalo was there today. But I cain't tell him straight. I might give somethin away, in my tone or my eyes or my face. So I says, There was two big dogs with the Tonton today. Creed called 'em ghosthounds.

Jack sits up straight, his eyes sparkin. That means DeMalo was there, he says. Them dogs never leave his side. He got 'em after Resurrection. Guess he don't feel too safe. Did you see him? Tell me he didn't spot you.

We was too far away, I says. There was smoke an noise an it was all confused ... no, he couldn't of. I sure didn't see him.

Outright lies. Half-truths. Evasions. Each time I open my mouth.

DeMalo bein there means that convoy was definitely somethin special, says Jack. Otherwise, he would of left it to his Tonton grunts like usual.

That's what Mercy said, I says.

Mercy, he says. Yeah. You can bet slaves notice things nobody else does. We gotta find out everythin she knows. Saba, d'you hear? You need to talk to Mercy.

Yeah, I says, Mercy, of course. I'm only half-listenin. Starin at a shimmer disc that hangs low beside me. At the play of moonlight as I spin it. Now I look at Jack straight. We cain't win this, I says. We're way outnumbered.

He frowns. That's old news, he says. We knew that from the off.

But now I know what that means, I says. What it looks like an feels like. We got six fighters, Jack, that's all. Emmi's a dead weight an now we got Mercy too. Tommo an Creed only jest escaped. Lugh nearly fell to his death. If we'd lost them, we'd be finished, an fer what?

It was our first op, he says. We learn an move on. We git better. Smarter. Yer talkin like we didn't win the action. We did.

They'll be rebuildin that bridge already, I says.

So we hit 'em agin, somewhere else, right away, he says.

It's the whole idea, you know that. We ain't many, but we can move fast. We make quick hits. Unpredictable. Time an agin.

Today was a waste of our effort, I says. An our firepower an our nerve. We ain't gonna win by killin people. Death only leads to more death.

Today will of shook DeMalo, he says. Another few hits like this one, he'll be scramblin to cover hisself. His losses mount up, he starts to look weak, people lose confidence in him. A few more start to bleed to our side—

That game's way too long, I says.

We need to step it up, he says. We'll hit the Tonton next. That'll hurt him the most. I got a plan to take out two checkpoints on the same night. Opposite ends of New Eden.

I'm tellin you, this whole idea's wrong.

It's right an you know it, he says. It's about who owns the future. One man or everyone. DeMalo or the people of New Eden. Fine, good, heal the earth, who wouldn't want that? Come together fer a common cause. Work together fer the common good fer a change, instead of each person guardin their own little patch. But as free people in charge of their own destiny. Not with the gun of a tyrant at their backs.

New Eden's too small, I says. There ain't that many places we can hide. He'll track us down before long.

You want the future to belong to DeMalo an his spawn?

Of course not, that ain't what I—

Cuz that's what'll happen if we all stand back goin, it ain't down to me, what could I do anyways, I'm too weak, he's too strong. You didn't do that when you was searchin fer Lugh. You took on the world single-handed to git him back. But … oh right, that was about family, warn't it? An, let's be honest, that's where it ends fer you, ain't it? When push comes to shove.

No, I says.

You should of left when I told you to, he says. After Resurrection. Yer jest holdin us back. You should leave us to it. His eyes glint ice, not silver. I take a quick swig of wine. Sweetness an fire, it burns his words down to my gut. There they churn thickly, sickly. We're silent, tight hearted, tight lipped. Then, not lookin at me, he says,

You want me to say the word, Saba? Give you permission to go? Fine. Go, the three of yuz, an good luck. There ain't no shame in it. You tried, but this kinda fight ain't fer you. Yer tied to yer family by blood an love. That means you'll rush to their rescue, no matter what, an that's dangerous to the rest of us. What happened today with Lugh? That jest proves it. Love don't make a good leader. It weakens you.

Jack's words click a trigger. In my head. In my gut. An I'm suddenly hot, my heart thumpin. Brothers. Sisters. Family. Blood ties. Mothers, fathers, children. Somethin new, unknown, starts to breathe deep inside me. With a tremble of excitement. A shiver of possibility.

Love weakens me. I repeat it, unner my breath, to myself. That's what Lugh's always said. What I never really believed.

Love weakens, I says aloud. Maybe not. Maybe … it makes me different. From you. From the rest of 'em. From DeMalo.

Okay, says Jack, but I don't see what this has to do with—

DeMalo knows about us now, I says. After today, he knows our drill – the quick hit an run – so he'll be thinkin what he'd do if he was us. He'll start thinkin like us. He'll probly even enjoy it, treat it like a game. After all, we are playin his kinda game. The violent kind. That's what we've all bin playin, all this time.

So? says Jack.

We did wrong today at the bridge. An DeMalo's wrong. What's right must lie somewhere else. Between us maybe. Or beyond us.

Or maybe not. Maybe what's right lies much closer to home.

So… I says slowly, what if we stop thinkin like him … an start thinkin … like me.

Like you? Jack's eyes narrow with sudden innerest. Go on, he says.

He'll be especkin us to blow another bridge, or a road or a checkpoint, I says. What if we don't? What if we change the game? Do somethin else? Somethin completely different?

Like what? says Jack.

I stole a horse today, I says.

Mischief, he says. Tricks.

No, I says, no, that ain't what I mean. It's more'n that, much more. Mercy said somethin … what was it? I know. *It won't take much to make their house crumble. It don't stand on strong foundations.* DeMalo ain't built New Eden on strong foundations, Jack. No families. No fathers an mothers with their children. He's split them all apart. It ain't natural. There ain't no … heart to it. To New Eden. It's jest this … idea. His idea. D'you see?

Okay, he says, but how does that change what we do?

I dunno ezzackly, I says. I gotta work this out. I got a strong feelin, Jack. An I don't jest feel it in my gut. It's my heart an my head too … all of me. Whatever this is, there's meat in it, I know there is. I gotta talk to Mercy. Yer right, she'll know things. I need to go.

Hey, hey, hang on. As I start to move, he grabs my arm.

I'm a great believer in goin with yer instinct, he says. But you got me thinkin too. Thanks to yer blunder at the bridge today, our hand's bin well tipped. Yer right, DeMalo will try to outfox us. I would if I was him. But here's what I think. He's the lodestone, Saba. The power here rests in him an him alone. One man. The Pathfinder, with his miraculous visions. This ain't the same as crazy Vicar Pinch an Hopetown. Without DeMalo, New Eden collapses. It's his plan, his ideas, the force of his will. Yeah, let's change the game. Let's cut it short right now. I'll go back inside the Tonton. I'll move quick before I'm discovered. I'm gonna kill him.

Another click of the trigger in my head. Say agin? I says.

I'm gonna kill him, says Jack. The sooner the better.

No, no, the bit before, I says. The Pathfinder with his miraculous visions.

Visions at sunrise. I seen 'em myself. Another secret I hold close in my heart. DeMalo led me there by the hand. To the bunker in the hill, to the room with white walls. Where he shared his miraculous vision. A vision of the earth before the Wreckers destroyed her. Sights wondrous beyond all imagination. Unfergittable as long as I live.

I says, You seen 'em, right? The visions, I mean. Don't all Stewards an Tonton go there, as part of, y'know, what's it called –

– initiation, sure, says Jack. I was set to go, but I got killed before I could. It all happens at this hill, at dawn. Hard by a place called Weepin Water. Nobody's allowed to talk about what they see an nobody ever does but – I tell you – afterwards, they all look at DeMalo like he's the sun itself. It must be somethin pretty amazin.

He is the lodestone, yer right, I says. An if there's any

heart to New Eden, that hill is it. We gotta go there, Jack. Right now.

Right now? he says. No way. Look at you, yer completely wired. No wonder with all that happened today, an you cain't tell me you got any shut-eye last night in that cave.

Sleep's a waste of time, I says.

Don't be stupid, he says.

All right, tomorrow. Weepin Water. I'll meet you at that hill jest after middle night. Bring torches. We're gonna git inside there somehow.

To do what? he says.

You said it yerself, information is power. We'll find out what there is to know about that place. It ain't figgered in our thinkin before. It should of.

Fair enough, he says.

An don't you do nuthin till then, I says. Not a thing. None of yer sneakin around, no dressin like the enemy. Promise me.

He smiles. Cross my heart an hope to die, he says.

His eyes gleam silver intent. As I start to git up, he grabs my hand, gives it a tug an I fall to him, deep in the fir boughs. How could I ever mistake him fer DeMalo? His scent is so surely of none but him. Warm skin an, faintly, warm sage. Like a whisper of wider lands. His end of day beard shades his face. I smooth its rasp with gentle fingers.

See? he says. We can be calm. Quiet.

I gotta go, I says.

You remember earlier? he says. When them flathead pigs was about to trample you an I swung down like a he-man to save yer life …

In yer dreams, I says.

… at great peril to my own, he says. I'd jest like to point

84

out that's the third time I've saved you from certain death. You see, there's this thing – I dunno if you remember – it's called the Rule of Three ... have I mentioned it before?

Once or twice, I says. I linger down his nose. Slightly crooked. Completely gorgeous. I'm glad I didn't punch yer nose, I says. I like it.

Don't distract me, he says. How it works is, you save somebody's life three times –

– their life belongs to you. I know, Jack.

All I'm sayin is, the pigs made it three to me. I win.

Yer pathetic, I says. Desperate. I trail around his lips, so smooth an warm. Them pigs warn't nowhere near me, I says. We're still two all.

He gathers me in. Desperate, huh? he says. I'll show you desperate. Our fingers twine, our legs tangle an his lips ramble roses all over me. Till I shiver an tremble with want fer him. Who's kissin you? he says. Who's touchin you?

You are, I says.

Say my name, he says.

Jack, I whisper. Jack. Jack.

Now kiss me, he says.

I kiss his name to his lips. His smooth, wine-sweet lips. I should go, I says.

You better go, he says.

Our kisses grow hungry. Our bodies heat.

There's a bark from below. It's Tracker. I break away with a gasp an peer through the branches at the sky. Jupiter hangs low in the east. The night's half spent already. I need to git back, I says. I push him off, sit up an start puttin my clothes to rights. He's made a heroic effort to undress me. You work fast, I says.

Yer a movin target, I hafta. Here, he says, lemme help.

I button, he unbuttons. I tuck, he untucks. I slap his hand. I'll do it myself, I says.

As I jump to my feet an do the job proper, he leans back on his elbows. I never do know what to especk when I'm with you, he says. But even so, I gotta say tonight's bin particularly unpredictable.

We live in unpredictable times, I says. Tomorrow night. Weepin Water. Don't be late.

I take hold of the rubber rope an whistle at Tracker to warn him. Then I leap from the platform. I let go as the ground speeds at me. I fall an land in a crouch. Tracker dives outta the way, startled. I scoop the spilled arrows, fill my quiver an shoulder my bow.

Take a different route back to camp, says Jack. An watch yer back.

I glance up. He's lookin down at me through the curtain of moss an branches.

How many nights to the blood moon? I says.

Countin tonight? He looks at the moon. I'd say … seven. Why?

I was hopin he'd say different. I was hopin Slim was wrong. Seven nights an our fates will be decided. It's all in my hands. It's all down to me. Tomorrow night, I says. Don't be late.

As I pass the bushes trampled by the pigs, I remember the mosstails from earlier. The panicky way they crashed from the woods across our path. Jack's words echo in me.

Somethin startled 'em. Use yer head.

If there was somebody followin us, Tracker would of found them. He'd of let me know. He'd of warned me.

86

Nero don't show.

As Tracker an me run through the woods, on a roundabout route back to camp, I look fer him. Seek fer him. Hope fer a sight of him. In the trees, in the sky, aginst the moon.

He should of come with Tracker to Irontree. It's strange he didn't. He loves Jack with true devotion. An he knew we was headed to meet him. Jack's the only one we ever run to in the middle of the night.

I stop to take breath atop a bare escarpment. From here, I can see fer leagues all around. It's a restless ocean of treetops. Frosted by the sharpness of the moon, they murmur of winter to come.

There's millions upon millions of stars in the sky. Night after night, they rush their brightness to the earth.

But Nero's shinin dark ain't nowhere to be seen.

I cain't really say this time's that much different from all the many times before that he's disappeared fer hours. More'n once, he's bin gone fer a couple of days. Nero's always had his own life, apart from me. A winged life of secrets an ancient crow ways, that calls him to do what he must. Still, this time, his absence gnaws at me. I'm jittered with unease. Why, I couldn't say.

I lay a hand on Tracker's head. Where is he? I ask him. Where's Nero?

He tips back his head an howls. A full-throated wail to the heart of the night. Three times he calls to his friend.

As the sound dies away, we wait. An we wait.

But there ain't no answer.

So on we go.

As we near Painted Rock an our feet start to slow, I signal our approach to the watch. Slim's creaky rustheap of a voice replies. You cain't ever mistake his birdcalls.

Tracker bounds on ahead, outta my view. Suddenly, the most unholy noise cracks the night. A shocked yelp that shatters to a high-pitched yammer. I run in fear towards the sound.

In a little clearin stands a tall bull pine. Tracker circles frantic in front of it. There's a crow spiked to the trunk. Jest above head height. Wings spread wide. Dead.

Nero.

My heart seizes. I stop. I fall to my knees.

Everybody's come runnin, weapons in hand. Their sleep broke by the racket. Ash lights the way with a torch.

Emmi screams when she sees him. Nero! No! She rushes to the tree, scrabblin to git at him. It's Nero, please, somebody help him!

I choke out one word. Lugh!

Molly runs to Em an grabs her, sayin, Hush now, honey, he's dead, poor thing. Come away.

An Lugh's here. On his knees. Holdin me. I cain't breathe. Cain't breathe. Nero. No. Ash, he says. Take him down, please.

She's the tallest of us all. Gawdammit, I'll kill whoever did this, she says. Light me, Tommo. He holds the torch close. With her pocket knife, she starts to prise the spikes from his wings. Fergawdsake, she says. Somebody shut Tracker up.

He's still howlin an yammerin his distress. Mercy soothes

him with soft words, soft hands. He quiets to a pitiful whimper.

Creed helps Ash, foldin each wing as she frees it. They're so careful. So tender. Makin sure they don't hurt him. They cain't. He's dead. He cain't be mustn't be cain't be please. Lugh holds me to him.

Hey Saba? says Ash. C'mere.

There's somethin in her voice. Tight caution. I stumble over to her. She lays him gently in my hands. He's a limp, heavy weight. Take a look, she says.

Tommo lights him with the torch. His sleek black body. His soft smooth breast. My heart lurches. The breast feathers shine full an glossy. Nero's breast don't look like this. His feathers is still growin back. From the wound that DeMalo's hawk dealt him. Fer a moment, I cain't take in what I see. Then the truth starts to smoulder.

Well? says Ash.

It ain't him, I says. This ain't him. The breast feathers. It ain't Nero.

They exclaim an crowd in to look. I couldn't hide that Nero'd bin injured. So I fixed on a likely tale of a hawk attack on him an me sneakin into a Settler's hut to steal a medicine bag to patch him up. More secrets, half-truths an outright lies. They all listened with one ear, if that. At the time, we had much bigger things to concern us.

My brain starts to tick. Clear an calm. This crow died natural, I says. Look, he's got a lump in his neck. Seems to be some kinda bubo.

Emmi shudders from weepin so fierce. Tears wet her face. Yer right, she says. It ain't him. But I don't unnerstand.

Somebody wanted us to think it was him, says Mercy.

But why? Em says. Who would do such a cruel thing?

89

The Tonton, says Tommo. They're the only ones spike like this.

If it was Tonton, we'd be dead, says Ash. Another Darktrees.

But I'm thinkin to myself, No, this is jest the kinda thing DeMalo would do. To send me a message. Prove to me how close he can git. How easily he could kill us the moment he wanted to. The next move in our endgame? Here it is.

Maybe it was one guy on his own, says Tommo.

That makes sense, says Molly. One guy couldn't take us all on, but he could leave a message. A warnin. You'll be the ones spiked next time. I'd say Tommo's right.

DeMalo could of had us followed from the bridge, I think. Or a lone man might of acted on his own. If there was somebody hid here in the woods, waitin fer their moment to play this foul trick, surely Tracker would of sniffed 'em out earlier. We beat patrols with him regular an often.

Ash, I says. You an Tracker did a sweep soon as you got here, right?

She nods. An there's bin one of us on watch the whole time, she says.

Not the whole time, says Creed. When I got back, there warn't no one on watch. Everybody was in camp.

It's my fault. Emmi's face crumples in misery. Saba told me to go back, she says, but then Lugh came an I didn't. I didn't. I'm sorry, it's all my fault.

Never give a child a grown-up's work, says Creed.

Lugh turns to him with a frown. You must of bin followed, he says.

I cain't see how, says Creed. I took a seriously snaky route back here.

90

We'll check jest the same, I says. Emmi an Mercy stay here. The rest of yuz, take yer track.

I whistle fer Slim to come down as we fan out an run circles around Painted Rock. It don't take long. It's all clear. Jest as we gather back at the campfire, Slim rushes through the gap, chest heavin from hustlin from the top of the Rock.

What's happened? he gasps. I heard the dog howlin an then all the commotion – oh lordy, no! He's seen the dead crow on the ground.

It's okay, it ain't Nero, I says.

Somebody wanted to frighten us, says Lugh. They managed pretty good, too.

You must of seen somethin, Slim, says Ash.

Not a thing, he says. It's bin quiet, I swear. Jest Saba an Tracker comin back, jest now.

Creed rounds on him. Stabs him in the chest with a finger. You must of missed 'em, he says. Stupid old man, yer useless, y'know that? You an yer gawdamn dress. The Tonton was right here an you didn't see 'em.

Creed, stop it. Molly snaps, hot as fire. Don't you dare talk to Slim like that.

Enough, I says. Who, why an where can wait fer later. We're outta here. I'm thinkin Starlight Lanes, I says. I look at Slim. Yer friend Peg the Flight. What about it?

Good idea, he says.

Besides Slim, we don't none of us know his junkjimmy pal Peg. But he's friendly to our cause an his place, Starlight Lanes, is in Sector Five. That ain't too far from Weepin Water an DeMalo's bunker in the hill. Good fer meetin Jack tomorrow night.

But Nero, says Emmi. Saba, we gotta find him! We cain't go without him! She clutches my hand, her eyes big with pleadin.

Nero's bin with me his whole life. He was huddled on the ground when I found him. A helpless scrap of skin an fuzz. He'd fell from the nest, his ma nowhere in sight. As I held him, his tiny heart beat quick time in my hands. He looked at me, I looked at him an I swear, he knew I didn't have no ma neether. We joined souls at that moment an fer always.

But Jack's voice speaks to me, Jack's words run in me.

Yer tied to yer family by blood an love. That means you'll rush to their rescue, no matter what, an that's dangerous to the rest of us. Love don't make a good leader. It weakens you.

I got eight other souls to consider. Standin right here. Waitin fer me to be the leader they need. To do what's best fer all, not jest them that's closest to my heart.

I'll bury this crow, I says. Creed, take Tracker once around the rock. Have a quick look fer Nero.

I'll go with, says Tommo.

Tommo don't jest lip read real good. His other senses lie higher than us who can hear. He's got cat eyes, cat feet an a nose fer anythin outta place.

Good idea, I says. The rest of yuz, strike camp.

They'd wakened her at dawn yesterday. The earthsongs.

Emmi had been dreaming of such things for many nights. Of the earth and the stones and their songs. And her touching them and being able to feel and hear and know their songs with her heart and her head and her body. And the songs leading her, telling her, teaching her. Not songs with words. No. No words.

Dreams. They were places where anything could happen. Life awake was nothing like a dream. At least, not until yesterday dawn. When she woke to a world and herself full of songs.

She soon realized no one else could hear them. Then she knew what it was. The call. She was getting the call. Auriel Tai got the call as a young girl, too. When light – her spirit guide – sang to her. Auriel's grandfather became her teacher. Now she needed a teacher. Auriel could help her to find one.

All day she'd asked Auriel to come, to find them. Pressing her message into the stones with her hands, into the earth with her bare feet. Not knowing if it would work or what she was doing. But hoping they might speak to any light that touched them. The sun, the moon, the stars. That the light would then speak to Auriel. Come to me, Auriel. I need you.

She needed her badly. There were so many songs, she couldn't make them out one from the other. Stonesongs, earthsongs, their night songs and day songs. Their songs that sighed like air through people songs. Like when Molly sang her lullaby.

But tonight in camp, lying there, listening, she realized one song had started to run through all the rest. Very faint, very small, but needing to be heard. If only she could understand what it meant.

As they started to pack up to go, suddenly she knew. It was a song of below. Of dark and alone and afraid. She told her bare feet to feel their way there. To take her to where the song began.

It don't take long. After more'n a month of this, day after day, we got the fast come an go down pat. Slim's carthorse, Duff, stands patient, hitched to the Cosmic. Molly an Tommo load Bean the mule with the ammo an other bits of fightin gear while the rest of us ready our horses. There ain't much talk. We're all shook by what's happened.

We can hear wolfdog howls as Tracker circles Painted Rock with Tommo an Creed in search of Nero. Though I know it ain't likely they'll find him, still I'm tense until they come back.

Tommo's face says all. Sorry, he says. No sign of him.

Mercy's jest about to mount Tam, her stolen pony. I hurry to give her a boost. She don't really need my help, but it's my first chance to speak to her since I seen Jack. The moon shades dark the tired hollows of her face. The scratches from Nero's attack. I could count every line, every wrinkle. But she sits tall, straight-backed, a queen in her slave collar.

I fiddle with the bridle. Keep my voice low as I says, I gotta talk to you. Alone. Soon as we git to Starlight Lanes.

Her eyes speak assent.

You comfortable there, Mercy? says Lugh. His voice makes me jump. I didn't realize he was so close.

Your sister's had a shock, she says. Look to her, won't you?

He hugs his arm around my shoulders. You don't hafta tell me, he says. He'll find us, Saba, he always does. He's probly jest off on some crow business.

As I sling my pack onto Hermes, I catch Tommo starin at me. He's kneelin, messin with his bootlace. The second our eyes meet, he ducks down his head. A flush floods his cheeks. My conscience gives a guilty start. I'd put from my head he tried to talk to me earlier. Lugh's right. I shouldn't of took his hand at the bridge.

Now, you know where yer goin, says Slim. Starlight Lanes, Sector Five. He takes a deep breath. His arm goes up to point the way. You head southwest from here—

Got it, says Ash. You told us twice already.

Well, he says, the sign's likely to be overgrown is the thing. There's snakecreeper grows fast as wildfire all over the—

We'll be on the lookout, I says. You better git rollin.

I told Peg the Flight all about you numberous times, he says, but, still, don't especk no warm welcome. Peg's a genius with the junk, but a notorious cranky old fish. Ergo, there ain't many drop-ins at the Lanes. Ideal fer a hidey-hole. Oh, an I meant to say. There's a Steward fella by Willowbrook's got a bad tooth I promised to pull. I'll swing by there an yank it out. Maybe stop a couple other places along the way. Gotta keep myself lookin bona fide. A wolf in sheep's clothin, that's me. A sheep's dress, I should say. Ha ha! Wouldn't that be a sight? A sheep in a frock.

Slim, I says. Go.

Walk on, Duff. He clicks at his carthorse an, with a cry of, See you anon! they're off. Inside the Cosmic his potion bottles clank in their cupboards as they bump through the gap an outta sight.

Eccentric he is, no question. But he's a medicine man among few such. So Slim's got value, he's official in New Eden. The five circle tattoo on his right arm says so. Still, it's curfew till sun-up fer everybody but the Tonton. An dawn's a while off yet. He'll hafta travel by one of the old ways till daylight. The slow, rough ones that wind an wander, that nobody much uses these days. DeMalo's new roads is the thing. The rest of us, we'll strike out wild. We'll probly reach Starlight Lanes well before he does.

I take a last glance around. The site's clear. I won't think about Nero. I won't I won't. We're all here, we're all ready to mount up. Apart from one. Where's Emmi? I says.

Nobody remembers seein her once we started breakin camp.

Molly says, That one's had her head in the clouds all day.

Dammit, I says. Why cain't she never do what she's s'posed to?

Lugh sighs. I'll go, he says.

Look who I found! It's a shout. Emmi's voice. We whirl around as she comes runnin through the gap. She holds Nero in her arms.

My heart bounds. Leaps. Nero! I cry.

Tracker makes a beeline, barkin like crazy. In the clamour of excitement that breaks out, I rush to her an take him. He greets me with caws of relief. Tellin me what happened, if only I could unnerstand. I elbow off Tracker, set to drown him with slobbery licks of joy.

Where'd you find him? says Creed. We looked, Saba, I swear we did.

As I check Nero to make sure he's okay, Emmi's breathless with the thrill of it.

I found him in a rabbit burrow tethered to a peg, she says. His beak was tied, so's he couldn't call fer help. He'd nearly got it off – he's so smart, he was rubbin aginst this sharp stone – but oh, poor Nero, it must of bin awful. He must of bin so afeared. He was sure glad to see me, I can tell you.

Where was this? I says.

Oh, over there a ways. She flaps a vague hand in no particular direction.

Unnerground, says Creed. Guess that's why Tracker didn't sniff him out. He ain't no burrow hound.

How did you know where to look? I says.

Em's a hopeless dissembler. She tries to meet my eyes, but cain't. Like a guilty dog that's stole the supper.

I dunno, she says. I jest kinda … felt where he was.

Felt, says Lugh. Airy-fairy. Come on, Em, none of yer mystical baloney.

It ain't baloney! I swear, she says.

Lugh gives me a frownin look. Jest then, there's a vexed squawk from my arms. Nero's head feathers stick up in mad spikes all over. Tracker's soaked him with swipes of his tongue. We laugh. I ain't laughed fer so long, I almost fergot how it feels. I pull Emmi in fer a one-armed hug an kiss the top of her head.

Thanks, Em, I says.

I'm really really sorry I didn't watch, she says. I feel jest awful, truly I do. But look, I brought you the tether cord. Here.

She hands me a short length of two-ply hemp twine. Plain, workaday cord that's seen plenty of use. The kind anybody pretty much anywhere might be likely to have on 'em. I shove it in my pocket. Where's yer boots? I says. Go put 'em on, yer as bad as Creed. Okay, we're on our way. Next stop, Starlight Lanes.

Nero would have managed to free himself before long. He'd tied his beak loose enough to make sure of it. Still, he'd hated doing it. Hated himself for doing it. Taking him, frightening him.

He'd rattled her. She thought a Tonton had followed them. That the dead crow and Nero proved they could get at her – at all of them – at any time, at any place. So what? She wasn't going to give up. Run away in fear. Had he really thought, even for a moment, that she'd do such a thing?

No. He'd stopped thinking. He'd lost his head. It was a shaming, stupid trick. Born of panic in the night-time woods.

He had to stay cool. Forget about DeMalo and just stick with his plan. It was simple and it would work. He'd follow her as she went to meet Jack. He'd look for his chance. He'd take it.

And his deal for their past and future would be done.

Our way to Sector Five takes us through the fells, with their acid springs an unsettled tors. It's a place of sudden echoes. Of long ago bloodshed, cold on our skins. The wind whines its claws over rock. There's bin a fresh landslip, a big one. We hafta dismount an help the horses pick their way through the shattered slabs.

I planted myself at the rear from the off, wantin to be alone with my thoughts. Not that I've had much chance. I carry Nero snug to my chest. He's buttoned inside my coat with his head poked out to see where we're goin. Tracker sticks like a burr, shovin his nose in, anxious to keep check on his friend.

Ash hangs back to wait fer us. How is he? she says. Hey, Nero. How ya doin, buddy? She reaches out slowly. He chitters nervily, beaks at her. It's okay, okay, I won't hurt you, she says. But he won't let her near enough to stroke him. Helluva thing, she says to me.

You said it, I says. I go to walk Hermes on, but her hand on my arm stops me. The hostile wind circles, snatchin at her forest of plaits. Whippin the manes of the horses. She stands foursquare aginst it, tall, shadow-eyed an sharply white faced. Like a shade of some old war, rumbled from the stones by our passage. Her fingers chill through my sleeve.

I bin thinkin, she says. An I don't like where it's took me.

The liar inside me takes a cagey step back. What're you talkin about? I says.

Come on, she says, you must be thinkin it too. It was one of us did that to Nero. Took him an tethered him.

I stare at her. It never crossed my mind, I says.

I don't wanna think that one of our own did it, she says. But I cain't figger how else to explain it.

DeMalo is how. But I cain't say. I couldn't ever say. None of us would dream of hurtin Nero, I says.

If somebody wanted to git at you, shake you, what better way than Nero? she says. An, I mean, we ain't ezzackly bin holdin hands an dancin in a circle. Yer in a spiky time, my friend.

Are you talkin about Creed? I says. You an him's best mates.

I ain't namin nobody, she says. I hate that I'm even sayin this. Maybe I'm wrong. But. You need to look into it. If it is one of us, we gotta know who. An why.

You ain't mentioned this to nobody else, I says.

No, she says. An listen, you make sure you suspect me too, okay? It could be I'm tryin to throw you off my trail here. Mind you, if I was, it's such a sorry attempt I'd hafta cut off my own head in shame.

No need fer that, I says. Okay, Ash. This stays between you an me.

She nods as she turns up her collar aginst the wind. We pick our way on through the rockfall. After a bit, Ash says, You know me, right? I ain't crazy or nuthin an … gawd knows I ain't got no imagination, but … I feel like she's still here. With us.

99

She don't hafta say who she means. I know. It's Maev.

An I see her, Ash says. Sometimes, I'll turn an I swear I see her. Jest fer a moment I catch a glimpse of her. An it's so real. It's like she's … caught in the light. In the moonlight. The sunlight.

Maybe she is, I says.

She's bin so tangled with my life, says Ash. With who I am, fer so long. It don't seem possible she's gone. An her an me, we had some … times together. Y'know what I'm sayin? Not heavy or nuthin – neether of us was like that – but…

Oh, I says. I guess I thought becuz her an Lugh—

Ash slants a smile at me. He, she … whoever, right? she says.

I'm sorry, I says. I know we don't talk about her enough. I jest feel too guilty.

Don't, she'd hate that, says Ash. She believed in you, Saba. She believed in this fight. Remember who she was, how she was, an take strength from her.

This time, when she puts out her hand, Nero lets her stroke his head. If only crows could talk, she says.

If only.

Mid-mornin. The northeasternmost corner of Sector Five. Sweat wet from a sudden heavy heat, we pick our way along a forest alley. Its single track winds through the grown-over ruins of a settlement. Here, the shape of man-worked stone. There, a peek of iron. The earth creeps an seeps. A slowtime tide of moss an bushes an trees. Sunbeams straggle through branches. Like I figgered we'd be, we're ahead of Slim. The alley's rutted deep with long use, but nuthin's passed along it today. It narrows as it heads fer a wall that towers high. The last gasp of some big Wrecker buildin, slowly bein swallowed by the great bloated bleb of crawlin forest.

Emmi's walkin jest behind me, with Tracker. I glance back. She's stood stock still, with the strangest look on her face.

What is it? I says.

She don't answer. Tracker whimpers an sniffs all around her. She's stopped next to a great stone, shafted through its heart by a determined hazel tree. She turns her head sharply. Stares at the stone hard.

Don't lallygag, Em, we must nearly be there. Emmi. C'mon. Quit dreamin.

The track ends at the high wooded wall. There ain't no sign of no junkyard.

Did we follow Slim's directions? says Creed.

Yeah, I says. But he did rabbit on. I might of missed somethin.

Mercy says, Did I not hear him say the sign might be overgrown? She nods at the wall, smothered by rambunctious snakecreeper.

Lugh an Creed scramble up, usin roots fer hand an footholds. They start tearin at the creeper. There's a sudden green flurry as we all join in, haulin an pullin. Then we stand there pickin off bits of creeper as we look at what we've uncleared.

A great, rusted fancywork archway. Over twenny foot high, it wracks an twists, saved from collapse by girders an logs. We stare at the sign that hangs from the middle. Hard

101

to say what it's made from. Nuthin that ever grew in the ground, that's fer sure. It was brightly coloured once, but long since faded. What looks to be a comet with a tail of stars smashes into bottles an sends 'em flyin. There's a bunch of letters that could be words.

Star ... light ... Lanes, says Tommo. This is it.

We stare at him in wonder. He reds-up furiously, shrinks from our close regard.

You can read, I says.

So? he says.

You never said, says Lugh.

You never asked, says Tommo. I got numbers, too. He reads the sign, slow an careful. Ten pin, he says. Twenty lanes. Great for a date. Come in and score. He struggles over the next bit, frownin with the effort. S, e, n, i, o, r, s. Sen-eye-ors? Seneyeors spec-ee-al rates Mon and Thur.

We wait.

That's all, he says.

What the holy hell does that mean? says Ash.

Who knows? It's Wrecker speak, I says. But this is the place. Starlight Lanes.

You read good, Tommo, says Lugh. Who learned you? Ike?

He shrugs. Tommo's life is split in two. Before Ike an after Ike. Life-after-Ike he'll talk about. Life-before-Ike he won't, not a word. When he learned to read must come from life-before.

Let's find Peg the Flight. Innerduce ourselfs, I says.

I lead us through the gates. We're quite the gaggle. Eight of us, sundry horses, a stolen pony, Bean the mule, a wolfdog an a nervous crow perched on my shoulder. Nero's stuck to me the whole way here. Hostile to anybody else that comes near him, quick to beak whatever bit of 'em happens to be closest.

Oh my! says Emmi.

The junkyard rises high in front of us. I ain't never seen its like. Countless piles an hills of scrap metal, some small, some large, with cranky paths that wind between 'em. There's a scatter of rackety low sheds an lean-tos. A flat-topped grassy hill rises behind the yard. In front of it stands the biggest junkpile of all.

A shack grows from it, clings to it. Made of flotsam an crazyjunk, thisses an thats of all sizes an shapes an descriptions. At a quick glance, I see car doors, goodyears, metal sheets, barrels, boards an logs. All put together any old way. It's a puzzle how it holds together. I never seen such a wackadoo place. Dozens of ladders an walkways sprawl out like a spider's web from it – down to the ground, up the junkhill, sidewise an every which way. There's ropes an chains an pulleys with buckets. Slides an chutes. Tracks an swings. Barrels an nets an wheels an flags. There's a raggedy wash hung on a line. An there's live birds in cages. Hunnerds of birds. Everywhere, birds. The air trembles with their trills an chatter. Nero caws to his cousins in their prison cells.

Molly shakes her head in amazement. An I thought the Lost Cause was a dump, she says.

So, where's this Peg the Flight? says Ash. An what kinda name is that anyways?

A camel mooches out from a nearby scrapmetal hill. He's a fleabit shambles. His hump slumps in defeat.

Look who it is, says Em.

Oh no, says Lugh. I fergot he was here.

It's Moses. He loathed us from the start. Five-time winner of the Pillawalla Camel Race, fer years he hauled the Cosmic fer Slim. When we had to take to country too tricky fer a camel, Peg the Flight took Moses on to haul his junktub. After the handover, Slim mourned through one endless, noisy night. With a keg of seed rye an long, confused songs about camels an brotherhood. We pretended sorrow, fer Slim's sake, but secretly we celebrated. You can only take so much camel spit.

He's seen us. He glares with unbrotherly malice.

He don't look too happy, says Creed. You don't suppose he blames us?

Don't be stupid, I says. Hey, Moses.

He bellows with rage. He charges.

He blames us, all right! shrieks Emmi.

We scatter fer safety, boy, girl an beast. Jest as we do, a giant bird comes barrellin straight at us from the sky. No, no bird, a flyin machine. But not a Wrecker flyer. A junkflyer. A revamp two-wheeler with metal wings an two windcranks. One on top, one behind. A skinny old fossil in goggles an a helmet wrestles with the stick controls.

Look out! I yell.

Moses turns on a dime an scrambles. I dive fer cover. We're all jest in time. The flyer smashes at speed at the scrapmetal hill. It explodes in every direction. The racket's so fearsome, you could hear it on the moon. As it starts to settle, we git to our feet an brush ourselfs down. Bean's honkin his head off in raucous alarm. Moses hollers back from wherever he's hid. Nero shrieks an swoops.

Welcome to Starlight Lanes, says Creed.

Everybody okay? I says. There's nods all around.

The pilot don't appear rattled in the least. Still wearin his goggles, his helmet cock-eyed, he chunters to hisself as he clambers around, checkin the damage to his flyer. There ain't nuthin but damage. It's completely wrecked. An now I notice that this particular scraphill's main scrap seems to be crashed junkflyer – bits of wing, wheels an so on. Sudden nosedives must be a regular event around here.

Ah … Peg the Flight, says Ash. Now I git it.

I call over. Hey there, sir? Hello? Are you okay? We're friends of Slim's.

He tucks the smaller windcrank unner one arm, slithers down the heap an hurries towards the junkhill shack, still talkin to hisself. Maybe he didn't hear me, what with the crash an the helmet an bein old an all. I chase after him, swervin an leapin through the scattered junk. Tracker an Emmi an Nero come too. We catch up an trot alongside.

I says, Excuse me? Sir? Peg the Flight? I'm—

Slim's girl, Angel of Death, yes yes, shut up, I heerd you, she says.

She. Peg the Flight ain't no sir, she's a ma'am. A scrawny old damsel, stringy as rawhide. Her tan skin droops in leathery folds. Her vulture neck pokes from high, narrow shoulders. Tattered britches flutter like feathers.

Sorry, I says. Sorry about the sir, ma'am, I mean, uh – Slim should be here any time. He ain't far behind us. He said he thought it 'ud be okay with you if we was to—

But she's gone. Nimblin one-handed up a rackly ladder, speedy as a spider. Still gabblin to herself nineteen to the dozen. Step by step, back to the start, basics, you goose, you fathead, she says.

Me an Em scramble up the ladder in her wake. Tracker's left below, whinin an barkin.

We follow as she scampers along a rope an slat walkway towards her shack. Easier said than done. It's a peril, with missin slats an patched in bits of frayed rope.

Beggin yer pardon, Miz Peg, but we'd like to stay here a bit, if that's okay, I says. If it don't cause you no trouble, that is.

Beggin my pardon blah blah blah! Peg swats her free hand about her head. As she rushes past the caged birds, there's a great hullabaloo of flappin an screechin. Yes yes, my dearies, I know, I know! Not long now to wait, my hearts! she cries.

She dives through the open door of the shack. She dumps the windcrank on a bench with some other rammel, barks, Quiet! at us an starts to scribble on the wall with a piece of chalk. Airflow, she mutters, turnage, lift, thrust. Step by step, back to the start. Basics, you goose, you fathead.

Ma'am? I says. I'd be grateful if, uh … well, would you look at that. I watch, spellbound, as a picture of a windcrank starts to emerge. Every last detail clear an sharp. Who'd think it of such a rattlepate old nonny? How far you flown in these things? I says.

She makes no reply, heedless to all but her task. Nero's followed us inside. Still more cautious than he would be usually, but he's far too nosy to resist at least a peek. Like the yard outside, the shack's a junkheap. But a indoor one. An a shipshape one. An it's all about flyers. There's spare parts in buckets an crates. Endless drawins an plans scrawled on the walls. This room seems to be the heart of the sprawl of buildins over the junkhill. I crane my neck to see the clutter of corridors, cranky stairways an other rooms that spider off from here. Through dozens of windows, big an small, sunbeams warm the dust of a thousand days gone. Peg's only comforts seem to be a rocker chair an a rusty stove swagged with webs.

A heap of fightin kit on a bench catches my eye. I pick out a couple of armbands an a jerkin an dust 'em off. They're Wrecker old, smooth an soft with age, but not bad fer all that. Good sturdy dark-brown leather with rusty metal plates. Well padded. Brass buckled. The jerkin looks to of stopped a few arrows in its time. It's got the wounds to show fer it. The armbands cover me, wrist to elbow. A good thing to have. Whaddya want fer these bits of armour? I ask Peg.

Them ain't fer tradin, she says. She don't even bother to look, she jest keeps on scribblin.

As I go to drop 'em back, she says, They're yers, meant fer you, kept fer you, put 'em on.

I pause. Cast a frown at her back. Crazy old coot. Then, Thanks, I says. I slip the jerkin over my head, slide on the armbands an do up the buckles. A perfect fit. All of it.

Emmi's bin silent this whole time. She's knelt by a table, starin in wonderment at a birdcage that sits on top. It's tiny. The size of my two fists together. Such dainty metalwork you wouldn't think possible. Vines twine the bars, burstin with leaf an fruit an flower. Inside, there's a metal finch perched on a swing. Scabs of colour tell of its painted beauty, once upon a long ago. What kinda person in what kinda world had time or cause to make somethin like this?

Nero flaps onto the table. He peers at the bird, his head tipped this way, that way. He croaks. Taps the bars gently with his beak.

Nero, don't, says Em. It's sleepin.

Wake it up, says Peg. The key, the key is the key to a song. She throws down the chalk an comes over, swipin her hands on her britches. Her crabby old fingers wind a key hid low on one side. There's a whisper of a clank. Then the tinkle of ancient spiderweb music. The finch's beak opens an shuts. It tips forwards an backwards, flickin its tail. As the song ends, it sits back on the perch. Its beak slowly closes. Frozen till the next turn of the key.

Oh, breathes Emmi. Make it sing agin!

Please, I says.

Sorry … please, she says.

Peg waves consent. Em winds the key an the song tiptoes through the dustbeams once more.

Them birds out there in the cages, I says. You should let 'em go. Birds need to fly.

Soon, girlie, soon. Me an them, says Peg.

A shadow falls over us. Tommo stands in the doorway. Slim's jest pullin in, he says.

Slim gives me a morsel of news on the quiet. He made three stops on his way here. One to pull the tooth at Willowbrook, one to lance a neck boil an one to treat a private complaint so gruesome his toes curl at the thought. He starts to regale me, but I hold him in check an the gist of it is this.

At each place he stopped, they told him the same. They heard from their neighbour who heard from his that the Angel of Death haunts New Eden. That her ghost comes each night with the starfall. She was seen last night. An the night before that. She's ridin the roads with her wolfdog an crow, seekin vengeance fer her death from any who cross her path. They're all unsettled. Worried what it means. Fearin it portends trouble soon to come.

I don't ever ride the roads. Nobody's seen me. In starfall season folks see haunts where there ain't none. I'll tell Jack about this when I see him tonight.

Luckily, there's more than jest junk at Starlight Lanes. There's a little coldwater washpond too. Round the back, through a woodland garden patch, an a nut glade an a stand of cottonwood. We find Moses an Hermes an Bean there, nibblin at the bark. Hermes would put up with anybody fer cottonbark. Even a foul tempered camel.

I'm amazed Peg could give us direction to the pond. From that ripe smell she trails, I took her to be a stranger to water.

Now with a ring of pale skin where her slave collar was – Peg had it off in a jiff, like Slim said she would – Mercy strips off her ragged hemp tunic. A shawl of thin whip scars shrouds her shoulders. She folds the tunic with care.

I'd of thought you'd wanna burn that thing, I says.

The day there ain't no slaves in New Eden, she says, I'll build a pyre an watch it burn.

She wades in fer a swim an a wash. I toss her my soapbundle. I don't look at her direct. I cain't bear to. That Mercy should be brought so low. The sight of her naked body, so scarred an gaunt, stabs my gut with red anger. This is DeMalo. I gotta remember that behind his clever words this is who he is. Mercy, jest one slave among many such as her. Like Slim's friend, Billy Six. His hard-worked land stolen an him spiked through the throat, nailed to a post like a trophy rat. Maev, dead. Bram, dead. The Free Hawks an Raiders, all dead.

You kill people to git what you want.

So do you. You've just done it again. Any violence is regrettable, but it's a means to an end. Did you weep when you destroyed

Hopetown? Did you lose sleep over any scum that might have burned in its flames? No. We are so alike, Saba.

Me, like DeMalo. I gotta shut out his voice. It's runnin through my head all the time. Confusin me. Twistin my thoughts. I can feel the heat rise to my cheeks. Mercy sees – not much escapes her notice – but she don't remark upon it.

You comin in? she says.

I bathe on my own, no offence, I says.

She takes that in, too, without comment. While she scrubs the dirt of slavery from her skin, I splash my hot face. Try to cool my hot mind. Drink down handfuls of water to calm the sick anger that roils my belly.

Once she's outta the water an rubbin herself dry with a clean sack, Mercy says, So, what is it you want to talk about?

Would you say love makes you weak? I says. That's what Lugh believes. Becuz of Pa, how he went after Ma died.

Mercy don't answer right away. Then she says, That's Lugh. What about you? Tell me what you believe.

I stare at my boots as I speak. As I think my way through each word. I seen both sides, I says. Not jest other people, I know it in myself too. I know how strong it made me when I was searchin fer Lugh. I couldn't of done what I did, I couldn't of endured if my tie to him hadn't of bin so strong. But I bin made weak by it too. I made some bad choices. On the whole, though? I'd say I'm stronger fer love, not weaker.

I couldn't have said it better myself, says Mercy. She sits down beside me, wrapped in the sack.

I raise my head to meet her eyes. I remember somethin you told me at Crosscreek, I says. You said my pa looked to the stars fer answers, but you look at what's here, in front of you, around you. I need you to tell me what you see, Mercy. Whaddya make of this place? Of New Eden?

110

Huh! She gives a little laugh. You sure do got big questions on your mind these days, she says. What do I make of New Eden. She thinks fer a bit, then she says, Things ain't always what they seem to be. People neether.

That ain't new, I says.

She says, Somehow … New Eden don't seem entirely real.

Them scars of yers look real enough, I says.

Of course, but, for instance, she says, them girls I tended at the babyhouse. Imagine that's you. Your family's driven away or killed – maybe right in front of you – but you're not. You get to live becuz you're one of the Pathfinder's Chosen ones. You're a Steward of the Earth now. You're dazzled by him. Convinced by him. The power, the violence, they keep you in fear.

Yes, I says.

Mercy goes on. You're paired with a boy you don't know. Sent off with this stranger to work the land an make healthy babies for New Eden. Before you know it, if you're lucky, you're pregnant to him. Maybe you cain't abide him, but you got no say in it. What do you think? How do you feel about it all?

My remembrance goes to the Stewards we killed. Buried in a shallow grave on the road to the Lost Cause. Eli an RiverLee. His dislike of her. Her fear of him. Her desperation to have a child. Knowin if she didn't, she'd be slaved. I think of RiverLee's precious silver necklace. Family reminders forbidden in New Eden, but she kept it, hidden, a secret. To remind her who she was, where she'd come from.

How do you feel? You tell me, says Mercy.

I feel awful about my family, I says. Why choose me above them? An I'm grievin them, I miss them, but I gotta hide how

I feel. I cain't talk to nobody. I hate the boy they paired me with. I hate him touchin me. He's mean. But if I don't have a baby, he'll turn me in an I'll be slaved. I feel afeared. I feel alone.

That sounds about right, says Mercy. An I'll tell you somethin. Girls givin birth, they always call for their mother. Your mother did. So do them Stewards. Not one wants her baby to be took from her. They try to hide what they feel – after all, the Pathfinder knows best, it's for the good of New Eden an Mother Earth – but I seen it in their eyes, their faces, every time. They cry in the night. An the ones who birth weak babies? They know ezzackly what's gonna happen. They know the child of their flesh, that they carried in their body, will be left out of doors to die. If the cold don't take it, some animal will. Maybe to feed its own young. Them poor girls, it just about kills 'em. One took her own life while I was there.

She killed herself, I says.

They don't let that get out, says Mercy. Not good for morale. Them Steward girls, they're breeders. Their wombs belong to New Eden. Natural feelins an inclinations don't come into it. Did you know they're expected to produce a child every two years?

Two years, I says. I didn't, no.

If they fail, they're slaved. An the boy ain't never to blame, she says.

What about them? I says. The boys?

They pretend to be men, she says. I can only imagine how they feel about never seein their own child. The Chosen of New Eden, they're all tryin to be who DeMalo says they are.

Pretend. That trigger in my head clicks agin. Things ain't always what they seem. People ain't who they seem. They're all tryin to be who he says they are.

So that's the Stewards an the babyhouse, Mercy's sayin. I

cain't say about Edenhome, I don't know it. Only, babies go there once they bin weaned.

Edenhome. Where they raise children to serve New Eden. Kids who was stolen from their folks. Weaned babies. When they turn fourteen, they become a Steward of the Earth an they're paired by the Pathfinder to breed an work.

Then there's slaves, says Mercy. Most like me, shanghaied. Some who used to be Chosen ones. Them that fell from grace with the Pathfinder.

One moment they're a Chosen one, the next they ain't, I says. That must give 'em food fer thought.

It don't go unnoticed, let's put it that way, she says.

An there's the Tonton, I says. Don't fergit them.

I ain't likely to, she says.

When you start to pick it apart, I says, when you start to look close, New Eden ain't what it looks like. But it's workin, ain't it? The Pathfinder's plan to make a new world.

In some ways, maybe, she says. The Stewards are well fed all the time now. That means more of the girls carry to full term. Word is that crop yields are up.

DeMalo's voice runs through my head.

I'm making difficult decisions every day. Allocating what scarce resources there are to those who can make best use of them. I'm behaving morally, responsibly.

Mercy an me sit silent fer a time, there by the coldwater pond. The sun on my skin feels softly, rarely kind. The same words churn in me, over an over. Mothers an children. Fathers. Brothers. Sisters. Family. People ain't who they seem to be. On the whole, we're stronger fer love. DeMalo's weakness. Our strength.

I realize that Mercy's watchin me, her eyes sharply curious. I take her neatly folded tunic an hand it to her.

113

You'll be buildin that pyre one day soon, I says.

There she is, by the twisted tree. Allis, my sunlight mother. We're alone, her an me, on the wide flat plain. In the grey at the edge of the world. The clouds hang low. The wind wails high. The tree gleams, bare an white.

At the foot of the tree is the gravepit. Rough an narrow an deep. Then we're standin beside it, my mother an me. I know what lies within. The body in rusted armour. Laid out in the pit full length. The head wrapped around with a blood red shawl.

Golden Allis. Gone fer so long. Sun hair, sky eyes, bright soul. But the dark-past-the-edge has vanquished her light. She drifts. She shifts. She fades.

Her feet of air step into the grave. She beckons, come with me. It's empty now. I follow her down. Into the down-dark earth.

Then water. On the rise. Up my bare legs. No, not water. Blood. It rises quickly. Blackly. Thickly. To my thighs, my waist, my chest. It grips me, I cain't git away. I slip an I'm chokin, I'm drownin, I'm chokin, cain't breathe, I'm—

With a jolt, I'm awake. Scrabblin at my throat. Pullin frantic at what's chokin me—

Saba, wake up! It's Molly's voice, urgent.

I cain't breathe! I gasp.

It's off, okay, I'm takin it off. Saba, c'mon honey, open yer eyes. Sit up.

She pats my hand gently. I blink. Made stupid by the sudden glare of sunlight. Blasted to life while lost in the darklands of dream. Molly kneels beside me. She holds the red shawl.

Uh! I shrink back. Take it away!

Okay, calm down, okay, it's gone. She pushes it behind her skirts, outta sight. You got yerself tangled in it, that's all.

My rattleheart slows to a rackety gallop. That was in the bottom of my pack, I says. How'd you git it?

Emmi gave it to me, she says. When Mercy told me she left you fast to sleep, I came to cover you, make sure you didn't die of sunstroke.

I stare at her dully. I didn't mean to drop off, I says.

I'm bone weary. My head feels thick. My body's heavy, like I'm weighed down by stones.

I'm sorry, says Molly. I didn't mean to disturb you.

No, no, I says. It's good that you did. I got thinkin to do. A lot to work out.

You hardly sleep at all these days, she says. You bein tired won't be good fer none of us. Here, lie down. Cover yerself with this. She slips the knot on her headscarf an hands it to me. It smells richly of the rose oil that softens her skin, that scents her hair. As she shakes out her curls, I make a point of not lookin at the W brand on her forehead. She sees me not lookin. She says, It ain't often I git a chance to air the war wound these days.

How can you make light of it? I says.

What should I do? she says. Cry fer the rest of my life? Molly of the Many Sorrows?

No, but – after everythin else ... Gracie an Ike an then – I dunno how you bear it.

You got battle scars. This is mine, she says. You know what it tells me? I'm a survivor. An if I ever need remindin why I'm here right now, why I'm doin this? One look in the glass does it. Not that I don't got plenty of other reasons. Ike, of course. An Jack. She hesitates a moment, then she

115

says, You never talk about him. Since he died, you ain't so much as mentioned his name, not even in passin. I know you gotta guard what you say with the others, but you know you don't need to with me. The hurt puzzlement in her eyes makes my colour rise. I know Jack's impossible, she says. Was … impossible. I know it was complicated between him an you. An maybe yer feelins warn't as strong fer him as his was fer you – I dunno, yer heart ain't none of my business an love ain't easy, I sure know that. What I mean to say is … what I'd really like, what I really need, is to talk about him. With you. That's all.

I'm silent. I sit starin at my boots while heat flags my cheeks. That was a sidewise reminder that Molly knows one secret of mine. She knows that the first man I lay with warn't Jack. But she don't know who. She'd never dream it was DeMalo.

The thing is? she says. The thought of Jack dyin never once occurred to me. Not once. Fer all the trouble he found or that found him. An the other thing is, besides me, Jack's th'only one who ever knew Gracie.

Her voice falters. Fat tears spill down her cheeks. Damn, she says. Sorry. She fumbles in her pocket.

I hate this. That I lie to everybody. Most of all, I hate lyin to Molly about Jack. She's our greatest guilt, him an me. Our biggest regret in this necessary deception. She, his dearest friend, who mourns him so deep. But she has to believe that he's dead. The more people who know a secret, the more likely it is to slip out. Jest a glance from her to me at the wrong time could git someone thinkin. I'd trust my little Free Hawk gang with my own life. But not Jack's.

An the fact is, I hardly dare mention his name myself fer fear I let somethin slip that I shouldn't. How I ache to unburden myself to her. To tell her everythin. About Jack, yes, of course. But, if I'm honest, about DeMalo too. Of anybody in the world, I think Molly's the one person who might unnerstand, who could help me make sense of it. Make sense of him an me. I want her to be my friend. I wanna be a friend to her. But it cain't be. Not now. Not yet.

Sorry, I never cry. Molly blows her nose on one of her useless little scraps of hanky. Well, I better head back, she says. Creed's probly lookin fer me to apologize fer the umpteenth time. He don't do nuthin by halfs, I'll give him that. I dunno if it was me slappin his face or what you said to him after, but the boy's contrite. No more declarations of love, no more proposals. Don't tell him I said so, but I quite like him now he's actin more normal with me.

She gits to her feet an dithers with brushin off grassy bits, tidyin her skirts an petticoat. I can tell that she's hopin I'll ask her to stay. To talk about Jack, as she so badly wants to. I sit, silent, with a miserable heart.

She's holdin the shawl in her arms. It's a shame you don't like it, she says. The colour suits you.

Shawls ain't me, I says. An I ain't easy with this one.

That's the truth, near enough. But it's a fishy excuse fer all the fuss I made. If Molly thinks so, she don't let on.

Who'd of thought? she says. The Angel of Death, shy of a shawl. Never fear, yer secret's safe with me.

I couldn't begin to try an explain it to her. I cain't explain it to myself. Why Auriel Tai's blood red shawl has wrapped through my dreams from the moment I met her. Why it's always swaddled round the head of a body. A faceless warrior in a gravepit. Or Lugh or Jack or DeMalo. An then, the unnerve of findin it in my pack. When Auriel an me parted at the Snake River camp, the shawl

117

was draped around her shoulders. Then somehow – some strange impossible how – when I was leagues an hours an more leagues away, I found it in my bag. It was hers, no mistake. One of her hairs was caught on it. Long an fine, the colour of pale fire.

Saba? Molly's watchin me with a little frown. If you really don't want it, I'll have it, she says.

I take it from her. No, it's mine, I says. See you later.

Dismissed, rebuffed, she leaves me. With a smile an a wave an a grace that I do not deserve.

Alone, I stare at the shawl. It is mine. Fer some reason, it seems to be mine.

I curl in the grass by the pool, my head pillowed by Molly's rose-scented scarf. Beside me, Nero nests hisself in the red shawl.

I tip into sleep an wake with a start. Like I'm on a cliff edge then fall off. Over an over. Agin an agin. My heart slams me awake each time I fall. Dark dreams trap me in shallow circles. Round an round. On an on.

Me on the hill above the bridge in the night. The Steward girl in the cart. Her face. Her smile. The spotted kercheef at her neck. The sound of the blast an the sound of screams an blood rains down upon me.

While Mercy's voice repeats an repeats. Paired with a boy you don't know. Pregnant to a boy you don't know.

Me an DeMalo. In the pool above the bridge. I'm in the water, in his arms. We twist an turn below the surface. Sunlight sparkles

above. His white shirt billows. His voice whispers. Think of it. A
child. Yours and mine.

From each place he kisses me, each place he touches me, a stream
of blood starts to flow. The water turns red. Hands pull me down.
Down down, the darkest depths beckon me down.

I go deeper, darker, as Molly's voice sings. Hush now, my baby,
an sleep without fear. Dream Angus will bring you a dream, my
dear.

Strands of hair wind from darkness towards me. Long an fair, my
mother's hair, like weeds it winds around me. Then she, her ghost
self, my white fog dead mother, wraps her arms around me an down
we go, down down down.

Dream Angus will bring you a dream my dear.

As I bleed. As I drown. As I drift away to black.

I come to with a shudder. Sit up quickly. Too quick. A
sleep of such dreams ain't no sleep at all. My skin's bumped
with cold. The day's fuggy swill is gone. The wind's
changed. A brisk easterly is busy at work, sweepin the dregs
of day into night.

I bundle Nero in the shawl, any old way, with him
squawkin protest till he struggles free an flies. I walk fast,
brisk, to wake myself. In the hope that my dreamtime cain't
keep up. I collect Hermes from the cottonwood glade. I'll
need him fer the ride to meet Jack tonight.

The racket from Peg's caged birds grows louder as I near
the junkyard. I hear music. Faint at first. As we follow its trail
through the yard, it settles to a wistful lament. Somebody on
a stringbox. A good player. Must be Peg. None of our lot
scrapes the strings. It ain't long before the deep smell of
cooked meat joins in. My mouth waters. There's a shout of
laughter.

The music an smells an voices tumble through the open

door of a ramshackle shed. Outside, there's a roastpit. The spit's empty, the rocks grow cool. Tracker slinks among the junkheaps, on watchdog duty. He greets us with a raised head an swish of his tail, then disappears agin, nose down, on his patrol.

Me an Nero go in. Rush lanterns hang on the walls of the shed. Splash warm pools of light over the dusty clutter. There's a big space bin cleared in the middle of it all. Peg hunches over a battered stringbox. Her skinny old arm's at one with her bow, haulin that mournful tune from its guts. Creed shakes his head in admiration as he plays along on his squeezebox. Molly an Slim an Mercy perch, uncomfortable, on barrels and whatnot. They're tryin to eat, but without much success. Emmi's in the grip of giddy excitement. She jigs an hops all around 'em, with her tongue goin clickety clack. They smile an nod. The fools. They don't know not to give her encouragement. They'll be trapped now till she tires or death takes 'em. Ash an Tommo know better. They don't meet her eyes, but keep their heads down an fill their bellies.

Lugh's right by the door. Eat tin in hand, he's pickin over the ravaged carcass of a spread you might dream of. An he's bein so fussy, he must be on his thirds. There's woodchuck roasted to tender flesh an crispy skin, boiled lilybulb with onions, nettlecake an more. I'm used to livin low, to hard fare. I'm only confused by plenty. Nero dives at the table. Lugh cries, No!, but too late. Nero's done a snatch an grab. He shrieks defiance as he settles on a rafter with a juicy big piece of woodchuck.

What's all this in aid of? I says. What's got Em in such a fizz?

Ah, there you are! Lugh turns quickly. It's a birthday party. Molly pulled it together. Ain't she a wonder?

Molly's birthday? I says.

No, stupid, Emmi's. She's ten.

What? I says. Today?

Last month, he says. You fergot, bad sister.

Ten, I says, good grief. Anyways, bad brother, you fergot too. Why didn't you come git me? You got grease on yer face.

You needed to sleep. He swipes with his sleeve an inspects me, narrow-eyed. I see you didn't, he says. Yer startin to give old Peg the Flight some serious competition in the ugly bag stakes. All tired an wrinkly an big dark circles—

I slap his arm. I am not wrinkly, you—

He plugs my mouth with a wodge of cake. You what? He blinks blue-eyed innocence at me as he nibbles on a lilybulb. Sorry, cain't hear you.

Saba, hey Saba! Emmi comes runnin. She pulls at my hands, hoppin an turnin me in circles. She gabbles full tilt, while I choke down the cake. Molly gimme a comb fer my hair – her very own favourite comb – an she says if I use it twice a day it'll make my hair grow beautiful jest like hers. I cain't wait, I already bin combin, can you tell? An Creed – guess what? He ate fire, he truly did, you should of seen! An then he pulled a button from my ear by magic. Here it is, look, he said it's mine to keep. An Ash gimme a gizmo knife an Slim gimme this special medicine necklace to stop the rickets an—

Rheumatics, not rickets, says Lugh.

I should know, it's my necklace, an it's rickets, she says. An Mercy says she'll make me a new shirt jest as soon as she finds one to cut down an we're gonna have dancin in a bit an—

Emmi! Tommo calls. C'mere!

She dashes off agin an me an Lugh follow. She stands in front of Tommo, her eyes shinin. He puts his empty eat tin on the ground. Creed an Peg stop playin to watch.

Keep still, Tommo tells her. Hands out. Eyes shut.

She squeezes 'em tight an stretches her arms straight in front of her. He reaches behind him. He brings out the dainty little birdcage with the tiny metal finch that sings. He places it gently in her hands.

Open, he says.

She opens her eyes. A gasp of wonder. Joy lights her face. Fer a second. A breath. Then it darkens to shocked dismay.

There's puzzlement all around. Raised eyebrows an baffled smiles. The cage is a rarely fine object. The best Tommo's got in his trade bag is a buckle.

That's quite the present, I says. It must of cost dear. What did you take fer it, Peg?

She waggles her head an shakes her bow. Never you mind, she says. The boy offered, I took, it's business, our business, his an mine, Miss Nosy Poke, not yers.

Tommo, you didn't. Emmi breathes the words in disbelief. It's clear she knows full well what he's traded. An she don't like it, not one little bit. An Tommo don't like her reaction. He scowls darkly. His cheeks flush.

No, says Emmi. You cain't.

C'mon, says Ash. What is it?

Tommo's glarin at Emmi. She glares back at him, her face scrinched with fury. There's a long, uncomfortable silence. I notice Nero makin free with the food table.

At last Mercy says, When somebody gifts you, Emmi, it's only good manners to accept with thanks.

Thank you, she says flatly. It's the best present I'll ever have.

No kiss, no hug, not even a smile. Fer the best present she'll ever have. Then Peg swings into a sweet old waltz an the strange moment breaks. Mercy starts collectin the eatin tins. Molly pounces on Nero to rescue the food. As she scolds him fer a thief, she feeds him tidbits.

Lugh says to me, What was that about? An how did he manage it? Tommo ain't got nuthin.

I know, I says. I ain't got the faintest idea.

Ash saves Tommo from his humiliation. She grabs him to show him how to waltz an then he's busy dodgin her clodhoppin boots, countin one-two-three over an over. With a courtly bow, Slim bids Emmi to dance. Despitin his bulk, he glides her around in elegant twirls an swoops. Emmi makes a big show of ignorin Tommo. Her pleasure in her first ever party is gone.

Did you speak to her like we talked about? I says to Lugh.

He grimaces. Sorry, I fergot. But, c'mon, let her be. Now ain't the time.

Now's jest the time, I says. I'll do it – don't worry, I'll be nice to her – but you owe me. We cain't be th'only ones don't gift her. Go rustle somethin up.

Where from? he says.

I dunno, look around, ask Peg, I says. We're in a junkyard, fergawdsake. I managed to find you that necklace in a landfill an I'd say it's pretty fine.

He grabs hold of it. The little green glass circle on a leather string that I gave him fer our last birthday. Eighteen year. He gives me a hopeful look as he says, Maybe I could—

You are not givin that to her, I says. Ungrateful swine. An don't go givin her yer spare bootlaces neether.

He wanders off an I ain't surprised to see him peer hopefully into a filthy old barrel. Like a birthday gift fer a

123

ten-year-old girl might be found in such a place. It'll fall to me to sort out but I'll make him sweat a bit first.

I catch Creed's attention an give him the nod. It's jest gone dark outside. Time fer him to join Tracker on patrol duty. As he sets aside his squeezebox an heads my way, Peg rackets into a lively reel. She saws at the strings, stompin time on a board with gusto. Poor Slim lets out a pained wail. Lugh takes pity on him an Em shrieks with startled delight as he grabs her an starts reelin her about the room. Good man, big brother. Slim staggers to a stool to mop his brow.

Creed's got me in his sights. His chin's set determined, like a man on a mission. I think him an me's about to have further words, probly on the subject of my character flaws. My body twitches to flee, but I stand my ground. I'll hafta put him off. I gotta leave to meet Jack at Weepin Water.

Molly's foot taps time as she helps Mercy clear the table. Creed passes by them an she touches his hand. She don't look at him. It's the briefest of touches an the light ain't good, but I know I didn't imagine it. An she was the one to reach. She was the one to touch. In the gloom, she must of thought she wouldn't be seen.

Creed looks dazed. Like from a knockout punch, jest before you hit the ground. He walks straight past me. I stare at Molly. She smiles an chats to Mercy as they work. She makes like she cain't abide him. Well. She did say it herself.

Life ain't black an white. People ain't neether. Family, friends, lovers. The longer I live, the more that I see, the less I know fer sure. Especially when it comes to matters of the heart.

So many secrets. Emmi an Tommo an now Molly an Creed. What else don't I know about? Far too much, I fear.

Emmi! I wave at her, shoutin over the fidget of Peg's fiddle. C'mere!

Molly, calls Lugh. We're two dancers down. Help us out.

This tame old jig? She shrugs. Why not? With a swish of red petticoat, she sashays over an he swings her into a dizzy whirl.

Emmi snails her way to me, in sullen obedience. What? she says.

Don't you what me, Miss Ten Year Old. C'mon, I says. You can help me saddle Hermes.

Hermes whinnies when he sees me carryin his reed mat an bridle. The wind hurries thin shreds of cloud across the sky. They shine whitely aginst the blue black of early night. The weather's changed. Feels like it's gonna be a cold one.

Em plunks herself down on a tangle of rusty iron. Nero's followed us outside. He busies hisself tryin to steal her new medicine necklace. I bin noticin how he is with everybody since he got caught an trapped in that burrow. He's okay with me an Em, but that's it. All others git pretty sharp shrift an he's most needle-tempered with the boys. Even Lugh that he's known all his life. That would jibe with a man snatchin him. My idea that DeMalo sent a Tonton to do the deed. To try an frighten me off. Push me towards early surrender.

Cut it out, Nero! Em gathers him onto her lap. She's got her shoulders hunched, like she's espectin trouble. Whaddya want? she says. I ain't tall enough to saddle Hermes, an you know it.

Oh? I thought you might be now yer ten, I says. Listen, Em, I got a special job fer you. Where I'm goin tonight, Nero cain't come. I'm leavin you in charge of him.

She brightens. I won't let him outta my sight, not fer a moment, she says. She gives him a hug. Poor Nero, it was awful, what happened to you. An that other poor crow. You know who done it, doncha? she says to me. I seen yer face.

Maybe I do, I says. I twitch the mat into place.

Are you goin after 'em now?

That ain't yer trouble, I got things in hand. But listen, Em, you gotta unnerstand that I need to know everythin that's goin on. No matter how small, no matter if you think it ain't important, you need to tell me. What did Tommo trade fer the cage?

Her face scrinches in misery. Torn between duty an friendship. I cain't tell you, she says. It's only important to him, nobody else. I made a blood swear I'd never say.

Swearin in blood, that's serious, I says. Must be pretty important.

Only to him, she says. Nobody else, honest.

I'll be the judge of that, not you, I says. What was it? Tommo ain't got nuthin of value.

Shows what you know, she says. Then she clamps her lips tight.

Now we're gittin somewhere, I says. He's had it hid away, huh? Somethin Ike gave to him?

I ain't sayin no more, she says. I ain't doin this to be contrary or vex you. I'm doin what's right. Lugh's told you his secrets yer whole lives an I'll bet you never told one of 'em, not ever.

Where he hid Pa's whisky, Pa's gun, Pa's knife. Lugh an me had a blood-sworn promise I'd never tell. Not even to spare him a beatin. So I never did tell. Not once.

If you make a promise, you gotta keep it, says Em. I learned that from you. You always keep yer promises, no matter what.

An so do I. You can torture me if you like, I still won't tell!

She pretends to lock her lips an toss away the key. I swear, the mulish defiance of her chin invites a swift kick to the seat of her britches. But she looks so tragic that my lips twitch as I slip Hermes' bridle over his head. I could always ask Peg, I says.

Go ahead, waste yer time, she ain't no blabber, says Em.

Don't smart off with me, I says. I'm outta time fer this, Em. You gimme yer word – yer sworn word it ain't important – an we'll call it quits. Jest this once, mind. All else, you gotta tell me.

She dumps Nero an scrambles down the junkheap. You got my sworn word, she says. She holds out her hand an we shake.

I hang on to it. We gotta be able to count on you, Emmi, I says. Know that you won't let us down. That means you follow orders at all times. When the day comes that you've earned our trust, that's when you'll have some leeway. Till then, you do as yer told, no questions, no fuss.

I'm sorry, she says. I should of gone back on watch when you said. I was jest so happy to see everybody back okay, but I know I acted like a little kid an I ain't that no more. I'll do better, I promise.

Yer a warrior now, a Free Hawk, I says. You got comrades who died becuz they believed that all people should live free. You an me an Lugh, we know what it means to lose our freedom. An you bin prisoner not jest once but twice. When they caught you an took you to Resurrection.

She meets my gaze, steady on. They kept me in chains, she says. Like they kept you in chains at Hopetown.

You acted the warrior then, I says. Yer my sister, Em. That means you got courage to spare. Yer strong an yer smart. We're gonna win this fight. We're gonna honour them that died fer freedom. Our pa fer one. Who else?

Maev an Epona, she says. Ike an Bram an Jack. All the Free Hawks an Raiders at Darktrees.

Well, you jest think of them – our friends an Pa, I says. An you'll know how to rightly conduct yerself.

I will, she says.

Y'know, you an me, we're a lot alike.

She blinks in surprise. We are? How?

We act first an think later, I says. But if we're gonna win here, if we got any chance, we gotta think first an then act. So. From now on, you an me keep cool heads, okay? Can you do that? Can I do that?

Yes, she says. We can. An we will. An I'll never let you down agin, never. She throws her arms around my waist. I love you best of all, Saba.

It always takes me by surprise. This hot, fierce love that rushes through me. Fer the sister I shunned so long. Denied to my blood so completely. I kiss the top of her head. Happy birthday, I says. Go have a dance.

She scoops up Nero but she don't go. While I make a last check of Hermes, she's givin it the old Lingery Lou. Some pretend fuss with her belt an general slormin around. She's clearly wantin to say somethin. Back at the party, Peg's playin Halleluja, I'm a Bum as everybody sings along. Slim's raucous bellow drowns out the rest.

Yer missin the fun, I says to Em. I'm pullin on my metal clad jerkin. I fasten its buckles snugly.

She says, I guess Auriel's probly on her way to the Big Water, huh? Her an Meg an Lilith an … all them people that fled New Eden?

Now I do the armbands. Three small buckles on each one. It's gittin late in the year, I says. They'd hafta git through the mountains before winter an it 'ud be a big caravan. I figger they'll

128

stay at the Snake till spring. How come Auriel's on yer mind?

Oh, no reason. Emmi shrugs. Jest … y'know, I liked her.

She's bein cagey agin. Uh huh, I says. I'll see you in the mornin. Keep Nero close. Don't let him outta yer sight. I swing myself onto Hermes.

Em grabs the bridle an blurts out, How I found him – Nero, I mean – I warn't bein airy-fairy, it was … the earth told me. She whispers the last few words, lookin at me with big owl eyes. Then she bolts. With Nero clutched to her chest, she runs back inside the shed.

I stare after her. Em's inclined to be fey. Airy. A dreamer with her head in the clouds. Always feelin this an feelin that. What Lugh calls her mystical baloney. Sometimes it's rubbish. Sometimes it ain't. It's as like to be one as the other. What that was about, I got no idea.

I click to Hermes an we're on our way. We leave the lights an warmth an good cheer. We leave Starlight Lanes as the cold night rises an I set a course fer Weepin Water. The lodestone of New Eden. The bunker in the hill. The room with white walls where DeMalo sees visions at sunrise.

I still couldn't say why I'm so certain we need to go there. But I am. I'm most certainly certain. Maybe I'm a bit airy myself.

He'd just lifted the bridle when a shadow fell over the stall. He dropped it back on the nail, careful not to clink the metal. He opened the gate and stepped into the yard, flooded by moonlight. It was Molly.

Oh! Her hand flew to her throat. You made me jump, she said. What're you doin?

Checkin on the horses, he said.

She went to Prue's stall to stroke her nose. No Hermes, I see, she said. I guess Saba's gone to meet her contact agin.

He bit off his frustration. Seems so, he said. Go, he thought. Please, Molly, go.

But Molly was in no hurry. Fussing Prue's ears, stroking her neck, she took in his coat with a quizzical look. Cooled down already? she said.

He had no hope of catching up with Saba now. He'd left it too late. Another chance blown. He shrugged off his coat and draped it around Molly's shoulders. Don't catch a chill, he said.

So gallant, she said with a smile. She smelled of warm summer roses. And, just like that, he was trembling. She always had that effect on him. Her smile, her smell, her beauty.

In a hot rush, he had her in his arms, pressed to the stable wall. And they were kissing. Touching. Hungrily. Breathlessly.

She pulled away. Put her fingers to his lips. Somebody might see us, she said. She was trembling now too. Oh gawd, she said, what you do to me. Every time. It ain't seemly.

You taught me, he said.

A frown creased her forehead. I shouldn't of, she said. We should never of started this. I never meant to, really, I didn't.

I know, he said. I'm a boy, we ain't in love, you still love Ike.

I want you to have what I had with him, she said.

Her breath brushed him sweetly. One of these days I will, he said. So I need to know how to please a woman. Yer teachin me. That's all this is.

They stared at each other for a moment. A smile began to curve her lips. Lesson time, she said.

Then she took his hand in hers. And she led him away to the woods.

Night Six

Me an Hermes come at the bunker from the north. I ain't familiar with this approach, so despite I'm on the lookout fer it, we come upon it sudden. So sudden that the shock hits me in the gut. We're on top of a low ridge among some trees.

Here it is. The little hill. In the middle of the sweetgrass meadow. It looks a hill like any other. You'd never think it held such a secret at its heart. The Wrecker bunker, deep within. The white room where DeMalo shares his visions of a long-fergot, long-lost world. The visions that I was witness to.

An here I am agin. I swing myself down from Hermes an look out over the meadow. Where he kissed me in a sudden summer rain. Where we ran through the grass, with my hand in his. Through the rain, through the woods, to his bed by Weepin Water. Where I gave myself to him. Took him fer my first. Where I lost myself in him an nearly didn't come back.

The hilltop's bin cleared of blackberry bramble. Gone, the rich fruit that smothered its slopes, that sweetened that hot summer day. The meadow's bin cut. The ground's hard with stubble, silvered an shaded by the moon. Shootin stars dash the night sky.

A nightpip kriks, quick an scratchy. Then it calls agin. Then, Saba! Over here!

I jump at the urgent whisper. It's Jack. He's crouched behind a bush not twenny foot off. He waves me to him, impatient. My cheeks burn as I make my way to him. Like he might of overheard my thoughts. The heartstone's warm. I didn't notice.

I leave Hermes in the trees with Jack's pony, Kell. He yanks me down beside him. What's with you? he hisses furiously. Yer stood there like a stooky an I'm pippin my damn head off. Shh! Guards comin.

As he speaks, two Tonton grunts lead their horses around the hill, one from each direction. They meet at the bunker entrance. A sturdy metal door set into the side of the hill, partly hid by a stray tangle of bramble. They take up position in front of it. They're armed to the teeth an then some.

I says, Tell me you brought yer Tonton gear.

Jack gives me the look. Did-I-jest-hear-you-right? You told me, he says, you never wanted to see me wear that agin.

Typical, I says. You never do what I tell you. The one time you shouldn't do what I tell you, you go an do what I tell you. Dammit, now you even got me talkin like you. Gimme that thing.

I snatch the long-looker from his hand.

So … I'll dress Tonton next time. Or not. He shakes his head, bemused. By the way, he says, I like the fightgear. It's very, uh … it's very.

I squint, tunin the looker. Oh yeah, I fergot, I says. You got a weakness fer violent women.

Only one, he says. I'm most particular.

The guards come into clear view in the looker. Hello, boys, I says.

They're too shadowed by the hill fer me to see their faces, but they're stickin close to each other, almost shoulder to shoulder. Rattled by the fallin stars, judgin by how often they look at the sky. Maybe keepin count of the unquiet

133

souls on the move, like Pa used to do with us. Their horses sense their mood an shift in restless unease.

Tell you what, says Jack. Middle of nowhere, middle of the night, two guards with full hardware ... DeMalo's got somethin in there he wants to keep safe. Well, there's only one way in an only one way to git in. He picks up his bow from the ground beside him. I'll take out the guy on the right, he says. You bag Lefty. I'll count three.

Wait, I says. A bird, starkly black, crosses the white face of the moon. It sails towards us. Nero, I says.

My gut tightens with irritation. Emmi. She's done it agin. She cannot be depended on. So much fer all her big promises.

Nero seizes the chance to buzz the guards. He knows an hates the blackcloaks. He drops silent from the night, straight at their heads. They cower with cries of alarm. As he swoops off, they huddle aginst the bunker door.

Guess they ain't animal lovers, says Jack.

They're afeared of him, I says.

Nero lands in a tree behind us. He drops on Jack's shoulder an beaks my head.

Hey! I jerk away. Okay, I'm sorry.

What's got him miffed? says Jack.

I'll tell you later, I says. I lift the looker agin. As I watch, one of the guards steps from the safety of the doorway. He checks the sky, firestick at the ready, probly to see if Nero's still about. I study his face, lit by the moon. He's young. An he's fearful. He says somethin to his mate. They're both well jittery.

Let's git on with this. Jack's loadin his bow.

No, I says. We don't need to shoot 'em.

An jest how do you think we'll git in there? he says. Ask 'em nicely? Look at 'em, Saba, they're trigger happy.

134

No, you look. I shove the looker into his hands. They're afeared, Jack, I says. You can see it. They don't wanna be here. They don't like the starfall, they're spooked by the crow, they're out here alone an they're young an green.

I see what you mean, he says. Maybe they heard the stories goin round about you. The fearsome Angel of Death an her miraculous escape from Resurrection. She killed ten men, twenny – no – thirty. It's all bin hushed up an she's still in New Eden. No, I heard she died in a blaze of fire. I met this guy, he seen her ghost with his own eyes. Ridin the night with her wolfdog an her crow, seekin vengeance on them that took her life.

It's you that's bin plantin them rumours, I says. I should of known.

I only fed what was already there, he says. Word spreads like wildfire in this place. The Angel of Death has a strong hold on people's minds. The unbeaten fighter who killed a king an destroyed his kingdom. Powerful stuff. We gotta use every advantage we have.

Jack? I says. I feel a haunt comin on me.

It's a waste of time, he says. If you don't wanna kill 'em, I will.

No. We're doin this my way, I says.

They're in such a high state of nerves already. So close to real terror it seems cruel to push 'em over the edge. I feel kinda sorry fer 'em. I feel kinda bad about doin it. But not so bad that I don't.

Jack sets the guards up. Unner strong protest, but he does it. Startin with wolf howls that – to my ear – barely pass muster, but they shake the guards pretty bad. As he does the wolf thing, he moves in closer, chuckin stones to rustle trees an bushes all around 'em. They're panicked to such a frenzy of gunfire, it's a wonder he don't git shot. But he keeps his head down an stays on the move. Meantime, me an Nero an Hermes make our way behind the hill an sneak into a good position right on top.

We don't have long to wait. Nature piles in on our side. She picks three of the brightest stars from the sky, loads 'em on her bow an lets fly. All three at once, side by side. In a show of unspeakable wonder, they scorch through the night like three small suns, their tails burnin fury behind them. The sky lights bright with their flash of fire.

Now. Go now. I throw Nero in the air. I haul the reins sharply. Hermes rears an squeals with his front legs flailin. Nero screams as he wheels above us.

It's the Angel of Death. Back from the dead. Flung from the sky as a fiery star.

The guards stare, mouths open, frozen with fear. Then their guns hit the ground as they rush fer their horses. They stumble an trip an yell. In a panicky scramble, they race off pell-mell. The drum of their hoofbeats fades to silence. An that's it. They're gone. We dared an we won.

Jack took a shot through the seat of his pants. He tells me next time I hold a target shoot he ain't available. Then he picks the padlock with ease an we go through the door in the hill.

I let Jack find De Malo's white room. I let him lead the way, with his rushtorch held high. After all, I'm s'posed to of never bin here before. I follow him down the steps, into the ground, through the long, narrow rooms with the bunks in the walls. Each room leads on to the next one. Our torches splash shocks of orange light over the rough, packed-earth walls, roof an floor.

It smells jest the same as it did that summer day. Musty an earthy an cool. It feels jest the same as it did that day. Heavy aginst my skin. I hate unnerground. My brow wets with sweat. An I'm back in our Silverlake storm cellar.

That eight by eight hole in the ground hacked out by my folks with pick an shovel. Their first home when they settled at the lake. Where they lived while they built the tyreshack. Then it was our shelter from wild weather. Bad enough we had to fret out the storms in there. But on scorch days too – when the sun flays the earth an all that cling to her – that cellar was our only refuge. It never bothered Pa or Lugh or Em. But it surely did bother me. I felt I was buried alive. I take a deep breath. I ain't buried. I'm fine.

This was a Wrecker bunker, says Jack. I seen somethin kinda like it before. It was a lot smaller'n this one, though.

I cain't tell him what I know about it. That DeMalo found ten skellentons here when he first discovered it an opened the door. Lyin on the bunks where they died. Probly shelterin from some calamity. One of the many that ravaged their world. If it was anybody else, you'd pity 'em their plight. Not the Wreckers. No pity fer them.

137

Jack says, We must be near the centre of the hill by now.

We are. We're in the tight little corridor. It squeezes us towards the white room. We're at the closed door. Jack opens it with caution an peers inside.

He says, Nuthin beyond here. You think this is it?

Must be, I says.

We're talkin in whispers. Like there's somebody here besides us. An there is. DeMalo. This is his special place. I got this crazy notion he'll be able to tell that we was here. Maybe right now, this moment, wherever he is, he knows that I'm in his vision room. It's foolish, I know. Impossible, how could he? But still. My heart's thumpin hard.

Well, yer the one with the feelin, says Jack. After you. He bows me through the doorway.

I step inside. Close it behind you, I says.

The darkness here is deep. Our torches dash at the shadows an retreat as we play 'em around the room. It's completely different from the rest of the bunker. Smooth white walls with rounded corners. Twenny paces across each way. A smooth white floor with a domed ceilin. It seems much bigger'n the last time I was here. Mind you, as well as DeMalo an me, there was a dozen Stewards an two Tonton guards in here.

Jack walks slowly around the room, scopin out the walls. What these're made of, I got no idea, he says. He runs a hand along them. Smooth an cold, he says. Still in good shape, after such a long time. Some kinda fancy Wrecker tech. They seem to be made in sections. I guess that's how they brought 'em in.

On these very walls, I seen light bloom to the dawn of day. Daylight brightened around us as the music of birdsong an stringboxes sweetened the air. All that was wonder enough. But it was only the start.

I touch the walls where I seen eagles fly. Where giant fish leapt through the oceans. Where herds of beasts galloped vast plains. Where forests an mountains an rivers an lakes an creatures an birds an people dazzled my eyes with sights of such glory that a lifetime ain't enough to think on 'em. To recall the rapture that shattered my heart. Even if I was to live a hunnerd year.

I stand in the middle of the room, like he did. I close my eyes. But I don't feel a thing. It's cold an it's dark an that's all. Without DeMalo, it's dead.

Nuthin, I whisper.

Jest a room where a man has visions, says Jack. People do. Like yer friend, the star reader girl. What did you think we'd find here?

I dunno, I says. There was somethin, Jack. There is, but I cain't git at it. It's like it's … jest at the edge of my sight or my hearin or— I let out my breath in frustration. I smooth the wall with my hand. I says, Auriel's th'only other person I know who has visions. Whadda you know of such things?

Me? He shakes his head. I hang with the lowbrows, he says. Readers of salt spills, entrails an ashes. Every last one a humbug. The only visions they have is from too much white lightnin.

DeMalo has his at dawn, I says. His visions, I mean. Ain't that right?

I think so, I dunno, he says. Listen, Saba. We came, we had a look, there ain't nuthin here. But, hey. It ain't bin a complete waste of time. I got my butt shot. You must be pleased about that.

I'm sure you deserve it fer somethin, I says.

Oh, I most certainly do, he says. He kisses me. Softly. Sweetly. C'mon, he says. Let's scram, we seen enough.

He waits while I take a last look around the room. So what was that about? That click of the trigger in my head an my gut. The tingle, the tremble of possibility. It grabbed me last night, so powerful, when Jack was talkin about DeMalo. The sudden certainty we needed to come here. That here we'd find some kinda answer. This was pointless. A fool's errand.

As we make our way back through the rooms with the bunks I says, So why d'you think the guards?

Jack says, Why the guards, why the dogs, why does he move from house to house, why does he only eat an drink what his hands touch an nobody else's...

Becuz I drugged him, I think to myself. Two drops in his wine from a tiny brown bottle. Eccinel, that's what Slim called it.

DeMalo ain't easy is why, Jack's sayin. We shook his throne when we blew Resurrection. He don't know when or where we're gonna hit him next.

All right, I says, I hear you.

We can trash his playroom, he says. You wanna go back?

No, I says, we'll leave it.

A cool night breeze stirs the earth air of the bunker. A little ways ahead, I can see moonlight stream down the stairs. Jack's up 'em an out like a shot. He hates these Wrecker places. Claims they're full of ghosts. I dunno about ghosts, but I'm more'n ready to git outta this tomb. I put a foot on the first step. What was that? From the corner of my eye I caught a gleam. My torch jest glanced on somethin. I cast about till I find what it is. My skin prickles all over.

The gleam is metal. A lock on a door. A lock that's bin sanded an oiled. The door's set well back in the shadows. You'd hafta to be lookin to see it.

Jack, I says. Git back down here.

It's a tumbler lock. Alone, I'd be outta luck. But I ain't. I'm with Jack. So I'm in luck. He's got a lifetime of scoundrel knowhow. Sure enough, he's cracked tumblers before. He protests, he wants to go, but I prevail. Jest a quick look inside, an we'll be gone.

He listens an turns. Listens. An turns. He woos that lock open. An we go through the second door.

This time, I light our way. Torch in one hand, shooter in the other. The ground beneath our feet slopes downwards. Gradual, like a long, slow ramp. Here, too, the walls an floor is hard-packed earth. The ceilin's shuttered with planks. Propped up with struts an girders.

I says, Whoever made this place didn't have comfert in mind.

Maybe they had to do it in a hurry, says Jack.

I take a closer look as we pass. There's signs of fresh repairs. Many of the shutter planks look new. It's bein kept in good order. We go down, down, deeper into the earth. The air grows cooler an thicker. I hate it. I sweat. I breathe deep.

Finally, Jack stops. Okay, we seen enough, let's go, he says.

As the words leave his lips, I take a step. There's a click-click-click-click. We're blinded by light. I shoot, on instinct, an dive at the ground. Wood cracks. Dirt rains down on top of us. My shot must of hit the roof. Probly smashed a shutter plank. As the din fades to silence an no one shoots back, we slowly git to our feet. We cough the dust from our throats. Stare as we brush ourselfs off.

Eight roundels of light cling to the walls ahead. Four line the left wall. The same on the right. They shine a straight path to a iron slab door. With a big iron wheel in the middle of it. Jack an me look at each other. His eyes gleam pale in his filthy face. His hair's dusted thick with dirt.

Door three, he says. Be my guest.

Sudden sweat wets my hands as I crank the wheel to the right. It moves smoothly. Well oiled, like the lock. There's a soft hiss. I feel the door sigh. I tug an it swings wide open.

Let's see what he's got in here, says Jack.

As we step past the door, red lights appear in front of us. They're scattered all over, high, low an in between. There's a lot of 'em, but they ain't bright. Not like the ones on the ramp outside. These murmur a dull glow. Like the last of a sunset on a cloudy winter day.

It's our movement that triggers the lights, says Jack. Somehow it sets 'em off.

We lift our torches. It's a room full of cupboards. Rows of cupboards. Heavy wooden ones, tall, with glass doors. Trunks an metal chests. Boxes an crates an barrels cut in half. Anythin that could be fitted with a shelf seems to be here. They're stacked an tucked an crowded together. There's shelfs in every single one. An every single shelf is filled with jars. Glass jars with lids.

The jars hold seeds. Seeds of all colours an sizes an shapes.

It's a seedstore, I says.

A Wrecker seedstore, says Jack.

He starts to move along one of the rows. I make my way down the next one. Starin, touchin. This feels like a dream. It don't seem possible there could be so much here. Some jars is full, right to the top. In some only a small handful of seeds. There ain't a speck of dust. It's all perfectly clean. Shelfs, jars, floor. The air is dry an cool. A bit musty but there ain't no damp. Each jar has a bit of old paper stuck to it with a hand-drawn picture of what the seed is. Flowers. Vegetables. Fruits, trees, grasses. With a figger of a man to show how tall it'll be, full grown.

I'm making a new world, one blade of grass at a time. Healing the earth and its people.

I wedge my torch between two metal cupboards. I take a small jar an hold it to the light. The seeds inside gleam. They're tiny an thin, a kinda reddish colour. I give 'em a gentle shake. They shift an sigh in their long, dry sleep.

Jack's voice falls dead in the muffled air. There's tree seed here, he says. If I'm readin these pictures right, they're good fer drylands. His torchlight bobs on down the row.

Now it makes sense. What DeMalo said to me. When he'd drunk the drugged wine an his guard was down. Jest before he passed out in my arms.

I wanted to tell you. I've found something amazing. If it's what I think it is, it's going to change everything.

He could reseed the whole earth with all this.

Saba, c'mere. Jack's voice sounds a tight, urgent note. With clumsy hands, I put the jar back where it came from. I hurry to find him at the far end of the room. It's clear of cupboards here. There's four tables bin pushed together to make one big table. Books an papers cover the top of it,

piled in neat stacks. There's stone fatlights to work by. A
chair. A cot with a blanket. An a half-empty bottle of wine.
DeMalo. He works here. Sleeps here sometimes, it seems.

Jack's lookin at the end wall. Starin up at it. There's
big sheets of heavy paper tacked the length of it. They're
coloured, mainly pink, yellow an orange. With thick blue
snakes an thin blue lines an blue splodges of all sizes. Words
in black. Numbers too. A lotta squiggly lines.

What is all this? I says,

They're maps, says Jack.

I only seen dirt maps before, I says.

Well, look on these real good, he says. He takes my
hand an pulls me to the furthest map on the left. This one's
New Eden, he says. Divided into sectors. See the numbers?
Weepin Water, where we are now, that lies south, right?
Sector One.

Uh huh, I says.

He puts his finger on the map. I figger that puts us about
here, he says. Got that? Okay. He tugs me along to the next
map. Here's New Eden agin, he says. You see the shape?
This is how it sits in the land all around it. It's the one an
only green patch. That must mean trees an growth. Becuz
we know all these yellow bits an they're bleak. We got the
Raze to the east, to the west lies the Waste, to the south –
d'you see? – here's the Black Mountains, an south of them
lies where Hopetown was, an here's Sandsea –

– Silverlake's there somewhere, I says.

It won't be on no map, he says. An here, to the north,
it's the Shield all the way to this big stretch of blue. Must
be water.

New Eden looks so small, I says.

He moves me to the next map. On this one, it's even

smaller, he says. On the next one, New Eden's jest a dot. Saba, d'you see? This is the world beyond. Beyond any place you an me ever bin. This is a world we never heard of, never dreamed of.

How come there's numbers all over? I says. They're everywhere. I go back to the second map. The Waste, I says. An the Raze an south of the Black Mountains. I glance about. From the maps with their numbers so tiny an neat. To the table with its stacks of papers an books. There's numbers on these papers, I says.

Numbered maps, says Jack. Numbered papers. There's numbers on these rows of cupboards. A number on every cupboard. Did you notice the seed jars have numbers? It's a plan, Saba. To plant.

I stand stock still. I stare at Jack, not seein him. Every hair on my head shivers. The tiny hairs on my arms. To reseed the earth, I says. This is what it's all about.

This is why the locks an the guards, says Jack.

The resettlement party, I says. This is why they was headed to the Raze. It explains the new bridge at the Eastern Defile.

It explains why DeMalo was with 'em, says Jack.

That worn leather bag strapped over his chest. His hand went to it, touched it from time to time. As if to make sure it was still there.

I bet he was carryin the seeds, I says. He wouldn't trust nobody else.

He'd wanna be the first to sow, says Jack. To teach the Stewards how to grow an care fer whatever it was.

One blade of grass at a time.

He actually meant it. He can actually do it. A new world. A healed earth. With grass an trees an crops to have food enough fer all. But not fer all. Only fer them he deems worthy. His Chosen ones.

My head's tight with tryin to make sense of this. I open a book. I stare at the letters I cain't unnerstand. The words they make tell DeMalo what to do. If only we could read these, I says. Tommo reads some. Maybe if we brought him here, he could—

That's detail, says Jack. We don't gotta read to know what this means. DeMalo will rebuild the bridge an be sowin seed in the Raze within a couple of weeks. He'll start with test beds, I figger. To see what takes an what don't. Hell, he might of done that already. He's planned this real careful. With this seedstore an his book knowledge an fear an guns to power the project – Jack sweeps a hand at the maps – he'll make everywhere jest like New Eden. A green paradise of slave labour, all controlled by him. Yes sir, yes my lord, yes my master, my king. With nobody old or sick or weak or anybody less than perfect. He'll decide who's fit to live.

While the hive pumps out endless Steward drones to work work work work work, I says. His Chosen Ones. What a lie. They're slaves too. You jest cain't see their chains.

We're silent fer a moment, lookin at the maps.

We thought it was jest New Eden, I says.

The tyrants I've known don't think small, says Jack. Their ambition is usually their undoin. But none ever sat on a arsenal like this one. If anybody can do this, he can.

We gotta stop him now, I says. Before it gits beyond us. There's numbers all over these maps. There won't be nowhere to run. Nowhere to hide. Nowhere to live free or be anythin or do anythin other than what DeMalo decides.

There won't be nobody runnin, says Jack. Fear's a powerful weapon. If people fear you, you control them.

Most of these New Eden folk ain't never known freedom. An they never will know it, unless we win it fer them.

I reach fer Jack's hand. It's warm an strong. A hand to hold on tight to. We stare at the wall. At the future laid out so starkly. A future earth, a future people controlled by DeMalo.

Yer right, I says. He can do this. He has the will, the belief an the power.

Case closed, Jack says. We kill him. I go back inside the Tonton right away.

No no, I need to think, I says.

About what? He looks at me in disbelief. How can it not be clear to you yet? DeMalo needs to go. Speakin of which, he says, we need to go. It's easy to lose track of time down here. The new guard shift'll show fer duty at dawn. We wanna be well away by then.

In silence, we crank the wheel an close the great door. We press the cracked roof plank into place an scuff away the fallen dirt on the ramp. If we don't leave cause fer him to look up, DeMalo might not notice the damage. Jack sets the tumbler lock dial back to where we found it.

Now the light from outside that streams down the stairs ain't moonlight. It's dawnlight. Pale an uncertain.

Told you, says Jack.

As I douse my torch, I hear it. Faintly. From inside the bunker. My heart jolts. Then it starts racin. I grab Jack's hand an make fer the stairs.

He frowns, pullin aginst me. Hang on, he says. I hear music.

I don't hear nuthin. We gotta go, I says.

He shrugs me off. Yeah, he says. Sounds like it's … comin from that room. You must hear it. Listen. There.

Faint but unmistakable. It's music. My eyes meet his. It's too dangerous, I says. Please, let's jest go.

He stares at me a moment. Then he takes off at a run. Towards DeMalo's white room.

I hare after him. Through the rooms with the bunks in the wall. I know this music. I heard it before. It's the sound of his visions. DeMalo. He's here. In the room. There ain't no guards, the bunker door's open. Anybody else would come lookin fer the cause. Not him. He's playin with us. Drawin us in.

I'm jest in time to see Jack reach the door. Reach fer the handle. His shooter held next to his head.

Jack! I says. Don't!

He dumps his torch. We're in total blackness. I inch forwards, feelin the wall. I got my gun at the ready. My throat ticks with fear.

A line of light glows as he cracks the door open. Then, slowly, slowly, it widens. Gentle light spills out. Light an birdsong an sweet stringbox music. That's all though. No outcry. Nuthin else.

Saba! Jack calls to me softly.

I hurry to join him, still tense, still alert. But there ain't no need fer our shooters. We're the only two people here. Jack stares in confusion. So do I, but fer a very different reason. Dawn glows on the walls of the room, all around us. The air that was dead is alive with music.

The light brightens an brightens to the gold of fresh

mornin. The music grows louder an quicker. The walls leap to life. Jack starts with surprise. An, jest like I remember from before, we're soarin above grasslands, lush an green, with a bird's-eye view of the world below.

What the hell is this? he says.

Great herds of beasts thunder the plains, with snow-topped mountains in the distance. It's still magical. Incredible. Unimaginably beautiful. Last time, I wept. This time, I don't. It's DeMalo's vision. But without DeMalo.

I got no idea, I says.

Jack's tried to touch one of the shaggy big-horned creatures as it leaps from crag to crag. Jest like I did when I seen it. Suspicion darkens his face. Visions, my ass, he says. This is Wrecker tech. That trickster sonofabitch.

Eagles fly beneath his hands as he feels the walls. Seekin to know how they work. Far from bein overcome like I was, he takes little notice of these glimpses of a long-gone world.

It's like the walls hold the memory of the past, he mutters. Somethin must set it off. With the lights, it was us, our movement did it. But this was playin already, so what triggered it?

Trigger. Light. Memory. Suddenly I remember. The tiny pinprick of light in the ceilin.

As it grows to a weak beam, I start to see DeMalo. He stands in the centre of the room, right unnerneath it. He lifts a chunk of clear, glassy rock. The light beam latches onto it. The rock begins to glow with a faint pink light. But not jest the rock. The whole room. The light grows stronger. Birds begin to sing.

DeMalo ain't here now. There ain't no rock. But still the birds sang. Still the day dawned on the walls of this room. I stand in the middle an squint at the ceilin. It's harder to see now the room's so bright. I can only jest see the pinprick of

149

light in the dome above me. If you didn't know it was there, you wouldn't think to look. You'd never notice it.

Jack, I says. Could it be triggered by light from outside?

He's beside me in a second. We stare up. You genius, he says. The first light of day sets it off. Somehow it gits in here, maybe ... through a pipe or somethin. I cain't hardly see that. What made you look there?

I dunno, I says. I jest looked up an there it was.

The music plays on. The lost creatures of the lost world roam the walls all around us. They fly the skies. They swim the waters. Lakes an rivers an the Big Water. What DeMalo called the ocean, the sea. I never thought I'd witness these sights agin. My heart cracks open wide, to fill itself with them. Greedily. Hungrily. I'm glad I don't hafta hide how I feel. After all, I'm meant to be seein it fer the first time.

It's beyond wonderful, I says. I would never of imagined this.

Wonderful fer sure, says Jack. But it ain't nuthin to do with DeMalo. If this is triggered by the dawn, it happens every day. All that Pathfinder malarkey. He ain't nuthin but a high-stakes con man.

He's lied, I says. About everythin.

Don't sound so surprised, he says. Anyways, lyin's hardly the worst of his sins.

We sat in the sweetgrass meadow that mornin. The Stewards, DeMalo an me. The breeze dried my tears as he spoke. Of the music on the wind that led him to this room.

As that new day dawned, I had the vision. Just as you've seen today. Mother Earth revealed to me, through me, the glories of our world as it was. And she revealed to me my destiny. You are the Pathfinder, she told me. I have chosen you to heal me.

We've all believed him so completely. That's becuz he

believes it hisself. He's told the tale so often, it's become the truth even to him. At what point does that happen, I wonder. That you start to believe yer own lies.

It's quite the make-believe he's cooked up, says Jack. The dream of Mother Earth reborn, DeMalo the big hero with his visions.

On the walls all around people walk an run an dance. Long ago gone. Long unremembered an long unmourned. The Wreckers. But in this moment, they live fer me an Jack. I think of the ten skellentons, lyin in them bunks. Whoever they was – man, woman, child – they closed the door in the hillside one day an shut theirselfs in. Knowin their refuge might well be their grave. That they'd seen the last of the sky.

Suddenly I git it. They go together, I says.

What goes together? says Jack.

The seedstore an this room with these visions, I says. They left it fer us. Fer those who might come after. When them people lay on them bunks fer the very last time, they died with hope. That somebody would find this one day. But they didn't mean fer someone like DeMalo to find it. A gift like this, a gift to the future, the chance to start over with them seeds … it's meant fer all of us. Not jest people, but the earth itself an every creature. It's fer the common good. The many. Not the few. They meant fer it to be used rightly an justly. These visions tell us so. Look!

Around the walls there's the young an the old. The strong help the weak. The healthy tend the sick. All manner of people together.

He's stolen this place, I says. He ain't no visionary. He's a thief. He's a liar.

Saba, says Jack. We better go.

His voice right behind me makes me start.

It's dawn, he says. The guard change. Remember?

He takes me by the hand an we run.

We ride into a strange kinda mornin. Uncertain day born of unsteady night. Short winds dash at us then die. Clouds threaten, then calm in a watery sunlight. At last a lumpy grey sky thumps down like a lid an sharp picks of rain razor us. It settles to a mean-tempered dank of a day. Jack jams his hat low an wraps his cloak high. Nero's quick to wriggle inside it an hitch a ride. Me, I got my coat an my sheema. But it ain't long before we're miserably damp.

It's all cloud an sharp rain inside of me as well. My thoughts clod an churn. Feelins spike me, slash at me. I try to grab 'em as they pass. Try to hold on long enough to take a good look.

One. DeMalo don't have miraculous visions. It's a trick. A cheat. He ain't who he says he is. He ain't what he says he is. He discovered the bunker an its secrets by chance. He claimed them fer his own an began to misuse them.

Two. He must be revealed fer the fraud that he is. Everybody needs to know about the visions. By everybody I mean the Stewards an the Tonton. The only way they'd believe is if they seen it fer themselfs. My Free Hawks an Jack's gang, we'll jest tell them what we found an they'll believe us.

Three. What's my next move? My next play in this endgame he's declared? Whatever I do, I gotta use what I know to our best advantage. I gotta be wise, be cool. Think, plan, then act. In the right way, at the right time, when he least especks it. But I got so little time, there ain't no chance in hell that I'll – stop, stop. Be cool. Stay calm.

Four. Four. It's unbelievable. It's shameful. But here it is. The cold stone of betrayal burns in me. I feel betrayed by him. By DeMalo. I feel deceived by him. I know this tight lump, hard right of my heart. I felt it when I thought Jack had betrayed me. You only feel betrayed if you place yer trust in somebody. If you believe what they tell you. I believed DeMalo. Believed him when he told me I was special. That I warn't like nobody else. I believed that meant he would tell me – me above all others – the truth. But he plays me jest like he'd play anybody. He baits his line an reels us in. An what was my bait? My arrogance, my self-regard an the weakness of my flesh fer his. I swear, when DeMalo hauled me from Weepin Water that night, he landed me on shiftin sands. Me, who used to think I stood on bedrock.

I realize Jack's stopped. That I'm stopped becuz he's leaned over to grab hold of Hermes' bridle. Guilty heat breaks on my skin. As if he might be able to hear my thoughts.

Sorry, I says. Did you say somethin?

I said, this is where we part ways, he says.

We're at HorseArch, in the middle of the boulderfield. The worn hindquarters of a stallion rear atop the crumbled stone archway.

Jack sits back in the saddle. He edges Kell away. Puts distance between us. His hat hides his eyes. He's only said one thing since we left the bunker. *Lucky fer us they was late.* That's when we'd reached the safety of the wooded ridge an looked back to see the two relief guards appear. Since then, not a word, an that's strange. Jack ain't no chatbox, but he's social. There's always some to an fro with him. It ain't like him to leave me alone with my thoughts fer so long.

You bin awful quiet, I says.

I got a lot on my mind, he says.

His distant tone slams the door in my face.

Yeah, I says, this changes everythin, don't it? The seedstore, the fake visions. D'you think I oughta tell Lugh an the rest what we found?

Not yet, he says. It's way too big. We'll keep it between us fer now.

Right, I says. Listen, I wanna meet with yer network today. You an me an them. Can you git 'em all together later on?

He says, I thought we agreed it was safer you didn't.

That was before all this, I says. I need to talk to 'em right away.

What about? he says.

Jest tell me where to meet you.

Sector Four, he says. At the watermill on the Don River. I'll see you there late afternoon. It's short notice, but I'll git as many as can come. With a click to Kell, he tugs the reins an turns to the north.

Hey, I says.

He looks back.

You got my crow in yer coat, I says.

I fergot, he says. He's asleep. He reaches unner his cloak. C'mon you, wake up, he says.

He picks him out an with a shake an a squawk, Nero takes to the air. Rain or no, he'll be glad to fly. He's bin tucked inside there fer ages.

Jack, I says.

He waits. His hat's still low over his eyes. I'm shut out.

He's shuttin me out. This ain't like him at all. Unease heats my belly. Sticks my words in my throat.

What's wrong? I says.

Nuthin. It's jest a lot to take in all at once. I'm gonna catch a little sleep, he says. You should too. I'll see you later.

I'm glad you was there, I says. That it was you an me. We always do make a good team. I wouldn't of wanted to be with nobody else.

He answers with a tip of his hat. Then he flicks the reins an moves Kell out. I will a turn of his head. Look back, look back, gawdammit Jack. I ache fer a smile. Or a wave.

Jack! I call. The fog deads my voice. They're melted to the mist as silent shadows. He probly didn't even hear me. Nero perches on HorseArch an caws his impatience to be gone.

He's right. I got much bigger things to deal with. I ride a thoughtful trail back to Starlight Lanes. I sort an sift an consider. All the words I bin hearin an speakin. What I've seen an thought an felt.

Whaddya make of this place, Mercy? Of New Eden?

Things ain't always what they seem to be. People neether. The Chosen of New Eden, they're all tryin to be what DeMalo says they are. Do you see? Not entirely real.

DeMalo an his visions. The bunker. The seedstore. It's the lodestone. He's the lodestone. Brothers an sisters an fathers an mothers. Stewards stolen from their families.

You're paired with a boy you don't know. Sent off with this stranger to work the land an make healthy babies for New Eden. How do you feel?

Natural feelins don't come into it.

They got no skills, no knowledge, no trust between 'em. They hardly know each other. It won't take much to make their house crumble. It don't stand on strong foundations.

Strong foundations. Family. Blood ties. Babies taken from the Stewards.

Not one of them girls wants her baby to be took from her. They try to hide what they feel, but I seen it in their eyes, their faces, every time.

Weak foundations. DeMalo's weakness. Our strength.

Think like me, like me, not him.

Jack an me at the Irontree. He nearly had me undressed an I never noticed.

Boy, do you work fast.

Yer a movin target, I hafta. Here, lemme help.

I button, he unbuttons. I tuck, he untucks.

Do. Undo.

When you start to pick it apart, their house will crumble. Undo it. Fast. Quickly.

What do you believe, Saba?

On the whole, I'd say we're stronger fer love.

Then I'm thinkin like me. Not like him.

The Starlight Lanes sign appears through the treetops. With its comet an stars an words that meant somethin to somebody, once upon a time ago. Then I catch sight of Molly. A little ways ahead, she slips from the woods onto the trail. She's all rosy aglow an not quite tucked in. The day's changed its mind since the mizzle of dawn. Now, early mornin sun sifts through the treetops. It gleams her hair golden as it rivers to her waist. Tied back, like always, in a tousled tail. She appears to have half the woods stuck in it.

A battered bucket swings in her hand. She swings her hips with cautious abandon.

Mornin, I call.

She jumps from her skin. She whirls around. Dismay gives way to a wide smile of welcome. I bin pickin mushrooms, she calls, holdin up her pail. Oh! Nero's jest landed on her shoulder. An a very good mornin to you, she says. Delicately, he picks a piece of moss from her hair. He gives it to her. Well, she says, thank you.

Followed by a leaf, then a twig, then another leaf. I've reached her by now. She's very pink an very flustered. I tell you, she says, yer so lucky to have short hair. Mine collects everythin. Moss an twigs an—

Men? I says. Or should I say boys? I swing myself down from Hermes.

Her smiles crumple to woe. Oh gawd, she says, I swear, Saba, I didn't mean fer this to happen. I had no idea. He jest—

Hey, I says. Calm down, it's okay.

It is? she says.

This is me, remember? I says. You of all people know I ain't in no position to preach. How could I return yer kindness to me with harsh judgement? An … he is handsome an charmin an, as we all know, he can be very persuasive—

Well, it warn't so much that as –

– as the fact he's bin after you since the moment he laid eyes on you. Yer only human, Molly, I says. Yer the loveliest, most gorgeous woman. You bin on yer own a long time. An I gotta tell you, it don't ezzackly come as a shock.

It don't? There's wary surprise in her eyes, in her voice.

I seen you, I says.

Oh?

157

At Em's party. You touched his hand.

Touched his hand, she says.

When he was goin on lookout duty, I says. You was at the food table with Mercy an he walked by you an you touched his hand.

Right, she says. You seen that.

I was th'only one noticed, I says. I didn't mention it to nobody an I won't. Molly, you so deserve happiness. Of anybody I know, you deserve it. Fer a night, a week, fer the rest of yer life. The only thing is— You gotta admit, it's bin pretty stormy with you two already an I jest don't want … I dunno, a lover's quarrel or somethin to cause more problems.

Say no more, I unnerstand completely, she says. I would never do nuthin to jeopardize this fight. I'll talk to him, to Creed. He ain't really my type anyways.

Oh, no, I didn't mean that you had to—

It's all right. She presses my hand an smiles. You can set yer mind at rest, she says.

Oh, Molly. Yer beautiful, weary brown eyes. Where hope's so faded an thin, I could weep. I seen her today, Moll. Jest fer a moment. The mornin sun caught her briefly in its light. Barefoot, her hair a golden river down her back. Cheeks flushed, eyes bright with possibility. It was you. It was her. The girl you once was. If only I'd come along the trail a bit sooner. Or passed a little later. She could of walked in the sun a bit longer. I'm sorry.

I kiss her on the cheek. Her skin's soft as dew. She smells musky an warm, of lovers in the woods. You better let Nero tidy yer hair, I says. But don't be long. I got somethin to talk to you all about.

I find 'em at Peg's flyer field. Tracker leads me up the hill behind the junkyard to the long stretch of scrubby grass on top. It's from here that Peg tries to make like the birds. This mornin, with the help of Moses an Bean an far too many ropes, they're all doin their sweaty best to launch her latest junkcraft to the sky. I call 'em to order, but they're so childishly excited that they won't be deterred. The whole thing's ridiculous an doomed. I give up. They won't be long.

Slim shouts advice from the safety of his slingchair. I sit an stare at the ground an think about what I'm gonna say. By the time Molly turns up with Nero an her leaf-free hair an Mercy, who she met on the path, they've managed to tangle the windcrank, the camel, the mule an all of them in a week's worth of knots an then some.

It's a moment's fun. The day's turned out fine. How I'd love to join them. Be carefree fer once. But my time's runnin out. I got a tyrant to topple.

This is a joke, right? Creed's ready smile ain't nowhere to be seen today. From his sullen mouth to boots that positively twitch to kick at somethin, he bristles spiky discontent.

A joke? I says. Far from it. It's the only way we can win.

Win? He looks around, with a half-smile that's more like

a frown. You hearin this, folks? he says. No guns, no bows, no blastpacks, no knives. We're gonna fight the man with – what was that you called it? Oh yeah – bad manners.

Disobedience, I says.

We're all stood or sat or sprawled in a kinda circle. Each accordin to their own state of mind. I'm on my feet, holdin fast to my ground. We're still on the hilltop at Peg's flyer field. She tends to her junkmetal love. Mutters an cackles as she untangles it from the mess of ropes an does things with spanners an bolts. Nero plays one of his favourite games. She puts somethin down, he nips in an steals it. She's so busy, she don't pay our talk the least bit of notice.

I says to them, It's like I said. DeMalo's built New Eden on fault lines. Lots of 'em an he don't even know it. The main one is he's broke families apart. That goes aginst nature. It goes aginst feelin an blood ties. He believes them things make fer weakness, but he's wrong. They're strong an they endure an we can use 'em to beat him. Mercy's told you about the babyhouses – how the mothers are when their infants git took from 'em. That's one fault line. Tonight I plan to make a little rumble there. If it works, if I'm right, that fault line will start to crack open. Then we'll go to work crackin open the other fault lines. The slave gangs. An Edenhome. We'll do it right unner their noses. They won't notice what we're up to till it's too late. Once we got enough cracks, at the right moment we make a big gawdamn rumble an the whole thing will break wide open. New Eden will crumble.

Silence. But what a clamour. Slim plucks at his whiskers. Ash works her boot heel into the dirt. Between the rest of 'em – Lugh an Tommo an Creed an Molly – there's frowns an raised eyebrows an looks an so on. From her seat on a rock, Mercy gives me a tiny smile.

A big gawdamn rumble, says Ash. What kinda rumble you talkin about?

I cain't say yet, I tell her.

You don't know, says Creed. You got no idea, do you?

A good leader responds an adapts, I says.

An that does make him smile. At last. You ain't a good leader, he says.

It's a lot to ask, I know, I says. This is a new idea. But don't dismiss it outta hand.

Creed laughs. Why shouldn't we? he says. We got a whole weapons dump ready an waitin. Hey, Slim, there's plenty of ammo in that secret store of yers, right?

Plenty, he says.

Why wouldn't we use it? Creed opens his arms to receive everybody's agreement. We're fighters, he says. It's what we know, what we're good at. We bin beatin the Tonton in straight fights all along. This ain't no different.

Why fight if we don't hafta? I says.

He says, That blast at the bridge must of done somethin to yer brain. It sure as hell rattled yer nerve. Ever since then, you bin all, thou shalt not kill. I tell you, that's hard to swallow, comin from you. They didn't call you the Angel of Death fer nuthin. Remind me. How many dead on yer dance card, dear?

Our eyes hold. He's gone fer the wound. Anger raises its head in me. Growls low in its throat. I silence it with a twitch of my hand.

I'll fight if needs must, I'll kill if need be. But it ain't smart to fight this fight with bows an guns an bombs. Fer three reasons, I says. Number one. Look at how many they are an how few we are. How few real fighters, I mean, not jest bodies – no offence to nobody.

Slim looks at Mercy an Molly. She means us, ladies, he says. The old, the lame an the slow.

Oh, I ain't always slow, says Molly. She's propped on her elbows, legs stretched out, studyin her bare feet with drowsy content. They're small an shapely an, fer feet, remarkably pretty. Creed eyes her like a hungry dog. Go on, Saba, she says. We don't take no offence.

If we keep this a gun fight, I says, they'll have the upper hand in no time an we'll be dead. Reason two. Even if we could keep 'em on the run fer a while, the terrain of New Eden don't favour guerilla action. Everythin's too close an we ain't got enough places to retreat to. Pretty soon they'll know where all our foxholes are an we won't have nowhere to hide.

I keep lookin at them, each one in turn. Tryin to read their faces, their eyes, as their thoughts turn an chase. Choosin my words with care. Slowin myself down when I start to talk too fast.

Reason three, I says. I bin learnin a lot about New Eden. From Mercy an other sources. Information has come my way about DeMalo. I cain't tell you no more right now, but I can tell you this. Knowin what I do, the smartest an best way to beat him is without a shot bein fired. An I believe it can be done. That we can do it.

I don't, says Creed. An I don't believe you believe it neether. The first sign of trouble, you'll be reachin fer yer gun or yer bow. It's who you are. Yer brother here says you was born with a bow in yer hand. I only had to see you in action once to know that.

Ash says, Sorry, Saba. I stuck with you all the way so far, but I jest cain't see how this would work. I mean, you even talk about bringin the Stewards onto our side... She shakes her head. It's a nice thought, but yer dreamin.

I never heard of such a thing – a fight with no fightin – an I'm a thousand years old, says Slim. Sorry, sister, I'm with Ash on this one.

Me too, says Tommo.

What about the rest of yuz? Mercy? I says. Molly? Where do you stand? Lugh? How about you?

Lugh says, Sorry, but I'm with the doubters. Even if it did work, it 'ud take ages.

I ain't so sure about that, I says. If we don't try, we'll never know. One chance to prove this can work. That's what I want. Tonight at the babyhouse. An if it works, you'll all support this. We'll roll it out fast. Babyhouses, slaves, Edenhome, the lot. Come on, Lugh. One chance.

He looks at me a long moment. Then, All right, he says. One chance. Me an Em'll support you that far. Right, Em?

My eyes tell him thanks. Emmi nods. She's kept her distance since I got back. Now she's usin Tracker as a shield between her an me. She coaxed him to sprawl over her lap. She hugs his neck, her face half-buried in his fur. She's ashamed over Nero. After all her sworn vows to do better. But I ain't gonna chew her out. I don't even give her the hard eyeball. I'm jest gonna leave her an see what happens.

Creed looks a world full of scorn at Lugh. Yeah, well, you would go along with her, wouldn't you? he says. Even if it was the most crackbrain notion ever. Which it is.

I wouldn't be so sure. Molly sits up straight, suddenly brisk. If there's somethin that runnin a hooch joint learns you, it's that there's more'n one way to settle a fight. So far, this one's gone down the usual dismal road. Ike's dead, Jack's dead an Bram an Maev an yer other friends too. I ain't ready to join 'em jest yet. She shrugs. We should try this. We'd be fools not to.

Well spoke, says Mercy. I'm with Saba.

I'll need yer help tonight, Mercy, I says.

Only if I won't be no hindrance, she says. No guilt on your side, no blame on mine.

Four aginst four. Slim digs in his pocket. Think I got a coin in here somewheres.

I says, This is too big to rest on a coin flip. I want everybody with me. If this works an we roll it out, we all hafta do it, believe in it, stick with it. Not jest one or two of us an the others go off with guns. I ain't crazy, I promise you. An this ain't some desperate idea I came up with becuz I lost my nerve. It's the only thing that makes sense. It is risky. It's gonna take more nerve an more smarts than anythin any of us ever done before. If I'm right, we could win without nobody gittin hurt. Please. One chance, that's all I ask. Tonight. One action. No weapons. Lemme crack open that fault line an see what happens. Whaddya say?

Slim slaps his knees. I say, help yer Uncle Slim to his feet. Tommo an Ash haul him from his slingchair. He grabs my hand, yanks me aginst his bulk an I'm fixed with his hard one-eyed stare. He says, We played a cool game of chicken with the Tonton that day, you an me. There ain't nuthin wrong with yer nerve, Miss Death. Go on, then. You show me somethin I ain't never seen before. Prove me wrong. Far as I'm concerned, you got yer chance. He lets me go. That makes it five to three, he says.

Six to two, says Tommo. I believe in you, Saba.

A smile breaks over my face fer him. Thanks, Tommo, I says. My breath starts to come more easy.

Ash stares at me. With a little frown that says I'm a problem she cain't work out.

Yer the one planted this idea in me first, I tell her. Back

when we first caught sight of Resurrection. That huge fortress risin up in front of us. A garrison of Tonton inside with their arsenal of weapons. All of them. Only five of us. It seemed so impossible we jest about lost heart. Not you. Tiny things can cause big trouble, that's what you said. We did. An we can do it agin.

She starts to nod. Skeeter bite brings fever, she says. Little thorn sticks in you, yer blood goes bad. All right. Let's see you do this thing. That makes you the only holdout, Creed.

Slim says, Jump off the cliff with the rest of us, son. You never know, we might jest sprout wings an fly.

Creed's bin eyes-to-the-ground, arms crossed over his chest, shakin his head from time to time. I don't believe this, he says. All of yuz. It's a complete waste of time. Go on, do what you like. He starts to walk away. He raises his voice, not lookin back as he says, When you crash, come find me an we'll talk about a proper fight. That's if I'm still around.

Creed! I call after him. One chance! C'mon!

He waves a hand in dismissal an disappears over the edge of the hill.

I got it! cries Peg.

We all turn. She's grabbed hold of the windcrank on the nose of her airbuggy. She hangs her weight to shove it around. It turns. Once. Very slowly. Then, very slowly, the whole thing collapses.

I'm headin down the hill to find a quiet place to think when Ash comes chasin after me. Wait up! she calls.

There bein only room fer one on the narrow, zigzaggy path, she has to stick behind me. As we pick our rocky way down, she says, Pretty wild idea. You changed yer tune some.

Whatever it takes, Ash. My mind's clear on this, I says. Like I said, it's the only thing that makes sense.

There's the scrabble of feet behind us. We look back to find Emmi an Tracker in pursuit. He flies past, leapin the rocks like a mountain goat, an disappears.

'Scuse me, comin through! As Emmi squeezes an elbows past Ash, her feet slide out from beneath her. Whoops!

Whoa! Ash grabs her collar to save her from a tumble. What's the hurry, ma'am?

Em clutches herself upright, hangin on my arm. She looks at me. With her clear as a summer raindrop eyes. I won't ever let you down agin, not ever, she says. I'm gonna step up, I swear. You'll see.

Then she's squirmed past, scramblin headlong down the path.

Hey! I call. Come back here so I can yell at you. Don't think you ain't in trouble, Emmi!

She's a rocket, that girl, says Ash. What's the trouble?

She let Nero go loose when I told her to keep him with her. Unreliable Em strikes agin. I shake my head as we go on.

Ash says, Hey, Saba? You thought any more about what I said?

Thought about what?

Nero, she says. Who might of snatched him like that. You must of noticed. He's okay with all us females – even Peg, an he don't know her. But he's still nervy with the boys – men – whatever. He don't trust 'em. That tells you somethin right there.

That bit of cord Emmi handed me. It's still in my pocket. I ain't gave it another thought.

I stop. I turn to her. So who're you accusin, Ash, huh? My brother? Tommo? Slim? Absolutely not. Never. An Creed an me, we might have our differences of opinion, but I've trusted him with my life. Jest like I have all of yuz, an you ain't never let me down. I got no reason to suspect any of yuz.

Who did it, then? she says.

She ain't gonna leave this, I can tell by her face. An I sure as hell cain't tell her it was a Tonton doin DeMalo's work. That would only lead to more questions. It's five nights to the blood moon. I could scream at her fer wastin my time like this.

Look, I says. I got a pretty good idea who did this an why. As her mouth drops open in surprise, I says, I ain't at liberty to say no more than that. I glance up at Nero, who's sailin around above us. There warn't no harm done to Nero an that's the main thing, I says. I don't wanna talk about this agin, Ash. I got a lot to do, a lot to think about.

She's lookin at me like I jest sprouted another head. Fine, she says, whatever. You got big things on yer plate. No problem.

I know her. I know how her mind works. Ash, I ferbid you to go pokin around, I says. There ain't nuthin to discover here, believe me. An I don't want you talkin to nobody about it, an I want yer word on it. I hold out my hand to her. C'mon, gimme yer promise, right now.

You are so wrong-headed on this, she says. But I stare her out till she shrugs with bad grace. On yer wrong head be it, then, she says. She grabs my hand an gives it her usual. A quick, hard tug towards her, like it's a stuck pump handle.

Ash's word is solid. With her promise to me handset, we carry on down.

I need Mercy with me at the babyhouse. I won't know ezzackly what my plan is till I meet with Jack an his New Eden rebels later today. But if we're gonna go baby stealin, we'll need somebody who's skilled with infants. Who better than Mercy? She also knows the workins of a babyhouse from the inside.

So I'm forced to tell her about Jack. She don't know him an she's only newly arrived among us, so she ain't had her prejudice set about him one way or the other. Unlike everybody else, I think I can trust her with this secret.

On our way to the meet spot, the watermill in Sector Four, I fill her in on Jack an his New Eden rebels. How Bram, with the help of his woman Cassie, had carefully an slowly put together a little gang. How they'd hardly got started when he got killed in action. How Jack took them over. How him an me work together.

Mercy don't say much. She nods from time to time. At the end of my piece she says, The heartstone burns for this man. Am I right?

Well, I says, you ain't wrong.

The mill's in a dip of a valley, on the shouty little river called the Don. The old waterwheel creaks its way around, like a crone with a bone complaint. The mill's greenly damp an ancient. The millstone rumbles inside. A white cloud of flour billows from a window.

Jack ushers Mercy up the steep stone steps. Ages of feet have worn 'em to a friendly sag in the middle. She holds tight to the rope handrail. I follow behind an glance at the river below. It's so clear I can see the stones of its bed. They gleam pale an round as faces. Long strands of weed stream around them like hair.

My heart slams in my chest. I grab the rail. Lean over to look. There. In the water. Lyin on the riverbed.

The current combs weed through her long wild hair.
My mother.
In the water.
Dead.
She lies, whitely dead, in her bed of pale stones.
Eyes closed.
A smile on her lips.
Like she froze while she dreamed of roses.
An I lie with her.
Me.
I'm there.
Cradled in her arms,
asleep.
Flushed with life,
a smile on my lips,
clasped in my dead mother's arms.

I rear back. My breath chokes in my throat.

Jack's halfways through the door. Wavin me on, wonderin why I'm laggin. C'mon, would you? He sees my face. What is it?

With a gasp, I look agin. Pale round stones pave the waterfloor. Weed strands wave an weave. She's gone. I'm gone. Not jest gone, never there.

Are you okay? he says.

I nod.

When the dead grace my days as well as my nights, it's a sign of my unquiet soul. But then … maybe I'm jest tired. I didn't sleep. That'll be it. That's all it was.

Saba, says Jack. They're waitin.

I straighten up. I try a smile. I'm comin, I says.

The great millstones have groaned to a halt. Their rumble still shudders in the air. Inside, a heavy mist of fine white flour drifts an sifts to the floor. As we pass through the millroom, we send it whirlin an dancin. Jack leads the way up a ladder in the corner, through a hatch to a room in the rooftop of the mill. It's small an seems crammed full of bodies. But there's only six of 'em. We three make it nine. The floor's bin cross-boarded so's the flour cain't sift through the cracks. A breeze trickles through a open window.

There's Vain Ed, the miller. Dusted flour-white from curls to boots. Handsome as george an none too bright. A mousy Steward couple, Manuel an Bo, with the quartered circle brands on their foreheads. Skeet, a runaway slave with a scarified face. His eyes fly to the pale skin that collars Mercy's neck. They seek out the long double x brands on her arms. You can jest make 'em out through her threadbare sleeves. Skeet an Juneberry – JB fer short – seem to be together. I'd say they're ages with Mercy. Skinny an tough with long hair matted into ropes, they smell of sweat an earth, of the woods they roam in secret.

From Jack, I know that JB's one of the last resisters of the Clearance. Some fled, like the folk at the Snake River camp. Some got killed fightin fer their patch. A few, like JB, took to the forest. Treedogs, they're called. Livin high among the branches, movin swiftly on foot to make trouble fer the Stewards who stole their land. Most of 'em's bin caught. Like Slim's friend, Billy Six, spiked to a post.

An there's Cassie. I bin dreadin this. Meetin her. I should of done it ages ago. Right away after Bram got killed. Instead I shirked it like the coward I am. I don't dare glance her way. She's perched at a open window with her arms crossed tight. But I feel her eyes burnin holes in me.

I speak my piece. The same kinda things I said to my Free Hawks. How New Eden's built upon fault lines. If we got them to shift, DeMalo's whole project would come crashin down.

Kill DeMalo, his whole project crashes down, says Jack.

Jack an me disagree on this point, I says. I don't say he ain't right. But that way leads to bloodshed. Not jest DeMalo's, probly all of ours an then some. Look, what I mean is … at the moment we're actin like DeMalo's power is somethin solid, like a mountain, to be chipped at with guns an bombs. The fact is, everybody in New Eden is the mountain. He stands on top of it.

Explain that, says Jack.

Okay, I says. What does DeMalo need to carry out his plan to heal the earth? One. He needs labour. The Stewards to work the land. The slaves to build the roads an do the work that breaks backs. Two. It's a plan fer the generations, not jest a few years. That'll take a steady stream of labour. So the Stewards hafta produce children an keep on producin them. Three. He needs the slaves an the Stewards to stay here an do what he decrees without question, so he needs the Tonton to enforce his will. He needs a helluva lotta people. Every single one of 'em makes up the mountain. His power depends on them completely. If they decide not to be that mountain no more, he'll have nowhere to stand. He'll fall. If even one bit shifts, the whole thing starts to weaken.

Jack listens. He takes it in, every word. I cain't tell if he's surprised that this is where my thoughts an feelins was leadin me. What fell into place as I rode alone from the bunker to Starlight Lanes. So clearly that I believe it's bin whisperin in me fer some time, only I was too busy fightin to hear it. I cain't tell what he thinks. It's a far cry from a plot to kill DeMalo.

As fer the rest of 'em, they stand aginst the walls, not lookin at me even once. With closed faces an probly closed ears. They couldn't make it more obvious. They're only here as a favour to Jack. Their loyalty lies with Cassie. Her man, Bram – their friend an leader – is dead thanks to me.

If I don't win her over, I got no chance with them. An I need their insider knowledge of the Stewards. But right now it don't look good. Not at all.

Cassie stares at me with naked despisal. Unlike the rest, she ain't took her eyes offa me. Not fer a second. She fills the air with such black hatred that I feel it closin around me. As I speak, I can feel myself gittin redder an redder in the face. I start to think how stupid I sound. How stupid I must look. My lips dry an I git more an more unsettled till I'm fumblin an mixin my words. An it ain't jest me. They're all shiftin, uncomfortable. Vain Ed elbows open another window.

Jack warned she'd be rough on me. I espected it. Figgered I even deserve it. But still. I ain't never bin flayed by ill will before. An I'm shocked at the change in her. Grief's clawed her soft round face. Gnawed the smile from her lips. Her pretty brown hair used to hang loose an wavy. Now it's scraped back, knotted tight, like a punishment. The circle brand on her forehead stands out starkly.

You got the power, I says. He can only rule if you let him. If you do what he says. If you stay obedient. D'you see?

I stumble to a finish. To thick silence.

Cassie curls her mouth in scorn. Fault lines, she says. Mountains. The mountain crumbles, DeMalo falls, an we all join hands an dance in the sun. Who'd of thought it could be so easy?

All right, I says. Tell me this. What's the one thing about this place that bothers the Stewards most? One of DeMalo's rules that people don't unnerstand or believe to be unjust. They might not say it, but they think it, feel it in their hearts to be unfair.

Silence. Mercy's eyes go around the room. They stop on Bo, the plain-faced Steward girl. She's lookin sidewise at her man. Manuel with the wispy beard. They bin huddled together, eyein me like I'm some creature they bin warned not to approach. I only jest now notice – Bo's got the tiniest start of a baby belly. She looks at me.

They take away yer baby, she whispers.

The attachment of parents to their child is powerful, says Mercy.

So if you was to … take yer baby back from the Pathfinder, from the babyhouse, I says, that would be a powerful thing to do. That would start to shake the mountain. Any mother an father doin that is bein disobedient to the Pathfinder an New Eden. They're takin a risk. A big one. Whoever does it is gonna have fear. But their desire fer their child will be greater than their fear. Once they have their child, an they've conquered their fear once, they'll start to lose their fear. He controls by fear. If people don't fear him no more, his power goes.

I wait fer a moment. To let all that sink in. To see if I can tell what they're thinkin. Have I got to them? Moved them?

Mercy an me's gonna go on a recce to the babyhouse tonight, I says. We'll take a child if it looks possible. I'm askin fer yer help. You know the girls here. We need yer inside knowledge.

Cassie laughs. A dry huff of breath, nuthin more. Us? she says. Help you? Work with you? What, you mean like Bram did? Becuz that turned out so well, didn't it?

I'm sorry, Cassie, I says. I am most truly sorry.

She says, Yer truly sorry an he's truly dead an his body's still unner the rock where you left it. An I'm paired with a new man, a stranger who sleeps in my bed an watches me with hawk eyes an that's how it goes in New Eden.

Vain Ed says, A woman whose man disappears fer no reason is suspect.

Cassie speaks with tight care. To her skirt, to her sleeves, as she tidies what's already perfectly tidy. You took everythin from me an now you want more, she says. You've had all yer gonna git from me. I let Bram go with you to rescue yer sister. He never came back. An you didn't even have the decency to come an tell me he was dead. I had to hear it from a stranger. From Jack. At least he knows how to treat people right.

Cassie never liked me, never trusted me, an she never made no bones about it. Now she hates me. Bitterly. I've known the lash of her tongue before, but I'm feelin a bit sick from this onslaught. I glance to Jack. He gives me a what-can-I-do? look. Mercy clasps her hands knuckle-white on

174

her lap. She cain't speak up fer me, I gotta take this on the chin. But her eyes steady my spirit.

That was wrong of me, I says. I should of come. An I meant to, but—

But what? Cassie's on her feet. She squares up to me. What? You had somethin better to do? she says.

No, I says, of course not. I'm sorry, Cassie, I should of come to you as soon as I could.

Well, you didn't, she says. You can pack yer I'm sorrys an take 'em to hell with you.

If I was you, I'd probly hate me too, I says. But hangin onto blame won't bring him back. It's no way to honour his sacrifice.

Sacrifice! she hisses. You dare talk to me about sacrifice! She lunges an belts me. Slaps my face so hard that my head snaps back.

Jack takes a step. Mercy half-rises. I stop 'em with a hand. Cassie stares aghast, eyes wide. She didn't plan to do that. Ed's arm goes around her shoulders. His jaw dares me to touch her. My cheek flames an stings. I'm seein stars. But I welcome the hit an the pain. I'll take 'em any day over the knife of her eyes.

I'm glad I didn't hafta meet you in the Cage, I says. I deserved that. Please, can we try to work together? I hold out my hand. She looks at it. She looks at me. She's set her face back to shun.

I am sorry, I says. I cain't ever repay what I owe you. I cain't ever make good yer loss, much as I want to. All I can do is try not to waste the chance that Bram gave us. I need yer help to do that. An, fer now, I believe you need mine. Please, Cassie. Let's try this. If it works like I hope, you'll all be able to carry it forwards on yer own. You won't need me.

175

She goes back to the window to sit an stare out at nuthin. She's finished with this. With me. That means the rest of them's done with me as well. I read on Jack's face what's all too clear. My past mistakes damn me completely. What made me think I could win Cassie over? Comin here was a mistake. An maybe a dangerous one. If her hatred is hot enough to betray me.

I says, DeMalo is weak, but he believes he's strong. Yer strong, but you believe yer weak. I nod a farewell. Let's go, I says to Mercy.

As Jack lifts the hatch door, she gits up from her stool. She hesitates, then holds out her hand to Skeet. After a moment, he takes it. We never did git innerduced, she says. My name is Mercy. My home is Crosscreek. A sweet green valley that sleeps in the sun.

Her words shift his gaze into memory. He says, quietly – like he's lyin in a bunk in a slave hut in the dark an he don't want the guards to hear, like a chant he says inside hisself, over an over – he says, My name is Skeet. My home's a cart. It's got yellow wheels an a horse called Otis to pull it.

Shared trials forge instant bonds. Mercy lays her other hand atop their clasped ones. He does the same.

The girl ain't perfect, my friend, she says. But she's cut from rare cloth. I've pledged myself to her, come what may.

He says, JB here's bin treedoggin fer a year or so. I bin with her a few months. We spoil a well, fire a hay barn, but they always come lookin fer us, beatin the woods with dogs. Sometimes they find one of our gaffs an fell the tree. We ain't gonna git no faster, eh Junie B? Someday, maybe soon, our luck'll run out. An they jest repair the damage an carry on an … funny, somehow I never stopped to ask myself if there might be another – maybe a better way.

When he's done, there's a awkward silence. That streamed

outta him as if him an Mercy's the oldest of comrades. Like they'd bin in the middle of a long conversation.

Maybe it's time you did, says Mercy. Maybe it's time we all did.

Their hands part. I move towards the ladder. I'll go first an guide her down safely.

Hey Bo, ain't there a girl went into the babyhouse a few days ago? Manuel speaks quickly, a bit too loudly. You know the one. I think she's nearby the new turnpike.

I pause.

You mean that – oh, what is her name? Bo frowns an snaps her fingers. Dian, that's it.

Vain Ed scratches his head. Naw, he says, that don't sound right to me. Cherry?

Y'know, now I'm thinkin it could be Eula, says Manuel.

You three wouldn't fool a child with that hopeless play actin. Cassie turns from the window. Her eyes meet mine in wary truce. Her name's Rae, she says. She's fifteen. She started havin pains a month before her time. I know her. I think she might go along with it. I'll come with you.

Thanks, I says.

What about Hunter? says Bo. You won't git out at night without him noticin.

Cassie's lips tighten. He's partial to a drink or five, she says. So long as I'm back by dawn.

My heart takes heart. The air starts to breathe. I don't chance a handshake, but I give Cassie a small nod. She may never fergive me. We may never be friends. She may never entirely trust me. I don't see all that as so bad. The only thing that matters is she's willin to try an work together.

We'll go as soon as it's dark, I says. You an me an Mercy an Jack.

Night Five

It's another night of rumpus in the sky. The stars chase about in fiery disorder. We came by the fieldways, around the edges, in the shadowland. But we probly could of took the roads, checkpoints an all. After dark in starfall season, most people bolt the door. They won't answer a knock fer fear of shades on the roam. Lurkin here behind the stables, with our pale faces an dark clothes, we might well be mistook fer haunts. Beheaded in life maybe, searchin fer our lost bodies. Essept ghosts don't breathe fog on a chilly night.

On the left there, at the front, Jack whispers. That's where the women stay. The birthin room's on that side too. There's a hallway divides the buildin in half. Runs straight from the front door to a door at the back.

Nursery's on the right, says Mercy. Plus beds fer the midwife an wetnurses. To the rear's Tonton quarters an a kitchen. Outside's a well, a privy an a woodstore. They'll git a food delivery every couple of days. That's it.

How d'you know all that? I says. You didn't midwife here.

They lay out all the babyhouses ezzackly the same, says Jack. An it's always four men on duty. A commander an three grunts. Four horses in the stable here. That means they're all inside.

We left our own horses in a scrubby hollow a half mile north. I'd be happier with 'em nearby but we didn't have the choice. There ain't no cover hereabouts to be found.

The babyhouse stands by itself at a flat crossroads. It's edged on three sides by little poplar whips. But it'll be years before they're high enough to make a windbreak, let alone one thick enough to hide in. This place is raw an new. Built only a few months ago, accordin to Jack. It's a low one storey with a bark an sod roof. Walls of board, mud an strawbale sprawl low an long. There's a sturdy barred door in the middle. Two windows eether side with narrow iron bars. They've closed the wood shutters inside, but light trickles out between the slats. I check 'em out through the looker, but cain't make out a thing. Here behind the stables, we're maybe fifty foot from the house.

Babyhouse, says Cassie. Baby prison, more like. D'you really think you can bluff us in there, Jack?

Oh, I can do that no problem, he says. It's what comes after that I'm worried about. Seein how we got no idea what comes after. He smiles his lopsided smile at me.

He seems more like hisself tonight. I'm mightily relieved, if none the wiser. I don't think I could of took no more of his cool distance. Tonight – unlike last night – he does have his Tonton gear on. An, fer the first time, I'm glad to see him in it. When I told him so, he jest raised one eyebrow. The fact is, he's our only chance of gittin into this place.

Mercy's padded Cassie with a pretty decent halfways along baby belly. Our plan at the moment – an to say it's rough is high praise – is fer Jack to pound on that barred door an say he's got a pregnant woman who's in a state. Mercy practised Cassie in signs of false labour an what to do when an it turns out she's a champion at pretendin to be in hysterics. Once they're inside, Mercy says the Tonton will leave the midwife to deal with her. An there's a good chance she won't blow the whistle when she sees Cassie's a sham.

Midwives hate their slavery, they hate what they're doin, an they hate the Tonton above all. From there on, it's down to Jack an Cassie what they do. So long as they don't use no weapons an nobody gits hurt.

I trust you, I says.

I'm flattered by yer faith in me, Jack says. An, as you know, I'm a great believer in wingin it. But even by my standards this is a very loose plan. Yer sure you wanna do this?

Cassie's got the final say, I says.

Let's move in closer, she says. Take a look through them shutters. See what's goin on.

Keepin low, we run across the yard. We flatten ourselfs aginst the house next to the window on the left-hand side. We edge in to peek through the shutter slats. It's one long room lit by wall lanterns. Two neat rows of beds. Only two girls. One, a big ruddy gal, hugely pregnant, lays propped up in bed. The other's a slip of a thing with a sweet, exhausted, frightened face. She ain't pregnant. She paces an turns. Starts an stops. Wearin a path in the floor beside what must be her bed. There's a small cloth-wrapped bundle set on it, like she's ready to leave. Her hands clutch together at her waist. Tryin an failin to stop the agonized claw of her fingers. She stares at the door to the hallway.

That's Rae, whispers Cassie. She must of had her baby.

A feeble wail trickles from the other side of the babyhouse. Emmi used to wail like that. Weak as a newborn mouse an no mother's milk to feed her. It's beyond a wonder that she lived.

Mercy shakes her head. Born before its time, poor thing, she says.

A collared slave, her face a careful blank, sits in a chair

beside the door. She's a great carthorse of a woman. That's why they picked her. Why she's here. To keep the girls on this side of the door. Rae goes to her, speaks to her, pleads with her. The woman shakes her head. No, Rae cain't go to her baby.

Rae turns away. You can see her tryin to git hold of herself, but she's crackin. The other girl holds out her hand, says her name. Rae runs to her an buries her head in her shoulder. She weeps as the girl holds her. As she strokes her back, talks to her quietly. She makes Rae sit up an dry her tears.

The shutters muffle their voices. The night-time flicker of the rushlight lanterns softens, blurs their distress.

Let's take a look the other side, I says.

We scuttle across the front door to the window of the baby room. Slowly, cautiously, we take a look. A room jest like the other. Only here, instead of beds, there's hopeful rows of small cots. They stand testament to DeMalo's belief in the future of New Eden. From here, we cain't see how many's full. But a Steward woman moves between maybe half of 'em, checkin on the infants inside.

The midwife, whispers Mercy.

The pitiful noise comes from a swaddled baby that another Steward holds to her breast. She's sittin in a chair, tryin to make it take a drink. But it won't grab hold. Its head flops away an it cries out its life in thread-thin complaint. Rae's baby, born a month too early.

Wet nurse, says Mercy. They only use women whose own baby died or was too weak an got exposed.

Mothers of the dead held captive. No chance fer them to mourn. Does it ease their sorrow some to see a child grow healthy from their milk? Fer them whose baby died natural, maybe. I could see it might help. But the women with feeble babies like this one? Who know the fate of their child? It must cut deep to their souls.

The Steward holdin Rae's baby buttons her shirt an holds it to her shoulder. She rubs its back, tries to calm it with her hands an her voice. She's got curly copper hair, a bit like Maev's. I'd say she's ages with me. If she had a baby that died, it might well of bin her first. Even to my eyes, she don't seem practised. Her gaze flicks anxiously to the two Tonton who jest came into the room.

The older man, dark-skinned, wearily handsome, is in charge. The other is a red-cheeked boy of about twenny. He looks too fresh faced to have the blood tattoo, but he must do. He stands post near the door while his commander speaks with the Steward wet nurse an the midwife. We cain't hear what they say, their voices are too quiet, but it's clear they're talkin about Rae's child. He makes them unwrap the baby from the swaddlin so's he can see it proper, take a good look at it.

It's a girl. A pathetic red scrap. Tiny sparrow arms. Legs you could snap between yer fingers. She's stopped cryin now. She jest lays there. I can hear DeMalo's voice in my head.

Whose children will best serve the earth? Those born to the scum of Hopetown? Weak children born to the weak? Or the children of these people?

Sometimes the strong give birth to the weak. An sometimes the weak grow to be strong.

That's jest how Emmi was, says Mercy.

Emmi. Born early, denied a mother's love to anchor her to the world, she barely hung on fer the first few weeks. Then, with Mercy's care, somethin inside of her kicked an she started to fight to live. The commander checks the child over. He speaks to the women some more. He turns to the young Tonton an flicks his fingers. The boy slips from the room.

The copper-haired wet nurse starts to swaddle the baby agin. The commander stops her. With urgent distress, they talk at him, her an the midwife. They've raised their voices, so I can make out, Another few days, an Please, sir. He cuts 'em off short with a raised hand.

He's decided, says Mercy. No hope fer this one.

After a few more words, the commander leaves the room. The young Tonton's jest comin back in an they exchange nods at the doorway. He comes over to the women. The wet nurse hesitates, clutchin Rae's baby to her. Then she gently kisses her head an hands her over, naked as she is.

I notice how carefully the Tonton takes her. How he supports her head with his hand. How he cradles her in his arms so easy, so natural.

An I think to myself, He's done that before. Maybe had a little sister of his own. Was happy to help with her, loved her. Not like me. To my shame, I never touched Em once. I blamed her fer Ma bein dead. Lugh was the one who helped Pa with her.

Suddenly, the pound of runnin feet. We all hit the ground. A second later, two Tonton appear from the back of the babyhouse. They head fer the stables. The moment they're outta sight, we scramble around the far corner of the buildin. We hold our breath. We wait.

The red hot quivers in me, strains to break free. My hand rests on my gunbelt – flew there at the sound of runnin feet. Essept I ain't wearin it. Fer the very first time since I left Silverlake, I ain't packin no weapons. None of us are.

No bows, no guns, no knife in my boot sheath. It don't feel right. I don't feel right. I notice Jack's hand rests where his gun ain't.

The Tonton haul a double bench buggy from the stables. One runs back inside to fetch a horse an they ease him into the traces an hitch him up. It's all done in double-quick time.

They're gonna take Rae home, whispers Mercy.

You know where she lives? I says to Cassie.

She nods. She's perfectly calm. I recall her steady nerve the night I first met her. When Jack snatched Emmi an it was only thanks to her an Bram's cool heads that I didn't git us all killed there an then.

While the Tonton bring the horse an cart to the front door, locks rattle, bars creak an it swings wide open. The commander walks Rae out, holdin her by the elbow. She hugs her little bundle to her chest. No sign of tears now. She wouldn't dare make a fuss in front of him. She holds her head high. Doin her best to act the way a Steward should.

The commander helps her onto the buggy's rear bench. He smiles an bows his head. She almost manages a smile back. She's made of stern stuff, this girl Rae. Whether that'll work in our favour remains to be seen. The two Tonton climb in an settle on the front bench. The grunt ridin shotgun lays his firestick on his knees. With a slap of the reins an a sudden jolt, the buggy rumbles from the yard an into the moonpath that lights the road north silver.

As the front door shuts, locks rattle, bars creak, we can see Rae's dark figger on the buggy's back bench. She twists around to take a long, last look. Then she turns to face the road ahead.

Don't worry, girl, I says. You'll see yer baby soon. Then

I says to Cassie, We ain't gonna need yer play actin after all. We picked the right night to come. You an Mercy git the horses. Wait fer us by the first bend along that north road. There's some rock cover there. Jack, yer with me. Let's go git that scrawny little baby.

The young Tonton's easy to spot. Easy to keep in our sights. The night's clear lit an the land lies flat an he's the only thing movin besides us. An the light breeze carries snatches of the baby's thin wail. So we hang back an keep low in case he glances behind him. Nero coasts along above us, but nobody'd give a second thought to a crow flyin by night. That's if they even noticed it.

With the Tonton's head start, he must be well on the way to wherever he's bin told to leave the child. I'm guessin it'll be some fair distance from the babyhouse. Far outta hearin range. Nobody could take the sound of a baby cryin outdoors all night long. Not even the Tonton. The speed this guy's goin, a sort of runnin walk, says he's in a hurry to git the job over with. From his gait, you can tell that he's hunched around the baby, huggin her close to his chest. He's probly got her unnerneath his cloak.

What a grim task. He must be bottom of the peckin order. We follow him fer half a league or so, along a path through the low scrub. It ain't worn ground, but it's bin trampled down enough to make easy goin. Then he's gone. Jest like that. Disappeared from view completely.

Jack snatches up the looker that's hangin around his neck.

Where'd he go? he mutters as he sweeps the night. Dammit. C'mon!

We belt across the plain. We nearly tumble down on top of him. He's sat cross-legged at the bottom of a dry little gully with the baby laid across his lap. We duck behind a boulder an peek out. The baby's whimperin now, but the steep rocky sides will blanket any sound she makes. The Tonton's took off his own sheema to wrap her. That's somethin he ain't meant to do. He's makin a tidy, careful job of it as well. His firestick's on the ground next to him.

He's sayin, Don't look at me like that. This ain't my fault. Yer too small an whose fault is that? Yers, that's who. You should of stayed inside yer ma till you was growed big enough. But oh no, you was in too much of a hurry. An fer what? Look at the pickle you got yerself into.

He talks to her like you would anybody. Jest normal conversation. It's the only way he can do this. Me an Jack look at each other. An, fer the briefest of moments, in the starfallen night, I see the father he was fer the briefest of times. Gracie's father. A girl child like this one. I always fergit Jack had a child. Only now does it occur to me that this might be hard fer him.

Okay, yer done, says the Tonton. He takes the baby in his arms an gits to his feet. I gotta put you somewheres outta the wind. You don't wanna catch cold. An we don't want them coyotes catchin wind of you. Over there? Good idea. He settles her in a nook between the rocks. There you go, look at that. Yer snug as a bug. Now listen to me, an this is real important, okay? You cain't cry, not a peep an I mean it. If a coyote was to find you— His throat works as he fights not to cry. Suddenly, he turns an scrambles up the other side of the gully. He rushes off into the night.

Jack an me do a silent finger count to ten. He stands slowly an checks with the looker. He's goin, he whispers.

You stay here, I says.

I pick my way down the rocks, takin good care every time I move a foot or a hand. I mustn't make no sound. But my last step sets off a slide of pebbles. I freeze. Stare up at Jack. He checks through the looker.

He's outta sight, he says. Go on.

The baby's started to mew agin. I hurry to her along the gully. She gringes a feeble protest as I try to winkle her out from where she's tucked between the rocks. I ain't quite sure how to go about it. I don't wanna hurt her by mistake. Shhh, I tell her. My hands feel clumsy. About as useful as feet fer the task. The Tonton's sheema seems to be caught on somethin.

Nero circles overhead, caw caw cawin. He probly don't like the baby's shrill laments. He ain't the only one. Does the little thing sound weaker or is it my imagination? Whatever, we need to git her to Rae as quick as we can.

I tug at the sheema an, bit by bit, I manage to wriggle her free. I reach in an take her. She don't hardly weigh nuthin. She's mainly bulky cloth. I turn to retrace my steps.

An he's here. The Tonton. Standin in the gully. Twenny foot away. His bolt shooter aimed at my heart. He gasps as he spots my birthmoon tattoo. The Angel of Death. Fear shards his face. He scuttles back. But his gun stays on me.

How did he creep up on me without Jack seein? Without me hearin him? He knows this place an we don't, that's how.

I raise my voice. I'm alone, I says. I ain't armed. *D'you hear me, Jack? Stay outta sight. Don't try nuthin.*

The Tonton's eyes widen. His breath's shallow an high.

He's heard the stories, the rumours. The ghost of the Angel of Death. On the prowl in New Eden. Set on revenge.

I know what you think but I ain't no ghost. I'm real enough, I says. Here. I reach out my hand to him. Go on, I says. Feel. I'm warm.

After a moment, he sidles forwards. His fingertips touch mine. A tiny nod. Show me yer clean, he says.

I keep my eyes on him as I move slowly an smoothly. I don't want him gittin jumpy on me. I lay the baby on the ground. I slide off my coat an throw it on the rocks. I open my arms wide an turn in a circle.

He moves in an does a quick pat down, holdin his shooter on me all the while. Lookin at me all the while. Like he still ain't sure this ain't some ghost trick. His face is a soft boy's face. His razor shaves peach fuzz, not bristles. He steps back. I seen the crow, he says. I thought he might hurt her.

The crow's mine, she's safe, I says. We look at each other, the Tonton an me. I seen you, I says. I heard you talkin to her. I'm gonna pick her up agin, okay? Don't want her gittin cold there on the ground. I crouch an scoop the baby to my arms.

Yer holdin her wrong, says the Tonton. You gotta support her head, doncha know nuthin?

Not much, I says. He's already holstered his gun an goes about settlin the baby proper in my arms.

Yer easy with her, I says. You got a little sister yerself?

His jaw tightens. His mouth too. That tells me all. Yes. But alive or dead, I dunno. Maybe he don't neether. That must hurt.

I got a sister, I says. She was born weak, jest like this one. But she grew an thrived an … she's somethin special.

Where you gonna take her? he says. When I don't

190

answer, he rushes on. I won't clype on you, I swear, he says. Apology – no, more than that – shame shades his face. This boy who shed tears over a baby that ain't nuthin to him.

I'm gonna give her back to her mother, I says.

You better hurry, he says. She ain't doin too good. She's awful small. He strokes the baby's cheek with one finger.

It don't hafta be this way, I says. Every blood tie cut. Mother from child. Brother from sister. Did they take her to Edenhome, yer sister?

I dunno, he says. Maybe.

What's her name? I says.

Then, it's like he suddenly realizes that he's standin with the Angel of Death, enemy of the people, talkin to her like anybody else. His face slams shut. He steps away. Head high, stood tall, he holds his clenched right fist to his heart. Long life to the Pathfinder, he says.

I bring my clenched fist to my heart. I spread my first two fingers in a V. Freedom, brother, I says softly.

Raw hunger spikes his eyes. Like a spark to a wick. His fist loosens. His lips part. Ohmigawd, he's gonna do it. He's gonna say it. *Say it. Go on. Freedom.* In the sky overhead, a star dashes itself to darkness. Hope sighs across his face an slips back in the shadows.

I says, The Pathfinder ain't what he says he is.

They really shouldn't let him out on his own. His face gives away his every thought. He knows he shouldn't believe such as me. But. He folds my words very small an tucks 'em away somewhere secret. To take out an ponder on later. I won't tell on you, he says. I promise.

Then he scarpers. Scrambles up the rocks an outta the gully, racin to git back to the babyhouse before they wonder what's takin him so long.

An Jack's slippin out from behind the boulder an scramblin down to help me up the slope. Possibilities brew in the gleam of his eyes. Huddle in the corners of his smile. As he gives me his hand, he says, Well.

As I take it, I says, Well, well.

My hands was sure itchin fer a gun, he says. That turned out innerestin, though.

Let's hope there's plenty like him, I says. The baby starts to grizzle agin. You take her, I says. I ain't good with babies.

Jack makes a sling around hisself with the ends of the sheema. Then, with the baby held snug aginst his chest, we head off at a fast trot north across the scrubland. To where Mercy an Cassie wait fer us. Where the north road takes a first bend.

Past curfew. Dead night. The stars rampage the sky. An all is quiet in Sector Three. Besides us, there ain't nobody afoot. The chill wind swings restless between north an east. My skin shivers. Maybe it's a fallen soul passin by. People believe that on starfall nights, they hitch rides on the back of the wind to wherever it is they're goin.

A wildcat on a field prowl fer mice pauses. Head high, he sniffs us, ever hopeful of a bigger meal. Then he carries on. The likes of him would easily take a baby left out in the open. She's asleep now, thanks to Tam's gentle jog an Mercy's heartbeat. She's cradled snugly in the sheema, tied around Mercy's chest.

The air whispers of winter soon to come. It mumbles the musty corn stubble back into earth. Murmurs on the tips of our noses an fingers. This'll be the first winter of my life that I ain't spent at Silverlake. If I last that long, that is. If I don't slip up fer DeMalo to crush me. But if I'm crushed, so will my people be. I look at the moon. It seems to grow fatter by the second.

I whisper to Cassie, How long away d'you figger the blood moon to be?

She says, Countin tonight? I'd say … five nights from now.

Jack hears me an frowns. I keep askin. Like time might be turnin backwards somehow. I gotta stop. He'll be wonderin why I need to know.

All's quiet at Rae's farmstead, like the land that surrounds it. The Tonton would of dropped her off an turned right around agin. Her an her boy – called Noble – farm ten acres. There's a sod an junk cabin an two rackety sheds. The tall wind pointer tacks to an fro with a metal click-click-click. Accordin to Cassie, their nearest neighbours ain't jest well outta sight but they'll be well outta hearin distance too. A baby's cry won't be heard.

Light bleeds out from unner the cabin door. Inside, a girl's cryin. Loud, body-wracked, heartbroke sobs. Here, with only her boy as witness, it's safe fer Rae to crack. The ugly sound of her pain warms hope in me.

Jack's keepin well outta sight. The fewer people who know about him, the better. Fer now, me an Mercy hang back in the shadows too.

Hermes tosses his head. His feet shift a restless demand to gallop. He longs to run flat-out over distance, across endless plains with big skies above. That's what he was born to. Not this closed-in land. Not this walkin in shadow edges, pickin through trees, this way, that way, around an back agin.

Yes yes, my dearie, I know, I know. Not long now to wait, my heart.

My hands soothe him, promise him. Come what may, he'll have his freedom. I'll make sure he ain't slave to no Tonton.

Cassie stands at the door with the baby in her arms, wrapped in the Tonton's sheema. My belly's twisted. My mouth's dry. Mercy squeezes my shoulder. My eyes meet Jack's. We're takin a big chance here. Much bigger'n we did at the gully. It ain't jest that I'll be proved right or wrong. Cassie's riskin her life. Liftin her mask. Obedient no more.

She straightens her back. Raises her head. She takes one deep breath an she knocks. Her gentle tap barely sounds on the heavy slab of wood.

Who is it? A man's voice raises from inside. Unwelcome. Suspicious.

Noble, it's Cassie, she says. Steward Cassie from Midway Rock.

Quick, heavy footsteps come to the door. Cassie? It's the middle of the night. What're you doin here after curfew?

Open the door, she says. Hurry. Please.

There's a fumbled rush as he lifts the bar, then a tall, husky lad fills the doorway. He lights the night with a rush lantern. There's a firestick unner his arm. Long life to the Pathfinder, he says. What's the matter? What's happened?

Cassie holds out the baby.

He stiffens. What's that? he says.

It's yer daughter, Noble. She raises her voice. Rae, I've got yer baby here.

There's a sharp cry, a rush of feet, then Rae's there. Her arms reach desperate fer the child. Noble blocks the doorway with his body so's she cain't git past. She pummels his back with a snarl of rage. How did you—? You stole her? he says.

Saved her, says Cassie. They left her in a ditch fer the night beasts to take.

Give her to me! Rae scrambles like a beast herself as she tries to shove past Noble. But he ain't movin an he's much bigger'n she is.

You shouldn't of took her, he says to Cassie. She must be a good fer nuthin or they wouldn't do that. The Pathfinder knows what's best.

There ain't a thing wrong with this baby, says Cassie. Nuthin that good care an love from her parents cain't make right. Look! She's perfect. She came early is all. Cassie pulls away the sheema, shows Noble her limbs, but he don't look. Not even a glance. The child starts to cry, woke by the fuss. Cassie covers her up agin an soothes her.

We don't want no trouble, says Noble. We ain't havin no baby here. Our only family is the Earth, you know that. If they find out, it don't bear thinkin what they might do to us.

He tries to shut the door, but with a No! Rae shoves herself between him an it.

They won't find out, says Cassie. I'm gonna help you. We're all gonna help you. We're gonna help each other. Everythin's changin, Noble. We ain't livin unner the boot no more. We can heal the earth, work the land, raise our children, an not at the point of a gun.

That kinda talk'll git you slaved or worse. Take her away now, I mean it, he says. Rae, hush, please! Cain't you see I'm tryin to do what's right here?

Rae's pushin him, pullin him. Let! Her! In! she says. Three words, each one jaggedly fierce.

I got a elder with me right here, says Cassie. She knows about babies. She'll teach you how to care fer her, what she needs. Most of all, she needs you. Her father an mother.

Ohmigawd, what're you doin? says Noble. What's happenin here? You can tell he's startin to waver. Fer the first time, he looks at the baby. Well how about that, he says. She's got a nose jest like my ma. In his voice there's both wonder an defeat.

She's made from yer own flesh an blood, Noble. She's yer child, says Cassie. I got some friends here I want you to meet.

At that, me an Mercy walk outta the dark into the light of the lantern. Noble sees my tattoo right away. Ohmigawd, he says. He tries to raise his firestick, but he's jugglin that an the lantern an keepin Rae an Cassie at bay an he was already on the verge, so his last defence crumbles.

With a cry of relief, Rae seizes the baby, Cassie slips past him an the two of 'em disappear into the cabin. I raise my hands an me an Mercy keep on comin.

We ain't got no weapons, Noble, I says. We ain't armed. We're here to help.

He flattens hisself to one side to let us pass. His face tangles in complete confusion. His hair's askew. I smile, friendly-like. Try to look normal, not ghostly. His gaze twitches to Nero, perched on the tree in his yard. To the starwild sky an the wind pointer as it chitters to an fro. Then he looks back at me, eyes wide.

I hitched a ride on the wind, I says.

I close the door behind me. Close it on two nervous people with a newborn child an Mercy to show 'em the way. I lean aginst the door fer a moment. I let out a long, thankful breath. One baby. One tiny crack. It worked.

Everythin go okay? Jack's low, husky voice rides the dark easily. I go to him. He's leanin aginst the shed, huddled in his cloak.

I'm okay, I says, but that baby's got problems. Her name's Lucky Star. Luck, fer short.

He winces. I know a tavern called the Lucky Star, he says. Scurviest dump in the livelong world.

I invite myself inside his cloak. Fold myself around his heat, his heartbeat. His arms circle my waist. But he takes his time, I notice.

So, he says. Ruthless killer sees the error of her ways. How does it feel?

Like this, I says. I take his face in my hands an I kiss him. With relief. With hope. With the newness of a day that I ain't never seen. With somethin my dustborn soul don't know the name of.

I wanna be with you tonight, I whisper. Jack, I—

He pulls away. His eyes pull the warmth from me as he says, I won't have too much to lose, d'you hear?

My bones take the stab. Quick an cold. I know what he means right away. He means he will not love me. He will not give all to me. He's lost all before. What he loved most dearly. His child. His Gracie.

Fer all he's said to me before, how he feels about me, he's drawin the line, steppin back from the line. But why why why? What's brought him to this? Only two nights ago, we lay together. In the bed he'd made of fir boughs. Maybe I didn't hear him right. Maybe he—

He sets me away from him. Out from his arms. When we was in that white room, he says. With DeMalo's fake visions. What did you mean when you said, them people in the bunks?

197

The smell of danger prickles my scalp. I don't remember sayin that, I says.

Well you did, he says. You said, when them people lay on them bunks fer the very last time, they died with hope that somebody would find the seedstore one day. What people in the bunks? How d'you know people died there?

But why? This is why. Ohmigawd, I let that slip. Does he suspect I was in the vision room before? One wrong word here, this could all break open. Be careful. Be very careful.

I really don't remember sayin that, I says. But, uh … I dunno, I guess I jest imagined what might of happened. Like you said, it was a lot to take in all at once. The seedstore an the maps an the vision room, the bunks. I s'pose I jest seen it all an made a story that made sense of it to me. Didn't you? Ain't that what anybody'd do?

I dunno, you tell me, he says.

An I'm thinkin, that don't sound like he believes me. Would I believe me if I was him? My mind dashes about, tryin to think what else I might of let slip. It ain't like him not to say what's on his mind. Not to chide me direct fer my sins. But then Cassie's comin outta the cabin an Jack's sayin, completely normal, like he didn't jest maybe very possibly stick a knife in me,

So, what next, Saba? More baby stealin?

I … uh … yeah, I says. Mercy's gonna see these two through the night. You'll be glad of her skills, so she'll stay on till you ain't got need of her no more. You should take every child they leave out to die. Return 'em to the parents, but only if they can be trusted. If not, you'll hafta keep the babies safe an well.

Okay, he says. But there won't be that many exposed. A handful at most. You'll need a lot more babies than that to make any progress. This'll take weeks. Months.

No, no, we bin talkin about that jest now, says Cassie. It's obvious what we do. In fact, Rae was the one said it. We'll need the help of the midwives to steal the babies to their parents. There ain't no Tonton in the birthin room, jest the midwife. Mercy says they ain't innerested in stillborns. They don't wanna see 'em. The midwife's in charge of the burial. So she reports a stillbirth an we take the baby. Cassie looks at Jack. Could you git Mercy back into the babyhouse she used to be at? The other midwife there was of the same mind as Mercy. She's sure that she'll help.

I'll think of a story to cover it, says Jack. Whatever Tonton was there when Mercy was, they'll be long gone. They're on constant rotation so's there ain't no time to build factional loyalties.

We'll work out how best to smuggle them away, says Cassie. We'll hafta make sure they don't cry, of course. Anyways, that's only our first thoughts on this. I'm sure once we dig into it, we'll have more. What if we have other ideas?

Talk to Jack, I says. If he agrees, then you do it. This is perfect, Cassie. It's jest what I meant should happen. You git the idea, you make the plan, you make it happen. All of yuz workin together. Not me tellin you to do this or that. All I do is set you off, set you thinkin in a different direction. Then you pass it on, teach the others. You become yer own leaders, d'you see? Cassie, you've changed yer life tonight. Rae as well, an Noble. One step. That's all it took an yer changin New Eden already.

Cassie's all smiles an bright eyes. We're the mountain, she says. An we're on the move. I didn't unnerstand when you explained this at the mill. I listened, but I didn't hear, not really. I had to see it fer myself. Do it fer myself. It's so simple.

Not everybody's like you, says Jack. Or even Rae, fer that matter. You gotta be careful with this.

An remember, no weapons, I says. You use violence even once, you'll be painted as the enemy.

We won't be able to keep this secret fer long, says Jack. A baby's cry carried on the wind could well be heard. Rumours here catch like a spark to dry wood. An there's always some toady wantin to gain favour with the local commander.

If Rae an Noble git informed on, says Cassie, if anybody comes to take their baby, they'll reach fer a gun. They won't let her be took without a fight.

That means we gotta move quick on every front, I says. Before there's a chance of word gittin out.

Before the blood moon, it seems. You keep askin when it is, says Jack. Why then?

Be careful. Be very careful.

Five nights ain't too far, ain't too near, I says. Probly jest about as long as we can keep this quiet. So we really gotta push. Move fast. The baby stuff's all up to you now. I'm steppin back unless you wanna bring me in fer somethin. It's slaves next fer you, Jack. I need you to play the Tonton commander an slip Skeet into a few slave gangs. A mornin here, a afternoon there. Quick, in an out. DeMalo ain't got no support with the slaves.

Some of 'em used to be his Chosen ones, says Jack. They might think to git back in favour by turnin informer. Skeet'll hafta be careful who he talks to.

I says, The main thing is, they need to be ready to move when they git the call.

Call to what? he says. Throw off their chains?

That's right, I says.

Okay, how? he says. When?

I'm workin on that.

You better work fast.

They need to stand tall, I says. Look the Tonton straight in the eye. Make polite, do what they say, don't give 'em no cause to come down hard. But look 'em straight in the eye. Man to man, woman to man. You act low, you believe yer low, an they do too.

High-minded words, he says. I'll pass 'em on.

Cassie says, I better git home before Hunter comes to. She looks at me. A smile warms her. What we done tonight, it's powerful. A kinda power I could never of imagined. Bram would be amazed. He'd be very pleased.

I'm choked. She didn't hafta throw me such a bone. She's a far kinder soul than I'd be in her place. This time she holds out her hand to me. I take it. Then she hugs me. Thank you, she says.

As she goes to mount up, Jack says, G'night, Saba. I'll let you know how it goes.

Like I'm anybody. Like my kiss didn't tell him, like my body didn't tell him, like we don't both know that I jest said to him, be with me Jack, burn with me till the dawnrise. His face is storm shuttered. This ain't how we are, him an me. It ain't how he is. Frantic hands rummage words on my lips. Quick, find the right one to make it okay. Remember, though, Cassie's in earshot.

Well done fer tonight, he says.

Please, say somethin else, please, Jack. No, no, of course, no, he cain't. Cassie's here an she don't know about us an she cain't know. But a look, he could manage somethin. I could manage some little thing.

Don't go, I whisper.

But he's already on Kell's back an they're already turnin their horses an then they're headin out along the field an I'm

201

standin in the yard an watchin them go. Cassie, back to her man who ain't Bram an her secret life that keeps her soul alive. Jack, to ride away from me when he shouldn't. Could I be readin this wrong? Readin too much into it? Nobody can be fine all the time.

Then I remember. The look on his face, in his eyes, as we listened to the Tonton with the baby. We all got wounds that will never heal. Jack's dead child is one of his. It must go deep. An it's bin pressed on hard this night. Maybe he jest needs to be alone fer a while. I gotta stop thinkin that everythin's always about me. I know full well that it ain't.

I know another thing, too. Whatever else I hafta own to, or cook a story to cover, Jack cain't never find out about me an DeMalo. I could never explain it. Never make him unnerstand. Some things are jest too big to fergive.

As I'm nearin home ground, with my eyelids at half-mast, I realize we didn't arrange our next meet. I need Jack, want him with me on the Edenhome recce.

I whistle Nero down an bring Hermes to a halt while I dig in the worn leather bag around my waist. I find the cherrybark roll that I'm after. A stick child in a square with a moon above. Meet me at Edenhome tonight. A arrow drives through the middle. That means be ready fer action.

Nero flaplands on my head. I pick him off an tie the roll to his leg. Find Jack, I tell him. Then I throw him back into the air. He banks north an with a caw caw of farewell, he beats strong an steady towards Jack.

I do need him on this recce. But – selfish as always – every time I see him, it's another chance to try agin. To try an git things right fer once.

An I'm in urgent need of somebody else too. I need Auriel. Auriel Tai. I need her an the best of her Snake River refugees. We need bodies in New Eden. We gotta rumble every last one of these fault lines. An fast.

The blood moon's comin at us quick.

I ride through the gate of Starlight Lanes as the first shades of dawn light the eastern sky. Slim's on watch in his slingchair. Though that heroic item is completely lost in his bulkitude of flesh an blue frock. As he struggles to his feet, it comes with him, attached to his backside. Lugh says one time it'll disappear up Slim's rear exhaust an bagsy he ain't gonna be the one goes after it.

Damn thing, he says. I swear it's shrinkin. He wriggles loose with grunts an curses. That knave, Bobby French, he's went an sold me a pup agin. A man pops wind when you handshake the deal, that tells you he's nervous. I should of asked myself why. How'd the politeness offensive go?

He ambles over to hold Hermes' head while I swing myself down. As my boots hit the ground I stumble. More tired than I know. Numbed by it all.

Whoa there! Slim catches my arm. Where's Miz Mercy got to?

I says, She stayed to help a Steward couple settle in with their baby.

His whiskery face cracks a wide grin. Hark at you, so casual! He grabs me in a one-armed hug. So, you bin baby stealin! Ha ha! He cackles with delight.

Finders keepers, I says. Somebody threw it out.

Ain't you the cool one, he says. An don't the bunny always come through? He waggles the manky old rabbit's foot at me. That'll teach you to mock, he says. I bin rubbin this old fella bare to send you luck. I wanna hear it all, soup to nuts, but later'll do. Go bag some zees. You earned yer beauty sleep tonight. He bows his head, with a fancy swirl of his hand. I shall attend to yer mount, oh great one, though I be but a mere humble vessel. Okay if I tell everybody mission accomplished?

When they wake, I says, that'll be soon enough. I need to see Ash, though, right away. Would you tell her I'll be in the grove? I head towards the forest garden an washpond. Oh! I talk to him as I walk backwards. Anythin to report?

Jest a heads up, he says. Creed's pressin me hard to show him the weapons dump at Nass Camp. He wants to know ezzackly how much firepower we got. That boy's brewin trouble. Best give him somethin dangerous to do right away.

Thanks, I'll think of somethin, I says.

You done good tonight, Angel, he says. Keep on provin me wrong. Who knows? I might even find I like bein a peacenik.

We smile at each other. I wobble as my heel hits a rock.

Oi! Look where yer goin, he says. With a salute, he trundles off with Hermes.

I duck inside the shed where I left my gear. I grab my bow an head fer the grove.

I zing the shots. Fast as I can. No time to think. Snatch, nock, pull, let fly. I scatter the target. Arrow by arrow. I'm tired. Off centre. Wobbly.

Lugh put up this big moss bullseye fer Emmi to practise. Tucked it outta sight in Peg's nuttery, hopin to spare her from all the Dutch uncles. But everybody swarmed on it, anxious to keep target trim. An any time Em twitched a finger she'd git don't-do-that-do-this, no, don't-do-this-do-that till she quit the grove in protest. Now she shoots at wormy apples in peace.

Oh, the relief of my bow in my hands. The rightness of my whiteoak bow. It cleaves to me like my own flesh. The gift of a dead man, Namid the Star Dancer. Warrior an shaman. Auriel's grandsire who lives in my dreams.

Arrow by arrow, I steady. Shot by shot, I move closer to the heart. I pull my self in. Shoot my self back to true. My hands, my eye, my body, my mind. Then, I'm on it. Hittin it. Time after time.

An everythin but the centre falls away. An it's simple. Perfect. No quarrel, no quibble, no trade-offs. No coldness in Jack. No lie upon lie that might betray me.

Hands start clappin. Behind me. I jerk at the sound an my arrow flies wide.

It's Ash. She stands there, clappin me, knee deep in a thick mornin ground mist. There's a smile on her lips, in her eyes. She's tall an solid an steady an familiar an I'm suddenly exhausted. Jest like that. My bow goes limp in my hands.

She comes up an hugs me. Tightly. Strongly. I lean aginst her. My throat tightens. Weak tears threaten salt trails. She steps back to give me a good lookin over.

The Angel has triumphed, she says. First time I ever bin woke by them words. Well. I'm proud of you. An so would Maev be. She told me to hang in with you, you know that? Mark my words, Ash. If anybody's gonna carve a new path, it'll be that one. If yer smart, you'll stick with her. That's what she said. She was right.

She thumbs my eyes dry with clumsy tenderness.

It worked, I says. I think this could really work. Was it hard, though, Ash. Much harder'n fightin. I had no idea.

You sent fer me, she says. I'm here an I'm ready. What's the job?

I didn't notice before. She's dressed fer the road. She's brought her pack.

I says, I need you to ride faster'n you ever rode before. I need you to—

Saba! Saba! Come quick! Emmi flies towards us, flappin in high excitement. It's Lugh an Creed! They're gonna kill each other! Hurry!

With a clatter of curses, Ash pelts off. An I'm right behind her.

It's a dustup at dawn. A two-dog fight in the junkyard. We hear the rumpus well before we reach them. Everybody yellin, Tracker barkin, Moses bellowin. Then the bangabout thundercrash of metal. They're brawlin on a junkpile.

Strugglin an tusslin. Throwin punches that mainly miss. Creed's split Lugh's lip. Lugh's blooded Creed's nose.

Make 'em stop! cries Emmi. Lugh! Look out!

Creed's grabbed him by the waist an hauls him down. Metal an iron. Slabs an sheets. Beams an girders. Edges to cut. Blocks to break bones. Stupidity times a million.

Ash yells, Gawdamn eejits! Git offa that pile!

Slim's in there shoutin at 'em an Tommo's tryin to grab a arm or leg to separate 'em, but it's too wild fer their safety an they beat a retreat.

What the hell's goin on? What set 'em off? I says.

Who knows? Slim mops his head with a kercheef. I'm in the stables, next thing I know, it's a brouhaha. Damn, I'm too old fer this.

I was asleep, says Tommo.

Creed's the more wily fighter, the victor of many a scrap. I know fer a fact this is Lugh's first punch-up. But he's taller an heavier an he ain't a bad wrestler. He's also wearin boots. Barefoot, on a heap of metal, Creed's on a hidin to nuthin. He must know it, but he's fightin like he means to win. They're breathin hard. Hot-eyed with fury.

Molly's yellin, Creed! I ain't gonna stitch you agin! Stop it! Lugh! Dammit, you two, stop this right now! Her colour's hectic. Her mushroom pail stands beside her. Another early mornin walk in the woods, it seems.

Any time now, there's gonna be blood, says Slim. One of 'em'll crack their head wide open. You better wade in there an break it up, Angel.

I'm already pilin in fast, shoutin, All right, that's it! That's enough!

Tommo an Ash help an between the three of us, we somehow haul 'em off the junkpile. Worked up past thought, Creed rushes me. I sidestep, hook his foot an he's down. He slams on his front an lays there, winded.

I says, Right, who started this? Lugh?

No reply. He won't look at me. Won't look at nobody. He wipes his bloody mouth with his sleeve, his breath comin harsh, his chest heavin. He's a fought-to-a-standoff mess. Shirt ripped. Britches torn. Scraped, bruised an drippin with sweat.

Creed's the same. Tracker's lickin his face, whinin. With a groan, Creed pushes him away. He rolls onto his back. Tommo helps him to his feet. He leans over, hands on knees, shakin his head. It's a wonder he didn't split his stitched shoulder wide open.

Creed, I says. You tell me, if Lugh won't. What's this about? Who started it?

He scowls as he dabs at his nose with his filthy shirt tail. Sullen silence from him too.

Fine, I says. I ain't got time to waste on you two. It's a draw. Shake hands an that's it.

They don't move. Gawdammit, I yell, be a man an shake hands!

They do. One quick shake, not lookin at each other.

Creed, I says, yer headin out with Ash. Git yerself cleaned up an ready fer the road.

He jabs his finger at me. Hotly angry. I do not do what you tell me to, he says.

I'm askin, I says. Please.

Why doncha send yer dear brother? he says.

I want you with Ash on this. She's gonna need yer help, okay?

C'mon, man, says Ash. Don't be a bigger ass than you already are. She claps him on the shoulder as she passes. See you at the stables, she says to me. We'll wait there fer orders.

Creed hesitates. His glance flicks between me an Lugh. Tryin to decide if he's lost face or not.

C'mon, Creed, I says. Please an thank you. With a curse, he heads after Ash.

I grab Lugh by the shirt an drag him outta earshot. He nurses his fist. He avoids my eyes.

That was a disgrace, I says. You put us at odds with each other, we're gonna lose this fight. An we won't walk away with a bloody nose, it'll be our heads on spikes. So think on that an whatever itch you woke with this mornin, consider it scratched.

He nods. I'm sorry, he says. I—

That's it, move on, I says. I turn to go.

Saba, he says.

I look back at him.

I need somethin to do, he says. I'm kickin my heels here, goin crazy ever since the bridge. Please. Lemme make it up to you. Gimme somethin to do.

I cain't hardly think, I'm so tired. I cain't remember when I slept last. I bin on the go the whole night. Then all this trouble an now, here's Lugh, askin me fer orders.

C'mon Saba, he says.

Okay. I got a recce tonight. Come with me, I says.

He goes off with Emmi to clean up an mend his wounds. Molly an Slim's already disappeared. There's only Peg an me left. I don't s'pose you know who started it, I says.

Who started, what's this, why oh why do bucks fight? Peg cackles an winks at me. She's bin hunkered down on a fender all this time. Parin her knobbly claws with a knife an watchin the fight like it's some travellin show. Whoops! I bin lookin fer that! She dives at the crashed junkpile, seizes a rusty crank an scampers off to her workshop.

Why do bucks fight. Why oh why, indeed.

I'm at the stables with Ash an Creed. Havin scared up provisions enough to keep 'em goin a few days, I fill their waterskins an help load their gear. While I do, I tell 'em the route to the Snake River. By way of the Yann Gap an the Wraithway an what they should tell Auriel about what we're doin here. You probly won't need to, I says. She's a star reader, she knows everythin. I want sixty of her people, the strongest an best she's got. Bring 'em to Nass Camp. You know where that is?

Slim told me, says Creed.

You two gotta go like the wind, I says. You cain't stop fer nuthin.

Fergit the wind, we're lightnin, says Ash. Jest as soon as we clear New Eden. Whaddya figger … four days all told? Us to the Snake an hustlin sixty of them to Nass Camp?

Two, I says. No more.

She don't even blink. We'll steal fresh horses on the way, she says.

Send me word when yer crossin back over the Gap, I says. I'll ride to Nass Camp an meet you.

What if they ain't at the Snake? says Ash.

Dig me a grave with a view, I says.

She looks at me, puzzled.

Never mind, I says. A feeble joke. If you don't find 'em, come back here fast as you can.

Maybe the punch-up got rid of some steam, maybe Ash

boxed his ears, I dunno. But there's the offer of a truce in Creed's voice – if not his eyes – as he says, Slim told us what you did at the babyhouse. I still think the whole thing's crazy, I still don't think it'll work, but I bin … persuaded to give it a try.

I kicked his butt, says Ash.

That's all I ask, I says. That you give it a try.

He sticks out his hand. We shake. Let's make tracks, he says.

He goes to mount his horse, but Ash grabs him, sayin, Hey, hey, not so fast. Yer a mess, fergawdsake. Why should I hafta look at you all bloody all the way there an back agin?

His hackles rise. A snap sparks on his lips. Then he takes off his precious frock coat, hands it to her, goes to the horse trough, vaults into it, dunks hisself whole an clambers out agin on a wave of water. He takes his coat, puts it back on an swings onto his horse, drippin wet. I'm ready, Ma, he says.

Fast as you can, I tell them.

We won't let you down, says Ash. Wish us luck.

I wave them on their way. Wish all of us luck, I whisper.

All quiet on the western front? says Slim.

He's leadin Moses along. An what a sight. Poor old Moses. He's bin decked out in a jaunty bell harness an straw hat to haul Peg's junktub around her circuit. As he shakes his head to try an throw off his bonnet, the bells on his harness jingle. He moans in despair at his plight. The King of the Pillawalla Camel Race has fallen low.

Now that's jest cruel, I says.

Don't git me started, says Slim. It's a crime aginst cameldom, pure an simple. So, tell me, what was that dog fight about?

Yer guess is as good as mine, I says. They're keepin schtum.

Well, he says, my guess would be that you got these young bucks forced to be around each other day after day. We're talkin high hormonals. Maybe the wonder ain't that they fought, but that they didn't have a barney long before now.

You could be right, I says. Creed an Lugh ain't never bin what you'd call friendly. Somehow they jest don't jibe. They're always talkin at cross purposes or doin somethin that annoys the other one. I sigh. The last thing I need is this aggro.

Somebody told you bein a leader was easy? he says. Give 'em somethin to do, Angel. Keep 'em busy. We all need to play our part in this. Every single one of us is jest as committed as you, each fer our own good reasons. You gotta involve us. We gotta see this happenin fer ourselfs. In fact, I'll remind you that some of us was already up to our necks in this with Bram, well before you come along. That's right, me an Molly.

An Cassie, I know, I says.

His head goes up. Like he's caught a sudden whiff of the unexpected on the wind. Cassie? he says. You tellin me she was with you last night?

I nod.

She's a rare 'un, that girl, he says. I'm glad to know she's okay. You better go git some shuteye. You'll pardon my frankness, but you look like hell. An no sleep makes fer bad decisions. Here endeth the lesson, amen.

Amen, I says. Thanks, Slim.

We all need to play in our part in this.

Gimme somethin to do, Saba.

In the corner of the shed, with the echo of discord still hangin in the dustbeams, I make a nest in the pile of our packs an curl up, wrapped in Auriel's blood red shawl. Quiet at last in the shadowcalm, my bones sink deep, my skin slacks with fatigue as I teeter on the cliff edge of sleep. Thoughts an cares, my restless days an nights of star flurry, fall away to the greedy dark of oblivion.

In the darkness of Auriel's tent, she sits by the fire in her shawl. Her pale wolfdog eyes turn to me. We all got our parts to play in this, she says. Jack. Yer sister. Yer brother. You an me. The wolfdog an the crow. Long before you was born, Saba, a train of events was set in motion. Fer you, all roads lead to the same place.

Bunkers an seedstores an visions in hills. An fall away, fall away to darkness.

Complaints from my body start to drag me awake. It grumbles at the lumpy hardness of my bed. Stiff neck, cramped arm, my back's got somethin stickin into it. An somethin heavy pins my feet down.

The hands of a dream try to drag me back. A dream of

Peg's birds. Nero had opened the doors of their cages. I followed their skysongs, chased after them to the seedstore, where I found 'em feastin on seed from the spilled jars. DeMalo discovered us there. He made me gather all the birds an put them in the jars. Even Nero. I wept as I closed the lids on their songs. He held me in his arms until the room fell silent.

I squint through gritty eyes. The sun's moved, but daylight still shifts through the slat window above. I got no idea how long I bin out of it. My dull head tells me too long an not nearly long enough.

The heavy weight on my feet is Tracker. As I sit, I pull myself free an he scrambles up. Next thing I know, his tongue's swipin at my face. All right, that's enough, thank you. I shove him offa me. Look at this mess, I tell him.

My bed of packs has collapsed. Between me probly shovellin at 'em in my sleep an now Tracker's big feet, they're scattered about. The top pack's fallen open an some of the gear spilled out. It's Tommo's. He's th'only one among us who'd bother to fold a worn brown shirt so neat. I tuck it back inside, along with the other stuff. Empty trade bag, his flint an steel, a coil of nettlecord.

Nettlecord. My hand pauses. I stare at it a long long moment. No two cords are the same. They speak of the hand of their maker. What Ash said, what I rubbished so quick, hisses inside of me darkly.

I don't wanna think that one of our own did it, but I cain't figger how else to explain it. If it is one of us, we gotta know who. An why.

I didn't look at the tether closely. It was night-time. I ain't looked at it since. I'm probly wrong. I should check anyways. I don't want to, but I must. I need better light.

Tracker follows me as I take the coil outside. There ain't nobody around. I pull the tether from my coat pocket. I hold the two side by side. The coil an the tether. They're the same. My heartbeat trips. I compare the cut ends. They match. They fit. The same hand made both. Cold stills my skin.

A cord tells its maker as surely as palmlines tell a life. From the loose work of a child's first cord to the roughness of one made in haste. Pa taught us cords early on, me an Lugh. How to make one. How to read one.

As my heart denies it, as my head decries it, my eyes declare they know who made this cord. I've watched him make an mend many times.

Tommo. It's Tommo's cord.

I make fer the nutgrove in a numb hurry. Tracker bounds on ahead. I'm dizzy, off-kilter, fuddled. Like I git when I've drunk too much whisky. When what's real seems dreamlike an distant.

Tommo would never harm Nero. He couldn't. Apart from a rare few people, his sympathy lies with creatures. An surely so. They won't ever misuse him fer his deafness, not like his fellow humans have. He's always got a soft word, a kind hand. Fer the horses an Tracker an Nero. Fergawdsake, he even thanks the animals he has to kill fer food. Thanks 'em an calls 'em brother. But I did wound him with my duplicity. Did I wound him so bad that this is how he wounds me back?

Peg waved a cranky claw towards the grove when I asked if she'd seen Slim. Too busy loadin choice bits of scrap on her junktub to waste words on me. On my way, I do my best to calm myself, smooth myself. I don't wanna give out that there's anythin untoward. I'm wrong. It's a mistake. I must be wrong. I gotta speak to Slim first, before anythin else.

I find him helpin Em with her bow an arrow target practice. They're a gentle sight, the old man an the girl. Golden an soft in the afternoon sun. Memory kicks in me, falters me mid-stride. Of a gold moment of my own, jest like this one. Wait ... no. Not a memory of my past. It's a memory from the walls of DeMalo's white room. A old man an a girl, laughin together in a kind afternoon, in a world that was lost long ago.

Still. If I was to secretly patch my own threadbare life with this small, unwanted scrap of memory, no one would know it ain't mine. I walk towards them, sayin, Fine shootin, Emmi.

She smiles, shy but pleased. I wish Jack was here to see, she says. He always said I had good aim. I still got a long ways to go. But I got the best teacher ever. She leans her head aginst Slim's arm. He ruffs her hair with affection.

It's clear he's bin helpin her fer some time. I had no idea. An I git a heart pang that it ain't me teachin her. Well, too bad fer me. I had every chance an never bothered. I hand her the tether cord. Is this the tether from the burrow? I says.

You should know, she says. I gave it to you an you put it in yer pocket right away. Why you askin me?

Never mind why, I says. You sure this is it? Take a good look, Em.

She studies it, frownin. Well, it's dirty enough, she says.

It's bin tied around somethin. It's pretty worn. I'm sure as I can be, I guess. It was dark, y'know.

I take it back from her. Okay, I says. Git back to yer practice. Keep on like this, you'll be outshootin me in no time.

Not yet, she says. Maybe one day. She steps her feet into place with particular care an starts firin at the moss target agin. She's much stronger in her arms an wrists an chest. Jack's right. She's got a natural eye. An her aim holds remarkably true. That's a surprise in a girl made of air.

I don't hafta give Slim the nod I wanna talk to him. He knows. He falls in beside me an we move among the trees so's we're well outta earshot of Em. I unsling the coil of nettlecord from my belt. I hand it to him, along with the tether. Tell me what you see, I says.

He takes his time, compares the two. Our eyes meet an hold. I see that Nero's tether was cut from this cord. An lookin at yer face, he says, I see you know who made it.

Slim wouldn't know the work of Tommo's hand. I don't s'pose he's ever seen it close enough. An Em didn't notice, she was too excited at the time.

I do know, I says. I don't want to, but I do.

He hands both back to me. I wouldn't rush to judgement. As you well know by now, things ain't always what they appear to be, he says. What looks to be guilt could be somethin else.

Such as? I says.

He shrugs. Somebody could of borrowed the cord. Whoever's guilty could be settin the cord maker up to be the fall guy. Don't gimme that look like I'm crazy. Yer a straight arrow, Miss Death, not everybody is. In fact, you shouldn't be talkin to me about this. Fer all you know, I could be to blame.

I'll take my chances, I says. What should I do, Slim? Help me out here, please.

He ponders the hazel bough above our heads fer a moment, drawin a hand down his bristly jowls. Then he says, Okay, lemme play devil's advocate. How much does it really matter? Our feathered brother's safe an well, no harm done, an yer plate's heaped high as it is.

I says, If we got somebody among us who's done this, we need to know who an why. They might be up to all sorts behind our backs. This could be a problem, Slim. A big one.

A traitor among us. One of us. These are my only people in the world. The poison I'm talkin burns in my mouth.

I cain't see it myself but, okay, says Slim, here you go. Do one thing about it. I ain't sayin what, that's yer decision. Do that one thing, quick an easy, then leave it, see what happens. Somethin's bound to. Remember, fer every action, there's a reaction.

Right, I says.

But don't jump to no conclusions, he says, an don't go accusin nobody, no matter what it looks like at this point. Bide yer time.

We ain't got time, I says.

The words let go their hold. They drop darkly from my lips. We-ain't-got-time. They land, light-footed, an they're off. Four words runnin to the four ways. North south east west. Gone. Never to be caught.

Slim's dead still. He sniffs the air, the warm kindness of the day. Grizzled old beasts, wily in the world, scent the comin storm while the children play on. I had the idea it might be so, he says. How long we got?

The blood moon, I says. Don't ask me no more.

Blood moon, he says. That's four nights from now.

If I was you, Angel, I'd gimme somethin to do, pronto.

I sent Ash an Creed to git Auriel an bring her to Nass Camp, I says. I'm countin on her still bein at the Snake with her refugees. You probly know some of 'em.

Most of 'em, he says. Seein how I bin here all my life.

We need the strongest of 'em back here right away, I says.

Nass Camp's a good call, he says. It's well offa the beaten track.

If you an Molly could go there an make it ready, I says. Git in some supplies on the way. They'll be tired an hungry an might well need yer doctor skills.

What's the plan once you got 'em there? he says.

Accordin to DeMalo, I says, they ain't good enough to live in New Eden. Accordin to us, they are. We're gonna smuggle 'em back in. Once they're spread about New Eden, we'll have everybody we need in place. Mothers an fathers, brothers an sisters, new babies, old neighbours an friends—

Then we make a big gawdamn rumble, says Slim. Jest like you said. I take it you know how that's gonna play out.

Fear slashes through me. I grab his hand. Clutch it tight to my chest. He's warm. Solid. Wise. I look at him. Sudden tears blur my eyes.

Hey hey, he says. What's all this?

I don't know, I whisper. Slim, I dunno what comes next. That's why I need Auriel, I need her right away. She'll know what I hafta do, she'll see it in the stars. We ain't got long, an it's gotta work or—

I stop myself before I lose it completely. I let go his hand. I scrub my eyes, swipe my nose, git my breath in control.

There's such concern, such compassion in his face. He goes to hug me, but I take a step back. Oh my dear, he says. What heavy burden you bear.

Please don't be kind, I cain't take it, I says. Jest tell me I ain't made a terrible mistake. Tell me we can do this.

He takes my hand in both of his. We will do this, he says. We are doin this. It's all comin together. I got faith in you, Angel. I always have done. An I ain't no fool, all appearances to the contrary. He kisses my hand. Me an Molly better go, he says.

Hurry, Slim, please, I says.

He's already on his way to the yard. He calls over his shoulder, with a wave an a smile, We're halfways there already!

Late in the game. The endgame. I know, I know, I cain't fergit it fer a moment. The blood moon's only four nights away. Tomorrow today will be yesterday. I'm fast runnin outta tomorrows.

An there might be a traitor among us.

Me an Tracker find Tommo at the coldwater pond. We find him bathin, his back turned to us. All around him, the still water shatters the sunlight. It dances his hair blue-black. Blazes him to sleek gold smoothness. This is a day to make the heart ache. Such unbearable beauty on the skin of life.

I kneel in the grass at the pond's edge an wash him a wave through the water. As he feels it, he whirls around. His eyes go wide. He dunks hisself to the neck. Excuse me, d'you mind? he says.

He's flushed dark red to the tips of his ears. His tone's so outraged that, despite my worries, my mouth twitches to smile.

Like I ain't seen him shirtless plenty of times. Or, fer that matter, caught a glimpse of his backside more'n once. He'll of seen the same of me. After all, we bin at close quarters fer months now. But I open my hands in apology. Sorry, I says.

Whaddya want? he says.

I move my lips slowly as I speak. So's he don't miss a single word. I want you to come with me tonight, I tell him. We need to check out Edenhome.

Okay, he says. Be glad to.

I feel like a heel. The lowest of the low. To ever think of suspectin Tommo, cord in his pack or no. He's kind. Gentle. One of life's good guys. An stout-hearted loyal to a fault. All Tommo's ever wanted is to belong. He'd never do nuthin to break bonds with us. Even me, no matter that I treated him rough.

It warn't till he met Ike a few years back that he broke bonds with his natural father. The man who left his young son at their camp, tellin him not to move from that place, he'd be back soon with meat fer the pot. The father who never came back. Who must of met with some mischance that took his life. We didn't learn this from Tommo, of course. Ike told us. An that was the full of what he knew. Ike figgered Tommo led a stray's life till he found his way to the One-Eyed Man stables one winter's night. Ike found him huddled in the straw, half-starved, an from that moment Tommo belonged with Ike Twelvetrees.

Now he belongs with us.

I realize he's said somethin. Sorry, I says, I missed that.

A little smile curves his mouth. Was there ... somethin else? he says.

My face flushes hot. I bin starin at him all this time an he's half-naked. He'll git the wrong idea fer sure.

No, I says. Uh … no no, that's all. See you later.

I git to my feet an head back to the yard. Aware that he's watchin me go. If that had bin anybody else, I'd say he was flirtin with me. Albeit in a bashful, not sure of hisself kinda way. But Tommo don't flirt. He's way too serious.

An he'd never play such a mean trick. Still. I gotta use my head fer this, not jest my heart an gut. We'll go to Edenhome tonight. I'll watch how he is. Drop a few hints. See what happens.

I follow the sounds of a hammer on metal an find Peg bangin some bit of a car into shape fer a washtub. She barks at me she's busy, she's promised it to some Steward fer quick delivery. But I ask her anyways. Could she hold off ridin her junk circuit fer a day or two an stay with Emmi while the rest of us go off? I ain't hardly finished when she's gabblin, Yes yes, why didn't you ask me in the first place? Which don't make no sense, but Peg rarely does. An quick as a wink she's downed tools an rushed off to the field on top of the hill. Any excuse to mess about with that aircrate of hers.

I fill my tin from Slim's never-stop stewpot. Then I climb the ladder to Peg's ropewalk. I sit myself down, hemmed in by birdcages, an look out over the Lanes. I'm dog-hungry. I shovel it down. But fer all my hunger, I'm done with it after a few bites. My belly's too jittered to eat.

I know not everythin is about me. But, when you git right down to it, I'm a uneasy sun fer anybody to be circlin. Particularly them I depend on most. Creed. Ash. Tommo.

Molly. Mercy. Slim. Even Emmi an Lugh. Somehow or other, my actions have scorched the souls of every last one of 'em. So far, I've jest about managed to keep 'em with me. But maybe not fer much longer.

Tommo an some nettlecord twine.

Don't rush to judgement. Things ain't always what they appear to be. Somebody could of borrowed the cord. Whoever's guilty could be settin the cord maker up to be the fall guy.

Who'd set Tommo up fer the fall guy? Who's bin hostile to me all along? Who'd love to see me fail? Who thinks we'd all be better off if he was in charge?

Be who we need or stand aside.

Creed is who. An, after all, it was Creed I sent in search of Nero. Creed who claimed he couldn't find him, even though a few minutes later Emmi found him in the burrow. Creed could of easily planned it an used Tommo's cord without his knowledge. An that look he gave me afterwards. Jest a flash an then gone. Like he was holdin a knife to my throat.

Who do I know least of everybody? Creed. Who would I trust least? Creed. Who does Nero go to least? Creed, Creed, Creed.

My thoughts turn an twist. I poke a bit of biscuitroot through the bars of the cage next to me. The little wallafinch prisoner flits about, chirpin.

If Peg's birds feel dismay at their jail-cell life, you'd never know. They sing jest the same. I got a strong desire to set 'em free, like in my dream. But Peg would boot us from the Lanes an that 'ud be our sanctuary lost. The finch don't want the food. I lift the latch an open the door. One bird. I'll chance the flack.

Off you go, I tell it. She'll never notice.

It hops to the door, then away agin, then back. Its head cocks this way an that. Its bright black eyes consider the new possibility in front of it.

Go on, I says. I'm doin you a favour. Do it. Go.

With a chirp it's off on quicksilver wings. To blaze out its fire of a life. A bird knows what to do with freedom. It's born knowin. I watch till it's gone from sight. Then I stand up an throw its metal prison. Fling it to the air with all the strength of all my hate fer cages. I watch as it tumbles, end over end, to land smash on the nearest junkheap.

One bird. One cage. It ain't nowhere near enough. But it's somethin. It's somethin.

Night Four

I set Emmi to work cleanin an oilin our weapons. It ain't necessary. We keep our gear in good nick. It's jest what you do. What everybody does, unless you got yer attic to let. But, keepin in mind what Slim said, it's good fer Em to feel useful somehow. She sure cain't be trusted with no more than this. I tell her to count our stock, oil the shooters, try makin a few new arrows if need be. I don't intend us to hafta use none of it, but better to be ready than not.

I leave her settlin into her task with good cheer. Peg keeps her company, warmin her gnarled root toes by the stove an puffin on a long clay pipe. Tracker's mad keen to come with us, but he's the best patrol fer the Lanes while we're all away. Slim an Molly made a quick start to Nass Camp.

As night begins to gather, me an Lugh an Tommo prepare to ride fer Edenhome.

I'm convinced now that Creed's to blame fer that trick with Nero. He was angry at me fer the mess at the bridge. Wanted to shake everybody's confidence in me jest that bit more. Look, she runs a sloppy ship, she let her sister off guard duty an the Tonton got that close to us we could of all bin dead. She ain't no leader. I am.

It all makes sense. It all fits. But I'll test Tommo. Jest once, jest a little. So I can say I did if Slim asks. Do one thing an see what happens. Action. Reaction.

I pretend I've mislaid my cord. I ask Tommo to borrow his. He hands it over with a smile. The very coil that a piece was cut from to tether Nero. I put it back in his pack right away. Tommo cain't ever hide how he feels. His big dark eyes always tell all. As he hands me the cord, they tell me that he's honest an true. That he ain't got nuthin to hide. Tommo didn't do it.

Creed did.

We ain't gone more'n a league from Starlight Lanes when a caw caw cracks the dusktide. It's Nero. He's a wide-winged blackness, coastin down towards me. My heart drops to my boots. I completely fergot. I sent him with a message fer Jack to meet me tonight. I bin frettin an thinkin about who might of tethered him an never gave a thought to my crow hisself. There's bin so much gone on, with the fights an all, an I'm so used to him bein around but not always seein him that he went right outta my mind. He's bin gone fer ages.

He surfs in to land on my shoulder an I hustle him into my arms. I quickly slip the bark roll from his leg. Shove it in my shirt without lookin. No need. Jack's returned the roll I sent him, but tied to Nero's left leg. That means he'll be there. At Edenhome.

My stupid stupid head. I don't believe it. I got Lugh an Tommo with me an Jack's gonna show too. The three of 'em. Together. With me. At Edenhome. No way, no no no. They mustn't find out about Jack. Slim was right. I was too tired. I must still be. No sleep means I make mistakes. Bad mistakes.

I'd stop right now an send the boys back if it wouldn't make 'em suspicious an cause ructions. What to do, what to do, what the hell am I gonna do?

Brazen it out. That's what. Or, as Jack would say, I hafta wing it.

Emmi had to move quickly. If she didn't hurry, the songs of their passing would fade and she'd lose them. She was going after them. She didn't have a plan, not yet. But she would.

So far, she'd been nothing but a trouble and a let down. A child when they needed a warrior. More than anything, she wanted to be worthy of being Saba's sister. She needed to honour the sacrifices of Pa and Maev and Epona. And Ike and Bram and Jack. Auriel's grandfather, Namid the Stardancer, was a warrior and a shaman. That's what she wanted to be.

Warriors proved themselves in the fight. She had everything to prove. She'd been working with her bow till she couldn't lift her arms for tiredness. Between that and the earthsongs to ground her feet, she was on her way to becoming a good archer. But Saba said they weren't fighting with weapons any more. They were fighting with cool heads. Thinking, then planning, then taking action. There had to be something she could do that nobody else could. That would allow her to stand tall among them, the living and the dead.

She and Peg were cosy sitting next to the stove, with the stack of shooters to be oiled and all else Saba asked her to do. Enough work to keep them busy into the great beyond, said Peg. We'll have a song, a song to sing us along.

She wound the key of the magical music cage. They watched and listened as the tiny finch sang. Then she told Peg she couldn't keep the cage. With a shrug, Peg gave her back what Tommo had traded for it. He'd be hurt, but not surprised. They'd argued back and forth since the night of her party. He knew what she thought and she was right. He couldn't give away something so precious. He'd thank her for it one day.

She started yawning. Not too much, just enough. Peg soon said, nighty night little bird. The old gal was yawning herself. With any luck, she'd doze off. She surprised her with a goodnight hug.

She went to the boys' sleepshed and left Tommo's bracelet inside his pack. On top of his things where he'd be sure to find it. He'd kept it hidden away for too long, like his memories. He should wear it. If you bring a hurt into the light, in time the light will fade it some.

Then she hurried to the girls' shed. She'd made her scanty arrangements earlier. As soon as she heard that Lugh and Tommo would be going with Saba to Edenhome. She didn't think Peg would check on her, but still. In the shadows, the blanket over her pack would pass for a girl curled up asleep. She'd packed the pockets of her coat with the necessaries, nothing more. Flint and steel, red gizmo knife, her birthday comb from Molly and a lump of nettlecake. She grabbed it and ran to the stables.

She'd be in serious trouble when they found she was gone. So she'd have to prove herself big. She couldn't fail.

Tracker stuck to her. He could smell adventure. He wanted desperately to come. But with everybody gone, he had to stay and be watchdog for the Lanes.

She woke Bean. She slipped a rope bridle on him and they rode through the sleeping junkyard. She moved quietly now, thanks to the songs. They sang her along the silent ways. Tracker saw them off, quivering nose to tail tip with desire.

Once she was outside the gates, she paused for a moment to listen. The ground still hummed of their passing. Good. They'd left a clear trail for her to follow. With sure hands, she guided Bean along it.

She was learning from the songs – earthsongs and stonesongs – spending her days with them, listening and studying, but there was so much she didn't understand. She needed to find her teacher. With all the messages she'd been sending Auriel, surely, surely she'd come soon. She was the only one who could help her.

The first starfall of the night caught her eye. Burning bright, some starsoul racing back to earth on urgent business. Or maybe, just maybe, it was Auriel. She could be travelling to her the quickest way possible. Hitching a ride on a shooting star. Streaking across the sky to land in New Eden in a perfect dazzlement of light.

No one could stop a shooting star. No one. Not even the Pathfinder or the Tonton.

We leave the horses in a mossy dell an move in on Edenhome by foot. As we softpad through the trees, my whole body's tuned fer any whisper of Jack. The skin an the blood an the bones of me listen. To the creak of a branch. The pass of a breeze. The sigh of the ground unnerfoot. Is he nearby? Is the heartstone slightly warm? No, jest wishful thinkin.

All the way here, I kept two bark rolls curled in my fist. In the hope that I might git the chance to send Nero with 'em. One of the rolls we ain't never used before. All it's got scratched on it is X. Which means we gotta axe our meetin. The other tells him to meet me at noon at High River Gorge in Sector Six. It's our closest meet spot to Starlight Lanes. A V with waves in the bottom. A small square box perched at the top of the V's right leg. Full sun directly overhead. But

Nero never touched down. He kept to the sky. I couldn't call him to me without suspicion.

I'm desperate to find out how Jack's gang is doin. To hear that everythin's rollin out fast like it needs to. It ain't that I don't trust him to hold the line. He will. He'll do the right thing, he won't blow no chances. So I do trust him an I believe, truly, that this is the only way we can possibly win, but...

But. This whole thing sits uneasy in my nature. So little in my control. So much to go wrong. So much to lose. An not usin bows or guns. The fact is, we live in a sticks an stones world. It's the only way that any of us knows. I fear that if we come unner pressure, somebody's gonna pull a trigger an that'll be it. Endgame over.

Nero plays the night sky above the treetops. He lofts an banks an scoops the chill winds, always circlin back to keep track of us.

Saba! hisses Lugh.

We bin halted by a fierce corral of barbwire. It hems in the grounds an buildins of Edenhome. A high, weak fence. The worst kind. Impossible to climb, even if you padded yer hands to the barbs. Only way through would be to cut our way.

Lugh's scopin the place with the long-looker. Guards, he mouths, an holds up two fingers. In a moment, two Tonton come into view. They approach from opposite directions. Must be on a loop patrol. They each got a armoured boarhound strainin on a short chain leash. They pass each other with a nod an continue around. Me an the boys look at each other. Their eyes a white gleam in their night faces. There ain't no gittin in here. Fence, guards, an dogs bred to kill with snap-trap jaws. We're stuck on this side.

Follow the fence along, I says. Check it out. Meet back here. Don't let them hounds catch wind of you.

Lugh splits right into leafy darkness an Tommo sifts away to the left. I prowl along the centre bit, back an forth, takin in the lie of the main buildins, the sheds, workshops, little barns an so on. It's tidy an clean an well-kept. The kids livin here – every single one of 'em stolen from their families – they're set to be Stewards of the Earth at fourteen. This is where they learn to not remember who they come from. Where they learn to believe their only family is the Earth, that the Pathfinder has chosen them to heal her. Where the stream of who they are is stemmed to carve another channel. An who they were dies to a trickle, then dries to dust.

Here, they're learned the kinda things Pa learned us. How to build an mend an cobble together, how to plant an tend an grow. An all the other day-to-day you need to know to git along. There's a junkbarn half built. The silent gleam of a duckpond. Patches of ground set aside fer crops. I wonder if they're usin any seed from the seedstore or if DeMalo's savin it all fer the tide of numbers on his great maps. Pushin outwards from New Eden to beyond an then beyond. They oughta be usin these woods fer a forest garden, but they'd never be able to keep tabs on the kids. Blink an they'd be lost to the shadows.

Gawdammit, Jack, where are you? My skin bristles, waitin fer the sound of a nightpip. If he came now, right now, I could hotfoot it, have a word with him an be back before the boys pitch up.

I tuck myself tight behind a tree an stare through the fence at the quiet dark of Edenhome. That woman from the Snake River camp. Her name's gone from me. The one half-mad with grief, who wouldn't give the body of her dead child

232

to be burnt. Her older girl, Nell, the ten-year-old stolen by the Tonton, she might be asleep inside one of these huts. I remember sayin to the woman, to Ruth – that's her name – I told her that wherever Nell was, she was bound to be watchin an thinkin an plannin how to git away. How to git back to her family. An she wouldn't give up till she did. I hope I was right.

C'mon, Jack, c'mon, c'mon. Where are you?

Suddenly, I smell DeMalo. I look panic about me, breath trapped, heart caught. Where is he? Where? I flatten myself deep to the tree, not breathin. Then I'm cursin myself fer ten kinds of fool. I'm only huddled aginst a juniper. That's the scent of DeMalo's shirt, his skin. I found sprigs of it in the chest where he keeps his clothes. I crush a needly twig. The cool dark smell fills me. But no warmth of his body to soften its bite.

The boys steal back. Lugh first, then Tommo. Still no Jack an we cain't do nuthin more here tonight. How we git these kids outta Edenhome is gonna be a harder nut to crack than stealin babies or slippin Skeet into a slave gang. The setup here, with the fence an the dogs an the guards, it gives us a whole different problem to solve. An not much time to do it. We'll need to come back in the daylight.

Fer now, we need to go. The chill wind's bin blowin in our favour all night but now it's restless, twitchy, on the change. I don't fancy our chances with them boarhounds if they catch our smell. We turn around an start to head back to the horses. Once we're at the Lanes, we'll talk it through. Lugh's good at unpickin complicated situations.

Nero's bin flyin guard duty above the woods all this time. He suddenly dives. Disappears into the trees. A few moments later, a bird calls. It's the krik of a nightpip. My heart jumps.

Jack. At last. Lugh ticks his head towards the sound. It comes from forty or so foot to the left of us. The heartstone's faintly warm. I sign to Tommo that it's only a bird, an we carry on. A nightpip callin in the dark ain't nuthin untowards. Nuthin to give rise to second thoughts.

Jack calls twice more. Nero caws an makes a fuss. Good. It sounds like he's tryin to flush out a smaller bird to make a meal of it. Agin, no cause fer suspicion. So. Jack sees Nero, he knows I'm here, but I ain't sendin no answer. By now, he'll know fer sure somethin's up. I hope he don't think I'm in trouble an come in search of me. Can I ditch the boys? I only need a few minutes. Jest long enough to find him an set another meet.

Nero lands on a branch by my head. A bark roll's tied to his right leg. I catch Lugh's notice with a click of my tongue. As he glances back, so does Tommo. I kneel an gesture that my boot's come undone. That they should go on, I'll be jest a moment.

I wait till they're outta sight. Then I seize Nero an check out Jack's message. He's sent two rolls. One with X to abort this meet. The other says to meet him at Deepwell Tower. That's our nearest meet spot to here. Not far, jest beyond two leagues northeast. An he's marked it as urgent. Urgent. He's never done that before. My heart stumbles over all the possible urgencies as I quickly retie both rolls to Nero's left leg. That's my reply. Unnerstood. I'll be there as soon as I can. Then I throw him in the air an he flaps off to deliver it.

I pull the unused bark rolls from my pocket an tuck 'em into my little leather bag. I won't be needin 'em now. I could of spared my poor nerves all this frazzle. I should know better than to fear that Jack might reveal hisself to the boys by mistake. He's far too canny a fish to go blunderin into a net.

He'd been waiting and watching since the day at the bridge. Hoping she'd make a mistake. But through all her shadowy travels, her comings and goings, and the secrets that hollowed her night by night, she hadn't made a slip, not one. Until today. When Nero showed up just after they'd left the Lanes, she gave a little start of surprise. Barely noticeable. But he felt a tug on his line. She took Nero in her arms, held him close for a moment, then let him go. Nothing unusual there. Apart from a one-handed fumble. She was quick about it. Most people wouldn't have noticed. But he did, waiting and watching as he was.

In the woods, she was edgy. Tension tightened her, crackled all around her. Then the sudden flurry in the trees with the birds. Then the stopping to tie her boot, telling them not to wait, just as Nero landed on a branch above her.

The blood roared in his head. She was up to something. Was Jack here? He had to find out. Time was short. He might never get another chance. As they headed back to their horses in the mossy dell, he cracked a few twigs to mark the way.

They'd mounted up, were just about to move out.

He jumped down, checking the ground all around, his pockets, his bag. Oh no, it must have fallen. He thought he knew where. He had to find it, couldn't leave it, he wouldn't be a moment.

He hurried back the way they'd just come.

He moved quickly, quietly, following the trail he'd marked. To the spruce where she'd knelt to tie her boot. Easy to spy its twisted stunt among the other, straighter trees, its paleness in the darkness. He didn't know what he was looking for. He didn't expect to find a thing. But he couldn't leave without checking the spot. Just in case. On the off chance that she'd left a clue. Anything. That she'd made a slip, a mistake.

He crouched low. He dared to light a pocket spill. Dangerous. But just for a moment, just long enough to play it over the ground where she'd been. Just in case. On the off chance. And there it was. A curl of cherry bark. Gleaming on the dark of the woodland floor. There weren't any cherry in this wood.

She had. She'd made a mistake.

As his heart drummed a warning of new darkness, his fingers unrolled the barkscroll. It had markings on it. A deep V. A small square. A full sun. He'd suspected. Now he had the proof. They were using Nero as a go-between. That little leather bag she'd started wearing at her waist, the one she never took off. It was perfect for carrying a stash of messages.

He doused the spill. He tucked the scroll deep inside his pocket. Carefully deeply safely in his pocket. As he stood up, a sweat of fear seized him. Weakened him. He leaned on a tree till it passed.

Then he hurried back to rejoin them. He'd study the message later. He'd figure out how their code worked, what it meant. Then he'd use it against Jack. And his deal for the future would be done.

From the top of a grandmother fir, Emmi watched them to-ing and fro-ing. She'd slung her boots around her neck and cat-climbed to the highest boughs to get a view. Reading its rough skin with her bare feet, like Creed would.

Nero found her right away, but she shooed him off. When he started dipping in and out of the trees, she inched even higher to find out why. She clapped her hands to her mouth. Her shout would have shattered the sky. His name leapt from her as he raised his head and the moon snatched the silver from his eyes. Jack! Not dead at all, but in New Eden. He must have been helping them in secret all this time. Probably nobody knew but Saba. She wouldn't breathe a word. With him on their side, they were bound to win. Jack always made everything okay. Oh, to be able to rush to him, to hug him. She hugged herself. Tears heated her eyes and fierce joy ached her heart. Just to know he was alive, that was enough.

And she knew this too. This was the place of the something. The something she could do that no one else could. That would let her stand tall among the living and the dead. She'd find out what it was in the morning. She'd work it out. Then she'd do it.

After they'd all gone off, she pulled her coat tight around and snugged into her sweet bough cradle. Nighty night, little bird. She whispered goodnight to her mother and father. The two bright stars above the Hunter's sword. Side by side, they'd shine guard on her till morning. Then she let herself sink to the nightsongs of the wood. The root-tangled, deep brown murmurs of long memory. They hummed her eyes shut and wove her to sleep and sang her through to the dawn.

We're nearly across the Slabway. A flat plain of granite open to the sky. Our horses begin to whinny an shy. Nero dives at us, screamin. A sting pricks my face. Then another. A saltsleet's about to hit us.

We're on the ground. It's a drill we know well. Grab the stormsheet, shake open an throw. Cover the horse, nose to tail, cords through the loops, pull an tighten. Nero, c'mon! He flies to my arms an we duck unnerneath. I grab the bridle. Hang on, I gotcha, I tell Hermes. I bury my face in his neck. An brace myself fer the hit.

A saltsleet comes with short warnin. It slams us with a shriek from the belly of hell. The world explodes all around. It's the bone of fury, the white eye of rage. A screamin madness of winds that whip. They batter the stormie. Snatch an savage it. In no time at all, we're soaked. Despite our covers, wet through. My clothes hang heavy, clagged with salt. Hermes quivers. I rub his neck with my cheek to soothe him, soothe myself. Nero trembles aginst my heart.

A saltsleet never lasts long. It's over in minutes. Gone as quick as it came. We creep out, white-faced an breathless an amazed. Hell's left some kinda heaven behind. The sky rises clear to the moon an beyond. Stars of salt, millions upon millions, glitter the cold body of the granite. Like a carpet of tears, flung from edge to edge of the night earth. Our feet crunch as we turn an turn. As we stare an stare in silence. A warm wind brushes our skin.

Then on we go. At the Shingle Cut crossways, jest shy of

middle night, I part company with the boys. They're used to my to's an fro's at all hours, but I tell 'em I got somewhere I need to be. That I'll see 'em back at the Lanes.

We go our separate paths. Them to the west an me northeast. Deepwell Tower lies a half league from here.

She was meeting Jack. She'd gone with the hurry of a secret lover.

He only just stopped himself from going after her. His hands twitched the reins. His horse responded. He had to pretend the mare had missed her footing.

He'd follow no longer. Now he would lead. With the help of the scroll in his pocket, he'd lead Jack straight to DeMalo.

He rode on. And he thought. And he planned.

Jack an me ain't never met here before. Deepwell Tower rises lone an lonely from a rubblefield. A crumbled brick finger that points to the sky. As I draw near my stummick twists in disquiet. We parted so badly last night. With so much unsaid between us. Was it really only last night? Every day seems a lifetime right now.

Nero calls to warn of our approach. Jack's pony stands patiently by the wreck of a doorway. I leave Hermes with Kell an duck through the shattered arch into a round room. It's twelve foot by twelve, no more. Mossy brick walls circle

239

high to meet the night. To gape open-mouthed at the sky. To let the moon softly wash them with its light.

Mind yer step, says Jack.

There's a well hole in the middle of the room. Lit by the shaft of moonbeam, it yawns widely, darkly deep. He leans on the wall the other side. Lookin like hisself fer a change. His own worn-out clothes on his back, his battered old hat on his head, his down-at-heel boots on his feet.

Yer message said urgent, I says.

There's a certain stillness in a person's body. A tightness, unmistakeable, that comes from once more knowin how all our stories end. When you see that, you know somebody's dead. An Jack ain't so much as glanced at me. He stares into the blackness of the well.

Who is it? I says. My voice barely comes out.

Skeet, he says.

A brief spark of thanks. I was braced fer him to tell me it was Mercy. Skeet, I says. How?

He looked a Tonton straight in the eye, says Jack. Man to man. Standin tall an proud.

Like I told him to, I says.

They shot him, he says.

I slump aginst the wall behind me. Skeet. Dead. I git a flash of him at the mill that day. As he clasped hands with Mercy an the fearsome mask of his scarified face softened to a smile while he told her of his life that used to be. The cart with yellow wheels an a horse called Otis. Another life – his – added to my scorecard. How many is that now? I'm losin count.

It's my fault, I says.

Now, at last, Jack does look at me. His moonlight eyes caught in the moonlight. Stop blamin yerself, you do it every time, he says. Give us some credit. We all know the risks an we choose to take 'em. Skeet lived on the edge fer a long while. It's sad. He'll be missed. He was a good man an we need good people. But he eether made a mistake or jest ran outta luck. That's how it goes. We all accept it.

I shake my head.

Yes, says Jack, an if he could, I know he'd tell you it was worth it. Listen, I managed to slip him in an outta two slave gangs. He started the whisper that change is comin. That the Angel of Death is back an they should be ready to move when you send word. An about the baby thing … a couple of 'em was jest too weak, they didn't make it. But the rest though, we bin real careful an, so far, that's gone okay.

It has, I says. How many?

Seven, he says. We've took every one they left out.

It ain't enough, I says. Did you git Mercy back into the babyhouse she was at? What's happenin there?

That plan her an Cassie cooked up, says Jack. Smugglin out babies they report as stillborn? Mercy did two. That's all we figgered was safe to do in such a short time without drawin notice.

We need more, I says. We gotta roll this out fast to the other babyhouses. You gotta move her on to another one.

He starts to speak, but hesitates. Like he don't wanna say what's gotta be said.

I straighten up, the skin of my hands pricklin trouble. What? I says. What is it? I hurry around the well an take hold of his sleeve. C'mon, Jack, tell me.

My urgency wakes the old echo in the stones. Jack waits fer it to settle before he speaks.

Mercy took Skeet's place, he says.

You should of stopped her, I says.

Why? Becuz she's yer friend?

She's lame, Jack. She's weak.

She wanted to, he says. She insisted. Said now that Skeet's gone, she's the only one who can do it an she's right.

We need her fer the babyhouses, I says.

That's all in hand, he says. The midwife Mercy worked with, I've moved her to Sector Seven now. It's rollin out, like you wanted.

I lean aginst the wall. Tip my head back aginst the cold stone. I'm blind to the night sky above. All I can see is Mercy's poor back. With its shiny white shawl of whip scars. I don't want her in the slave gangs, I says.

Too bad, she's there an there she stays, he says. We're all committed to yer plan. This is what it looks like. Losses an wins an riskin our lives fer what we believe.

I know, I says. Well, I cain't say I'm surprised. I'd be more surprised if she didn't. Good thing she kept that raggy old tunic.

Speakin of raggy, what happened to you? He feels the salt-heavy wet of my coat. Yer soaked.

Oh yeah, I says. A saltsleet caught us out on the Slabway. Guess it didn't make it this far.

A shiver runs through me. I'm suddenly chilled.

C'mon, take that off. Here, have mine, he says. He shrugs from his coat an wraps it around me. It's warm from his body. It smells of him. There, that's better, he says.

Earlier… I says, at Edenhome, I — I'm sorry, it was my fault the boys was there. I was tired, not thinkin straight. It could of bin bad.

No harm done, he says.

I need yer help, I says. I cain't think how to git in there or even if we should. If you got any ideas, I could sure use 'em.

Later, he says. You do look tired.

It's this place, New Eden, I says. It's closin in on me. I feel it. Circlin me, tighter an tighter. All these trees an roots an neat patches of land an tidy parcels of sky. There ain't no long views. That's the worst of it, I think.

There's some of us set our course by the horizon, he says.

Lugh likes it here, I says. I'm quiet fer a moment. Then I says, If you could go anywhere, Jack, right now, where would you go?

Somewhere I ain't never bin, he says. I've had too much of land, I'll tell you that. Did you notice at the top of that map in the seedstore? Nuthin but a big stretch of open water. Ran right off the edges. There was a river marked. Flowed north into it. I'd find that river an follow it along till I reached that big stretch of water. Once I hit it, I'd find me a boat an jest keep on goin.

He pulls the coat collar around my neck. His reluctant hand lingers. Then it strays up my throat to wander my face. I watch him watch me as he touches me. As we stand in the pale light of moongrace. As I drown myself deep in his silverlake eyes.

Don't look at me like that, he says.

Don't touch me like that, I says.

I told you how it stands, he says.

You did, I says. I remember.

I press him to the wall, gently. I undo his shirt an smooth it away. An I bless my lips to his heart. To the red risin sun crudely inked on his flesh. His Tonton blood tattoo, that he earned servin justice on two wicked men. My lips crawl the scar road on his chest, hard won in the service of friendship. He was safely away but turned back to save Ike. Got flayed near to death by a hellwurm's claws. The tattoo, the scars,

243

they're beautiful to me. They confess the man that he is. I cain't see the wounds inside of him. So I honour the ones I can see.

His skin shudders an jumps beneath my mouth. Stop, yer gonna kill me, he whispers.

I ain't even started, I says.

I won't ask why he stays, why he touches me. What's changed in his mind since his coldness last night. I cain't risk runnin up aginst my shames, my lies. I'll jest take this fer the moment, fer the gift that it is. The heartstone burns fer him, strong an fierce. Like it did from the start. When it seared him fer always to who I am.

Our shadows move together in the starfired night. But we're gone to sunlight, him an me. We're gone to sweet grasslands beyond the horizon. To high skies an merciful days of gold. Where, fer one bright moment, I truly am what he once told me I was. Somethin good an strong an true.

We're skin to skin. Breath to breath. My sins roll away to the beat of his heart.

There's now. There's here. There's him an me.

In this broken world that's enough.

As the red line of dawn bleeds blue night into mornin, Jack halts Hermes by the blasted thorn. Here, we're a safe distance east of the Lanes. I press myself tight to his back. Kell stands quietly, tied on behind. From a birch copse nearby, a blackbird spills a full-throated welcome to the light. Somehow it knows that each dawn's a rare wonder to be praised. That's the only, only sound. A hush lies deep in the bones of the world.

We're still. To move would break this shimmer on the edge of time. I beat my heart with Jack's heart. I breathe my breath with his breath. The morn blooms slowly, silently around us.

He speaks. Softly. An behold, this day I go the way of all the earth.

We ain't said a single word from the tower to here. Like we might be able to slip past our lives unnoticed.

The woman who raised me, he says. Sometimes she sat night-watch on the dyin. That's what she'd say when she closed their eyes.

It's beautiful, I whisper. Say it agin.

An behold, this day I go the way of all the earth. This 'ud be a fine moment to go, he says.

We listen to the blackbird. The air tastes sweet, like a pineforest stream. Nero croaks from his perch on the thorn tree. A humble crow song to the sunrise. No less heartfelt fer bein so plain.

The day starts to wrap around us. Jack slides down from Hermes an unties Kell. I take off his coat an hand it to him. Our moment outta time is done.

That's the first he's made mention of his childhood. I'd like to know about the woman who raised him. Her name, if she still lives, if she was kind to him. I'd like to know what happened to his folks. He knows so much about me. I know so little of him. No matter. What difference would it make?

He lays a finger on the heartstone at my neck. He smiles his crooked quirk of a smile. The one that makes my knees weak. Surprised it ain't burned itself out, he says. So. Edenhome? Tonight?

I think so, I says. I'll send Nero.

I reach down my hand. Fer what, I dunno. A last touch, a last kiss, a last word.

He takes it in his. He bows his head to rest his lips on my palm. G'bye Saba, he says. Then he swings onto Kell an turns fer the north. An I head to the Lanes, where time awaits me.

Before first light, Emmi climbed the tall bull pine next to the fence. A garden patch stood just the other side. She hid herself deep among its branches, tucked herself close to the trunk. She'd watch and listen and learn. To find out what the something was that only she could do. Then she'd wait for her chance, for the right moment to do it.

She watched the boys and girls stream from the bunkhouses in silent single file to the long, low building. She counted at least fifty kids. All ages. The littlest looked about four. The biggest ones, twelve or thirteen. Some of the girls had chests. She'd never seen so many children together before. Every one had been snatched from their family. She knew what that felt like. She heard the clatter of spoons on eat tins. Breakfast time. She ate her nettlecake while she waited for them to finish.

Then they filed back outside and a man – not a Tonton – blew a shrill blast on a tin whistle. He shouted at them to get into their work groups. After they all did that and cried, Long life to the Pathfinder! they were soon busy with their chores. Tending beasts, climbing ladders to mend roofs, checking for eggs in the duck house by the pond, filling buckets of water at the well to wash floors, working on the half-built barn. There were black-robed Tonton moving about, but she didn't see too many of them. There were other grown-ups, too, like the man with the whistle. Working with the kids, showing them how to do things the right way.

One group headed for the garden patch below her, carrying hoes and shovels, rakes and buckets. Without a word, they set to work. Hoeing and pulling weeds. Digging the earth, turning it, raking it smooth.

After a bit, she watched one girl in particular. Studied her closely. About her age, strong and sturdy, with numbers tattooed up her arm like all the others. Fiery red hair in a long neat plait and dark eyes that kept looking, looking around her while she worked. Looking for what? Maybe her chance?

The girl paused, frowning. Her head turned towards the woods and she scanned the trees. As if she knew she was being watched. Slowly, she hoed her way right to the fence. Making sure nobody was looking, she picked a clod of couchgrass from her weed bucket and tossed it through the mesh of barbwire.

It landed with a thud beside the bull pine. In the safety of its branches, Emmi held her breath. Was this the right moment? Or a trap? She twisted off a pine cone and held it to her chest, clutched it to her hammering heart. What would the Hopetown Emmi do? That smart survivor of hard knocks and fear? She tossed it to land at the girl's feet.

The girl stared at the cone. Her eyes flicked up to the tree.

Emmi tossed down another cone.

Who's there? the girl whispered.

Me, said Emmi. My name's Emmi. I'm here to help you.

I'm Nell. The girl started hoeing again, talking quickly in a low voice. There ain't nobody lookin. They won't hear if we're quiet. I gotta git outta here, Emmi, she said. I gotta try an find my folks. Can you really help me?

I'm gonna help all of yuz, said Emmi.

247

She looked along the fence. A cage for the kids, that's what it was. High and tight and wicked barbwire to rip anybody climbing it to shreds. In Hopetown, Saba climbed the bars of the Cage to escape. She fought her way out from the inside.

That arm tattoo, said Emmi. Did it hurt when they did it?

Not so bad I couldn't stand it, said Nell.

Okay, she said. Spit on the devil an swear me yer true. That you won't say nuthin to nobody. No matter what.

Nell spat. I swear, she said. What're you gonna do?

You'll see, she said.

Emmi shinned down the pine and slipped a silent way through the trees, staying out of sight but always skirting the fence. It landed her at the road. She walked its cheerless song to the front gate of Edenhome.

There she stopped, her boots still hanging around her neck. The Tonton on guard duty was walking the fence, away from her. She grabbed the gate bars and rattled them. As he came running, shouting, with his firestick aimed, she raised her hands in the air. They were trembling a bit. Her stomach had the jitters. She was only a kid, they'd expect her to be afraid. She wasn't afraid. She was nervous. And excited.

She'd been a prisoner of the Pinches at Hopetown. A prisoner of the Tonton at Resurrection. She'd survived, become stronger and escaped, both times. She wasn't just the sister of the Angel of Death. She was a Free Hawk. A warrior for freedom and justice.

As the guard pulled the gate open, she held her clenched fist to her heart. Long life to the Pathfinder, she said.

And, just like that, she was in. She was in. She was doing the something that no one else could.

There'd be another something soon. The big gawdamn rumble. Saba had promised. She would listen and learn. She'd watch and wait. And when Saba gave the word, she'd be ready to move.

It's all strangely quiet at the Lanes. Tracker comes runnin to meet me. But not a soul answers my calls of hello. Every shed's empty. No sign of Peg. Jest her jailbirds twitterin in their cages. Lugh! I call. Emmi!

There ain't nobody down none of the alleys between the junkhills. The piles of wreckage see all the comins an goins, but they ain't inclined to say what they know.

Where've they all got to? I says to Tracker. Emmi! I yell. Lugh! Gawdammit. Lugh!

I rattle the rope of the yard bell. It yelps awake in a splash of white clatter. Nero's sailin about fer a bird's-eye view. He caw caws jest as Lugh ambles into sight, whistlin an sloshin a pail of water at his side. What's the panic? he says.

I bin callin fer ages, I says. Where is everybody?

I dunno about nobody else, he says. I was seein to the horses. You must be starved. I'm gonna cook a big pot of root mash. Hot an wholesome, jest like yers truly.

I thought you gave up yer life of crime, I says.

It don't hardly seem possible there could be a worse cook than Molly. But Lugh is it. You let him near a cookfire at yer peril. His root mash is especially vile.

Ungrateful brat. You'll eat it an thank me nicely. He grins wickedly as he pecks my cheek in passin. We can talk plans fer Edenhome, he says. I got a few ideas.

Yer cheerful, I says. Where's Em?

He walks backwards to answer. She was gone by the time I got up, he says. Must of headed out early fer one of her wanders in the woods. She'll show when she's hungry. You better go give that coat of yers a wash, git the salt out. I did mine first thing. It's a good dryin day.

Yes, Mother, I says.

Hot mash in a flash, he says. I'll ring when it's ready.

Spare me the pain, kill me now, I mutter.

He heads fer the cookhouse, almost trippin over Tracker. Any sniff of a tidbit, he's windin between the cook's legs like snakevine. A taste of Lugh's root mash oughta cure him of the habit.

Me an Nero make our way to the washpond. Halfways there, we meet Tommo comin towards us. He's on his way back to the yard, eyes fixed on the ground, hands stuffed in his pockets. Frownin like he's got a heavy load on his mind. Nero buzzes him to catch his attention. He starts when he sees me. Colour patches his cheeks. We stop, a couple steps apart.

Yer deep in thought, I says.

I bin lookin fer Em.

She won't of gone far.

After that awful night at Resurrection, Tommo made sure him an me never found ourselfs alone. He was that hurt an angry. An I was so ashamed of myself, I steered clear of him too. But this makes two days in a row that it's bin jest us on our own. An somethin's changed in him. In fact, he's bin changin ever since the bridge.

He stands his ground in front of me now. His gaze meets mine steadily. No uncertainty. No resentment.

I've owed him a real apology since that night. Fer far too long. I might not git another chance like this one. I planned an practised in my head what I would say. I take a deep breath an set off. That night at Resurrection, I says. Kissin you like I did. I knew what you'd think. That it meant I cared fer you like you cared fer me. It was selfish an mean. I can be like that. It ain't somethin I'm proud of an I'm tryin to improve my character. I would like to say that I'm sorry, Tommo. Yer a fine person. I should never of done it. I apologize most sincerely.

You told me sorry then, he says.

It was too soon, I says. The hurt was too raw. It's simmered between us all this time. I'd like if we could lay this to rest. I hate that I hurt you. That I lied to you. I care fer you.

Lemme guess, he says. Like a brother.

A dearly loved brother, I says.

I love you like a man loves a woman, he says. He jest says it. So simple. Like he carries the words in his pocket, jumbled up with a clasp knife an string an other oddments.

I didn't plan fer this. A wave of heat crawls my neck. Please, don't waste yer love on me, I says. I lied to you, Tommo, treated you wrong. You only think you love me. I'm th'only girl you know. If you met some other ones, you'd change yer mind, you would. You jest need to meet other girls.

Think what you like, he says. I know my heart.

He steps in close an before I realize his intent, his warm lips is on mine. He kisses me. A slow, tender melt of a kiss. In no way clumsy or unsure. Not like the twice he's kissed me before. If I desired him, craved him, such a kiss would slay me. As it is, it takes my breath away. Our lips part.

Jack's gone from our lives, he says. He was never good fer you. You only did what you did becuz he'd hurt you so bad. I'm constant. I ain't goin nowhere.

I'm dumb fer a moment. Then, not knowin what else to do, I stumble on with my pathetic little piece. If I could go back, I would, I says. I'd do it all different. I'm ashamed every time I think of that night.

A ghost of a smile lifts his eyes. His mouth. Are you done? he says.

Yes, I says.

Whaddya want from me, Saba? He says it patiently. Like I'm a fractious child.

I want you not to love me.

That ain't how love works, he says.

All right then, fergiveness, I says.

He shrugs. I fergive you.

Three words. I asked fer them. An they weigh me down like a drowninstone. Serves me right fer thinkin I'm so smart. That I can have everythin on my terms. It's only Tommo, that's what I thought. I'll say the right things, I'll apologize, an we'll be back to where I want us to be. Friendly an easy. But I didn't reckon with him. With him bein different, that is. This new purpose in him, this new strength. This toughness that never was there before. Tommo's eyes always looked inwards to his past. Shaded, clouded by all he that won't, or cain't, speak of. But there's a sharpness in his gaze now, a clearness.

He says, There may come a day when you look kinder on me. We won't talk of this agin. Unless you change yer mind.

The boy that he was is gone fer sure. His dignity slaps me with my own smallness. With a bow of his head, he carries on past.

I stand there, dismissed, feelin worse than I ever did. I wish I'd kept my mouth shut. I handled that so badly. *I want you not to love me.* I am a fractious child. So stupid an clumsy. When it comes to Tommo, I cain't git nuthin right.

Damn damn damn, I says softly. I don't want the burden

of his love. It weighs me down far more than my guilt ever could. I wish Molly was here. She knows about men. She'd tell me what to do.

Then Tommo hisses, Saba! an Tracker's suddenly, outta nowhere, streakin circles around me, silent with raw wolf urgency. Warnin there's some badness afoot. He races back towards the yard an from a standin start, we're runnin, me an Tommo, tearin up the trail behind him. The red hot slams in to speed my feet. Lugh. It must be Lugh. He's in trouble.

I grab Tracker's collar an we duck behind a junkpile near the cookhouse. We catch our breath. Our bodies burn the fierce heat of sudden fear.

A Tonton points a gun at a man on the ground. He lies face down, hands behind his head. Black hair, stocky build, dusted with the red of New Eden roads. There's a strange horse, travel stained, must be his. Somethin flickers in me. Do I know this guy? Two horses, shiny with polished kit. Tonton mounts. So where's the other Tonton? Then Lugh walks outta the cookhouse. He's got his hands in the air. Behind him another Tonton, proddin Lugh's back with a firestick. Two Tonton. Present an accounted fer. What the hell're they doin here?

Then the guy on the ground's bein yanked to his feet. Shock kicks my stummick. It's Manuel. The Steward I met at the mill. He must be here to see me. Somethin so important that he chanced the roads by night an broke curfew. The Tonton patrol must of spotted him an followed him here.

My eyes meet Tommo's, my hands open in panic. I ain't got no weapon. He shakes his head. Nor does he. Think, Saba, think. Any second now they're gonna be rakin up Lugh's sleeve, checkin fer a arm tattoo that ain't there. An when they don't find it, they'll shoot him, no questions.

I look around us. Junk. Nuthin but junk. Useless, worthless – I stare at the pile next to my head. No, no good, not that one neether – yes! That'll do. I take hold of a sheet of battered metal, some bit of a car I think. I signal Tommo to do likewise. They're jest big enough to give us decent cover. We hurry, hurry but make no noise as we loop bits of string into rough handholds. A shield each.

We got surprise on our side. Nuthin else.

I point Tommo to his man, the guy with Manuel. We raise our scabby shields. I count us in silently. One. Two. Three. Then we charge, shriekin wild mayhem. High pitched an crazy. I go straight fer the Tonton with Lugh. He's off balance, startled by the racket. Tracker streaks past me, leaps an bowls him over. His gun goes sailin. As he's scramblin up, I hit him at top speed. He flies backwards. I crash land on top of him, shield first. That does him. He's out.

Lugh's grabbed the gun. Help Tommo! I yell at him.

It's a messy scrum on the ground with Tommo, Manuel an the other Tonton strugglin an kickin. The Tonton clings to his gun like grim death. Then, somehow, he's scrabblin free an on his feet. His gun swings towards Manuel. Jest as I yell, Look out! Peg comes harin outta nowhere. She scuttles up behind him, swingin the yard bell by its rope. She sledges him such a body whack he goes spinnin around full circle. Then she belts him to blankness with one clonk to the head. He hits the ground like a tree.

I reach down a hand an help Manuel to stand. He's a little bit dazed an a lot outta breath.

What is it? I says.

I got a message, he gasps. Fer you. He rummages in the pouch at his waist. It was left in a safe drop, he says. One of our lot picked it up late last night.

Fer me, I says. How d'you know?

He hands me a folded piece of cloth. There's a shootin star marked on it in charcoal. That's you, he says.

The rumpus in the sky's down to me, huh?

That's the word goin round, he says.

I unfold the cloth, a torn off bit of shirttail or somethin. There's a single star an a circle with a tiny circle on top of it. I study it a moment. Then I tuck it in my pocket.

Okay, we're on the move, I says. Lugh, Tommo. Strip these two jokers an put on their gear. I need a Tonton escort. We're goin by road.

We leave Peg an Tracker to hold the fort. Wherever Em's sloped off to, she ain't gone far. All of her stuff's here. It's in a fine old mess. Tracker's pawed through it. He was after a stale bit of jerky she had stashed, but sicked it up after a few chews. She helped herself to a chunk of Peg's nettlecake, so she must plan to be gone fer most of the day. No doubt she'll be moochin about the woods, singin to herself like she has bin of late. Molly puts her oddness down to growin pains.

Manuel's still callin his grateful humble endless thanks to Peg fer savin his life as we ride through the gates of Starlight Lanes.

We dump the two Tonton along the road a ways an empty a keg of Molly's hooch over 'em. The best use ever fer the vile stuff. If they're lucky, they'll come to an run off before one of their comrades stumbles on 'em. They'd be hard pressed to explain. Where their horses an gear went, fer one. Fer another – an a damn sight more awkward – how they come to be lyin in each other's arms, wearin nuthin but lady dresses, an stinkin of rotgut drink.

I'll probly git it in the neck from Slim fer stealin two of his late mother's frocks. But from what he's told us, Big Doe was a rakehell in her day. I figger she'd approve an then some.

So we dare to ride the roads in the daylight. It's the fastest way to where we gotta go. The northwest corner of New Eden. It was Slim sent the message. The circle with the tiny circle on top. That means one of the lethal pinballs that we used to blow the Causeway an Resurrection. They come from the arms dump at Nass Camp. The single star is Auriel Tai, the star reader.

Auriel's there, at Nass Camp. If Ash an Creed found her so fast, she must of bin on the doorstep of New Eden. The question is, did she come alone? Or did she bring her people from the Snake River? An if she did bring 'em, how many?

They asked Emmi a lot of questions. Where she was born and when. Who her parents were, how they died. Things like that. She only had to lie a bit for most of those. Did she have a brother? No. A sister? No. In a little room on their own, a woman who reminded her of Mercy called her dear and looked her all over. Teeth, ears and

eyes. Hands, feet, hair and skin, strength and straightness of limbs. Her height was checked to a mark on the wall. She had to say if she'd ever had this fever, that sickness, quite a list.

Then they tattooed the numbers on her arm. It hurt. It took a long time and burned like fire and bled and hurt a lot. She didn't cry though. She wouldn't let herself. She screwed her face tight and thought about Saba. How she never cried after that first time they made her fight in the Cage. Never, no matter how much they hurt her. How she didn't cry when the hellwurm ripped her shoulder and Jack stitched it. This was nothing compared to all that. To shed even one tear would be shameful. So she didn't. Not one single tear.

Today our boldness works. Tomorrow it might not. Today the weather's set to unsettle. Uneasy nights give birth to uneasy days. The sun rises to brood darkly red. Not long after we leave the Lanes, a cold fog rolls in from the north. But the sun will not have its power denied an burns the mist red, like a thin blanket of fire.

There's a spare few rigs on the road. Otherwise, the land's silent as we roll our way northwest. Tommo an Lugh ride up front. Manuel an me follow behind. He drives a little cart of Peg's, with Hermes tied to the rear. I sit on the bench beside him, muffled in Auriel's shawl. Unner Molly's green dress, my belly billows with its pad of corn husks. We're Stewards of the Earth. Our Tonton escort of two's bin charged by the Pathfinder hisself with makin sure we git back home as soon as possible. I'm a precious cargo, pregnant with the first set of twins in New Eden. Nobody'll dare to ruffle us.

A sudden thought has me grabbin Manuel's arm. Don't say a word about Jack, I whisper. Not to nobody, okay? It's important.

He slants me a look of dark-eyed closeness. I ain't no talker, he says.

Despite the risks of road travel, it beats crawlin through the backwood trails. We make decent enough progress, so far as caution an conditions allow. I should be champin at the bit to go flat out. But we'll be there soon enough. Too soon.

At a few of the checkpoints, the Tonton go through the right drill an want the right password. Lugh's ready with it, all thanks to Jack's network, if he only knew. Mostly, though, the day makes them careless. Not keen to leave the warmth of the guardhouse stove. Single guards run out at the last moment. A quick glance at the brand on Manuel's forehead, at my swollen belly, an they're liftin the gate an wavin us through. Strange nights of starfall an ghostfear followed hard by strangeweather days means people stick close to their fires. Even DeMalo's Tonton. A reminder, if I need one, that yer only as strong as yer weakest man.

An I think of the young Tonton at the babyhouse. His heartsickness at leavin the baby out to die. *Freedom, brother.* That raw flare of hope in his eyes. *I won't tell on you, I promise.* It cain't only be him that's got a conscience. There must be other Tonton who feel the same. But enough of 'em to make a difference when the time comes?

What time though? When? An where? Auriel will tell me. Auriel will know.

All my roads lead to the same place, she said. It's my destiny. That's what she said. Well, I bin walkin my roads, takin one step at a time since that terrible day I left Silverlake. An I'm still walkin an I still don't know where all of this is leadin me to. The babies, the slaves, the seedstore. DeMalo's false visions. The blood moon's comin. I hafta finish this somehow. If I put one foot wrong, it'll be the end of us. But I cain't see what to do next. I ain't got no certainty. I won't till I can speak to Auriel.

My destiny. Is that what this is? What I'm doin? I didn't choose it, but that ain't how destiny works. Auriel said that long before I was born, a train of events was set in motion. Auriel said … Auriel said. Destiny or no, one step at a time has led me here an will lead me on. An this is happenin an will be, an whatever will be I mustn't fear. Jest like Pa told me.

They're gonna need you, Saba. Lugh an Emmi. An there'll be others too. Many others. Don't give in to fear. Be strong, like I know you are.

The lack of him suddenly knifes me in the chest. Not the hollowed-out man he was after Ma went. But my handsome young father, so strong an steady. I'd crawl into his arms as nightfall came. An I'd listen to his heartbeat an feel him breathe an know I was safe in the world. Now all I can do is hold fast to his words. Hold fast to myself. An go forwards, step by step, on this road that only I can walk.

No matter what comes. Whatever will be.

My time ticks away. Only three nights to go.

Night Three

The dark comes upon us early. It takes us by surprise. The fog ain't lifted all day. It's made heavy weather of our travel. By middle afternoon, the sullen red sun dies. We're muffled in misty darkness.

Even if it warn't too dangerous to go on, nightfall means curfew in New Eden. We pull off the road an make a camp among the trees.

I take first watch while the boys sleep. My mind circles in a swamp of shallow fears. I hear whispers in the fog. Movement in the black heart of the night. Lugh relieves me when I done my time.

I lie down, close my eyes an try to sleep. But rest won't come to me. What comes to me is

the faint, far-off sobs of a child.

The dry rustle of bones hung in trees.

I wait fer the night to pass.

We pause at the crossroads where we hijacked Slim. The one with the sourfruit trees. We're in the bleak nowhere now. That means little danger of discovery. The boys shed their Tonton robes while I strip off Molly's dress an dump the corn-husk belly. I ain't felt like myself since Peg helped me tog up. That was yesterday mornin already. Manuel climbs down from the cart to stretch his legs. We pass around waterskins an wet our dry throats.

There's a harsh beauty to this place. It seems like somewhere in a dream. A white hotwind sky that scalds yer skin. The great forest of red pine frozen to stone an the baked cracked red earth. The scattered remains of light towers. A hazy shimmer of mountains far north.

I have a fancy that our voices linger in this place. That that moment of decision still murmurs in the dust, echoes in the frozen pine branches. All of us hot an quarrelsome. Arguin over which way we oughta go. Me determined to press on to the Lost Cause with nuthin in mind but to find Jack. Lugh pullin in the opposite direction. Anxious to turn back, to head west to the Big Water. If we'd done as he wanted, Maev might still be alive. I wouldn't of fallen to DeMalo. We wouldn't be speedin now towards the sharp end of our lives.

What should I whisper to myself? Here at the crossroads of the past? What should I tell myself to do? Listen to Lugh an turn back? Or forge onwards, though I know what lies ahead?

I catch Lugh's eye. I can tell that he's hearin our voices too. But did we, do we, ever really have a choice? It seems our course was set long before that crossroads moment.

They're gonna need you, Saba. Be strong, like I know you are. An never give up. Never. No matter what happens.

I won't. I ain't no quitter, Pa.

I buckle on my jerkin an armbands. I tie Auriel's shawl around me like a sash. I ain't no quitter. One step at a time, I'll see this thing finished. I ain't got no fear on my own account. But fer them that I love, I fear plenty. If that makes me a bad leader, so be it. I look at Lugh an Tommo. I says, You know that you ain't obliged to come with me.

But they're both swingin theirselfs onto horseback an Manuel's jumped in the cart, reins in hand, ready to move at the word.

C'mon then, says Tommo.

Let's go, says Lugh.

So I swing myself up onto Hermes. An I lead us on north to Nass Camp.

Our landmark looms into view. The rusted stub of a single light tower leg. Ash is perched on the topmost beam. The moment she spots us, she shouts out somethin, then swarms down the leg to the ground. Nero sails off to greet her. By the time we roll to a stop, Creed's appeared. As the boys an me dismount an Manuel halts the cart, he strides towards us with a big white grin. Ear rings janglin, coat tails flappin, his hair wild tossed by the wind.

That smile better mean they're here, I says.

You ask an the magic man delivers, he says. He takes my hand an ushers me forwards.

Don't believe him, says Ash. They was already in New Eden. We met 'em jest after they'd crossed the Yann Gap.

Creed flings his arms wide. Behold, he says. Yer army!

We're lookin down a mild slope into Nass Camp. I dunno what I espected, but it warn't this. A dry flat valley of white rocks, bright in the middle day sun. The strangest rocks I ever

264

seen. A close-packed clutter of cones, pillars, mushrooms an chimleys. Small, large an every size in between. Some rise many foot high in the air. They've bin carved by human hands into honeycombs of caves, nooks an holes. But it ain't the rocks that drop my jaw. It's what's camped among them.

Good gawd, says Lugh. He sounds as numb as I feel.

This is everybody, I says.

Every last one of 'em, says Creed.

The Snake River camp has picked up an moved here. Their flotsam skellies, teepees an ragtents scatter all about between the rocks. Their carts an horses an other beasts. They've took over some of the caves as well. I spy Auriel's patchwork tent. Dogs chase. Children play. I hear Moses, in full-throated bellow of complaint. I spot Slim at the same time he spots us. He raises his hand an shouts welcome. A few kids start runnin towards us. Then everybody begins to move in our direction.

How many? says Tommo.

A hunnerd twenny three, says Ash. That's accordin to Auriel. An she should know.

I feel instantly sick. Seein 'em all here like this, all together, it hits me. They're my responsibility now.

Over the Yann Gap, says Tommo. But we wrecked that bridge.

There's a new one, says Ash. The Pathfinder's bin busy. An not jest the bridge. They also cleared the Wraithway of yer pals, them skull collectors. How's about this, Saba? Struck dumb, huh?

Dumb. Shocked. But I take in what she says. DeMalo's built his bridgehead to the west. Of course he has. The maps in the seedstore roll out in my mind. The land an the waters, to the west, east, north, south. All of it DeMalo's to control.

Take me to Auriel, I says.

By this time the kids is on top of us. Grubby urchins, gabblin an leapin with excitement as they help with the horses an cart. Then they're all upon us. We're swept along in a tide of warm bodies towards the camp. These people who've trekked from the Snake River. What a difference from the first time we met them there. With fear-filled faces an weapons in their hands, they would of done us mortal harm had Auriel not stopped 'em. They'd fled fer their lives from DeMalo an the Tonton. An they knew about me, the Angel of Death who'd razed Hopetown to the ground. Him an me was one an the same in their eyes, bringers of misery an death.

Now they're wantin to shake our hands. There's nods an smiles an the chatter of hopefulness surrounds me. I reckanise quite a few. They're dry folk, these people, parched in body an spirit. Stand 'em next to the fresh green Stewards, they'd look poor specimens indeed.

Who are the best stewards of the earth? The old and weak? The sick? Or the young and the strong? There isn't enough clean water or good land to go around. You know that.

DeMalo's words hiss in me. Slither in dark corners. Be silent, be gone, yer his thoughts, not mine.

Make way! Make way! Slim sails a path through the crowd, belly-first. Molly follows in his wake. His gappy grin stretches ear to ear. Whaddya say, Angel? Does all this put yer mind at rest?

I cain't believe it, I says.

We'd barely got here ourselfs when they pitched up, says Molly. They caught us on the hop. But they jest set to without no fuss, diggin latrines an all else.

A wiry little man pardons his way through. He's got a

woman with worn red hair by the hand. They've both bin
edged sharply by a lifetime of want. They got springtime years
but wintertime faces. I don't s'pose you remember us, he says.

You s'pose wrong, I says. How are you, Ruth? An—

Webb, he says. Webb Reno, ma'am. Ruth's hangin on,
ain'tcha girl? Not givin up, jest like you told her to. You
did us a great service that time. We come to help you fight.
I mean me.

I'm glad to see you both, I says. What about food? I says
to Slim. An water?

Only waterhole's half a league off, says Slim. Moses don't
mind playin water carrier.

We didn't have time to collect much in the way of
provisions, says Molly. With what they brought, there's
enough fer a few days. I tell you somethin. She leans in close
an lowers her voice. Some of these folk ain't in the best
shape, but every last one of 'em's hell bent on doin their bit.

Beg pardon, ma'am, says Webb Reno. But d'you think
there's any chance we can find our girl they took? Our Nell?
It's all Ruth lives fer, me too, to have her back with us.

That trigger inside my head. It clicks agin. Nell. The same
age as Emmi. If she's still alive, she'll be at Edenhome. We
need a way in there. Maybe this man is it. I says, I cain't
promise nuthin. But let's talk about it later.

When yer starved of hope, even lean words can make a
meal. A spark leaps in their flat, faded eyes.

Oh, thank you! Thank you! Ruth seizes my hand an kisses
it before I can stop her.

I ease from her grasp, gentle as I can. I says, If the day
comes that I earn yer thanks, Ruth, offer me yer hand. I'll be
honoured to take it. Hand to hand, eye to eye. That's what's
fittin between people.

I surely will, she says.

The crowd surges us towards Auriel Tai. I can see her waitin in front of her tent that's bin pitched atop a small rise in the land. The same high-peaked tent made of tatters an patches that I remember so well from the Snake. The wind twitches at her long black shift.

I ain't met everybody on this earth there is to meet. Still, I know there cain't be none other like Auriel. This star reader servant of the light. Sixteen an fine boned as a sparrow, with skin the clear white of a watery moon. Her milkfire hair hangs loose to her waist, threaded with feathers an beads. A dark eyeshield covers her eyes. Any glint of light – the sun on water, say – can set her off in a vision so fierce she'll be laid out cold on the ground.

Auriel knows my black water. She knows it like nobody else. In night skies an lightnin, she's read me. Past an future. Mind an soul. She's roamed the grey plains of my dreams.

I knew what she looked like. I knew her to be sixteen. But her power is such that since I left her at the Snake, my memory's changed her to someone more like Mercy. A older woman with long knowledge of the world. A little spray of shock hits me at the sight of this small girl.

As I stop jest below her on the slope, Nero lands on my shoulder. I can feel the press of bodies behind me. All of my people. All of her people.

She stands there quietly. The chatter stops dead. She raises her voice so none miss her words. They fall clear as spring rain upon a lake. The hotwind dies down, as if soothed by the sound.

The starworld is unsettled, she says. Change in the skies foretells change here on earth. The stars told us to leave our Snake River camp. They sent us here to this place. They sent us to be of service to Saba. My Snake River friends know this land well. It was their land before the Pathfinder came. Before he stole it from them an named it New Eden. He stole their children, their hope fer the future. He killed an enslaved their loved ones. Their friends an their neighbours. They fled in fear of their lives. Yet here they are, returned. Prepared to risk all in the hope of real freedom. The stars say that hope lies with Saba. We wait upon her command.

She motions fer me to come to her. As I go up the slope, settin Nero loose to fly, my Free Hawks crowd behind me. Slim an Molly, Ash an Creed, Tommo an Lugh.

I glance back at them. I'll see her on my own, I says.

Lugh says, But surely I can—

On my own, Lugh, I says.

He stops with a frown. He has a iron dislike fer Auriel, forged in his soul by our star-scarred life. He despised her the moment he set eyes on her at the Snake. Thanks to our misbegotten father, he's always spat at the very mention of star readin. Auriel ain't no never-was, not like Pa. But despite that she proved to a certainty she ain't no fake – maybe becuz she did – Lugh will not give her credence. He'd claim disbelief even if she raised our mother from the dead right in front of him.

She's holdin the tent flap open. As I'm about to duck inside, she lays a cool hand on my arm. Where's Emmi? she says.

Not here, I says. She's back at base.

Auriel goes completely still. Jest fer a moment. Like that warn't the answer she espected. Then, Come in, Saba, she says.

The tent of a shaman ain't jest her home. It's the place where seekers come. To hear her speak startold secrets of their lives. To journey drugged dreams born of strange powders on the fire. It's odd to see Auriel's tent here in New Eden, jest as it was at the Snake. The cot, the stool, the chest, the little table. All of it plain, rough stuff. By the firepit, her rocker chair an tin box of dream powders. Their smell hangs thick in the air. Sweet an sharp an strange.

She settles in her rocker like thistledown. I pull up the stool an sit, facin her.

The hotwind that was leashed by her voice now roams free. The tent walls billow an snap. The harsh light of middle day's softened here inside. It's safe fer Auriel to take off her eyeshield. I know what I'll see, but a tiny shock thrills me jest the same. She's got eyes like Tracker. The palest blue of a thin winter sky. Uncanny wolfdog eyes.

I wait fer her to speak. She don't say nuthin. She jest holds me with her steady gaze. I feel a red heat wash my neck. She knows about me an DeMalo. She knows about my tangle of lies. Of course she does. I so wish she didn't. Auriel's all air. She skims above the ground. Not fer her the hot earth of bodies. The drag of unwanted desire.

She told me I'd meet DeMalo. She told me to beware of him. She begged me to stay longer with her, so I'd be more prepared. She said other things, too, an I shrugged her off. All I could think of was goin after Jack.

I should of heeded you, I says. You warned me about him. You said he would know my shadows. He does. I

... I lay with him, I – why am I sayin this? You already know.

The time's short, she says. The blood moon draws near. What would you have my people do?

I give a little laugh. What would I have them do? I says. You know very well. Go onto the farms, back to the land. An I gotta git them kids away from Edenhome – if Webb Reno's girl is there, she'll be the key – but I need you to tell me what I gotta do after that. I bin thinkin an tryin to work out that final move that'll bring all these things together an bring DeMalo down. I know that's what's gotta happen. The babyhouse, the slaves, how I needed these people from the Snake – that all came to me pretty clear. But after Edenhome, I cain't see nuthin. It's jest blackness. I bin so badly needin to see you, Auriel. Even you probly got no idea how much.

To my dismay, my voice wobbles. I gather it up an carry on.

Jest ... please, I says. All I want is fer you to tell me what I gotta do to finish this.

I'm sorry, she says. I cain't.

A chill runs over my skin. Of course you can, I says. It's my destiny. You told me so yerself. You said long before I was born a train of events was set in motion. You said all my roads lead to DeMalo an you was right, they have. An you told me – an my pa did too an he warn't much of a star reader – you both said, all these people would need me an they do. An you said I mustn't give up an I don't. Yer grandfather knew about me. He gave you his bow to give to me. So, I don't unnerstand. I jest need to know this one ... this one last thing becuz I hafta git it right. So I need you – please – to tell me ... please tell me what I need to do, Auriel. If this is my destiny, you must know.

Things ain't the same as they was, she says. That's why the tumult in the stars. You've changed so much, Saba. Yer changin all the time, so quickly. You ain't the same girl you was at the Snake. You ain't the same person you was two days ago, yesterday, this mornin. Who you are is yer destiny. As you change, so it changes. Do you see? Yer remakin yer destiny, rewritin it as you go, every moment of every day.

I am?

Yes, she says. The future is yers to shape.

I make my destiny myself, I says.

By the choices you make, she says.

But — there's too much at stake, I says. So many lives. I dunno what De Malo's got planned. Here's all these people an— How will I know if I'm doin the right thing?

The right thing is to do what yer doin, she says. Take one step at a time. Moment by moment, step by step, that's how you got here. That's how you'll git there. An in every moment, as you choose, stay true to yerself. Who you really are. What you believe. You ain't like nobody else.

There's silence between us a long moment.

That's all you got to say to me, I says. When I ask fer yer help, when I need to know, when—

I hafta stop fer a moment. The hot tightness of fear has my voice.

This ain't nuthin, I whisper.

It's everythin, she says.

My head's poundin. The hotwind circles the tent. I can hear the chatter of voices outside. I feel distant from myself. Like I ain't in my body. The tent walls bluster an threaten. In an out. They close in on me. There's a roarin sound in my ears.

I stand. So does she. She reaches up to my face. Her

fingers rest on my birthmoon tattoo.

Never lose sight of what you believe in, she says. Never, no matter what happens. What one person does affects the many. We're all bound together, Saba. All threads in a single garment of destiny.

As I halt from the tent, the wind blasts at me, hot an gritty. I'm numb. I cain't believe it. Auriel cain't help me. I bin countin on her to see my way clear. Two nights to the blood moon. Two nights.

What now?

What do I do?

The voices shout at me from the bottom of the hill. Everybody that was there when I went in to see Auriel is still hangin around. Her people. My Free Hawk gang. All waitin, eager to be told what comes next. Where they're goin. What's gonna happen. My heart starts to pound. I need to think. I head away from them, fast as I can.

They come rushin after, yellin questions at me.

When do we fight? cries a man.

We don't, I says loudly. I don't turn to look. I keep walkin.

We need guns, calls another man. Bows an arrows.

No weapons, I says. This ain't no blood vengeance.

We got guns in plenty. It's Creed's voice. More'n we'll ever need, right here beneath our feet. Tunnels full of 'em.

I turn to face them. I said, no weapons! I yell.

A great furore erupts. Then why're we here? We'll go it alone! No weapons? That's crazy.

I raise my voice to be heard above the noise. It's the smartest an quickest way to win this fight!

Climb up where they can see you. Here! says Slim. On the cart!

Peg's little cart stands nearby. The one I rode here in with Manuel. I hesitate a moment, but Slim an Tommo's already seized me by the elbows. They hoist me into the back of it. Then the crowd's surrounded me an before I can pause to think, I'm launchin headlong into speech.

There won't be no fightin, I says. There ain't no need to. At least, not the kinda fight you think. The smartest an quickest way to win New Eden is not to fight at all.

I turn as I speak, so's everyone can hear me.

DeMalo makes out that he's powerful, I says. Unbeatable. I'm here to tell you that he ain't. He's weak an grows weaker by the day. He don't know it. He cain't see it. An it's happenin right unner his nose.

I look out on the sea of faces. They're silent. Listenin. The hotwind whips at our clothes an hair. I feel the red hot risin high in me. But not to fight. To convince them.

The people of New Eden are slaves, I says. Each an every one, make no mistake. They may not wear iron collars an iron chains, though many in New Eden bear that injustice. But they all wear the slave bonds of fear. So long as we live in fear of this tyrant, we'll always be his slave. Right now, at this moment, the people of New Eden are castin off the slave chains of fear. Yes. Yer children, yer friends an yer neighbours. DeMalo don't know it. DeMalo cain't see it. An it's happenin right unner his nose.

I raise my voice. I lower it. I speak slowly, then fast. My hands reach out to them. All eyes stay upon me.

How're they doin it? I says. They're comin back together is how. Quietly, quickly an stronger, much stronger, than ever they were before. They're mendin what he broke apart. What did he break? Family. Friendship. True community. Why did he break it? Becuz he fears it. Becuz it's stronger than anythin he could ever make. It's stronger than he could ever hope to be.

Here in New Eden, they're joinin hands once more. In peace an hope an strength. Mother an child, father an child, sister an brother, slave an slave, neighbour an neighbour. Joinin their hands in true community. Becuz hands joined together break iron chains. But they need more hands. They need yer hands.

Everybody here today. Every man, woman an child. All of you. An me. Our destinies have brought us together. In this place, at this time, to end this tyrant's rule. To end the rule of all tyrants over us. We cast off our fear. We cast off our chains. We move forward in hope with joined hands. Tonight we go east. To freedom. An the future!

The crowd erupts. A thunderous great roar shakes the air. Then they're cheerin an whistlin an clappin an reachin up to grab my hands.

I stand there. I'm dazed by the heat an the noise. The red hot's suddenly gone an I'm altogether done in. I only jest finished speakin. But I cain't fer the life of me remember what I said. Tommo an Manuel help me down from the cart.

I ain't never heard speechin like that before, says Manuel.
Roustabout stuff, says Slim. A bit short on detail but—
Gather our crew, we'll do that now, I says.

We take ourselfs off to a quiet place among the rocks. I stay on my feet. I think best on my feet.

275

I tell 'em what I've planned. That Manuel, Creed, Ash an Slim will work together. They'll go with sixty of these folk, the strongest men an women, into the heart of New Eden. They should be slipped back onto farms where it's certain they'll be safe an welcome. One or two of 'em fer each farm, no more. The idea is to plant 'em around New Eden as wide as possible. They should work, help with chores, become part of daily life. Well away from any Tonton or nosy pokes. We're bringin back together what DeMalo's put asunder.

They perch on odd-shaped rocks or sprawl on the burnt yellow moss that covers the ground. They're all watchin me. Listenin. There ain't no sign of dissent.

I'll leave the details to you, I says. But you'll need to work fast.

How fast? says Creed.

We need 'em in place by the blood moon, I says.

Tall order, says Manuel. Not impossible.

Ash takes a last draw from a redclover ciggy stub. Whadda we do when they're all set up? she says.

Make sure it stays quiet an trouble free, I says. I'll git word to you as soon as I can.

Wait fer the big gawdamn rumble, right? says Slim.

Yeah, I says. That's the one.

He sat there with the rest of them. No one looking at him would be able to tell how alarmed he was. He'd been so sure this idea would go nowhere. But it was gathering speed. Growing, spreading, out of control. If he didn't move fast, his plans would be in ruins.

This course they were on was dangerous. Way beyond reckless. It bore all the marks of Jack's hand. She was so in his sway, she was doing his work for him while he hid in the shadows.

It was time to make his move. To finish this. To finish Jack.

Where you headed, Saba? says Molly. She puts her arm through mine an walks alongside. Lugh an Tommo's with her. I shake her off.

We need to start right away fer Edenhome, I says. Me an these boys an … whatshisname, that guy. We gotta find a way in there. It's the last thing I gotta set up. His little girl might be there, she's Emmi's age. Webb Reno, that's his name, he's gonna help us. I gotta speak to him.

We'll let him know, she says. Right now, you need to rest. Yer tired, my darlin.

An in that moment the concern in her lovely face so instantly, so painfully reminds me of my mother that the rush of lost memory makes me dizzy. They dive to steady me.

Leave be, I says. I shrug 'em off.

Molly says to Lugh, You do know she ain't bin sleepin.

We stopped fer curfew. I could swear she slept, he says.

Saba, says Molly. Did you sleep last night?

Yes, I lie.

She's lyin, says Tommo.

A woman starts to rise from a pit in the ground. Right in front of us, at our feet. She's got long fair hair. Her name sounds in my heartbeat. Ma, I says. I take a step towards her.

You know yer ferbid to go down there, she says. That's twice now, Davy, you got a swat comin. You better not of touched nuthin. She's climbed out an set a lit lamp on the ground. She hoists out a wriggly little boy by his armpits. She notices us. Her face creases in dismay. So sorry, she says. He won't do it agin. She snatches the lamp an rushes him off, scoldin him fiercely as they go.

I step, step to the edge of the pit. I look down, down to its blackness. It yawns

rough an narrow an deep. I know what lies within. The body in rusted armour. Laid out in the pit full length. The head wrapped around with a blood red shawl.

The wind flurries the shawl ties about me. I bend towards the dark. Tip my heavy head to the hush of cool earth.

There's blood in there. Look, I says.

It rises in a tide from the red heart of the earth. If I step in, it'll take me. It'll drown me.

There ain't no blood, that's a gun store, says Lugh.

Him an Tommo take my arms. They move me away.

I got somethin to help. Come with me, says Molly.

Not long, she kept saying. A few hours. No more.

It ain't ezzack, y'know, said Molly. I'll do my best. From a tiny stone bottle she tipped the merest, barest blink of a teardrop. This is pure silence, she whispered.

No dreams, said Saba.

Not a one, I promise.

Molly weakened it three times in water. Saba drained the cup, then lay down. Short minutes later she was out. She slept like a child, curled on her side, bathed in a soft pool of lantern light. The dark fans of her lashes lay heavy on her cheeks. The little carved-out rock den hushed around them, dry and cool.

That was fast, he said.

An I hardly gave her nuthin. She ain't bin sleepin or eatin, it's hit her hard, said Molly. I figger it'll take her through the night. She knelt beside her, arranging the blanket around her shoulders. She smoothed away the tiny frown between her eyes. It's a heavy burden she bears, Molly said. There's few could do what she's doin. I couldn't. Nor could you, I warrant.

Nero had flown into the den with them. He hovered about Saba, making anxious crow noises. Molly picked him up. I know, she said. You jest wanna help. But you gotta leave her now, she's sleepin.

C'mere, Nero. He took him from her. He stayed quiet in his arms as he smoothed his feathers.

After his fright at Painted Rock, they'd had to work hard to win back Nero's trust. The men, that is. Softly softly had finally won him around. An offensive of tidbits, coaxing and gentle words. They'd all been at it, so he didn't stand out from the rest. It seemed Nero didn't know who'd snatched him. Only that it was a man. He was still ashamed, but relieved.

You must be hungry. Molly smiled at him. Follow the cookin smells an somebody'll feed you, she said. I'll stay here with Saba.

This was it. His heart quickened. I won't be long, he said.

A woman gave him some damper and corn porridge. He found a

quiet corner, away from curious eyes. While Nero ate his fill, he took four things from the pouch on his belt. A length of string, a thin peg of charcoal, the cherrybark scroll she'd dropped in the woods and a small roll of oilskin.

Molly had handed him a gift. Not just a few hours' sleep, but a whole night. It was late afternoon. They'd be on the move again the moment Saba woke. That would probably be around dawn. His timing would be tight. But he had to chance it. He was depending on Nero's speed. And his need to get back to Saba as soon as possible. Luckily, the changeable hotwind had died. So that wouldn't slow him down.

He pondered for a bit. He made a few careful marks on the scroll. He drew the same marks on the piece of paper rolled inside the oilskin. After he'd rolled the skin back up and tied it with string, he put it safely in his pouch.

Then he waited till Nero had finished and wiped his beak clean on a grass tuft. You missed some, he said, and picked a fleck of corn from his head. As he tied the scroll to Nero's leg, he noticed that his fingers were trembling. He stood, cradling Nero's warmth to his chest.

Find Jack. Nero, find Jack, he said.

Then he gave him up to the air. The great black wings began to row steadily. Onward, westward, he watched. As their future beat towards the sun's red blaze.

Night Two

Once they were lying on their hard bunks, before sleep took hold, Emmi did as she'd done last night. Her first night at Edenhome. She spoke quietly but clearly, so every girl in the bunkhouse could hear. She said,

My name is Emmi. I come from Silverlake. My folks was Willem an Allis. I got a sister an a brother. He's got blue eyes, the same as me.

She started them off, then they took it in turns, up and down the bunks and around and along, keeping strictly to order. Their name, where they came from, who their people were. The more timid ones whispered so you could hardly hear.

It's what Mercy had done, when she was in the slave gangs. She'd talked to Mercy a lot. Told her how afraid she'd been when the Pinches snatched them. When Saba was taken from her to fight in the Cage. When the Tonton took her prisoner to Resurrection. Mercy said she'd been afraid when they slaved her. Saying her name and where she was from helped her remember who she was. And it helped the other slaves too. It helped keep them strong. The kids here were prisoners as much as the slaves.

Last night, as they'd settled in for sleep, she knew she had to do the same. Even though such talk was forbidden. They had no family now but Mother Earth. They only lived to serve her. Emmi had no idea if the girls could be trusted. If anyone told on her she'd be set for a beating. Like the boy at supper yesterday. He couldn't sit for the pain, couldn't eat. He was made to stand at his place,

282

red-eyed from crying, a warning to them all. So, before she could lose her nerve, she just dived in and did like Mercy. When she'd finished, there was a long silence. Then, from the bunk below, Nell began to speak who she was. After her, the rest followed on.

And nobody told. Not yet, anyway. But secrets would be hard to keep in this place. The only safe place for a secret was inside your own head, shared with no one. If only they knew. She had the biggest secret of all inside hers.

Soon Saba would come. The Angel of Death was coming to free them. To take them back to their families.

As their voices murmured in the dark, her hand went to it cautiously. That very afternoon, she'd been sent for a hammer. And there it was, in a dark corner on the floor of the shed. It must have fallen and nobody noticed. In the leap of a heartbeat, it was in her hand and she'd tucked it in the waist of her unders. Now she pushed it out of sight, into the space between her bunk and the wall. Her stolen treasure. A wire cutter.

Another big secret that no one could know.

I come to with a stone-heavy head. Dull an dull-witted. Fer a long moment, I cain't place where I am. There's the wide sound of rainfall. The smell of damp cool. The wash of grey dawnlight on smooth pale stone walls. I'm in the den. Nass Camp. Dismay jolts me. I must of slept through the night. I told Molly clearly, a couple of hours, no more. She's still here. Sat on the ground, leaned aginst the wall with closed eyes. Has she bin watchin on me the whole time? She starts awake at the first sounds of my stirrin.

It's rainin, I says.

Jest started, she says.

You coshed me, I says. Slowly, stupidly, I start to sit.

No, no, don't move. She props me up aginst her shoulder. Here, drink this. It'll help clear yer head. I sip from the cup she holds to my lips. It's water. With the faintest hint of somethin bitter. That dose I gave you was nuthin, she says. But you was on yer last legs. It hit you hard.

I says, One dose to sleep, another to wake. How often d'you do this, Moll?

She gives me brown-eyed blankness. I know that look. I should mind my own business. Drink it all down, she says.

I drain the cup, to my dry throat's relief. How often d'you do it? I says.

Hardly at all these days, she says. I save it fer the big stuff. Y'know – she gives a little shrug – when life jest gits too much to bear. You do look better fer a night of rest.

I may thank you fer it later, but not now, I says. I should of bin gone ages ago. Gimme a hand up.

Outside, a chill grey world rains an rains. Steadily. Patiently. The ground's turnin to mud. I find Nero huddled half asleep on the dry of a ledge. Webb Reno's there too. Crouched on his haunches with a little cloth bundle, shelterin unner his drippin cloak. He jumps to his feet. Ready when you are, ma'am, he says.

No more ma'am, please. I'm Saba, I says. You kissed yer wife g'bye, Webb?

Well, sure, he says.

Go kiss her agin. I got a couple things to do.

Nass Camp's bin awake fer some time, includin Lugh an Tommo. I got a hunger on me fer once. They take me to a shelter that's bin rigged fer cookin. A stringy old fella fries

284

me a tin of corn porridge. While I share it with Nero they tell me how the war parties slipped away in the night one by one. Slim an Creed, Ash an Manuel an their peaceful army of sixty souls. They couldn't wait to be gone, Lugh says, their hearts was so fired by what I said.

It was stirrin stuff, says Molly.

I cain't remember more'n bits of it, flashes. It's hazy in my memory, like I dreamed it. I ain't never bin a good talker, but it's strange what you can do in the moment. It won't be long now till some of 'em show up to New Eden farms. What I'd give to be there. To know right away if this works. It has to work. What can I wish by? The stars, the sun? Maybe Slim's old rabbit foot. No doubt he'll rub it enough fer all of us.

The moment I sat down to eat, a gaggle of silent kids gathered to stare. I can jest see 'em from the corner of my eye. One tow-headed chancer, braver'n the rest, edges closer, bit by bit. Till I can hear his breath, shallow an nervous, at my elbow. They're puttin me off my grub. I growl an they scatter, shriekin with terrified delight.

After food an sage tea, I'm anxious to be gone. My head's clearin, but the weather sure ain't. I wrap my sheema around an pull my coat collar up. As I splash to an fro in the mud, gittin Hermes ready, I realize I ain't seen Auriel this mornin. I better say g'bye before we ride out.

Lugh an Tommo walk their horses towards me, wavin that we need to go. They're in their Tonton gear, lookin smart. Black knee robes, polished boots an kit. Webb follows behind on a pony. With him along, I figgered on travellin to Edenhome the roundabout ways. Far safer. But I didn't figger we'd be so late to set off. An cross country will be rough goin in this rain. Do we dare try our luck on the roads agin?

In that silent way of hers, Auriel appears by my side. A patchwork parasol keeps the rain off. In such murk, she don't need her eyeshield. Her pale eyes flare like ice in the gloom. I came to wish you luck, she says.

I'm sure I'll need it, I says.

I got every confidence in you. She hesitates a moment, then she says, I don't think you know this. We wouldn't of made it in time if it warn't fer Emmi.

Emmi, I says.

The starfall told us to come, says Auriel, but when I started gittin her messages, we hurried here quick as we could.

What messages? I says.

They came through the light, she says. But they started in the earth.

Speak plain, I says. I ain't got time fer this.

Yer sister's had the call, she says. Emmi's a shaman, Saba. She's an earth speaker. An I'd say a powerful one if this is how she starts off, without no teacher to guide her.

I stare at her, speechless. Emmi, a shaman.

Saba, calls Lugh. We need to go.

Don't worry an don't dwell on it, says Auriel. It's a wonderful thing. I'll see her right. D'you have all you need fer now?

Fer the first time, I notice the clothes she's got on. The same long black tunic she wore yesterday. I'm that much taller'n her, it would hang on me like a robe. A black Tonton robe.

There is one thing I could do with, I says.

So far an no further. The first four checkpoints went easy. Lugh shouted out the password as we drew alongside an after a second shout, sometimes a third, the lowliest grunt would run from the guard hut. He'd splash through the chill rain an mud to lift the barrier. Then, wait, wetly sullen, fer us to pass through. Three Tonton with our prisoner, Webb, chained at the wrists. We hardly even got glanced at.

Now it seems we're outta luck. Our fifth checkpoint. The start of the Sector Eight Eastway. The guy that comes runnin is keen-eyed an bright. An what right away attracts the notice of them keen eyes is me. An, in particular, my boots.

They're knee high, like the ones Tommo an Lugh wear. An we're all of us muddy an wet through. But my boots is brown an scuffed. Not like theirs, black with a high shine. Which is how Tonton boots oughta be. None of us gave a thought to it. I damn myself fer a hasty fool. Danger bristles my spine as his gaze takes me in, head to toe. My hands tighten on the reins. Both my gear an Hermes' kit is well offa the Tonton mark.

I'm ridin at the rear. He ignores Webb, on a pony in front of me. Goes directly to Lugh an Tommo, ridin side by side at the front. Careful, boys, take care, we cain't fail now. I can see the tension in their backs, in their shoulders, as the guy circles, givin them an their horses a good look. He takes his time. Not bothered that the rain drips from his chin. That his hair's plastered to his head. He pauses beside Lugh. Says somethin to him. Lugh says somethin back. Then he goes to Tommo an checks him over. Says somethin to him. Tommo nods.

I've had to let the boys wear weapons. They wouldn't pass fer Tonton if they didn't. Shooters, knives, ammo belts, the works. I don't want we should hafta use 'em, but—

Then I sag with relief. He's liftin the barrier an wavin us on. I nod as I pass by him, but he don't look my way. His eyes is fixed on the guard hut. Whatever the boys said, it's turned his notice. From my dodgy gear to the comferts of a stove. Maybe a sly tot to warm his blood.

We're through. Now, no stoppin till Edenhome.

His body was trembling as they rode on. He'd done it. He could hardly believe his luck. The moment she said they'd go by road, he'd known this would be his chance. His best and probably his only chance to get the message to DeMalo in time. After they'd been waved through the first four checkpoints, he'd started to fear that he wouldn't manage it. That the whole thing would fall apart. And he dreaded the moment of being stopped, of making his move. So much could go wrong. What if DeMalo hadn't set it up like he said he would?

But he had. It worked just as they'd discussed.

He'd moved, just a little. Shifted so the Tonton could see what he needed to. The grunt's eyes widened. He knew who he was. Then, as they rode on, he let the little roll of oilskin drop to the ground. The grunt would look for it, find it when they were out of sight. Then the message would be rushed to DeMalo.

And Jack would be gone from their lives forever.

We're back where we was three nights ago. In the shelter of the woods lookin through the fencewire at Edenhome. We left our horses in the same mossy dell. We was three that night-time. This day-time, with Webb, we're four. The rain's stopped at last. The sun cooks the world to a close, damp warmth. Steam rises from the trees an our clothes as the water melts to the air. About the only place that ain't heavy with wet is the woodland floor beneath our feet.

The same cain't be said of Edenhome. The open ground between the buildins is a lake of mud. A straggly trail of ankle-deep bootprints runs to the half-raised junkbarn. A handful of older boys work with a man who ain't a Tonton. We can see a few kids an a couple of women walkin on boards between the beast sheds. The ducks quackle complaints as Nero teases 'em from his perch on their house. It appears everybody else is keepin indoors. The sound of kids' voices raised in song spills from a open window. Saws an hammers racket in a workshop. There's movement inside the two bunkhouses. There ain't no fence patrols, no sign of the armoured boarhounds. They're fer night watch only, it seems.

Beside me, Webb's got a death grip on the looker. He scans it back an forth, twitchy with hope that his daughter might be here. The door of the right hand bunkhouse stands open. A girl with a bucket appears there. She empties it in a slow stream onto the muddy ground below. After her, there's a little parade of girls. To an fro, they come an go. Ditchin dirty water, emptyin dustpans, shakin rags. They're on cleanup duty. Four girls in all. But no sign of copper-top Nell.

Nero caws insults. The ducks quack their fury.

We're wastin time, says Webb. He lowers the looker, shakin his head. Let's check out them sheds an barns.

Hang on, I says. A girl with blaze-red hair's jest appeared in the doorway of the bunkhouse.

Webb whips the looker onto her. Yes! he hisses. It's her!

She flings out the dirt from her dustpan. With a glance at the duckpond commotion she's gone in a swish of long red plait.

Webb grabs my arm, his face fired with joy. That's my Nell! It's her! She's here!

Emmi! Nell laughed. You should see this crow! It's out there drivin the ducks crazy.

The other four girls carried on with their chores. Wiping down the bunks, scrubbing the floor on their hands and knees. Emmi stared at Nell, her heart pounding. A crow. Could it be? She dropped her broom with a clatter and ran to the door. Yes! It was. It was Nero. Circling above the ducks, teasing them. She had to stop herself yelling his name.

She stepped barefoot into the mud and stared at the woods the other side of the fence. Was Saba in there? The trees grew too thick and it was too far to see. But she had other ways of knowing. She crouched briefly, her eyes closed, and pressed her hands through the mud to solid ground. She was already used to the earthsong of this place. A low sad murmur. Always the same, day and night. Now

290

her hands and feet brought another song to her. The same one she'd followed from Starlight Lanes. They were here. Saba and Lugh and Tommo. The song was coming from the woods.

This was it. Jest like Saba had promised. This was the big gawdamn rumble. And she was ready. She was ready to move.

We draw back a bit an talk in whispers. Nell's inside. That's the first step. I'd feared Webb might be the excitable sort, that I'd hafta rein him in, but it turns out he's steady. An he claims his Nell's steady too. I hope so. She'll need to be.

Lugh starts tellin us this plan he's cooked up. It's way too complicated an won't ever work. But I keep my mouth shut. Let him have his say. It'll gimme some time to think this through. I glance at Nero, who's jest lofted into the branches above. He's so well trained as a messenger, he might be the key. Meantime, I'll keep my eye on what's happenin. You never know what lucky chance might arise. I train the looker on the yard.

I catch the last flash of another girl, as she disappears back inside the bunkhouse. By her size, it's one we ain't seen before. That's four girls plus Nell, an now this one makes six.

Emmi ran back inside and scrambled onto her bunk.

As a couple of the girls rushed to mop the tracks of mud, scolding

291

her in low, furious voices, Nell said, Emmi? What is it? What's up?

By now she'd pulled the wire cutter from the gap next to the wall. She jumped to the floor. Listen, she said. Listen! There ain't much time! The girls fell silent and stared at her. At the cutters she held in her hand.

You stole that? said Frankie.

What do I care fer stealin? she said. My real name's Emmi of the Free Hawks. I defeated the Tonton at Resurrection an Hopetown. My sister's the mighty warrior they call the Angel of Death. She's here, right now, in the woods with our fighters. They're gonna take you back to yer families. An I'm gonna git you outta here. She held the cutter high. We're gonna escape through the fence.

I know! said Nell. The buckets! We'll pretend to weed. She seized the nearest one and dumped out the water. Here! She shoved it at Bly, who was standing there, open mouthed. Well, are you comin? she said.

Yes, said Bly.

Me too! Frankie jumped to her feet and emptied her bucket.

The Angel of Death! Lin clutched her scrub brush to her chest. Only just eight and timid to the bone, she'd do whatever her friend Runa did.

Don't be afeared, she won't hurt you, said Emmi.

Runa dumped out their buckets, saying, Me an Lin's comin too. But today ain't a garden work day. Becuz of the mud. An there ain't no weeds to weed.

Now that the moment was here, Emmi was surprised at how cool she was. How calm. Just like Saba had told her to be. If we do it like we mean it, she said, nobody'll say boo. They'll think somebody else told us to weed. We walk there in a line, like normal. Nell goes first. Me last. When we git there, stick close together, right next to the fence. If there ain't no weeds, pick the mud. Frankie,

you keep watch. The rest of yuz, cover me while I cut the wire. Git
ready to move fast when I tell you. If we do this quick an quiet,
nobody'll even know we're gone. Don't worry, I done loads of
escapes. You ready?

They all nodded. Their eyes were wide and excited and fearful.

She put the cutter in her bucket. Let's go, she said.

As I sweep the looker back to the bunkhouse, Nell slips out
the door, bucket in hand. A little line of girls follows behind
her, different ages an sizes, all carryin buckets. They're
makin a straight line fer the garden patch in front of us.
Webb's right, his Nell's got a determined look about her.

Quick, this might be our chance, I says.

They hustle to crouch beside me. Look! says Tommo. At
the back there!

I train the looker on the girl bringin up the rear. My heart
stops. That stubborn chin. Them eyes. As big an blue as the
sky.

Emmi! says Lugh. What's she doin here?

Ohmigawd, I says.

The penny drops. Why nobody could find her the other
mornin at the Lanes. She was gone. She was already here.

She followed us, I says. The other night. She's bin here
ever since. C'mon, we need to git closer.

We dodge our way to a big bull pine that crowds the
fence next to the garden patch. The girls squelch their way
through the mud an kneel near the wire, close together.
They start dumpin handfuls of wet dirt in their buckets. I

stare, puzzled fer a moment. Then I realize. From a distance, it'll look like they're weedin. This ain't no lucky chance. Em saw Nero. She's got a plan.

Lugh an Tommo huddle close to me. They know we're here, I whisper. Lugh mouths it to Webb, behind the tree next to us. He nods.

There's one girl on watch. She keeps checkin to see if anybody's takin notice of 'em. Nobody is. The ducks paddle on the pond. The junkbarn work party bashes an clatters a good seventy foot away. Emmi scuttles right to the fence. She takes a wire cutter from her bucket an starts snippin. She has to use both hands.

Emmi, I hiss, it's me! No, no, don't look. Stop what yer doin an listen. What the hell're you up to?

She keeps on cuttin. Whaddya think? she says. I'm cuttin the fence so these can escape. That's why yer here. I told 'em so.

Emmi, stop! I says. We need more'n six to git out. D'you hear me, Em? Stop!

She don't pay no heed. On she snips. We still okay, Frankie? she says.

All clear, says the girl on watch.

While they're talkin, Webb's sayin to me, I dunno whatever else you got planned, but my girl's comin outta there right now.

Nell's head shoots up. Pa, is that you?

It is, but you hush, girl, he tells her. Play it steady.

While they're goin on, Lugh's whisperin to me, I want Em outta there, Saba.

Listen, I says, there's more at stake than—

Nearly done, says Emmi. I'm through. She throws down her cutter. Help pull it back, she tells Nell. Careful, mind yer fingers. They bend back a flap of wire. She's cut a hole big enough fer a child to slip through. Go, Nell, quick!

Then it's all happenin. All at once. All too fast.

As Nell bellies through the fence an Webb grabs her into his arms, Em's sayin, Now you, Bly, an the blonde girl's wriggled through the hole an Tommo's pullin her behind the tree with us.

At that moment Frankie, the girl on watch, says, Emmi! He seen us! He's comin!

A boy workin on the barn's noticed what's happenin here. He pelts towards the girls as fast as he can. Judgin by his speed, he aims to join 'em, not to stop 'em. The man in charge shouts, Where you goin? Git back here!

Other kids workin on the barn start to run this way.

Suddenly the man twigs. There's kids escapin through the fence. Jest as he opens his mouth to yell, Lugh pulls Tommo from behind the tree. Lugh raises his arm an shouts, It's okay! We got 'em!

The man sees what he thinks is two Tonton. They seem in control of the trouble. He stops dead, not knowin what to do.

Meanwhile, Emmi's goin, Lin! Runa! Come on!

The littlest girl's froze to the spot. I cain't! she says. They'll catch us! They'll beat me! She takes off, back towards the bunkhouse. Lin! her friend cries an races after her.

Em's sayin, Frankie! Quick! An Frankie's scramblin towards the fence an crawlin through. By now, the barn boy's scant feet away an Em's callin to him, Hurry!

Emmi, come through, that's enough, says Lugh.

But she's wavin the other barn kids on. Faster! she hisses. C'mon!

The barn man's sniffed a big rat. He's yellin fer help. Runnin fer help.

Go! I tell Webb an Tommo. We'll see you back at the Lanes.

Webb lights out fer the dell where we left the horses. Nell an Frankie stick close on his heels. Tommo grabs my arm. Emmi! he says.

He's grabbed me with our hands high, in front of our faces. A thin silver band circles his left wrist. It's got marks etched into it. Jest like DeMalo's bracelet. I look at Tommo dumbly. Why is he wearin it? How'd he come by it?

Saba! He shakes me. What about Em?

We'll git her out, I says. Lead the rest of 'em to the Lanes. Take the girl. We're right behind you.

Then he's runnin fer the horses, pullin the blonde girl by the hand.

An Lugh's sayin, Emmi! Now! but she's urgin the kids from the barn through the fence. They race off to scatter to the woods an beyond. Five, six, seven of 'em.

Emmi, c'mon, that's enough, I says.

The barn man's brought a Tonton to help. They come runnin towards us. The Tonton's got a firestick. Stop! he shouts. Don't move!

Emmi! says Lugh.

She dives fer the hole. Me an Lugh haul her through. We turn an start to run. I did it, Saba! I really did it! she cries.

Yer my girl, Em, I says. Yer the best. Come on! Run!

We're runnin an pullin her along by her hands. Lugh one side, me the other.

There's a crack.

I feel the shot hit her.

The blast throws her forwards. I hold tight to her hand. She goes limp between us. We stumble.

Lugh! I cry.

Keep goin, he says.

What're you doin? I says.

He's shiftin her to my arms, drawin his shooter, turnin around to go back. Run! he says. Run, Saba, run!

I scoop Emmi up an I run an I run an she's heavy so heavy an I don't dare think I jest run an run as fast as I can with her so heavy, an Nero flyin above us callin out an

behind me Lugh shoots, then he shoots agin

then he's poundin after us an he snatches Em from me an we're runnin fer the horses with her clutched to his chest

an I'm runnin beside him an holdin her hand an sayin to her, Em yer okay, it's okay, but her head's slack an I know it my body knows it, an her eyes is empty an I know our Em's dead but she cain't be she cain't

an – Please, I'm goin, please oh please oh please, an Lugh's goin, Shut up shut up gawdammit

then we're at the horses, Webb an Tommo's set to leave, with the kids on their horses, an Tommo sees Emmi, right away he knows the truth an, No! he cries out, like he's bin shot too

an the girls, her little friends, they all bust out weepin

an Lugh's somehow, I dunno how, he's got on his horse without fer a moment lettin go of Em an now he takes off with her, rides fast through the trees, but not the way he should be, not towards the Lanes

an there's Tommo sayin, Where's Lugh goin

an I tell him, Tommo, ride fast, don't stop

an him an Webb they ride off with the girls an I jump onto Hermes an head after Lugh an

my heart beats Emmi

Emmi

she's dead

Emmi
Emmi
she's dead.

Lugh rides like a demon. At first I think he's jest ridin wild. But he's headed somewhere fer some reason. I follow over fields, down roads. Plenty see us. None stop us. Two in dark robes at full gallop.

Keep my body tight. Like stone. If my bones, if my blood, if my skin don't know, then it won't then it won't then it won't be true. Not Emmi, not her, no, never. She's our light, she's our hope, Lugh an me.

I cain't feel. Don't feel. Won't feel.

The sky turns dark. The rains come agin. Heavier this time than last. The roads turn to rivers. The fields turn to lakes. I'm soaked to the bone. I don't feel it. Rain on. Rain me gone from this life.

We ride south fer a time. Then I notice where we are. I know this approach. High River. A creek in a dark rock gorge. With a small Wrecker place on its banks. Me an Jack met here once. I hear its roar before I see it. Bloated by rain, the river's in flood spate. It runs high an fast, brown with mud.

Lugh don't falter. He don't slow. This is where he's bin headed. He gallops down the slope an I follow.

As Lugh hauls up his horse yellin, DeMalo! DeMalo! four armed Tonton surprise us. They run out from behind the buildin, two on me, two on Lugh.

Why're we here? I says to him.

They don't seize him. One guard grabs the bridle as Lugh leaps off, slidin Emmi down into his arms. At gunpoint, the other guard takes Lugh's weapons belt, but he has to do it on the move becuz Lugh don't even notice. He's already walkin towards the doorway yellin, DeMalo! Where are you?

Lugh! I shout. Wait! Stop! My heart pounds danger. He knew DeMalo would be here. But how? Why? This ain't right. I'm down from Hermes, holdin out my arms, sayin, No weapons, I'm clean, to the Tonton. They check me over quick, then I run after Lugh.

No trouble from them. They've had orders. I don't like this. Not at all. Two of the Tonton follow behind us.

Lugh! What're we doin here? Lugh! I says.

We're through the door.

DeMalo! he yells.

He takes the stairs of rusted iron two at a time to the room above. It's a shattered shell with a junk metal roof. A web of rough props keeps it upright. Bare remains of walls an pillars crumble from the iron skellenton. Black firescorch patches the floor. A broke ladder leans aginst a pillar. On one of its rungs, DeMalo's hawk, Culan, huddles hooded an silent. Four great holes gape where windows used to be. Nero lands in one of 'em. He spies the hawk, his old enemy. He caws a challenge. Culan shifts nervously.

DeMalo stands at the room's far end. Starin out at the rain, at the river below. He turns as we come in.

She's dead! Lugh yells. He rushes at DeMalo, Emmi limp in his arms. His face seethes. He's wild with grief an rage. Aware of nuthin but DeMalo. Yer men shot her, he says. A little girl! Look at her, gawdamn you! She's dead!

I'm draggin at his arm. Lugh, we cain't be here. C'mon, let's go.

If my men shot her they must have had reason, says DeMalo.

You sonofabitch, what reason? I says.

She's a child, says Lugh. What harm could she do? He stops fer a moment, overcome. His chest heaves as he gasps in air. This ain't how it was meant to go, he chokes out.

Your sister was your responsibility, says DeMalo. If you play the game, be prepared to lose. I did tell you.

I stare at him. The blood pounds in my ears. You told him, I says. When? What game? I turn to Lugh. We rode straight here, I says. You knew he'd be here. What d'you hafta do with this man? Lugh! I shake him. Tell me!

He rips hisself from my grasp. He heads fer a cracked stone table.

I look at DeMalo. I wanna know, so you tell me, right now, I says.

He dismisses the guards with a wave of his hand. His face smooth an blank, as always. Your brother and I met, he says. Just after you'd blown up my bridge. We discovered that we share a mutual interest in traitors. One traitor in particular. Your brother said he could deliver him. In return for a plot of best New Eden farmland.

What're you talkin about? I says.

A certain rotten apple in my Tonton barrel. A friend of yours, I believe, says DeMalo.

Jack. He means Jack. He cain't do. Nobody knows Jack's alive.

Lugh's bin layin Emmi on the table. Carefully. Like she's asleep an he don't wanna wake her. I go to him. What does he mean? I says. What've you done?

Nothing yet, says DeMalo. He hasn't delivered. I'm here at noon, he says to Lugh, as your message instructed. So where's the traitor? I don't see him.

Please, Lugh, I says, tell me you ain't done a deal with this man.

She'd never of bin in that place if it warn't fer you. Lugh's breath shudders from him as he tenderly wipes mud from Emmi's face with his kercheef. Her empty, dead face. She was so desperate to live up to you, she'd of done anythin, anythin to earn yer praise, he says. We should of gone west like I wanted to. Why couldn't you have a care fer her? He smooths her rain-soaked hair. Why couldn't you have a care fer me? Becuz of him, that's why. He's got you so in his spell, you cain't think fer yerself, you jest do whatever he tells you. Don't think I don't know who's bin callin the shots. This whole thing, it's all bin his idea. Well, I've seen to him. I've seen to Jack.

Jack's dead, I says faintly.

He looks at me. Give up the lie, he says. I've known all along.

I look at him. At Lugh. My brother. My golden heart. He's betrayed me. As I betrayed him. My skin shrinks to my bones.

He'll be here any time. As Lugh speaks to DeMalo, his eyes don't leave mine. Saba's message told him noon.

You sent a message from me, I whisper. With Nero.

I'm a busy man, I can't wait, says DeMalo. No traitor, no land.

I don't want yer gawdamn land, says Lugh. I wanna see him hang. He's ruined our lives. He can pay with his.

The floor seems a long way away. I cain't feel my hands or my feet.

DeMalo's back at the window. He stares out. Let's hope it doesn't rain tomorrow night, he says. I always look forward to seeing the blood moon.

He don't hafta say no more.

If you keep on, more people will die. People you care about. Your sister. Your brother. My offer's good until the blood moon.

Formal surrender. Hand in our weapons. Fer Lugh an the others, safe passage over the Waste to the Low China Pass. No doubt a small army of Tonton to escort them, an bound in chains all the way. But they'll walk free into the mountains an beyond.

If I marry him. That's fit. It's just. I'll atone every day fer Emmi's death. I trade my freedom fer theirs. That, at least, I can give them. Since the moment I met DeMalo's eyes at Hopetown, I knew. Somewhere, some day, somehow, it would come down to him an me in the end.

I'd of thought the red hot would of took me by now. Emmi dead. Betrayed by Lugh. Trapped by DeMalo at last. But I'm calm. It's like I'm watchin everythin from a distance. Like I ain't in my body. I know it's the kindness of shock. I listen to myself speak.

Safe passage fer Jack as well as the others, I says.

DeMalo turns his head to look at me. I need to make an example of him, he says.

Jack too. Them's my terms.

Terms? says Lugh. What're you talkin about?

I hear but don't hear him. I'm starin at DeMalo. I've jest realized. It was that turn of his head. Jest like Tommo turns his. Now I'm distant from myself, I can see it so clear. The eyes, so dark they're almost black. The high cheekbones. The full lips. They are so alike. The silver bracelet on his wrist. It's the same as Tommo's, the very same. Of course. They're father an son. Tommo's dead father is DeMalo.

How impossible. How unmissable. I couldn't see it before. I was standin too close.

Saba, says Lugh. What terms?

Terms to save yer life, I says.

All right, says DeMalo. Safe passage for your grubby little band of rebels and Jack.

Safe passage? says Lugh. He's a traitor. A dead man. We made a deal.

DeMalo an me don't take our eyes from each other. An I see them to the Pass, I says.

No treachery on some lonely road, he says. All right. Agreed.

What the hell is this? says Lugh. Saba, what's goin on here?

DeMalo wants me. I believe he wants me unbroken. So he'll keep this promise. Whatever else happens, Lugh will be safe. An Tommo. He believes his father dead. I won't tell him otherwise. Mercy an Molly. Ash an Creed. Slim. Jack. I'll make sure they go far far away from this place. Through the mountains an on. To the chance of a a decent life.

Not Emmi though. Too late fer her. This world always comes to blood. I should know that by now.

We surrender, I says.

I accept, says DeMalo.

Surrender? Lugh breathes out the word in disbelief. You what? He grabs my shoulder an spins me to face him. Safe passage fer Jack? He spits out his name, digs his fingers in my arms. There ain't no safe passage fer Emmi, he says. She ain't goin nowhere ever agin. It's his fault she's dead an yer so blinded by him you cain't see it. We'd be long gone out West if not fer Jack. We'd be safe an settled an she wouldn't be dead. He's stolen our future. He's kept you here an he's stolen our future an he's ruined us. We was ruined the moment you let him in yer life. You think I wanted to do this? Make a deal with this man? I only did it to save you, to save our family. Everythin, all my life, all I've ever done is fer you an Emmi. An you'd give safe passage to Jack with our sister lyin here dead? Damn you, Saba. Damn you to hell!

He shoves me hard. I stumble an I fall. Nero flies towards me.

Lugh's rushin to the door, yellin, I'll see to him myself!

At that moment, Jack appears. Brought in by two guards. His hands tied behind him. He takes in the scene at a glance.

Here's the traitor, says one. He shoves him in the back.

Jack staggers forwards. Lugh dives at him. Jack twists aside an hits the ladder. As it crashes over, the hawk, still hooded, panics. His great wings flap. His talons slash at the guards. They cringe, cry out, fling their arms. A wild shot blasts the roof. Rubble showers down.

Stop! DeMalo runs to catch Culan. Stop! You'll hit him, you fools!

I'm on my feet by now, grabbin Nero, tellin him, Go! As I launch him towards the fray, he screams vengeance on the hawk.

Lugh's got Jack by the neck, chokin him. He hangs backwards, halfway out the window. But Jack's fightin.

304

He struggles, scrabbles, off balance with his hands trapped behind him. Rain pours down on them. Lugh's enraged. Strong way beyond his strength.

I haul at Lugh's arms. His coat. Tryin to pull him off Jack. I hook one leg an he staggers to the side. Jack tips. I grab fer him. Too late. No! I yell. I lean through the window. He lands in the river. It rages him, swirls him away.

What've you done? I shout at Lugh.

He's on his feet, lookin dazed.

A gun thuds. A bolt slams him in the back.

No! I scream
as his arms fly up
as he twists
an falls
to my arms.
Then we tip
we topple
out of the window
down to the river below.

We hit the water. Lugh on top of me. Down we go
down
down
down.

I hold his shirt tight. We're wrenched an turned. We're ripped an tumbled apart.

I'm thrown to the surface. Gasp in the rain. I look fer him. I scream his name, Lugh!

Lost to the roar of the river. His name, my voice, my cry. The current grabs me. Sweeps me away. A stout branch swirls past. I seize it. Agin an agin, it saves my bones as I'm flung towards the rocks of the bank. I shoot over rapids. Outta the gorge into a wooded valley.

Nero screeches above. I look around, frantic. I spot Lugh near the bank. He's caught in the roots of a fallen tree. Sprawled, face down in the water. Jack's there too. He's jest pullin hisself from the river. Lugh! I yell. Now, at last, the red hot kicks me. It rages me, burns me as I struggle towards him. As I fight myself free of the current.

Then I'm there. Grabbin hold. Haulin myself out. Jack's tryin to drag Lugh free.

Don't touch him! I yell. Lugh! I'm climbin, scramblin among the tangled roots. Give him to me! I'm grabbin fer Lugh. I'm here, I'm here, it's okay now, I says. I'm lookin, touchin, checkin him over. There's some blood where he got shot, not much. An Jack's helpin me. Turnin him into my arms so he's laid back aginst me.

Yer gonna be fine, I tell him. An he's so brave, he don't make a sound. I hold him in my arms, hold him close. Not a mark on his beautiful face. I kiss his birthmoon tattoo, the same as mine. Look at you, I says, yer perfect. I lace our fingers together. I lay my cheek aginst his. He's fine, I tell Jack. He's okay.

I hold him so tight. So tight to my heart. I'm shakin. I'm shiverin.

You'll never guess, I says. We're goin to the big water. You an me an Em, it's all arranged. We can leave right away. If I hadn't of bin so stubborn, if I'd of listened to you, we'd be there by now. But we'll git there, I promise, we will.

I hafta stop fer a moment.

I need yer help, I whisper. You see … I made some mistakes an – you always know what to do. You always took care of me. I should of told you before, I should of – please don't leave me. Please. I cain't be without you. I dunno how to be without you in the world.

Saba. Jack's crouched beside us.

He's sleepin, I says.

Jack kisses my temple. He ain't asleep, he says.

Emmi's dead, I says.

I know.

I stare down at the river. Brown water rises, tugs at my feet. Drownin's easy. So they say. If you don't fight it. I could slide in, with Lugh in my arms. Before the pain comes. Before it takes me.

He's gone.

Gone.

My golden heart is gone.

The sound of shoutin comes muffled through the rain.

They're comin, Jack says. Saba, we hafta run. We cain't take him with us.

I look at Jack. He's soaked an filthy. His eyes bloom like stars in his muddy face. The rain sheets down upon our heads.

Find that river you talked about, I says. That stretch of water at the top of the map. Find a boat, like you said, an keep goin. I don't trust him to keep his word about you. The rest of 'em he will, but not you.

Saba! DeMalo's voice, his men's voices grow closer. Saba! They're all callin my name.

You did a deal with him, says Jack.

It's me he wants. Only me. He always wins, I says.

Jack's drawn back. I see his face change. As some kinda truth starts to dawn in him.

He didn't even hafta lift a finger, I says. All he had to do was wait. I did this myself. To all of us.

What deal did you make?

To marry him, I says.

His eyes harden to ice. You bought our freedom in his bed, he says. You'll pardon me if I don't thank you. You should of listened to yer brother. Listened to me. Left this place, like we told you to. I always knew you'd funk it at the first deep cut. But I never once thought you'd betray us.

I'm doin this to save you, I says.

I didn't ask to be saved. None of us did. I thought you unnerstood, he says. What we're doin here is bigger than any of our lives.

It's over, Jack.

All that's over, he says, is you an me.

Then he's gone. Disappeared to the rain.

Saba! It's DeMalo's voice. Urgent. There she is!

I hold Lugh tight to my heart. I slide with him into the river.

Then the pain
—sudden
—ecstasy
—of pain.

After

My eyes open to daylight. I lie on a bed. In a room I
don't know.

DeMalo's the first thing I see. In a chair, by a window,
dressed in white, he sits an reads a book. Outside, the sky
is blue.

Lugh, Lugh with yer eyes so blue
I could sail me away on yer eyes.

I turn my face to the wall.

You're awake, says DeMalo. At last.

I hear him git up. Hear him walk.

A door opens. He says some words. The door shuts. He
walks.

The floor is plank. The door is oiled. His feet an voice
fall soft.

He moves his chair beside the bed. A quiet creak as he sits.

How are you feeling? he says.

It's whitewashed stone. The wall.

Do you remember what happened? he says.

The room feels warm. My mouth feels dry.

I got there just in time, he says. The river almost had you.
You were bleeding badly. In terrible pain.

The door opens an shuts. Someone's come in. He stands.
Moves away. She's awake, he says.

Firm footsteps. Work-rough fingers lift my wrist. Take
my pulse. I turn my head. It's Mercy. Her eyes warn

me not to betray us. She lays her hand on my forehead.

Fever's gone, she says. Her pulse is fine.

This is Mercy. She's been caring for you, says DeMalo.

He don't know that I know her.

You miscarried, lady, says Mercy. I'm told you had a bad shock. I expect that's why. Still, it often happens with the first one. Sometimes you don't even know you're pregnant.

Miscarried. Pregnant. Jest words.

She straightens up. She says to DeMalo, Like I said, Master, your lady needs to put some flesh on her bones. Plenty of rest an proper food, that'll soon set her right. I oughta check her over, now she's awake.

She stands, hands folded, eyes lowered.

Of course, says DeMalo. I'll leave you alone. Sleep, he tells me. I'll see you tonight.

Mercy sits on the bed. She takes me in her arms. Holds me. I'm sorry, she says. So sorry.

DeMalo sent out searchers. To find the best midwife in New Eden. The Tonton tracked her down by word of mouth. She was brought here in greatest hurry. She stays to this room, her own room, a sluice room an the kitchen. Wherever she is, a Tonton's with her. None must speak to her but on matters of my care. It's a fine house, one of several DeMalo moves between. Plain but comfortable.

She don't know New Eden well. All she knows is we're somewhere southwest. The house stands in grassland with views to nowhere. At the end of a long track from the road.

311

DeMalo went in the river to save me. I bin here five nights an five days. At first she feared I had no will to live. DeMalo ain't hardly ever here. She got the idea there was trouble elsewhere an he was called away to deal with it. She wonders if our work got discovered. She fears fer our people.

Nero's about. He comes an goes through the window. Mercy taught him to lift the latch. Tracker found his way here from the Lanes. He ain't seen by day but he howls in the night.

My brother an sister lie in graves, side by side. DeMalo raised stone cairns above them.

That's what she tells me. No more. Not yet. She don't say the words agin. Pregnant. Miscarried. She don't ask me no questions.

I don't speak.

I don't cry.

I'm white.

I'm bones.

Stripped bare.

I wake. It's dark. There's a fire in the hearth. The room's lit by rushlight. DeMalo sits by the window in his chair. He stares at the starfall night. A glass of blood dark wine in his hand.

I can hear the howl of a wolfdog. Tracker, not far off.

Star season, he says. Superstitious fools. They think this tumult is all down to you. The Angel of Death. He don't turn his head. He must of heard me move. That wolfdog's been howling for hours, he says.

I sit up an push off the blanket. I'm wearin a long shift. It's thick an soft. He's come to my bedside. He offers his hand. I look at it. Then I take it. I'm shaky as he helps me to a settle seat by the fire.

Covered dishes keep warm on the hearth. He sets one on a low table. Hands me a fork. Eat, he says. You must be hungry.

It's scrambled egg. I take a small bite. He props hisself in the corner of the settle. One knee up, one foot on the floor. He's poured me some wine. He watches me sip it.

You're too thin, he says. Too pale. Our wedding day will be the first great event in the history of New Eden. I need you to look in bloom. I'll speak to the woman, to Mercy. She's bound to know a trick or two. He holds his glass to the firelight. Stares at its blood red richness. I scour New Eden for the most skilled midwife, he says, and where do they find her? In a slave gang. It beggars belief. With the babyhouses full to bursting all the time, we need every midwife we can get.

The babyhouse I seen was half full.

While you've been resting, I've been busy, he says. A wedding likes this takes much planning, preparation. It's going to be extraordinary. Magnificent. It will bind us all together. One family, serving, healing the earth. This will be the true beginning of New Eden. The story will be told for generations to come.

He takes my hand in his. He looks tired. But beautiful. By the fire an lantern light, he's burnished gold. Like Tommo in the sunlight that day.

I've waited for you. Now I have you, he says. Say my name.

Seth, I says.

He pulls me to him. Gathers me close. No, he says. Like you said it then.

Then. When I gave myself to him. I look in his blackwater eyes. An I whisper his name like he wants me to.

He goes to kiss me. I turn my head, slightly. With one finger to my chin, he brings me back to him. An I know the dark country of his mouth once more. The drug touch of his hands. The heat of his body. He leaves me cold. He stops. So ungenerous, Saba, he says. I'll forgive you. This time.

He shifts back to the corner of the settle. I stare straight ahead as he looks at me. You'll grow your hair long, he says. I want to see it against your skin. Now eat. I won't have wasted food.

I lift my fork. Make myself eat another bite. He drinks his wine an watches me.

My men rounded up your rebel crew, he says. What was left of them. Three people in a junkyard. One's the crazy old junk woman, I'm told. The Steward couple were easily found. Dealt with on the spot. We few, we happy few, we band of brothers. Small wonder you were ready to surrender. And, before you ask, no, you can't see them. They're somewhere secure until after the wedding. Don't worry, I intend to keep my word. I have no wish for a resentful wife. What is it they say? A little kindness goes a long way.

He toasts me.

So ... how do I rate your performance? he says. In this little endgame of ours. You were always going to lose, no matter what you did. Was it unfair advantage that I set your brother against you? You must know that I always have a safety net. I'm sorry to say ... you rate low. I expected much more. I give you a week and the best you can do is free a few children from their intolerable life of three meals a day, a warm bed and a meaningful future. They're all back at Edenhome in any case. And as for that sentimental trick of returning infants to their parents, I don't suppose they'll be thanking you now. He stares at me a long moment. There's the tiniest of frowns between his eyes. Disappointing, Saba, he says. And perplexing. You've caused me some ... inconvenience, that's all. And rained your own blood upon your head. Your lover, the traitor, is the only one not accounted for. If he drowned, he'll wash up downstream. If not, he'll be found and dealt with.

He pulls somethin from his pocket. Shows it to me. It's my little leather bag with the barkscroll messages. He says, Nero as go-between, I presume. That's more like it. He tosses the bag on the fire.

Safe passage fer Jack too, I says. You promised.

What? he says. You'd have your brother die for nothing?

A single tear shames me. Tracks down my cheek.

He watches me as he drinks. What is this? he says. Self-pity? Guilt? Or is it grief?

It's somethin in the way he asks. Not to taunt me. He wants to know. An at last I git it. His unreadable eyes. His smooth, blank face. Not blank becuz he's hidin how he feels. Blank becuz he don't feel nuthin. Kindness. Guilt. Grief. Self-pity. They're jest words to him. He's learned to say them at the right time.

We marry in two nights and one day, he says. Cry until then if you must, but no more. He empties his glass. I'll have no red-eyed bride, he says. We're not made of common dust like the rest. We have a destiny, you and I. Together. There's much to be done. I have plans.

He kisses me agin. A hard kiss, like he owns me. Next time, we'll know who the father is, he says.

He gits to his feet. Goes to the door. It opens an closes. He locks it behind him. He's gone.

I sit. I stare in the fire. A sudden rattle at the window makes me jump. The gleam of black feathers in the lamplight, through the glass. My heart quickens.

Nero, I says.

He's lifted the latch, like Mercy taught him. Silently, carefully – they mustn't know he's here – I open the window an bring him in. I can hear Tracker still howlin nearby. I lean out into the night. There ain't nobody around. I whistle softly. Once. Twice. I wait. I wait. Then I see him by the light of the moon. A silver-grey streak, racin through the field towards the house. He flings hisself at the wall below me. Stretches on his hind legs to his full height. Hopin to try an reach me. But three bone-breaker floors stand between us.

All I can do is look down an whisper to him. I'm okay, it's okay, I'm here. I tell him what a fine fellow he is. He whimpers, but knows not to bark. Then I tell him to go. He mustn't be found near the house. DeMalo would never hurt him. He's kindness itself to any creature not human. But the Tonton cain't be trusted not to harm him.

I close the window an take Nero in my arms. Bring him to my fireside chair. I cradle his warmth to me. Breathe his smell to me. He rubs his beak on my neck. It's jest you an me now, I tell him. They're gone. Jest you an me.

I say the words. I still don't feel what they mean.

We sit fer some time. An I begin to think.

The two Tonton we left in the road. They must of led the way to Starlight Lanes. Three at the junkyard. Peg an Tommo an Webb. De Malo said, the Steward couple, dealt with on the spot. The Tonton must of tracked down Manuel. His woman, Bo, would be judged guilty with him. But only those two from Jack's rebel gang. That means they didn't talk before they died. Before they died. That leaves Molly an Auriel at Nass Camp. Slim an Ash an Creed still somewhere in New Eden. Jack, who hates me, on the run. Maybe they all hate me.

The Snake River folk on the farms ain't bin discovered.

He's made plans fer our marriage. Preparations. Extraordinary. Magnificent.

I look to the fire. My leather bag lies in the ashes. I pick it out. It's singed an blackened. But the scrolls inside ain't bin burnt.

I eat the eggs. Some cornbread. A sliced breast of duck. I drink some wine.

I set Nero free in the night. Then I go to bed. An I sleep.

I wake to find Mercy movin about. Fillin a tin bath with hot water. She drops in oil of thyme. When I'm scrubbed, she washes my hair with soapwort. As she's tippin rinse water over my head, DeMalo comes into the room.

There's a Tonton jest inside the door. No doubt to make sure me an Mercy don't plot. But we're behind a low screen to be private.

317

DeMalo comes around it. Without a nod or a look to me or a by yer leave, he says to Mercy, I want her blooming by tomorrow. Rosy cheeks. Bright eyes. Do you understand?

She nods. A decoction of archangel, she says. Cures melancholy. That's what she needs. I'll hafta gather some.

Find it, he says. Do you know where to go?

I believe so, she says.

My men will take you there now.

I wanna see where you buried them, I says.

He looks at me.

Please, I says.

After tomorrow, he says. That's soon enough. That reminds me. DeMalo reaches in his pocket an pulls somethin out. He was wearing this around his neck, he says.

He tosses an I catch it. Lugh's necklace. The little ring of green glass, threaded on a leather string. I gave it to him fer our last birthday. Eighteen year, it was.

I'll spend tonight elsewhere, says DeMalo. I won't see you now until we wed.

He leaves. Mercy an me look at each other. I git outta the tub an, as she dries me with a sack, I says to the Tonton, Empty the water, would you please? When he hesitates, I says, You heard the Master. She needs to go right away.

I stand aside, wrapped in the sack. He hurries over, not lookin at me. He seizes the tub, takes it off to empty it. I go to my bed. Pull my leather bag from unner the straw pallet an dump out the scrolls inside. As I start to sort through 'em, I whisper to Mercy, There's a safe message drop near the watermill. On the Don River, where we met that day. D'you know the one I mean?

I do, she says. I'll find some archangel thereabouts. It grows most places. It's our luck he don't seem to know that.

I've found the scroll I want. I press it into her hand.

Could be they don't find this in time, I says. We don't even know if they're still usin the drops. Or they might find it an … ignore it, I dunno. I don't really know what I'm doin, I jest have this idea. I could be wrong, but—

I'll see to it. Don't worry. As she tucks the scroll in her bosom, she says, I'm glad to hear yer voice agin. I was startin to think you'd lost it.

Please be careful, I says.

I ain't got this far bein careless, she says.

With a smile an a nod to reassure me, she slips out the door. She'll be gone fer some while.

The house is quiet. Nobody comes, nobody goes. I stare out the window. I sit an I think.

I hold Lugh's necklace in one hand. I hold the heartstone in the other.

I cain't let myself feel. Not yet. So I do what I did in my Hopetown cell at night. When the dreams woke me. When the fears took hold. I imagine the world all around me is dark. I go deep inside my self. Shrinking my self down to one point of light. Where I'm safe. Where I'm strong.

I'm one point of light an I ask,

Who am I?

What do I believe?

Never lose sight of what I believe in. Never, no matter what happens.

What one person does affects all of us.

We're all bound together. We're all threads in a single garment of destiny.

I make my destiny myself.

By the choices I make.

Mercy won't be back. That's all they'll tell me. She must of bin caught tryin to leave the message in the drop box. I dunno if she's alive or dead.

But somebody, maybe her, picked the archangel. It was brewed an brought to me in wine. I don't touch it.

Tomorrow, I marry DeMalo.

A strange slave woman wakes me in the grey time. As the night turns towards dawn. She's bin sent to dress me to be wed. As she lights every lantern in the room, I see the gown that's bin laid at the foot of my bed. It was put there while I slept.

It's strange. Wonderful. Extraordinary, like he said. A queenly gown. Long to the floor. Tight sleeves to the wrist. Laced up the back. The colour of rich wine. Made of heavy soft cloth. It's old. Wrecker old. It's bin garlanded with fresh flowers, with real leaves. With feathers an polished stones. There's a circle of twisted gold fer my head. No boots. That means he wants bare feet.

Nero taps on the window. I let him in. I wash my face an hands. The woman combs my hair. She's shy. Won't meet my eyes. Her name, she tells me, is Fan.

In silence, she laces me in. The gown fits me perfect. Of course. He's seen to it. Fan's brought rose petals in oil. She rubs 'em into my cheeks an lips. I must have bloom. The flush of joy. That's what he wants. Today, appearance is all.

In New Eden appearance is all. The lie dressed as truth. Slavery dressed as freedom. Me dressed as DeMalo's bride.

The same someone who brought the gown left a tall lookin glass aginst the wall. When I'm ready, Nero comes to perch on my shoulder. We stare at the stranger who stares back at us. In the lanternglow light, the circle gleams gold on her black hair. Her eyes glitter huge an dark. The gown fits her like a skin. The neck's low at her bosom. The skirt trails behind her with a hush. The stones catch the light. The feathers gleam.

Beautiful, says Fan. Like a forest spirit.

Nero starts to caw. He scolds, heckles me, bobs up an down. He's right. She ain't me, this stranger. I ain't her. She ain't real. She's some idea of DeMalo's that fits into his grand plan, his great story. With him, the powerful, wise father of New Eden. An her, the earth mother. An the Angel of Death is dead at last. Killed by him. Like her sister an her brother.

Dead I may be at the end of this day. But I ain't dead yet.

I ditch the gold circle. Haul on my boots. I strap on my armour over the dress. The metal plate jerkin an armbands. It puts poor Fan in a twitch.

If there's blame, I'll take it, I says.

She dithers about me, the heartstone in hand, anxious to hang it around my neck.

Not that one, I says. The green glass.

I wear the necklace I gave to Lugh.

Then we go outside. Nero takes to the air. It's cool an clear an windy. Three shades short of dawn. I find a guard of eight Tonton lined up to escort me. Hermes waits in the

321

middle. He looks splendid. He's bin groomed like never before in his life. He shines an gleams from ears to hoofs. He tosses his head when he sees me.

I pause. My gown's tight. I'll hafta ride sidewise. DeMalo's thought of this too. A Tonton comes towards me to lift me onto horseback. I reach down an grab the hem. The old cloth tears easy. I rip it to my thighs. Then I swing myself onto Hermes.

Nero flies above me as we move down the track. Then Tracker appears in the fields alongside. The Tonton horses shy, the Tonton go fer their guns.

He's with me, I says. He won't harm none. I whistle fer him to come an he runs beside Hermes.

When we reach the road, we turn east.

East to the sunrise. East to Weepin Water. East to the bunker in the hill. An DeMalo's magnificent dawn vision.

His secret. His half truth. His outright lie.

I start to hear the faint throb of drumbeats. Many drums bein played together. The faint glow of torchlight colours the sky. As we git closer, the drums grow louder. Their fast, earthy beat urges us on. The hubble of voices warms the air.

The wind's brought great rollin banks of grey cloud. They clash an tumble an break overhead.

Me an my Tonton escort stop on the low ridge that overlooks the torchlit meadow. The sweetgrass meadow with the bunker hill in the middle. It's thronged with hunnerds of people. Stewards of the Earth, scrubbed an polished. There's plenty of Tonton about. Fer them, too, it's a day of celebration. At the foot of the hill sit the children from Edenhome. Kept apart from the rest by a line of Tonton. Low junktents ring the meadow. Through their smokeholes, the smell of food billows from cookfires. It seems that a feast will follow.

I see what's kept DeMalo so busy. He's completely transformed the hill. On top of it stands the white vision room. He's had the walls an floor an ceilin moved, piece by piece, then put back together atop the hill. The front of it stands open to the meadow so's everybody can see inside. Jack did say it was made in sections. Only DeMalo could do such a thing. I should be amazed, but I ain't. I know his singularity of purpose.

Extraordinary. Jest like he said. All here will witness his miraculous vision. Most of 'em will of seen it once before. In a small group, inside the bunker, at the start of their new life in New Eden. But today they'll witness it together. At the dawn of this marriage day of great joy.

The story will be told fer generations to come.

Everybody's seen us. They've all seen me. They fall silent as I follow the front four Tonton. The back four bring up the rear. The drums beat our way down the ridge. The crowd falls back, clears a path fer us to the hill.

In this broody dawn of torchlight an drums, crow on my shoulder, wolfdog at my side, people ain't certain if I'm real or not. The Angel of Death. Slayer of kings. She who rides the night with starfallen souls. Superstitious fools, DeMalo called 'em.

A few brave ones dare to dart forwards. To touch her dress. Her boots. The murmur spreads. She's real. She's alive. Captured. Conquered by the Pathfinder. Jest like them.

323

The drums. The spectacle. The crowd. The tang of flesh, sharp with excitement. I feel the hot clench of red start to burn in my belly.

It's the Cage at Hopetown as I entered to fight. It's the gauntlet, that snakeroad of drug-crazy hands, eager to pull me apart. It's Freedom Fields on that midsummer night, with Lugh staked out to burn. It's the beat beat of fear, the beat of sticks on stones as I came to the Snake River camp.

I look fer any familiar face. Cassie, even Vain Ed the miller. But none do I see. It's a blur of bodies an torchlight.

DeMalo meets me near the foot of the hill. He's dressed all in white. Of course. Britches, shirt an cloak. His black hair gleams. His skin's golden in the torchlight. His face tightens when he sees what I've done, what I'm wearin. The rip in the magnificent marriage gown. My armour, my boots, Lugh's necklace.

My beautiful bride, he says. His smile don't reach his eyes. You brought your own entourage, I see, he says. I set Nero to fly. I slide down from Hermes. The wolfdog stays here, he says.

A flick of his hand brings a Tonton with a cord. I slip it around Tracker's neck. Go, I tell him an he's led away.

Then DeMalo holds out his hand to me. High. With ceremony. I lay my hand in his. He grips it painfully. He turns us so we face the crowd. As the drummers drum an the dawn creeps closer, the Pathfinder an his warrior bride move around the hill slowly. So's all can look up an admire them.

It wouldn't be obvious to nobody else. It is to me. DeMalo's ill at ease. The first time I ever seen him so. You wouldn't know from the calm of his face. But his eyes keep goin to the sky. To the clouds that tumble an shadow. Even as I wonder why, the answer comes to me. He needs the

324

clear light of dawn fer his miracle. Dawnlight to trigger the Wrecker tech of the white walls. I know he won't of left this to chance. He will of tested it. Probly more than once. But the master of control ain't got no control over Mother Earth. When it comes down to it, he's at her mercy like the rest of us.

DeMalo never loses. He always has a safety net. But not today. The biggest day of all. His whole body's tense. I feel it through his hand.

Disarm yer opponent if possible.

I look at him. Our eyes meet. I squeeze his hand. Fergive me, I says. The dress is beautiful. I ain't bin myself the past while.

He nods, distracted. We'll have our handfasting after the visions, he says.

It's nearly dawn. The clouds have finally started to move, swept westwards by the wind. The sky behind looks clear.

It's almost time, he says. As he leads me up the hill, Stewards an Tonton begin to fill its slopes. They want to be close to the show.

Know yer battlefield. Locate yer allies.

Nero's perched on top of the vision room. My belly tight with nerves, I scan the crowd once more. Then I see them. Down to my right. Off to one side. Tommo, Peg an Webb. They're guarded by Tonton. Roped at the wrists.

I thought they was in prison till we married, I says.

DeMalo don't even glance their way. I want them to see this, he says. So they're left in no doubt whose side you're on.

By now he's properly on edge. His eyes fixed to the sky, as the clouds move away. Slowly. Slowly.

You'll stand at my side, he tells me. We've reached the top

of the hill. As our hands part, his silver bracelet catches my eye. He goes to git into position in the centre of the white room.

I pause beside a Tonton. I point to Tommo. That prisoner, I says. The boy. The Pathfinder wants him here, right now.

The Tonton pelts off down the hill, shovin his way through the gathered crowd. I wait till I see him seize Tommo an start rushin him up the hill.

I walk into the white room an stand near DeMalo. He's in the centre, directly beneath the pinhole in the ceilin. He holds the great chunk of clear crystal rock, ready to raise it fer the light to latch on. It ain't necessary, the walls do the work. But it looks good. Adds to the mystery.

At last it's a cloudless sky. This marriage-day dawn is on the break. The drumbeats stop. The torches go out. A hush falls. Heavy with anticipation.

Tommo arrives at the top of the hill. Him an the Tonton outta breath from their haste.

The dawnlight's about to hit the pinhole.

I speak loudly to DeMalo. I have a marriage gift fer you, I says. A bracelet to match the one you wear.

As he glances at me, distracted, I'm givin the nod to the Tonton. He thrusts Tommo forwards into my arms. Tommo looks at me, bewildered. Fergive me, I says.

I grab his roped wrists. I raise them high. I show DeMalo the bracelet. The identical twin of the one he always wears. He stares at it. He looks at Tommo. His face turns ashy pale. Tommo stares at him in shock. At his father, so long believed dead. Father an son. Their likeness is strong. Seen here together, their kinship cain't be denied.

An the vision has come to the smooth white walls. The bloom of dawn colours. The soft song of birds. The low sweetness of music.

A murmur of unease runs through the crowd. They all know how the visions come to life. The Pathfinder raises his crystal rock to receive them. The visions are playin. But the rock ain't raised. The Pathfinder's starin at this boy. Clutchin the rock to his chest. How is it possible? What's goin on?

Tommo frees hisself from my grip. He takes a step towards DeMalo. Confusion an wonder war on his face.

You said you'd come back, he says. I waited fer you, Pa. I waited an waited. All these years I thought you was dead.

His words ring out among the smooth white walls. Everyone in earshot hears them. Tommo's voice is rough an hoarse. The unmistakeable voice of a deaf boy.

It's the Pathfinder's son! His child! a man calls from somewhere on the hill nearby.

I nearly cry out his name. The surge of relief is so great. I stop myself jest in time. It's Jack. He's here. He came after all.

Word spreads. It spreads quickly. Down the hill. Through the meadow. Son? The boy's deaf. Listen to him speak. It's his son. The Pathfinder's son is deaf.

A woman shouts out, The Tonton killed my sister becuz she couldn't hear!

At the same time, there's a risin buzz about the visions. The walls play without DeMalo. The grasslands, lush an green. The eagle. The mountains. The herds of beasts roamin the plains.

The visions are fake! It's Wrecker tech! shouts Jack. He ain't no Pathfinder. He's a trickster. A liar.

Nero starts to screech. The crowd erupts to confusion an anger. Some of 'em surge towards us. The Tonton run to form a line. They push back aginst the bodies with their firesticks.

DeMalo ain't moved. He's frozen. Blank-faced. Clutchin his chunk of crystal rock.

Speak to me, Pa. What happened? says Tommo. Why didn't you come back? Look fer me?

Answer yer son, I says. Answer these people. Tell us. We all wanna know.

His face changes. From nuthin to rage. In the split of a second. Wild, black rage. He drops the rock, pulls a knife an lunges at Tommo.

I dive at Tommo too. Knock him to the ground. DeMalo's knife slashes my arm. Tommo's back on his feet. DeMalo goes fer him agin.

I seize the crystal rock.

I raise it high.

I smash DeMalo in the head.

One heavy blow to the back of his skull. With the swing of my full weight behind it.

He goes down.

Like a stone.

He don't move.

I'm on my knees beside him. Feelin fer life. My fingers wet with his blood. His head's crushed. A mess of hair, blood an bone. Tommo's with me. He helps to turn him over.

Seth, I says.

He's dead.

Words need sayin. So I do.

An behold, this day I go the way of all the earth.

After a moment, I close his eyes.

There's silence. From the crowd. From the Tonton. The visions play on. The music plays on. Nero drifts quietly above.

I look at Tommo. I'm so sorry. I didn't plan that, I says.

He stares down at the father who denied him. He would of killed me, he says. He was ashamed of me. That's why he left.

I touch Tommo's face. He had wrong ideas, I says.

Yer arm's bleedin, he says.

Only now do I remember the knife caught me. The point ripped my sleeve. Sliced my skin, not deep. I'm fine, I says. It ain't nuthin.

The Tonton ain't known what to do all this time. Now a couple of 'em move towards us, their guns pointed. They falter. They stop. They turn away.

Becuz there's somethin happenin. In the meadow below, Stewards cry out. They're startin to run towards the ridge. Me an Tommo stand slowly. I cain't believe my eyes.

A tide of people flow down from the ridge. Slaves in their collars. The Snake River folk who went back to the farms. I see Creed an Ash an Slim. There's Molly an Auriel with the rest of 'em from Nass Camp. Women from the babyhouses with infants in their arms. Many others, Stewards, carry babies as well. People call out as they spot friends an family. They run. They embrace. There's tears an laughter.

It's what we wanted. It's what's right. I'm glad fer them all. I only wish I could feel it in my heart.

A Tonton grabs me. Shoves a gun in my back. Another Tonton's grabbed Tommo.

What's the plan? I says.

Wait fer orders, says my guard.

So we stand there, the four of us, an watch the reunions. Watch as the children from Edenhome run free, lookin fer their brothers, sisters, mothers, fathers, anyone at all they know. I cain't miss Nell's copper hair. She's found Webb.

Him an Peg are free of their bonds. Deserted by their Tonton guards. An Tracker's bin set free too. Peg's got hold of him. She raises her hand when she sees me lookin their way.

When did you know? says Tommo.

I turn my head to find him lookin at me. Not till Edenhome, I says. When I seen yer bracelet. I cain't believe I didn't realize before. You are so like him.

If it was Seth's child I lost, it would have bin brother or sister to Tommo. What a very strange thought that is.

His eyes shift away, then back to me. You called him Seth, he says.

Keep quiet, says my guard.

We'll talk later, I says.

A few commanders shout orders, but the Tonton're fallin apart. Some throw down their guns an walk away. Some find theirselfs bein disarmed by Creed an Ash, Vain Ed an other Stewards. They don't put up no resistance.

Tommo's guard spots a Tonton commander walkin up the hill in our direction. Sir! he shouts. Prisoners here, sir. Awaitin orders.

The Tonton commander is Jack.

As he comes towards us, he says, Release all prisoners an stand down.

Stand down, sir? says my guard.

That's the order, he says. We're disbanded. This is over. No more Tonton. As Jack speaks, he throws off his black cloak. Unbuckles his weapons belt. If yer amenable to society, he says, there might be a place fer you here in New Eden. There's a man down there'll tell you what comes next, what you hafta do. His name's Salmo Slim. You cain't miss him.

They hesitate, jest fer a moment. Then they're gone without further ado.

Tommo's already got Jack by the hand. I might of known you wouldn't stay dead fer long, he says. Then, with a glance at the two of us, he heads down the hill.

He didn't ask about Emmi or Lugh. He must be able to see it in me.

An we're alone. Me an Jack. With Seth lyin a few foot away. We don't look at him. We move outta the room an a few steps down the slope. The noise of celebration fills the mornin air. The late autumn sun shines bright. There ain't a cloud in the blue blue sky.

We stand a little bit apart.

The day's turned out fine after all, says Jack.

I'm sure I got you to thank fer all this, I says. I didn't know what I was gonna do. Thank you.

You set it all goin, he says. Once it got started, it was amazin how quick it went. Like a runaway horse. I had to hold it back some. We needed the ... what did you call it? The big gawdamn rumble. You gave us that, no question. Talk about wingin it, though. That was hairy, even by my standards. But you did it. I didn't ... really believe it would work. I would never of thought of it. Congratulations.

I nod at the scene below us. It's them you need to congratulate, I says.

We're talkin as if we're two strangers.

He turns to look at the walls of the vision room behind us. Silent now. Jest white walls. Nuthin more.

You was in this room with him, he says. In the bunker. Before you an me went together. That's how you knew about the light. His eyes go to DeMalo. Then to me. You owe me the truth, he says.

It was when I believed you'd turned aginst us, I says. You was at Darktrees. You sent me back the heartstone. I didn't unnerstand why, you know that. An then you took Emmi an Lugh warn't there an – I was in a bad way. I fell, Jack. I didn't wanna be caught, but he caught me. He was the only one there.

I cain't look at him.

Jack's silent. You did ask how I'd feel if you'd bin with somebody else, he says. I had no idea you meant him.

It got very … complicated, I says.

I can only imagine, he says.

I'm jest about to say somethin. I dunno what. Maybe

I never loved him, I love you, always you, can you ever fergive me fer my lies an deceit

but a horde of people come rushin up the hill. Ash an Creed an Slim an Molly. An Tommo agin. An Cassie. There's Webb an Ruth an their coppernob Nell. An Vain Ed the miller an JB, the very last Treedog. I'm grabbed by them an swept away down the hill in a wave of celebration an laughter. Come on, Jack! cries Molly. Come with us!

I look back but he's already gone.

New Eden

It fell apart so quickly. So completely. DeMalo's New Eden. I was right. He did build it on fault lines. He was right. The story will be told fer generations to come. It jest won't be the story he intended.

New Eden it will remain in name. But in spirit an body, it's already startin to be somethin else. Somethin good an right an hopeful.

There's much mournin to be done. Much healin that's needed. Much atonement to be made fer grave wrongs. Much fergiveness to be granted from some bigger place within us. Fer many, it's like bein wrenched from a dreamworld where they've long bin held captive. Such was the power of one man. His vision, his passion, his belief, his will.

The people of this New Eden will need courage an faith. They must be strong enough never to be followers agin. Healin the earth an all who share her is the work of many lives an it will take many lifetimes. DeMalo said that. He was right.

At the centre of New Eden will be a council of nine wise women. The first council they choose includes Mercy, Auriel, Molly an Ash. They've chosen well. They try to choose me, but I won't be chosen. My warrior's part is played out. The strength of New Eden, their future lies with them, the people. An them alone.

There's a few here can read, Tommo among them.

They're startin to discover the secrets of the seedstore. That gift from the past to the future, which is now. I'm hopeful fer New Eden. Fer the earth an the sky. The water an the trees. The beasts an the people.

If I'm hopeful fer myself, I hope fer no more than this. That beyond the horizon, somewhere, someday, I can live with myself an what I've done. I cain't ask fergiveness fer the highest of my sins. Them I'd beg it of are dead.

So I ain't fer this land no more. I'm done here. I hafta move on. An keep movin.

I stand with Mercy as she burns her slave rags. A great pyre is built. All the slaves' clothes are placed upon it an we all bear witness to the fire. Black smoke billows upwards an fades to the blue.

I say what needs sayin to them I love. To those I'll carry always in my heart. I tell the truth, at last. All of what I did, to all of them, all together. None of it's easy. I don't come off well. I ask fergiveness from that bigger place within them.

Lugh's part in this, I don't say. I tell them he took Nero, in the hope I'd be frightened an give up. His care was only fer Emmi an me. Everythin he done was fer love of us, to keep us safe. That's all they ever need to know.

I spend a long time with Tommo. Jest the two of us, alone. He tells me of his life before Ike. What he remembers of his years with his father. I tell him what good things I can of Seth. We talk of Lugh an Emmi. We talk of his feelins fer me. An of my deep care fer him. He tells me how he asked Creed fer advice on how to win me. By the end, he's emptied his dark eyes of secrets. By the end, we've reached some kinda peace.

Then we go to the hilltop meadow where Seth lies. Tommo buried his father hisself. Jest him, with his own hands. That's how he wanted it to be. Together we plant a young ash tree at the grave. Its roots will grow strong among his bones.

Molly seeks me out. It was Lugh that she lay with in the woods. How strange. How very strange. That them two should come together. He, who hated Jack, an she, who loves him. It started between them jest after Resurrection. Their hurt brought them together. They never spoke of Jack. It warn't no great love match, but they cared sweetly fer each other.

I'm glad Lugh had Molly in his life. That he knew her light an her strength. She tells me of his tenderness to her. How it fell like balm upon her soul. I'm glad that she knew him to be kind an good. An I'm the first to be told her secret. She's with child. Lugh's child. He never knew. She never got the chance to tell him.

A tiny spark of hope lights within me.

When I've made my farewells an packed Hermes up, I do the one thing I've left until last.

I go to the twisted old oak where they lie. My golden heart, Lugh. An my Emmi. I loved her well. But too late.

The children of my mother an father. Dead an buried in the short days of the year. When the light fails early an things perish.

I've bin told an now I see it fer myself. Their cairns are covered with tributes. Posies of late flowers. Bunches of berries an autumn leaves. Grasses an ivies an polished stones. Beautiful things of the earth. I could wish they'd bin burnt on a pyre so their souls could rise free to the stars. But I know they'll find their way there somehow. An it's fittin that they be in the ground. Since they gave their lives fer this land.

I cain't leave them here without me. We three must lie together, somehow.

I scrape a narrow pit between them. In it, I bury the Angel of Death. I lay my armour that never saw a fight. My metal-plate jerkin an armbands. An, obedient to the dream that's haunted me so long, I put Auriel's red shawl on top. I cover it with earth an pile stones above. Nero watches from the top of Lugh's cairn.

Auriel's voice comes from behind me. Her cool, clear voice, like a mountain stream. Every people need a place of visitation. Every people need a story, she says.

I git to my feet. They've all gathered quietly while I bin workin. Auriel. Mercy an Tracker. Molly. Ash. Creed. Slim. An Tommo. Tommo, of course.

A long time ago, says Auriel, when the land was sick an hope lay dyin there was twins born at midwinter. A girl, dark as the night. A boy, light as the day. An so it goes, she says with a smile. I can tell you, that cairn in the middle will soon rise high above the other two.

That ain't a sight I wanna see, I says. It's time fer me to go.

I cain't look at their dear faces. I give Tracker a last kiss on his head. Then I go over to Hermes, sayin, No long goodbyes. We already said what needs sayin.

No fuss, we promise, says Slim. We knew you'd try to sneak off. We're jest here to wave you on yer way.

I swing myself onto Hermes' back. I steel myself to look at them. One long last time.

Ash is red-eyed from cryin. Gawdammit, Saba, she says.

Molly rests one hand on her belly where my brother's child now grows. Creed stands next to her, a few foot away. Their bodies incline towards each other. Neether one of 'em realize.

The heartstone hangs cool around my neck. You don't own a heartstone. You jest become its keeper fer a time. When it's led you to yer heart's desire, you pass it on to someone else.

I pull it over my head. Molly, I says. This is yers now.

I throw it to her. She catches an looks startled. It's hot, she says. What does that mean?

Look beside you, I says. Then pass it on.

We raise hands in farewell. Hermes moves out. An I ride away from my life.

A league gone from Weepin Water, I take pause at the first crossroads I come to. Nero circles above.

I ain't got no plan. No more plans.

The day's fine an warm. The sun's soft an kind. The wind blows strong from the south.

With the wind at yer back, you go further, faster.

I turn Hermes to the north. To the top of the map. Then I dig in my heels. An we fly.

I find the river all right. The one that flows north to wide water. I follow till it opens to the sea. I stop when I run outta land. On a harsh granite cliff on a sunny afternoon with a view that rolls on to ferever.

I jest wanna see where he's gone.

I jump down from Hermes an walk to the cliff edge.

I had no idea. I didn't know. How the air of the sea would smell. That I would taste it, fresh an alive. That my blood would quicken at the sight of great water. How it hisses an bucks where it meets the land.

Flocks of white seabirds wheel an call. Nero replies from the landward side. I take out the looker an set it to my eyes. I jest wanna see where he's gone.

The sun tips the water with fiery dazzle. I squint as I scan the view.

An my heart trembles in my throat. A white boat. A white sail. It's him. It's Jack. I never thought to see him. I was sure he'd be long gone. He's makin slow but steady headway, west to the sunset. Two miles out from where I stand.

Jack, I whisper his name. Then I'm runnin along the clifftops. The sudden fire of hope speeds my feet. Jack! Jack! I cry. I'm shoutin an wavin. But on he sails. He cain't hear me. I slow to a halt.

In sight. Outta reach. What would I of said to him anyways? Nuthin that could make much difference.

Hermes followed me. He shoves me gently with his head. My timin always did stink when it comes to him, I says.

I take the reins. We start walkin back inland. Nero soars

above the rough rocky shield. All at once, he starts to caw. Then he spears on ahead an disappears from sight.

Soon a shrill clamour splits the quiet. A dark cloud appears on the horizon. Movin steady in this direction. It looks like a flock of birds. I stop an lift the looker to my eyes.

It's a flock of birds, right enough. A vast swarm of songbirds. An, right in the middle, the biggest bird of all. Peg the Flight, in helmet an goggles. She flies with the birds in her flyin machine.

You should let 'em go. Birds need to fly.

Soon, girlie, soon. Me an them.

She did it, I says. I don't believe it!

I leap onto Hermes an we gallop to meet them. She spots us comin an waves. When we reach her, I turn Hermes an we keep pace below. She ain't more'n thirty foot above. I look up at her. Peg! I yell. Peg! Where you goin?

She cups a hand to her ear an shakes her head. She cain't hear above the racket of the birds. A wild notion grabs hold of me.

I point to the water. I point to my chest. She shakes her head agin. She don't git it. The water. Me. The water. Me. Then she gits it. Thumbs up. She rummages at her feet an tosses down a thin rope. It's tied to somethin at her end.

I race on ahead. I stop a ways back from the edge of the cliff. Jump down from Hermes, dump my gear an quickly strip off all his kit. His bridle an reins, the mat on his back. Good thing I know how to swim, I says.

I throw my arms around his neck. Thank you, I says. I won't fergit you. Not ever.

Peg an her flock pass above us. Headin seaward. Nero leads the way.

I snatch my bag an bow an chase after them. The rope flies jest above the ground.

I'm runnin an runnin Peg's shoutin gonna miss it she clears the cliff edge an I'm runnin hit the edge an I

leap

    fly

       reach

           gonna miss gonna

                    stretch reach reach.

I grab it. I got it. The rope. The flyer jolts as my weight pulls it down. It wobbles. Dips. Falters. There's a sudden roar as Peg slams some gear into play. The flyer steadies an we're headin out to sea.

An I'm free. I'm flyin with the birds. Nero flaps along beside me. He caws to let me know his opinion of my madness.

No wonder you do this, I says.

I can see Jack's sail in the distance. I shout up to Peg. She peers down at me. I motion her in his direction. We bank around slowly an head west in pursuit.

I look back at the land one last time. Hermes stands where I left him. He's watchin us go. I wave. He waits a moment, then gallops away.

Down below, in his boat, Jack hears the racket of the birds behind him. He turns to look. He gapes as we pass overhead.

I give the rope a tug. Let Peg know I'm gittin off.

Holdin tight to my gear, I jump. The water's cold. My boots heavy. But it turns out my skinbag makes a float. Peg leans out, looks back to check I made it. I wave. She waves back. Then her an her flock turn landward.

Jack's dropped the sail. I kick my way to the boat. Soon I'm alongside. I look up at him.

What a coincidence, he says. Not a hint of a welcome in his voice, on his face.

No coincidence, I says. I followed the road. It brought me here.

If I pull you in, that'll make it three to me, he says.

Save someone's life three times, their life belongs to you. The Rule of Three.

It's yer call, Jack, I says.

How did you find me? The heartstone? he says.

I look into his eyes. His silver moonlight eyes. The still calmwater heart of him.

I don't need no stone to find you. I'd find you anywhere, I says.

He hesitates. Then he reaches down an hauls me aboard. While he raises the sail an gits us unnerway, I empty my boots, strip to my skivvies an wring my clothes over the side.

As I lay all my gear out to dry, Nero flutters down to the prow. He spreads his wings wide an caws.

I didn't figger on it bein so social out here. Not to mention domestic, says Jack.

I thought you'd be long gone, I says.

So did I. Turns out boats ain't so easy to come by, he says. I had to play a two-day dice game fer this tub. I lost all my clothes four times. If I hadn't of cheated, I'd still be there. Bare an boatless.

Now there's a picture, I says.

A smile lurks in his eyes. If yer after a husband, fergit it, he says. I seen what you did to the last one.

No husband, I says. Jest drive the boat, Jack.

Drive the boat, he says. Aye aye, captain.

I settle back an lift my face to the sun. The bands that bind my heart will break soon. I know that. What better place to cry a sea of tears than the sea.

Jack steers our boat on with steady hands.

He looks at me over his shoulder. You got any particular direction in mind? he says. The wind's changeable this time of year.

We'll go where it takes us, I says.

An we do.

Him an me.

We do.